Praise for *Beautiful People*

"In a word—yum."

—*Times of London*

"Wendy Holden has made the raunchy romp her own."

—*Glamour*

"When she's good, she's very, very good, and *Beautiful People* finds Holden on steroids. Unmissable."

—*Daily Mirror*

"Fantastic escapism."

—*Heat*

"Hilarious tale from a bestselling author."

—*Look*

"Sizzling with energy, this is Holden at the top of her game."

—*Woman & Home*

"Sinfully enjoyable, literary cheesecake."

—*She*

"Thank God for Wendy Holden. *Beautiful People* is exactly what a girl needs."

—*Daily Mail*

Beautiful People

wendy holden

sourcebooks
landmark

Published by Sourcebooks Landmark, an imprint of Sourcebooks, Inc.
P.O. Box 4410, Naperville, Illinois 60567-4410
(630) 961-3900
Fax: (630) 961-2168
www.sourcebooks.com

Originally published in somewhat different form in 2009 in the UK.

Library of Congress Cataloging-in-Publication Data

Holden, Wendy
  Beautiful people / Wendy Holden.
       p. cm.
    1. Celebrities—Fiction. 2. Hollywood (Los Angeles, Calif.)—Fiction. 3.
Chick lit. I. Title.
  PR6058.O436B43 2009b
  823'.92—dc22

                                  2009039305

            Printed and bound in the United States of America.
                  VP 10 9 8 7 6 5 4 3 2 1

Also by Wendy Holden

Farm Fatale
Bad Heir Day
Simply Divine
Gossip Hound
Azur Like It
The School for Husbands
The Wives of Bath
Filthy Rich

Chapter One

SAM SHERMAN, HEAD OF the Wild Modelling Agency, strode through Covent Garden. She was on her way to a lunch appointment with Jack Oeuf, an arrogant but indisputably rising French photographer. She walked quickly. Oeuf was famously no fan of waiting. No photographer was. Unless people were waiting for them, which was, of course, a different matter.

Sam did not particularly look like a fashion person. As she saw it, that crazy, spiky, shiny, short stuff was best left to those younger and more in fashion's shop window than she was. The models. The designers. The stylists. The muses.

Sam's style was muted: middle of, rather than ahead of, the curve. She was curvy too, as well as small, which was why her own modelling career had literally been cut short. In addition, her face, with its round eyes, full cheeks, and rather prominent teeth, had a suggestion of the hamster about it, although there was nothing of the small, amenable pet about her business acumen. This was formidable and frequently ruthless. Combined with this was Sam's sure eye for a new face and her confidence and accuracy in predicting trends. As a result, Wild was one of the biggest and most successful model agencies in London.

Sam, who had been a teenager in the seventies, generally stuck to a classic rock 'n' roll look of white shirt teamed with black waistcoat and jeans. Today her jeans were tucked into high wedge-heeled boots of sand-coloured suede, rendered vaguely Native American with the addition of coloured beads. Her beige woollen wrap with its fringed edge billowed about her as she walked, and the bracelets that filled the bottom half of each of her forearms rattled.

Sam walked everywhere. This was not because she was fond of exercise—she wasn't. And there was certainly nothing pleasureable about picking one's way along the uptilted pavements of Endell Street and wincing at the deafening noise of the various drilling gangs engaged in the refurbishments this part of London constantly underwent. Sam walked because it made good business sense. It was more difficult to spot talent from the back of a taxi and more difficult to get out and run after it if one did.

And spot it she must. Modelling was a competitive business. The Wild agency might be one of London's biggest and most successful, but new agencies were always snapping at her heels, competing for the best girls and boys. Wild needed a constant stream of new talent. As Sam walked, her round, hamsterish, hazel eyes, ringed firmly with kohl, swivelled from side to side between centre-parted curtains of heavily highlighted shoulder-length beige hair. As ever, she was on the lookout.

Sam crossed Long Acre and walked purposefully down Bow Street, past where the vast bulk of the Royal Opera House blazed white against the blue sky. In the narrow shadows of Floral Street, a skinny girl with a graceful carriage caught her attention, one of the ballerinas, Sam assumed. Well, she had a good figure, but oh, dear God, that nose...no, no, no.

She entered the road where the Tube station was. But there was nothing promising among the crowds either outside it or drifting aimlessly across the cobbled marketplace among the face-painters, cartoonists, bracelet-weavers, jugglers, buskers, human statues, and all the other theatrically inclined losers who daily congregated here. No, the beautiful people really weren't out this morning. Sam found herself positively wincing at the unsightliness and dinginess of those she walked among.

Everyone looked the same: acne, terrible hair, short, thick legs in stonewashed jeans, white trainers, and nasty black windbreakers. Tourists, without a doubt, many gathered in an awestruck, giggling, and mobile-phone-snapping ring round a street entertainer. Sam paused to watch the Afro-Caribbean man limboing under a stick placed on top of two wine bottles. His physique was good, but his features were all over the place.

Which, of course, in some cases could work or could be fixed. Some things could be fixed: teeth, hair colour, skin problems. Weight, especially, could be fixed; not that one was allowed to say that these days, with all the fuss over Size Zero. But behind the scenes, a model's life went on as before. The drugs, the self-denial, the workouts, the worry. Nothing had changed. That could not be fixed.

The early summer sunshine continued to beat cheerfully down, but Sam, behind her sunglasses, hardly noticed the way it polished the cobbles, warmed the butterscotch stone of the eighteenth-century market buildings, and made the great white pillars of the Royal Opera House gleam. That was not the sort of beauty she either noticed or cared about. One could hardly give it a business card, ask it to come in for test shots, and subsequently launch it as the face of the moment. One could not make money from it.

A few lanky, blank-looking British girls were swishing their hair and dawdling self-consciously along in tight, low-waisted jeans and skimpy tops. But none of them looked like the next Lily Cole.

God. The lunch. Jack Oeuf. Sam glanced at her special-edition Cartier Tank watch and saw that she needed to get a move on if she was going to reach the restaurant on time.

"Ow!" Sam's progress was now halted in the rudest and most uncomfortable of manners. A great physical blow to the front of her lower pelvis stopped her agonisingly in her tracks. Reeling with the suddenness, eyes watering with the pain, she realised she had walked straight into a bollard. She gripped the metal post tightly with her silver-tipped fingers and breathed in hard.

"Are you, um, alright?"

Sam, red-faced and agonised, glanced crossly at the person who had materialised beside her. He was very tall, his face hidden beneath tangled, dark blond hair.

"I'm fine, thanks," she managed tersely. She had no desire to discuss the damage to her intimate regions with some unknown, callow youth.

The untidy blond head nodded. He now pushed his hair back to expose his face and, instead of the zitty and misshapen bunch of teenage features she had been expecting, Sam found herself looking at one of the handsomest boys she had ever seen.

He was about eighteen, Sam reckoned, and with all that delicious boyhood-ripening-to-manhood quality: smoulderingly sexy with those narrow eyes, those huge lips, that big Adam's apple. And yet still innocent with that smooth skin, that touch of fresh pink on his cheekbones, that endearingly puzzled expression...

"Look, are you sure you're okay?" the boy asked, unnerved by the way she was staring at him.

Sam nodded. She was more than okay. She was revelling in this boy, feasting on his looks. There was a golden glow about him, of classical gods, of mediaeval angels, of youthful Monaco male royals with big pink lips and blond hair blowing in the Mediterranean breeze. And more than that, of Armani campaigns, Ralph Lauren, Chanel—oh they'd love him. Who wouldn't? And that voice; it had that just-broken quality of being deep and squeaky at the same time. Better still, it was posh, which the French and Italian designers especially loved. They'd got into that whole English public schoolboy thing in the eighties, and they'd never got out of it since.

Her eyes scoured his body: amazingly tall, broad-shouldered but slender. Long legs and arms; nice hands. Pale; a quick blast in the spray-tan would do him no harm at all. But otherwise he could well be the discovery of the century. Compared to what he could mean to the agency, earn for the agency, banging into a bollard was a small price to pay.

"I'm a scout," she smiled at him.

"Not my sort of thing," he muttered, shambling from foot to foot. "I've never been any good at putting up tents."

Sam gasped in annoyance. "Not that sort of scouting. I own a model agency." She flared her nostrils. "Have you," she asked the boy, "ever thought of modelling?"

At these words, she knew, almost every other teenager currently drifting through Covent Garden would punch the air with delight, their ambitions realised; their careers, as they saw it, made. But this boy said nothing. He continued to look blank and seemed frozen to the spot, his beautiful green eyes dilated with shock.

Beaming, Sam tipped her head to one side. "Yeah, I know," she nodded. "Your dream come true, eh?"

He did not reply, disappointingly. She would have liked to hear that public-school accent again.

Sam pressed her thick, rather fishy lips understandingly together. He was obviously overwhelmed. It was, of course, a great moment in any young person's life. "Well, look, I'll just give you a card. You think about it, talk to your mother about it. And then give me a ring…" She rummaged in her bag for a card.

She registered, with injured surprise, the complete lack of recognition in the boy's face as he took it. The agency's famous logo, the roaring panther, was something he had evidently never seen before. Most kids she showed this to lit up with excitement. Some even whooped.

Sam felt suddenly full of doubt. Not about his beauty, but about whether asking him to get in touch was the best idea. There was something clueless about him, which was all to the good in a model, but it might be advisable not to leave the ball in his court.

She really didn't want this boy to get away. He was extraordinary. And Wild was not the only agency who had scouts out all the time, all over London. The risk of him being snapped up by someone else was just too great. No, she'd take him back to the agency herself, but, bugger, damn it, she couldn't. She had this lunch with Jack Oeuf.

Sam stared furiously into the convoluted depths of her Birkin. Then the answer hit her. She'd phone a colleague. Stacy, a Wild scout, would, at this very minute, be patrolling Oxford Street Topshop. It wouldn't take her long to get here, and she could then take this boy back to the agency.

The downside of this plan, of course, was that Sam would be late for Oeuf and he'd be furious. But, she decided, now feeling back in control, she'd promise him first dibs on the next face of the moment. The one now looking at her with alarm and confusion written all over it.

"I think you've got an amazing future in modelling," Sam now told the boy. Unexpectedly, the huge trainer-clad feet opposite herself suddenly moved. With incredible speed, the boy ran off into the crowd and, within seconds, had disappeared from sight. But not before Sam, with the presence of mind that had got her where she was in life, grabbed her mobile from her bag and snapped what could be seen of his departing face with its camera.

The boy shot through the middle of Covent Garden market. Through the rows of painted, novelty cuckoo clocks and triangular candles, past the hippies sitting cross-legged on the steps eating beans with plastic forks out of polystyrene cartons, past the woman who may or may not have been an opera singer but who was belting out "Nessun Dorma" in an earsplitting vibrato nonetheless. He ran as if wild animals were after him, or the Wild Model agency, which seemed even more fearsome a prospect.

The boy's brain rushed with fear, his heart was pumping, and from time to time, he looked behind him. The hamster-faced woman had not followed him however.

Now slowed down from a run to a fast walk, the boy found himself before the large church in the piazza. The huge neoclassical building with its gilded clock and pillared portico was in deep shadow; the shadow of the building itself stretched out across the cobbles in front. There seemed, to Orlando, to be something protective about it; he darted gratefully into the gloomy refuge between the church's blue door and the thick, brown sandstone pillars in front of it. He sat down on one of the broad, brown stone steps and waited for his heart rate to return to normal.

He wasn't alone for long. A gaggle of girls appeared, passed from the light into the shadow of the church, and walked by him rather too closely. From his school, the boy recognised, heart sinking.

"Look," said one of them, nudging the others. "It's Orlando. Looks even better out of school uniform, doesn't he?" They all giggled.

Orlando ignored them and watched with relief as the girls passed out into the bright sunlight on the other side of the shadow. Then his heart sank as they stopped, hesitated, and giggled before turning and, giggling again, re-entering the shadow and coming past once more. They were leggy, with lots of eye make-up and long blonde hair, which they swished about while looking coyly at him through it. Exactly the type of girls, Orlando reflected, staring hard at the step, who would never have given him a moment's notice before.

Before…

Before his appearance had changed. He looked different now from how he had looked a year ago. A year ago, and many of the years before that, he had been average height and above-average chubby and pimply. Girls had not given him a second glance; he had never had a girlfriend, although he had got on well with the shyer, less swishy-haired, less self-confident ones. And this had suited him just fine. He had been plump, pimply, unremarkable—and content.

But in the year since then, his appearance had radically changed. He had no idea why. Or how. He had not started to go to the gym. He had not started to use any cleansing facial products. But for some reason, over the last twelve months, he had grown taller, much taller, and so fast that his bones ached in the night. He had also slimmed down, become quite skinny, in fact.

His pimples had disappeared of their own accord, his thinnish lips had suddenly become fuller and pinker, and his eyes seemed to have receded under what were now heavy, dead-straight, brooding brows. A prominent Adam's apple appeared in his newly thickened throat, and his dull, unremarkably mousy hair, which he had never cut much anyway, developed blond streaks all by itself and now swished in a golden curtain about his neck without him having to put anything on it or even brush it all that much.

And so, without particularly wanting to—without remotely wanting to, in fact—the eighteen-year-old Orlando, who had never been interested in women in any other way but friendship, now realised with dawning horror that he was of great interest to them. And they wanted a lot more than friendship.

They stared at him all the time, wherever he went. And Orlando found that he disliked being stared at because he was handsome. That he hated being looked at, full stop. And so he protected himself as best he could. He narrowed his eyes beneath his great level cliffs of brow and hid under his curtain of hair. He pushed out his full lips in go-away defiance. He slouched, he brooded, he muttered, he maintained distance. But this just made matters worse. Women and girls stared at him even more.

And now one of them had asked him if he wanted to be a model. It was hard to think of anything he wanted to be less.

Chapter Two

"Give my love to the Queen," Dad shouted from the other side of the train window, his voice faint through the thick glass.

"I will!" Emma laughed, not caring if the other people in the train car stared. Let them stare.

As the train pulled out of Leeds and her parents' faces, half proud, half anxious, slid past, a mighty wave of excitement passed through her. She was going to London. To seek her fortune, like Dick Whittington in the books at the nursery she worked at. Or had worked at.

She fought through the jumble of people and luggage at the end of the carriage. "Is anyone sitting here?" she asked a grey-haired, grey-suited, grey-skinned man, whose pink newspaper was not only the one colourful thing about him but who also occupied an entire four-seater table area. If he'd paid for all four seats so he could spread out his *Financial Times* to the max, then fine, Emma thought. But she doubted this. He didn't look the extravagant sort.

"No," the grey man admitted. From behind his glinting glasses, he scanned Emma as she edged into the seat, feeling, despite herself, rather self-conscious. Of course, she didn't care a button what a stuffy, miserable, old wrinkly like that thought about her looks, but even so, it would be wonderful to have the kind of whippet-skinny figure that allowed one to slide swiftly into confined areas. But her build required a little more room.

Of course, she wasn't fat; far from it, but she wasn't thin either.

She defied anyone not to be plump when they lived with her parents, however. Mum put out two different types of potato every Sunday teatime—roast and mash—and there was always pudding and custard to follow. And Emma had never known the biscuit tin to be empty, even in the most difficult times, and there'd been a few of those. In fact, the leanest times were when the biscuit tin tended to be at its fullest.

But physical appearances didn't matter so much anyway, Emma reminded herself—not in the business she was in. It was how good you were at your job—and she was very good at hers. Too good in fact now, with all the extra qualifications she'd spent the last two years getting at night school. Especially as Wee Cuties, the nursery in Heckmondwike that employed her, was uninterested in keeping up with the latest educational theories. It was time to move on. And, without mortgage, without fiancé, there would never be a better time to do it.

Should she stay, she would probably remain at Wee Cuties for the rest of her life, as most of her colleagues seemed to be planning to—the ones, that was, who were not planning to defect to the soon-to-be-completed supermarket, which was rumoured to be offering better wages and longer holidays. And while Emma sought both, she sought also excitement, challenge, and possibility, none of which were normally associated with supermarkets.

And so it was, when first her eye had fallen on the ad in the *Yorkshire Post*, that a thrill of recognition had gone through Emma. The ad leapt out at her immediately. "Nanny Sought. Smart Area of London. Well-behaved Children. Excellent Pay and Holidays." With shaking hands, she copied down the details—Dad hated his paper being vandalised.

The train was hot. So that it would not crease, Emma removed the pretty fawn jacket with its nipped-in waist bought, along with the skirt, especially from Whistles for the interview. In the shop, the pale brown had perfectly complemented the chestnut shoulder-length hair that was, Emma felt, her best feature, with its flash of red threads in the sunshine. She crossed her feet in their smart, low-heeled brown pumps at the ankles and tapped her fingers on the new matching handbag. Perhaps she looked too smart, but better to be too smart than too scruffy. After all, Mrs. Vanessa Bradstock, the mother who would be interviewing her, had sounded very grand on the phone.

Stepping out of her carriage in St. Pancras International, Emma's gaze swung automatically upwards to the great glass arc of roof flung above the station, through which poured sunlight from an optimistically blue sky.

London was as fast moving and purposeful as a colony of ants. To the right and the left of her, people swarmed off the train, darting towards the shining chrome barriers in a jostling, heaving mass, weighed down with rucksacks and briefcases.

All the rush and running made her feel she should run herself, and Emma found her pace quickening past the glossy shops in the terminal; no scruffy cafés these, but smart bookshops, glamorous French patisseries with aluminium chairs outside, and fashionable florists whose chic bouquets arranged tastefully round the door bore price tags that made Emma gasp. She lingered in front of the great glass window of Hamley's toy store, her eyes running greedily over the big, shiny, colourful, wonderful things on the other side of it. The idea of bringing a small present for her future charges—if the interview with Vanessa Bradstock went well—came to her. Emma ventured inside, amid the lights and pounding music, and quickly picked a little stuffed pink cat for the girl—girls always liked cats—and a small rubber train for the boy. She had yet to meet a boy who didn't like trains.

❖ ❖ ❖

Emma looked just right, Vanessa thought gleefully as she opened the front door. Fat, in other words. Size twelve at least, to her own carefully preserved ten. Fourteen even, at a pinch, and there was certainly more than an inch to pinch there. Oh yes. Emma was certainly not the long drink of water Jacintha, the last nanny, had been.

One should always employ fat girls. They were so grateful and had absolutely no self-confidence. This girl, with her brown hair—not a highlight to be seen—and almost make-upless face had low self-esteem written all over her.

"You're late," Vanessa said challengingly. Best make it clear from the start who was in charge.

"I'm sorry," Emma said immediately, even though she did not consider the fault to be hers entirely. It would have helped a great deal in finding the house—one of a row of red brick Victorian terraces with pointed roofs and small front gardens—if she had known it was in Peckham and not posh Camberwell, as for some reason had been put on the letter.

"My last nanny's father was a peer of the realm," Vanessa loftily informed Emma. "She was excellent. So if you get this job, you'll have some very big shoes to fill." She glanced at Emma's shoes and twitched her lips disapprovingly. They looked plain and brown and possibly from Office Shoes.

Emma's reaction was not what Vanessa had expected. Instead of looking cowed and terrified, as had been the intention, this girl from the north turned her brown and direct gaze on Vanessa and asked her, in a quiet yet steady voice, why Jacintha had left, exactly.

Vanessa, while unpleasantly startled, nonetheless realised she had to give an answer. The windmills of her mind whirred in panic as she searched for one. That The Honourable Jacintha had left to go and work for the family of a famous writer had been a bitter blow. A more famous writer, Vanessa corrected herself; she herself had a newspaper column and was extremely well-known. In media circles. Her lack of influence in more general circles had been unpleasantly illustrated by Jacintha's resignation.

"The Honourable Jacintha had been with us for some time," Vanessa hedged. "It was time to move on."

"How long?" Emma asked steadily.

Vanessa pretended to think hard, as if the answer—six weeks—had somehow been lost in the midst of much more pressing concerns. "Three months," she asserted, with an imperious toss of her head that warned Emma that she proceeded any further down this track at her peril.

Emma added the toss to her store of impressions about Vanessa. Her main impression was that she was rather cross and unhappy looking. But why was a mystery. Her house was big and roomy, if not particularly tidy. She clearly had money. She was also very attractive, slim in a close-fitting white T-shirt and long purple denim skirt, her pink-sequined flip-flops revealing tanned feet with red-painted nails. Her shining blonde hair was brightly streaked, but so finely it looked natural, and much chopped about in that artful way that only real good hairdressers could pull off. She had big blue eyes, which were pretty, if bulgy. And good skin, even though her face was rather red. So what did she have to look grumpy about?

Perhaps Vanessa was unhappily married. Perhaps with an overbearing alpha-male husband. Yes, that could be it.

"Sit down," Vanessa said, sitting on the edge of the battered mock-Georgian sofa.

It seemed to Emma that—beyond the obvious about driving licence (yes) and criminal record (no)—Vanessa was soon struggling for questions to ask her. She subtly took over herself, conducting her own interrogation of her employer to be. Vanessa seemed to know little about her children. She had no idea what Hero and Cosmo, as the children were apparently called, liked to eat, what books they liked to read, what games they liked to play, or whether they had special words or names for favourite people or things.

The husband Vanessa may or may not have been unhappily married to worked, it emerged, for the Foreign Office and had been sent to Equatorial Guinea, wherever that was. He would be back in several weeks. "So you see, I really need someone urgently. Now," Vanessa emphasised, skewering Emma with those bulging blue eyes.

But it did not seem to Emma that this urgent need was reflected in the salary offered, which was low. On the plus side, she would be living in, and while she had not been expecting luxury, the fact that the tall house seemed to get colder the further up you got was discouraging. Even more so was the tiny bedroom at the top she was shown into, with the peeling wallpaper, collapsing curtain rail and light fitting that appeared to be masking-taped to the wall and ceiling respectively. Next door was the children's bedroom and, next door to that, the playroom. The "nursery suite" was how Vanessa referred to the whole.

Emma went back downstairs with Vanessa, full of uncertainty. Should she not get out now? Go home? She could always write off for other jobs, after all.

"You can start immediately," Vanessa offered. Or, possibly, instructed.

"But I haven't seen the children," Emma pointed out quickly. If they were awful too, that would decide it.

"Hero! Cosmo!" bawled Vanessa.

The children appeared at the door. Hero, the solid little three-year-old, had a solemn little face and hair so flaxen, so impossibly white, that it seemed lit from within, a silver flame. Cosmo, at four, had eyes that were deep, sunken, and anxious, and his hair was a caramel pageboy, striped with lighter gold. They regarded Emma suspiciously, but that, she felt, was understandable enough, especially if five nannies had come and gone in the last twelve months.

"Ask me if I'm a passenger train or a freight train," Cosmo demanded suddenly in a low, growling voice.

Emma thought of the toy train in her handbag. She had been right, after all. Was there any little boy who didn't like locomotives?

Vanessa rolled her eyes. "God. He's absolutely bloody obsessed with trains. Just shut up, will you, Cosmo? You've driven all the nannies mad with this. Another reason why they've all left," she groaned at Emma.

But Cosmo, ignoring his mother, was looking at Emma expectantly, his blue eyes round through his blond fringe. She sensed it was some sort of test. She smiled, stooping down to his level, and felt the difficulty of doing so in wobbly high heels and trousers that bit at the waist and round the thighs. She looked into his uncertain little face. "Are you a passenger train or a freight train?" she asked, obediently.

Cosmo shuffled his little feet on the carpet. His fingers were joined together and pointing forward, and both arms were revolving by his sides, imitating the moving parts of a locomotive.

"I'm a passenger train," he told her now, his four-year-old face entirely serious.

"Can I get on you?" Emma asked.

"No," said Cosmo, causing Emma's heart to sink rather. Her initiative had been rejected.

"You can't get on me," Cosmo added, earnestly, "because I'm a special train. But you can look at me. Woo woo!" And with that, the little boy steamed out of the sitting room.

"See what I mean?" steamed Vanessa. "He wants to be an engine driver. I ask you, is that what I'll be paying millions in school fees for?"

Emma looked at Hero.

"And Hero's obsessed with cats," Vanessa added, as if this too was a crime.

Emma hardly heard. She was looking into Hero's blue eyes, in which she had spotted an unmistakeable, hungry look that was nothing to do with food but everything to do with the need for affection and attention. It twisted her heart.

"I'll take the job," she said, reaching for her handbag. "And, actually, I've got a couple of presents for them."

Chapter Three

In an apartment in Los Angeles, a phone was ringing loudly beside a bed. As his short, fat fingers made contact with the receiver, Mitch Masterson, actor's agent, squinted at the alarm clock beside his bed.

Who the hell was ringing him this early?

As if he couldn't guess.

Mitch groaned. Last night had been the annual get-together of the Association of Motion Picture Actors' Representatives, an annual red-letter day in the agenting industry that provided unmissable opportunities for networking. Mitch had done so much networking he'd been barely able to stand up at the end of the evening. And now his throat burned, his eyes ached, and his head felt as if someone had stuck a sword in it. The last thing he needed was a call from Belle Murphy.

The day had barely started, and it was a nightmare already. If only he could send it back and get a refund. Or swap it for another one. But no, it was here. Fingers of daylight as thick as his own were poking bluntly and insistently between the wenge-wood blinds that Mitch's interior designer assured him gave his apartment that breezy, Californian, young-stylish-single-guy-with-money-to-burn feel.

Californian as in originally from Cataract, Tennessee, that was. Young as in forty-four. Single in the divorced sense. The money could be better too—Associated Artists was a super-successful agency, sure, one of the biggest in Hollywood. But he was only one of its medium-ranking agents. Nor was he stylish; frankly, he was fat and irredeemably scruffy. His ex-wife had likened him to Humpty Dumpty. After he fell off the wall.

"Hey, Belle, baby!" Mitch struggled to sound as if no call could be more convenient or more delightful.

As usual, Belle didn't waste time on pleasantries. Such as asking Mitch how he was or apologising for waking him up. "You heard from Spielberg yet?" she demanded, her shrill, high-pitched voice drilling the tender insides of Mitch's ear.

Of course, he hadn't heard from Spielberg. Nor was he likely to. The casting director was an old girlfriend and had allowed Belle to try out more to get her off Mitch's back than to put her in the film. No one wanted to put her in a film. In a meeting room in the offices of Associated Artists, a room in which no client ever set foot, was a league table of those the company represented. The Fame Board covered an entire wall and was adjusted each day, like the FTSE and the Dow Jones, to reflect clients' comparative status. On this cruel, if accurate, measure of exactly where she stood in Tinseltown, Belle was currently near the bottom. And yet this time last year, she had been at the top, Associated Artists' number one, most important client.

Even the CEO of the agency had answered her calls then, and at great length. She'd been sent Christmas, birthday, Thanksgiving, Halloween, and every other imaginable kind of present from the agency, including some "just because we love you." Or, to be more accurate, just because of the hit film *Marie*, in which Belle had played Mary, Queen of Scots.

Mitch allowed himself a transporting moment of remembered joy at this most purple of patches. Belle had carried all before her—literally; the costume department had certainly made the most of her assets. Her take on the doomed, impetuous monarch, all plunging cleavage and passionate four-poster scenes, had been a stupendous success. For several months, Belle had been one of the hottest actresses in Hollywood. Her smouldering red pout had sizzled from the cover of every magazine. But then had come *Bloody Mary* as a follow-up.

Mitch still had no idea why Belle's studio had imagined that a film about an uptight, pyromaniac, religious nutcase was a suitable vehicle for her. No doubt he should have advised her against doing it, but the enormous amount of money the agency had pocketed over the deal had clouded his judgment, as was often the case in Hollywood. The film had bombed, or gone up in smoke, to be more accurate, and now Belle was colder than yesterday's breakfast.

"And what about Ridley Scott? Sam Mendes?" Belle was screeching now. "Have they got back to you?"

"Not as such, baby, but you know they're both pretty busy. Mendes has, ah, um, you know. Kids and stuff…"

"*Kids?*"

"Yeah. You know how busy kids keep people." Mitch was improvising as best he could. "Can't get to the phone or anything…"

"*What?*"

Mitch wondered why he didn't simply put the phone down on her. Any other agent at Associated would have done so, recognising that Belle needed them far more than they needed her at the moment. What complicated things for Mitch was that he felt sorry for her.

He would never have admitted it to either his bosses or his colleagues. It was probably a sacking offence. It was certainly the last thing an agent should ever feel, he knew. And, no doubt, it was the reason he had never got any further than he had.

He simply wasn't ruthless enough, Mitch knew. He empathised. He winced at the way the Hollywood machine chewed people up and spat them out. And although what had happened to Belle was anything but unusual—he'd seen it many times before—that didn't make it pleasant.

And what made it worse, Mitch thought, was that he felt

personally involved. To blame, even. He felt guilty that he had not objected to *Bloody Mary* as soon as it was mentioned. That he might have had a hand—a very big hand—in Belle's fall.

Because fall she most certainly had. Even though this time last year, after the sensation of *Marie*, she had been hotter than the earth's core, twelve months was an eternity in Hollywood. Since *Bloody Mary*, Belle couldn't get arrested in L.A. Mitch even feared her studio was about to drop her.

Studios were laws unto themselves, and Belle's studio, NBS, with the workaholic puritan Arlington Shorthouse at the helm, was more of a law than most. It could afford to be—it had a box-office hit rate second to none in Hollywood and was reportedly planning its most audacious assault yet on the multiplexes of the world.

There had been nothing definite yet to confirm that a space saga, provisionally entitled *Galaxia*, about an imaginary universe of robots, spaceships, and fabulous creatures with improbable names along the lines of the blockbustering, all-conquering *Star Wars*, was being planned by NBS. But the rumours were insistent enough for Mitch to wonder if there was anything in it. If there was, the timing could hardly be better for Belle. She needed something—and fast—to turn things around for her.

The fact she was dating Christian Harlow, an actor who had been unknown before he had hooked up with Belle and now was widely tipped to be the new Brad Pitt, was certainly not that something. It was, Mitch thought, fairly obvious that Harlow would dump Belle just as soon as she'd outlived her usefulness.

"Relax, baby," he pleaded with Belle, although he knew there was as much chance of this as of the Californian sun going out.

"I'll call Steven today. Yeah. And Sam too. And Ridley, sure, yeah, mustn't forget him. No. Yeah. No. Promise. See ya." Thankfully, he shoved the receiver back in its cradle and dived back into the refuge of his hot, stewy, and rumpled bed.

Chapter Four

Burdened by luggage, James Bradstock walked slowly down the street leading to his home. He had not seen it for several weeks. Not since setting out on the fact-finding mission in Equatorial Guinea on which his employers in the Foreign Office had seen fit to send him, and from which he had just returned. Not necessarily with the requisite facts, James was aware; the brief had been vague, to say the least. The only things he felt entirely confident about coming back with, in fact, were the pair of pencils with little carved dolls on the top for Hero and Cosmo.

As he went through the small front gate, James felt happy and excited. He had thought of the children constantly while he was away: little white-haired Hero with her serious gaze and determined character, and impulsive and passionate Cosmo. He longed to feel their small but strong little arms around his neck and their faces snuggling into his.

He wondered whether they had grown—but, of course, they would have; there would be something wrong otherwise—and what new words Hero knew. There was sure to be a new interest, as well. When he left, it had been Thomas and trains still, as it had been for some time, but Cosmo might well have discovered something else since. Music, perhaps. He knew Vanessa was starting them on music appreciation classes at—of all places—the Royal Opera House and had high hopes of them becoming virtuosos.

He was looking forward to seeing his wife nonetheless. She scared him rather, but he loved her and was proud of her. Slim, blonde, and always smartly turned out, Vanessa was better looking and better dressed than most of the other Foreign Office wives, most of whom looked like their husbands, only rather more masculine. The fact that Vanessa had a career of her own—her newspaper column—made her even more exotic and special.

James had spoken to Vanessa from the airport and had learnt, rather to his disappointment, that she would be out for the early part of the evening he arrived home. She had a charity-ball committee meeting to attend at which some crucial issue, such as the sandwiches, was being decided. But the nanny would be at home, the new one who had been engaged while he was away. The fact she was still there was, James felt, encouraging.

"She's…okay then, is she?" he had asked his wife earlier.

Vanessa had inhaled disdainfully. "Bit fat and northern, but no, not bad."

Fat and northern, James mused after she had rung off. Well, that sounded good to him. The last nanny, Jacintha, had been all sharp elbows and painfully thin calves. She had been painfully pretentious too, full of references to her ancient and venerable family.

Vanessa had loved the thought of someone who claimed to trace her ancestry back to the Conqueror wiping Hero's bottom. But Jacintha had always made him feel as if the whole family was rather beneath her. Anything—fat, northern, or whatever—was going to be an improvement on that, James felt as he opened the front door.

The first thing he noticed was that the house smelt much cleaner than usual. It smelt of nice baths, shampoo, and talcum powder. It also looked tidier than he had expected—tidier than he ever remembered seeing it, in fact. The great bulging bundle of children's cardigans, bags, coats, and other paraphernalia, traditionally attached in a clump to the hall coat hooks like some multicoloured wasps' nest, had disappeared. One or two coats in regular use hung demurely there instead. James' gaze dropped to a row of children's shoes, neatly arranged and beautifully clean, beneath the coats. His eyes widened. The children's shoes were usually in a muddy heap of wrong sizes and missing other halves. This had been the case throughout the reign of all previous nannies.

It was now that he noticed the delicious smell. James ventured into the kitchen, which, unusually, was pin-neat. On the shining draining board, whose metal surface he did not recall ever seeing before, so choked was it normally with clutter, were two small plates, two sets of spoons and forks, two cups, and a baking dish, all washed. On the otherwise empty and spotless kitchen table, a delicious-looking macaroni and cheese, browned on top and evidently homemade, sat cooling in the twin of the empty baking dish.

He noticed with approval and surprise the two cloth napkins rolled up in their rings and placed tidily to the side. Most nannies instantly gave up trying to impress proper table manners on Hero and Cosmo; not this one, it seemed. His gaze now took in a small bowl in which a few pieces of broccoli, evidently leftovers, had been placed. James did a double take. This nanny could not only cook but had managed to get the children to eat vegetables. And not only vegetables. Broccoli.

The house wasn't silent, James realised now. He could hear something upstairs. A voice, but not one he recognised.

He slowly ascended the threadbare sisal staircase. The sound seemed to be coming from the direction of the large, rather shabby bedroom that Hero and Cosmo shared and the adjoining and even shabbier upstairs bathroom.

James paused outside the children's bedroom door. Someone was speaking loudly and dramatically in a strange accent. It didn't sound northern though. It sounded French.

James was puzzled. Although Vanessa occasionally decided that the children needed lessons in conversational French, he hadn't realised she had done anything about it. He glanced at his watch and felt even more puzzled. If French wasn't off the agenda and a teacher had been appointed, what was he or she doing here at half-past-seven at night? Without Vanessa being around? What was she thinking? He knew she took her charity committees seriously, but this was ridiculous.

James grabbed the round, wooden handle of the white-painted door and pushed it open.

The French accent stopped immediately. James peered into the room.

The next minute, he was bowled over by small bodies running at him full tilt. "Daddy!"

James pulled them to him and hugged them hard. They had both grown, he saw from an initial glance; their faces seemed to have lengthened, especially Cosmo's. They had obviously had their baths, being dressed in their pyjamas with their hair neatly brushed.

He had almost forgotten about the strange French voice, but now he saw that, sitting on Cosmo's bed, was a girl of about twenty with a very pretty face and shoulder-length brown hair. She looked perfectly normal in build, not at all fat, and wore black trousers and a white polo shirt. Her skin was creamy, with reddish cheeks like apples and a pair of large brown eyes that were looking at him enquiringly.

"I'm so sorry," James apologised. "Emma, isn't it? We haven't met. I'm James, Cosmo and Hero's father." He ruffled their neatly brushed heads. "Actually, I hadn't realised you were French." Had he heard Vanessa wrong? Had she said "France" instead of "northern"? But surely the telephone line, even from Equitorial Guinea, couldn't be that bad.

From her comfortable perch on the bed, Emma regarded Vanessa's husband with interest. He was not what she had expected. Not the sleek alpha male she had pictured at all, but tall, thin, be-spectacled, and apologetic, his collar awry and his glasses wonky.

"I'm not French," she smiled. "I was just giving one of the characters in *Chicken Licken* a French accent."

In the dim recesses of James' mind, something stirred. "Oh yes," he said, uncertainly. "That chicken. It goes and tells everyone. It tells Cocky Locky. Is that right? Chicken, um, Licken meets, um, Cocky Locky?"

"And Turkey Lurkey," Cosmo interrupted eagerly, his eyes shining beneath his smooth pageboy fringe. "And Emma does everyone in the story with a different voice."

Emma saw the children's father was frowning slightly, his eyes moving about as if searching for something.

"What's the matter?"

"Oh. Um. I was just wondering. You don't seem to be using a, um, book," James said eventually.

"I don't need a book. I've read it so often to children that there'd be something wrong if I didn't know it off by heart. Time for you two to go to sleep anyway," Emma informed her charges.

James watched as Hero slid a pair of tired white arms about Emma's neck and was carried to her small bed in the corner and laid down with the utmost care. He did not remember them being so tactile with Jacintha, nor Jacintha being so solicitous.

James looked round the bedroom. The furniture had been rearranged in a more sensible, harmonious way: the children's beds had been pushed further apart, and stuffed toys had been arranged in one corner to look like a tea party. Up on the walls were the embroidered names in frames that his mother, a keen needlewoman, had done when the children were born, but which Vanessa had always declared too naff to display.

A comfortable-looking chair had appeared from somewhere. Various lamps had arrived; the harsh, overhead light that had been in operation seemed to have been retired. Emma had achieved far more during her first three weeks in her job than he had in Equatorial

Guinea, James reflected guiltily. But then, Emma obviously had a sound grasp of what she was supposed to be doing.

"I'll leave you to say good night to them now." Emma slipped past him out of the door, a clean, scented soap smell trailing in her wake. "But I'd leave the lamp on for a while. Hero's afraid of the dark, as you know."

James blinked back at her, stifling the instinctively honest response that this was news to him. Jacintha had been obsessed to the point of hysteria with completely dark rooms being crucial for proper sleep. At her behest and at great expense, they had fitted black-lined curtains and blackout blinds in the children's bedroom, but here was Emma, saying none of this was necessary and with Hero looking more relaxed than he had ever seen her.

"By the way, if you're hungry," Emma said as she passed him, "there's a spare macaroni and cheese in the kitchen. I was going to freeze it, but I like to cook the children something fresh every day, so you're welcome to it if you want it."

James blinked. He was beginning to wonder whether this woman was real or a happy vision. She seemed too good to be true.

Chapter Five

IN AN APARTMENT MORE lavish than Mitch's, and in a better part of Los Angeles, a thin, blonde woman slammed down the bedside phone angrily. Damn Mitch for not picking up. Okay, so she'd spoken to him this morning already, only five minutes ago, in fact, but he was supposed to be her agent, at her beck and call. Her call, certainly. Belle was not sure what her beck was.

Still, there were compensations. If Mitch didn't want to pay her any attention, others would. Beside her, across the rumpled expanse of oyster-coloured satin sheets covering the vast bed, a handsome young man stirred. As she watched, Belle's artificially shaped and filled chest, balancing like two melon halves on its thin ribcage, swelled further with pride, albeit this time completely naturally.

He was like a young lion waking, she thought fancifully, admiring the muscled arms—smooth, tanned, and lightly oiled—as they moved upwards, pulling the powerful chest and stomach with its clearly defined six-pack into a stretch. Everything below this was twisted up in the oyster satin, but Belle knew what lay beneath well enough: the powerful thighs, the tight buttocks…she felt a sudden hot rush in which the thrill of ownership combined with lust.

If Christian Harlow wasn't the hottest man in Hollywood at that moment, she'd like to know who was. And he was hers. All hers. Of all the women in Hollywood, he had chosen to be with her. She couldn't be all that washed up, could she?

Her smile widened as Christian lifted his head from where it was squashed into the oyster satin pillow, revealing that impossibly handsome, deeply tanned face with huge lips and black hair, so very black that it had navy lights in it, dropping into smouldering eyes of a different blue, an intense, swimming-pool blue. The face that currently had all of Hollywood excited, Belle knew. That was starting to appear on the front of the men's magazines. All thanks to her. She had given him the contacts he had needed to make his dreams of being a Hollywood star come true.

Christian looked at her, and, as always, just as she had the first time she had met him, Belle felt a tightening in her groin, a rush in the mouth, a tingling in her nipples. He was a prime piece of beefcake. The best.

Their meeting had, she remembered fondly, been a classic lady-and-tramp situation. Or perhaps lady and cramp. It had been at a film industry party where Christian had been a human sculpture, painted silver and striking a pose which, he explained afterwards, had given him chronic leg ache.

He had soon recovered, however, and, that same night, Belle discovered Christian's ability to give her orgasms so intense they made her teeth rattle. Even after all the veneering, which seemed a double achievement.

She watched admiringly as the blue eyes opened for the first time that day, looked straight into hers, and, right on cue, creased in a smile.

"Hey, baby," Christian breathed. He had arranged his features into their usual smouldering, impenetrable pout into which undying devotion or cynical lack of interest could be read with equal ease. Belle always chose to read the devotion. But what Christian's silent smoulder was actually saying was that she really should get some clothes on.

He liked slim—who didn't—but making love to Belle was like screwing a set of steps. And while the odd nip and tuck was fine by him, there were more nips on Belle than a colony of goddamn crabs. It wasn't that Christian particularly prized authenticity, but there was nothing remotely natural about this woman. Belle was all fake, from the cascade of white-blonde hair tossing constantly about and the equally unremitting blaze of veneered teeth to the stretched skin of her face and the exposed and prominent rounded domes of her breasts—with a gap between them you could park a motorbike in.

Belle always denied she had had surgery, but Christian knew the signs. He didn't think she'd had a fanny tuck yet, but she'd definitely had lipo on her bottom that might have gone to the filling in her lips. And so every time her mouth sought his, Christian wondered if he was quite literally kissing her ass.

"You look gorgeous," he assured her.

There was a growl from beside the bed. Christian raised himself on his elbow and looked with dislike at a small, brown dog with a very big diamond collar. Belle's pet Chihuahua, Sugar, was, as usual, staring at him with enormous and very prominent black eyes.

Caninus interruptus. The dog had got him off the hook. Belle clearly wanted servicing, even though he'd done enough of that last night. Yet Christian could still not look at Sugar with anything other than hatred. He was aware that the animal returned his feelings in full measure.

How could anyone love a mutt like that, Christian wondered. Sugar was bad-tempered and vicious. Belle spoilt it rotten, and it wasn't grateful in the least. She lavished it with love, which it did not return one iota.

Belle swung her thin, brown legs off the bed and scooped the dog against her naked breasts. "Sugar!" Christian watched scornfully as she lavished the dog's bony skull with kisses. "This morning," Belle crooned, "I'm taking you to the dog beautician for a manicure."

He drew himself upright against the pillows, pulling up his powerful legs and letting them fall open with just a swatch of oyster sheet covering his manhood. This was less for reasons of modesty than fear that sight of his organ—of which Christian was justifiably proud—might rouse the dog to some act of jealous and irreversible savagery.

Belle licked her lips. Her eyes on the satin heaping between his legs, she put the dog carefully on the floor. But as Sugar growled warningly, Belle paused in her slithering progress across the sheets. "We'd better not, baby," she said to Christian in tones of breathy apology. "It might upset Sugar."

"Oh, for Chrissakes," snarled Christian, impatient with the whole idea of the dog's importance, as well as the idea he wanted to have sex with this scrawny tramp yet again. He'd performed for the last time last night, knowing that this morning he was going to dump her.

Belle had outlived her usefulness, and it was time he moved on to someone who could get him through the final bit of the journey: right up to the top of the Hollywood ladder.

Christian's eye, sufficiently deep set to hide how small and sly it actually was, caught the row of acting awards, gold masks, wreaths, globes, and lumps of engraved glass that stood proudly on the two mirror-panelled nightstands at either side of Belle's bed. He felt a twinge of envy. He'd have all that too, one day. It was all in front of him, Christian thought, his blue gaze sweeping appreciatively down the front of his massive, oiled, and waxed pectorals to the thick stem of his manhood. Which, from now on, would be servicing someone else. Someone more useful.

Because it was all over with Belle now. She had let her career hit the skids with a turkey film. And so he had to move on for the good of his own career. How was that his fault? She had no one but herself to blame. He was only doing what anyone in his position would do at the moment.

"We can have some time together later," she said, as she wound an arm around his neck. Christian felt her silicon breasts squash unpleasantly against him. He remained rigid, however. "It's over, baby," he muttered into the brittle, musky-smelling, white-blonde hair massed against his lips. "We're over."

He felt her convulse with shock. "Over?" Belle gasped disbelievingly.

"I've gotta move on," he explained.

"Move on? Move on from me? But why?"

"Look, baby. It's business, yeah? Only business. No offence. Nothing personal."

Belle's eyes were bigger than he had ever seen them. He had not imagined, given the constraints of her facial surgery, that so much stretching was even possible. "Business?" she managed to force out. "Nothing…personal?"

"This is Hollywood," Christian said. "So you were huge last year. But a year's a long time in showbiz. You're losing it, and now you've lost me." He put his handsome, heavy head, with its great ridges of cheekbone, on one side and gave an apologetic grin. "It's just the way things are, baby."

"Don't leave me," Belle wept, stretching out her thin arms to him in abject and heartfelt appeal. "I thought…I thought…you loved me."

"Loved you?" His amazement was genuine. Didn't she know? No one loved anyone in Hollywood. They just had sex with them; that was all.

Chapter Six

THE MEMORY OF THE beautiful boy haunted Sam. With his amazing pale-green eyes, touched with yellow, not to mention all his other attributes, he remained with her as magnificent salmon do with the fishermen whose hooks they have slipped. The fact that she had managed to snap him on her mobile phone only increased the sense of him being the one who got away.

Sam pored over the image. She had spent most of the week since it was taken at Wild's sister agency in New York and was haunted in her absence by the fear that rival scouts might have snapped the boy up in the meantime.

At the first opportunity, which happened to be the Friday following that when Orlando had escaped her, Sam rose from her desk at around the same time she had the week before. Her logic was that the beautiful boy might have to cross the piazza again at the same time, that he had some regular reason for being there.

With this in mind, her PA, Nia, had been instructed to book today's lunch with a magazine fashion editor, one recently appointed to an important glossy, in the same restaurant in Covent Garden in which Sam had met Jack Oeuf the week before.

"I'll be back at two-thirty," Sam called as she left. Nia, a thin-faced brunette with shining, black shoulder-length hair and dressed in regulation Wild black polo sweater and black capri pants, flashed her boss a slightly knowing smile. Nia knew, just as Sam did, that a return before three was highly unlikely.

There was, Sam felt as she left, something rather insubordinate about Nia.

In Covent Garden, Sam had given herself a few extra minutes to dawdle in the piazza. Carefully, she stepped round the taped-down, chalked renditions of Marilyn Monroe and St. Paul's. She didn't want to risk another mouthful from the pavement artists, who clearly had artistic temperaments, if no other attribute in that respect.

"Visualising" success had always been one of Sam's buzzwords. She firmly believed that if you could imagine something to yourself, it would then happen. She had visualised seeing Orlando again so many times that the possibility he might not, after all, appear was unthinkable. Nevertheless, as the gilt-faced clock of the actor's church boomed one, the lunch hour, Sam found herself having to think it.

She glanced at her watch. There was always the possibility that the new fashion director would be late at the restaurant, thus giving her a few more minutes. This prospect faded as Sam reflected that Genevieve was not the late type. Fashion directors fell into two categories: those who looked like messy bedrooms and those who looked like research scientists. Genevieve was in the latter category, a stick-thin brunette with dark retro spectacles, severe hair, and plainly cut clothes in shades of aubergine, charcoal, and moss. She was also extremely organised.

Swinging her beige cashmere angrily over her shoulder, Sam moved crossly off. Her glance swept, uninterested, over a group of rickety schoolgirls with narrowed, much-eyelined eyes and miniskirts exposing long, white skinny legs. Although that girl there, about twenty, walking purposefully along by herself, with reddish-brown, shoulder-length hair and a pale blue cardigan, she was interesting. Remarkably pretty, with thick, shining hair and a sweet, open, heart-shaped face. Milkmaidy. Healthy. Fresh. A milkmaid moment in fashion was long overdue, Sam found herself thinking. But, of course, the girl wasn't tall enough and she was far too fat.

❖❖❖

Emma was coming to meet Cosmo and Hero from their Friday morning music appreciation class at the Royal Opera House.

As she entered the foyer, grand, high-ceilinged, and blazing with mirrors, she slowed down. The children were not out yet, but the other nannies were already there. The other nannies, who looked after Hero and Cosmo's friends and acquaintances, invariably made Emma feel uncomfortable.

It wasn't just that she was the newest of the circle. She was so unlike them as well. The other nannies were so poised and polished: slim and groomed, all high heels and skinny jeans, their shiny, swishy hair caught up with sunglasses. And the most poised and polished of them all was Totty de Belvedere.

Totty looked after a gloomy-looking child called Hengist Westonbirt. The first time Emma had seen Totty, at a children's party, she had wondered how, given the exigencies of car seats, nappy changing, fiddly buttons, bathtime, and the rest of it, Totty managed to maintain such impressively long and manicured nails. Perhaps she had an assistant. For her part, Totty had asked Emma what part of Eastern Europe she had come from.

"None. I'm from Yorkshire," Emma had answered, looking Totty steadily in the eye.

"Oh, God. Sorry!" Totty had clapped a hand with long manicured nails to her lipsticked mouth and squealed with laughter.

The children were now coming out of the auditorium, but only Hero and Cosmo looked pleased to see their nanny.

"Woo woo!" chortled train-mad Cosmo, steaming across the carpet beneath the huge and brilliant chandeliers. Hero, meanwhile, lispingly informed Emma that the orchestra had played her favourite film tune.

"'Chitty Chitty Bang Bang!'" exclaimed Emma delightedly.

There was a scornful noise from behind. Emma turned to find herself staring into the tiger-yellow, much-mascara'd eyes of Totty de Belvedere. "What is it about kids and 'Chitty Chitty Bang Bang'?" Totty swung back her striped blonde hair scornfully. "Hengist's obsessed with it too." She shot a look of deep dislike at her charge, who was shuffling unhappily along beside her.

"Poor Hengist," Cosmo remarked as they walked out into the sunlight of the piazza. "I don't think he likes Totty very much. She isn't very nice, is she?"

Chapter Seven

"ARE YOU ON FACEBOOK, darling?"

The voice came from the other side of Orlando's bedroom door. As it happened, he was watching morning children's television. A pair of chirpy northern presenters with gelled hair were sitting on a purple sofa and bantering with someone dressed in a bright-yellow chicken suit.

The door opened, and his mother came in. As usual, she was dressed in clothes designed for someone several decades younger than she was. Georgie was small and thin and proud of the fact she could get into Miss Sixty jeans like the slimmest of teenage girls. She was wearing them today with a flimsy purple blouse. Her make-up, as always, was immaculate. Georgie's face was thin and rather rabbity with over-plucked eyebrows, but she made the most of what she had, as she believed everyone should.

"Oh...you're not on Facebook..." Georgie sounded disappointed as she stumbled in her high-heeled sandals on the piles of trainers and hooded tops that lay scattered over Orlando's bedroom floor.

Facebook. Orlando groaned silently. Georgie was obsessed with the social networking site. She kept up with fashion and trends with an energy that amazed her son, who did neither, but Facebook was a special interest, with its opportunities for demonstrating social one-upmanship. His mother was a hopeless snob, Orlando knew, but hopeless in the positive sense that she was too kind-hearted, too spontaneous, and too nervous to make a real success of snobbery, as well as utterly lacking the visceral instinct that made the flint-eyed parents of some of his school peers so terrifying, and, in some cases, the peers themselves.

Nonetheless, Georgie had badgered him mercilessly to get his own Facebook page, sending him endless "Georgie Fitzmaurice has invited you to join…" messages from her own account and making her friends, also in their mid-fifties but all keen Facebookers, do the same.

Orlando secretly thought Facebook a boring waste of time, the acme of insincerity, a magnet for neurotics and the socially insecure. He held out as long as he could, but his email inbox had become so choked with invitations from mature ladies that the site crashed every time he launched it. He had had to give in.

After that, whenever curiosity got the better of him and he was actually on Facebook, Georgie seemed miraculously to know and would appear, as she had done now, lean over his shoulder, and try to catch a glimpse of who his cyber-friends were.

"Orlo!" she would exclaim. "You've only got ten friends! And half of them are mine! Shouldn't you have three hundred or something? I hear that's the normal minimum. Tania Whyte-Oliphant was telling me yesterday that Ariadne—she's the part-time model, going to Cambridge—has over six-hundred friends on Facebook! And Eliza Cocke-Roche gets poked over a thousand times a day!"

"Mum!" Orlando would groan. He absolutely didn't care about Facebook. But he did care about his mother, and to see her stooping to such levels was far more distressing than his cyber-unpopularity…

Facebook, however, had been the first indicator of his recently altered status. Some time before he grasped the extent to which his looks had changed, Orlando was puzzled to find that his inbox was suddenly full of people proposing themselves as cyber-acquaintances. None of them were middle-aged women either.

From having ten friends, Orlando suddenly began to find he had twenty, then fifty, then a hundred, then hundreds and hundreds.

Most of them were girls. Some he knew: girls from his own school, sisters of his school friends, girls in the sixth form. But many, many, he didn't. He had scrolled through, dumbfounded. There was page after page after page of them, some extremely pretty, with long blonde hair and big pink smiles. Others smouldered from behind black tresses. All seemed to be staring at him expectantly. Orlando was scared of all of them. What did they want?

As the numbers spiraled towards the thousand mark, Orlando stopped going online, terrified of his mother seeing the hugely increased figures. Her excitement would have been excruciating.

"Aren't you a bit old for this?" Georgie was gesturing at the television, where a giant purple cat was demonstrating how to make pineapple-topped pizza.

"Yes," Orlando agreed readily. He had no idea why he was watching it either. He had a vague inkling that the world of children appealed to him more and more as he got older and the pressures of adulthood revealed themselves. But he could not have said this to his mother, nor would she have wanted to hear it.

Neither had he said to his mother that a model agency had approached him. This was because he could easily picture her indignation—with him. So desperate was Georgie for him to be a success at something that she would have phoned Wild up on the spot and offered his services.

As Orlando reached his late teens, the fact that he was less and less the child his mother had hoped for was becoming more and more obvious. Of course, he loved her—as he did his father—very much, and he knew that she loved him. But he also knew that she found him annoying. As she saw it, Orlando knew, he resolutely refused to make the most—or indeed, anything—of the opportunities she lavished on him. While Orlando, although he tried to feel grateful, was increasingly, bleakly aware that he had not wanted these opportunities in the first place.

The expensive private school, for which his parents had scrimped and saved to send him, was the most glaring illustration of this. It maddened Georgie that the only determination Orlando had shown in regard to Heneage's was in relentlessly not trying to become friends with the sons and daughters of what his mother called the movers and shakers.

"You never get asked to anyone's house for the weekend," Georgie wailed at one particularly frustrated moment.

Actually, he often got asked these days, but he was careful to make sure his mother did not know he had refused. The frantic, competitive social fray revolving around whose smart house everyone else was staying at in the holidays—or which festival in the grounds of whose grandparents' castle everyone was heading to with their tents and Temperley party dresses—filled him with horror.

He was not academically gifted either and was further hampered in success of this nature by what had been diagnosed as borderline dyslexia and by more than borderline lack of interest in either the subjects or his teachers. So far as the teachers were concerned, the lack of interest was mutual.

Despite the staggering fees that his parents paid to make sure the most was being got out of him, most teachers wrote Orlando off immediately and told Georgie and Richard that he simply was not trying.

These teachers seemed, Orlando had noticed, to make more effort with the equally unmotivated children of richer and more famous parents, but he had never mentioned this to his mother and father. It had suited him to be left more or less to his own devices at school.

Now, however, Orlando heartily wished he had made more effort. He had taken his A levels at the start of the summer, and the results were due in the middle of August. They would be terrible, Orlando knew. It was largely to stave off thoughts of this future misery that

Orlando currently spent as much time as was possible in his bedroom watching chubby twelve-year-olds throw pies at each other.

"I came to show you this," Georgie beamed, waving a coloured picture at him. She picked her way over the trainers.

The image was of a long, low house in golden stone with a red roof. It had a patio with big white sunshades on it and was surrounded by cypresses. There was a blue sky and a swimming pool in the foreground.

"What is it?" Orlando asked.

"A farmhouse in Tuscany!" Georgie trilled. "I've booked it. For the whole of August."

"Great. You and Dad deserve a break."

As did he, Orlando felt with a surge of joy. And this was one he had never even dared hope for: being left alone and unbadgered by his mother when the exam results came out.

"You're coming too, of course, darling. There's plenty of room. And a pool!" Her voice might be light, but Georgie's eye, Orlando saw, was steely. And he knew of old that resistance to the iron will of his mother was not an option. His chin sank onto his chest in a defeated attitude, and, as his mother fussed around picking up T-shirts, he sank glumly into the beanbag.

Then a thought occurred to him. Perhaps Italy could be an advantage so far as his A-level results were concerned. The middle of the Tuscan countryside might be somewhere the long arm of the examinations board was unable to stretch to reach.

Might, but probably not, given his mother. She would have the date from the school; she would no doubt ring up on the day. And he had a feeling the results could be texted.

"Oooh, almost forgot." Georgie turned at the door. "The Faughs are coming for dinner next week." She wagged her finger playfully. "So don't go out. Jago and Ivo will be dying to see you."

Italy faded instantly in the face of this much greater threat to happiness. A burning, unpleasant sensation swirled through Orlando.

He had never liked his parents' friends, Hugh and Laura Faugh, and liked their sons less.

"It's so nice that they're your own age," Georgie fluted.

Orlando couldn't imagine why Georgie thought Ivo and Jago were his age. They were two years older at least. She really should overcome her vanity about wearing spectacles.

"They're such a good influence. Such nice, tidy boys. So well dressed," Georgie added, her gaze hooking on Orlando's oversized black T-shirt with its glow-in-the-dark, printed-on skeleton ribcage. He shrugged. So his clothes were tacky. He didn't care. He had bought this T-shirt weeks ago in a pound shop; it had appealed to his childish sense of humour.

The Faugh brothers, he knew, would never have worn such a thing, nor did they ever go in pound shops; facts that raised his T-shirt even higher in his eyes. The last time he had seen them, at a House of Commons garden party Georgie had dragged him determinedly along to, they had been wearing tight, dark-blue designer jeans with visible creases and high waists, all straining over the twins' large bottoms. Tucked into the jeans—and also into the underpants beneath, Orlando suspected—they wore merchant banker striped or checked shirts, open at the collar to expose a gold chain and with double cuffs and cufflinks. Tied around the twins' shoulders had been cashmere pullovers, jade for Ivo and ginger for Jago.

"And, of course, they're so clever," Georgie reminded him now. "Both at Cambridge."

Behind the curtains of his hair, Orlando grimaced. Cambridge was a word that struck fear into him. He had been dragged to the town several times over the past year by his mother, positioned in front of various spiry college entrances, and instructed to admire them.

"Wouldn't you just love to go there?" Georgie had demanded, eyes blazing with ambition. Orlando had taken one look at what seemed an endless stream of self-satisfied geeks coming out of the front entrance of King's and thought that no, actually, he wouldn't. Even if, given his academic record, there was a hope in hell of him going to Cambridge as anything other than one of the tourists that seemed to throng outside the innumerable tea shops, he wanted to go there about as much as he wanted to go to Italy. At the age of eighteen. With his parents.

❖❖❖

Downstairs, Orlando's father Richard was thinking about the Italian holiday too. He felt uneasy.

Georgie often made him feel uneasy. She was his childhood sweetheart and wife of nearly thirty years. But while he loved her devotedly, she had never been happy with his rank-and-file MP status. Georgie had always nursed ambitions for him beyond anything he had wanted.

These had never been fulfilled, however. He had remained a backbencher and would, Richard suspected, always remain one. He had long since resigned himself to the fact that he would never be a power in the land, but he was aware that Georgie hadn't.

"He's thrilled!" Richard heard Georgie trilling. She was back downstairs from breaking the holiday news to Orlando.

Richard felt a clutch of panic. "But darling, it's awfully expensive."

Georgie's expression was defiant and defensive. "I had to act fast. We haven't got anywhere else lined up. Have we?"

Her husband flinched at this full-frontal attack on his lack of social influence. For all his twenty years as a Conservative Member of Parliament, he had failed just as spectacularly as his son to bond with anyone who might have a suitable holiday home. Like Orlando, he had not tried, because, like Orlando, Richard had a built-in aversion to the types of people who swaggered about bragging about their wealth and influence. The fellow members of Parliament that Richard liked best were just like him: hardworking backbenchers struggling to maintain a place in London, as well as a constituency one.

Some MPs, of course, lived in their constituency and used cheap hotels when staying in London, but this option was not open to Richard. He represented a particularly unfashionable swath of Hertfordshire—albeit with one or two smart villages—in which Georgie flatly refused to live. Which was why Richard was now struggling to maintain a large, if battered, Highgate terrace house. Given their financial circumstances, hanging on to it sometimes felt like hanging on to a balloon in a Force 10 gale.

There was also the upkeep of a small flat in the constituency. Richard wished he had suggested to Georgie that they holiday there. It might be on the High Street and above a Chinese takeaway, but at least it was free.

He looked dumbly at his wife now. It didn't really matter what he thought about the villa; it was a fait accompli anyway. And given that their household outgoings were no longer as enormous as they had been, the expense was more bearable. There would, for example, be no more school fees for Orlando; he had taken his A levels this summer, and they could afford a little financial leeway. It would, in fact, be their first real treat holiday for fourteen years, since Orlando had started at prep school and his education had started to dominate the budget.

To what end, Richard was not sure. His only son had never been academic, a fact that had emerged early. Personally, Richard had been all for Orlando going to the local state primary, which had a good reputation. But Georgie had had other ideas. "Contacts!" she would insist. "He has to make contacts. Good contacts will get him through life."

Of course, Richard mused, household expenses could easily go up again if Orlando went to university, as his mother was determined he should. Personally, Richard rather hoped that he wouldn't.

Better the boy should leave and do something useful with his life, although goodness knew what. Not politics, obviously; too many family resources had been sacrificed to that already.

"Oh, by the way," Georgie added, as she clacked off across the kitchen tiles in her high heels, "I've asked the Faughs for dinner next week."

"Oh, my God," was her husband's response. He looked as if he were about to be sick.

"Richard!" Georgie's eyes bore into him. "Hugh's one of your closest friends!"

"That's stretching it," Richard muttered, sensing again that resistance was useless.

Hugh Faugh. Why on earth did Georgie persist in believing he was a close friend? They had never been close friends, even though their lives had, at one stage, run quite closely together. They had entered Parliament the same year, young Conservative MPs still wet behind the ears, or as wet as Hugh's ears ever got considering, or so Richard always suspected, he blow-dried his thick, black, shiny hair to give it that characteristic full, upward-sweeping look.

"Hair gets votes," Hugh had once told him in that booming, confident, maddening way in which he said everything. He had swept an unimpressed look over Richard's even-then-thinning, greying scalp and his pale, dry, nondescript face with its monkish features, and raised one of the virile, black eyebrows marking his own highly coloured, handsome, if rather heavy, face.

Had his underperforming follicles, Richard occasionally wondered since, stood in the way of Parliamentary favour? Would a more thickly populated pate have ensured election to the great offices of state?

But he knew in his heart that it wasn't killer hair he lacked. It was killer instinct. Certainly, soon after entering Parliament, his and Hugh's careers had dramatically diverged. Hugh, the more forceful and swashbuckling of the pair, had immediately disappeared into a cloud of glory with never a backward glance, gaining promotion after promotion, while Richard Fitzmaurice, bar the odd Commons committee, had never really moved off the backbenches. He had contented himself with being a well-thought-of constituency MP, which was, as he reminded himself many times through the years, what he had, after all, been elected for. That this wasn't well thought of by Georgie was just one of those things.

Great friends with Hugh, Richard thought with uncharacteristic sourness. Oh, absolutely. Great friends to the extent that Hugh, recently promoted to the Shadow Cabinet, had taken to stalking past him in Westminster corridors without even acknowledging him. But Georgie had been beside herself in delight to find that her husband's former university friend was now so elevated, and this, Richard suspected, was one of the reasons she had invited him for dinner.

Of course, Hugh would have accepted with alacrity. Not the least cause of Richard's disquiet was the fact that Hugh, or "Freebie Faugh," as he was known in the corridors of power, was notorious for his interest in all things complimentary. He was famous, in particular, for the zest with which he proved there absolutely was such a thing as a free lunch—and a free dinner as well.

Thank God, the summer recess was coming soon, Richard thought. Time for a change of scene. Time for Italy.

Chapter Eight

"Am I speaking with Mitch Masterson?"

"Yeah," Mitch drawled, not bothering to conceal the fact that, contrary to his doctor's instructions concerning his increasing weight, he was chewing on a jelly doughnut as he spoke. It was his second jelly doughnut, as well. And he had just had lunch into the bargain.

"I have Arlington Shorthouse on the line for you," the female voice said.

Her words electrified Mitch. His hand jerked in shock, and the coffee he was about to swig to wash down the last of his second doughnut now landed on the front of his shirt. His eyes watered, and he wanted to scream as the scalding liquid made contact with his nipples.

There were many reasons why NBS Studios, of which Arlington was head, could be calling him. At least fifty reasons: Mitch had upward of fifty clients after all, and they were all actors. But it was the fact that Arlington himself was calling that rang alarm bells.

Arlington, even though he was a well-known workaholic and famously hands-on, only called agents directly for two reasons. One was because he wanted to launch a career. The other was because he wanted to end one. Mitch, for whom thoughts of Belle Murphy were never far away, had a sudden, sickening, guilty feeling that had nothing to do with jelly doughnuts.

"Good morning, Mr. Shorthouse," he said meekly, as if his own good behaviour could somehow mitigate for his client and earn her a reprieve. And yet it wasn't a surprise that the end had come.

Since being dumped by Christian Harlow, Belle had hit the ground running—literally, and more than once after oblivion-seeking, champagne-fuelled benders in nightclubs that had been mercilessly covered by the press.

Day after day, Mitch had opened the tabloids to find, to his despair, lurid photographs of his former star client struggling, blind drunk, in and out of limos in wisps of dresses with a glaring absence of underwear. All of which would have been unlikely to impress the only person, apart from the state attorney, who mattered. This was the teetotalling and puritanical head of her studio, who felt his stars should be paragons of American virtue at all times. Arlington Shorthouse, the man who was ringing now. Doubtless to knock Belle's career on the head.

Arlington's next words, however, knocked Mitch as flat as Mitch could be knocked, given that he was sitting up at his desk. "We're making the *Galaxia* movie," the studio head announced in the quiet, ominous voice that could, Mitch imagined, freeze vodka solid. "We start shooting in the summer."

Mitch blinked. That was sensational news. Of course, many studios had tried and failed with space sagas since George Lucas had brought out *Star Wars*. But NBS's track record meant it had a very good chance. It was a prospect almost as dazzling as the sunshine.

It was also a relief. The news was clearly connected to one of his actors, and Belle, for all her troubles, was the best-known actor on his books. Arlington could hardly be ringing about anyone else. Perhaps he wasn't about to fire her, after all.

"You've got someone I want to offer one of the two main roles to," Arlington said.

A main role? Holy crap. In the darkness below his striped shirt, beneath his flabby upper arms, Mitch felt a nuclear glow of moisture. Sweat gathered on his forehead. Belle's career was saved, and his own was too. She'd be back at the top, the biggest movie actress of the day, probably the best paid too, which was the bit that interested Mitch. And would interest the Associated Artists CEO, when it came to doling out the promotions.

And not before time. Mitch had been passed over not once but many times too often recently, and there were other unpleasant reminders of the extent to which his status had slipped within the company. Associated's thrusting, younger agents, who felt they were too important to handle anything other than superstars, were increasingly palming off their smaller or older clients on him. Thanks to people like Greg Cucarachi, who was one of the palmers-off in chief, Mitch's list was currently thick with duds, small-timers, old-timers, and also-rans, and he had heard that some of the other agents sneeringly referred to him as "the graveyard."

The graveyard! Ha! He'd show them. With one of his clients a star in the new *Galaxia* film!

"Who is it?" Mitch asked, his voice smiling.

"Darcy Prince," replied Arlington Shorthouse.

Mitch's mind instantly dissolved into a fog. He felt he was standing over a bath and watching the pictures that had formed of Belle and himself—on the red-carpeted entrance to the Kodak Theatre, the Oscar-night paparazzi going crazy—disappearing down the plughole.

"Darcy Prince," he repeated, with a calmness he did not feel.

Darcy Prince? Who the hell was that?

Mitch groped about in the mist in his mind, panicking that Arlington had rung the wrong agency, that someone else was going to get this big chance, and wondering about the chances of finding this Darcy Prince and taking him or her on anyway, all in the next few seconds.

Then, with a great rush of relief, he realised that he did, in fact, represent Darcy Prince. He remembered the name vaguely; it had been in the latest sheaf of hopeless cases dumped on him by Greg

Cucarachi the other day. Mitch had filed the slim sheet of details away without even reading them, never expecting he would ever have to. Now, with the receiver containing Arlington tucked unsteadily under his flabby, stubbly chin, Mitch shot again in his chair over to his filing cabinet, trying to open it silently and fish out the details with trembling, sweating hands.

"Darcy Prince!" he said in musing tones, whilst frantically shoving his stubby hands into overstuffed folders that cut his fingers. Was it a man or a woman, he wondered.

"Yes. I was just in London, and I caught Darcy in a play there," Arlington remarked. "What was it called?" he mused.

"Er…" gasped Mitch, screwing up his eyes as he tried to remember what was currently going down in the British capital. *Mamma Mia* was all that came to mind. Was that a play, strictly speaking? And if it was, was Darcy Prince in it? He should know, of course, should have the information at his fingertips, being her agent.

"*A Doll's House*. That was it," Arlington said, his thin voice faintly warmed with self-congratulation. "She was impressive."

A Doll's House? Was that some kind of Bratz musical, Mitch wondered. But at least he was now straight on one thing. She! She! Darcy was a woman. He had secured the crucial information on gender.

And now, miraculously, he had also found Darcy's details. He scanned them eagerly.

Name:	Darcy Alethea Desdemona Prince
Nationality:	English
Address:	43 Montague Mansions, Wilton Street, London SW1
Age:	24
Education:	St. Paul's Girls' School, London; Girton College, Cambridge (BA Hons—first class—English); Royal Academy of Dramatic Art (RADA)

Mitch could see why Greg had dumped her on him. There was nothing remotely Hollywood about this woman. She had never even made a film. No doubt, whatever two-bit London agency represented her—it obviously wasn't a big one—had one of those deals with Associated in which they paid the American agency to handle their clients' L.A. interests.

These were known as "drawer deals," because the dark inside of a filing cabinet into which they were immediately shoved, never to be extracted, was usually all these British clients saw of the famous bright lights of Hollywood. And at Associated, most of these unfortunates were shoved in filing cabinets in Mitch's office.

Acting career: Ophelia in *Hamlet*, Cambridge Shakespeare Company, 2005; Cordelia in *King Lear*, CSC, 2006; Viola in *Twelfth Night*, RSC, 2007. Nora in *A Doll's House*, Orange Tree Theatre, Richmond, 2008

Mitch blinked. This was all way off the usual Hollywood acting resumé. Most of the women he handled didn't mention their education or early experience, and not without good reason.

"She's gonna be the next Keira Knightley," Arlington asserted.

Mitch felt his excitement peak. Keira Knightley. So Darcy looked like her? Wow. Keira Knightley was one hot babe. Thin, and maybe a bit flat-chested. But definitely hot.

"I want her to play Princess Anatoo," Arlington was saying in his cold voice. "She's the young Grand Duchess of the Galaxy who must enlist the help of her dead father's supporters, the Kinkos, to overcome the evil that threatens her and her realm, the Kingdom of Anoo."

"Darcy's your woman," Mitch said confidently. "If ever anyone had Grand Duchess potential, it's her."

"Yeah, well, it's not cut and dried yet," Arlington snapped. "I think she'll be great, but she needs to meet with the director."

"Oh, sure," said Mitch, warmly. This, of course, would be a technicality. If Arlington wanted the film to go ahead with Darcy in it, then go ahead with Darcy in it the film duly would. The director was hardly likely to make a difference. "Who is the director?" he asked, as if mattered.

"Jack Saint," said Arlington.

"I thought he'd retired," Mitch said, his spirits slumping slightly. It had been a loss to the studios, no doubt, when the celebrated Saint had bowed out last year with an unparalleled string of successes behind him. The agenting industry, however, had breathed a sigh of relief. Saint had been an extremely difficult person for their clients to work for. He had wanted them to act, for a start. He had begun each day's shoot with an improvisation session that had proved almost more than the average Associated client could bear.

"He had," Arlington returned. "But I persuaded him out of it with enough money and the chance to out-Lucas George Lucas. He's always been pretty competitive with him. Can you get her over here by Friday?"

"Sure I can." Mitch's confidence shot back. What choice did he have? He absolutely could, even if he had to go over there, to—he glanced at the resume—43 Montagu Mansions, Wilton Street, London SW1, and drag Darcy back by the scruff of the neck. Which, of course, he would not have to. No one in their right mind was going to turn down a chance like this.

Chapter Nine

IT WAS, AS ALWAYS, gone midnight before Darcy Prince, her pale face scrubbed of make-up, her black hair drawn back into a roughly brushed ponytail, emerged from the stage door of the theatre. She felt, again as always, drained after yet another performance of *King Lear*, in which she played the troubled monarch's fatally honest and tragic youngest daughter Cordelia.

The part was exhausting enough, but equally harrowing was the proximity, for more than three hours, of the naked, swinging, and shriveled testicles of the septuagenarian actor playing Lear and giving it his all in every sense.

Fortunately, his playing Lear semi-naked was interpreted by both critics and audience as a metaphor for the exposed and vulnerable predicament of Shakespeare's tragic king, rather than the blatant exhibitionism Darcy suspected it really was. And, of course, this publicity was helpful; the production was by one of London's least famous, most experimental directors and in one of the city's smallest and least well-known theatres. Basically, it needed all the help it could get. Still, everyone in the play was passionate about their work, passionate about Shakespeare and the theatre, and this was all that mattered to Darcy.

Leaning against the bus stop, watching taxi after taxi go by, all enticingly lit up in front with that glowing yellow rectangle, Darcy wondered whether she was being slightly hard on herself. With the allowance from her grandmother, she could easily have afforded to take one of them. She dismissed this as a weak moment. Struggling actresses couldn't afford taxis across town at nighttime rates, and she was determined to live within the means of her earnings—the absolute Equity minimum, not what inherited money made possible.

She was equally determined to make her own success, not trade on the name of her family. And, within the theatre, the Prince family had quite a name. Her paternal grandfather, Sacheverell Prince, had been the Hamlet of his day despite looking, in all the pictures Darcy had even seen of him acting, like an irascible middle-aged man with a moustache. A far cry, she had always thought, from the volatile and indecisive teenage boy of Shakespeare's play.

Her own mother and father were among the most celebrated classical actors of their generation and extremely politically committed. As a child, Darcy was taken to far more demonstrations than she ever was birthday parties and once suffered terrible fright at the sight of her father in handcuffs—by his own volition, it was quickly explained to her—and attached to the railings of a bank that had interests in the then-ostracized South Africa.

At home, the kitchen seemed permanently full of people with impassioned eyes thumping the big wooden table, and, throughout her childhood, Darcy had rarely came home from school without wondering what ANC activist or Soviet defector would require her to give up her bedroom this time. Although some, admittedly, had seemed to prefer that she remained in it, an even less inviting prospect.

Darcy had detected from an early age the fact that neither her mother, Angharad, nor her father, Caractacus, held her grandmother in particularly high esteem. Anna de Blank, Angharad's mother, had been a very successful light film actress of the forties and fifties, starring in Ealing comedies and Disney films. She had made the family fortune, although no one, it seemed to Darcy, was terribly grateful.

Personally, she and the chain-smoking, purple-haired old lady, who drank at least half a bottle of champagne a day, had always got on tremendously well, although performing her grandmother's old song-and-dance routines at home was, Darcy had quickly discovered, frowned on.

Theatre at Granny's may be fun and frivolous, but that at home was terribly serious and important. Both her parents had impressed upon her the fact that they were political artists and that she should be, too. "The theatre is the only thing," Angharad would declare in her trademark dramatic, husky voice, and Darcy would agree—as indeed she believed—that it was.

Nonetheless, there were times, such as now, when the weight of ancestral expectation pressed heavy on Darcy's slim shoulders. Playing Cordelia had meant seventy-hour weeks during the rehearsals, of which she had never missed one, and now that the show had started, she worked six nights a week plus matinees on Friday and Saturday.

Eventually the night bus came. Whenever her fellow actors asked her where she lived, Darcy always said West London, as if it were Shepherd's Bush or Hammersmith, and not, as it actually was, a penthouse in Queens Gate, a mere smoked-salmon-sandwich's toss from the gates of Hyde Park and with a fine view of Kensington Palace and the Round Pond from the roof garden. Turn around, and you could almost shake the hands of the classic-figure reliefs circling the great dome of the Albert Hall.

Alighting at Kensington Gore, Darcy went down Queen's Gate. Despite the traditional, white-porticoed appearance of the entrance, you got in by using the electronic keypad beside the front door, or at least you did if you were Darcy and the occupiers of the two luxury flats below the penthouse. If you were Florrie, the nightclubbing German princess on the first floor, you forgot it almost every time, and, irrespective of the invariably late hour, simply hammered on the door and shouted until someone—usually the long-suffering Brazilian plastic surgeon on the ground floor—got up and let you in.

A sweeping, red-carpeted staircase with mahogany banisters rose up the entire six floors of the building, but Darcy, who lived in the penthouse, took the old-fashioned cage-style lift at this time of night. Pressing the lift button and hearing the doors clang shut somewhere above, Darcy allowed herself to luxuriate in the cosseting feeling of home.

But what made this impressive place home to her had nothing to do with the fact that flats here were expensive and sought after. To Darcy, the apartment had for years simply meant her beloved grandmother. Anna de Blank had lived to the age of eighty-five and left it to her favourite—and for that matter only—granddaughter upon her death two years earlier. Whereupon Darcy, resisting heroically her mother's pressure to sell the place and donate the proceeds to one of her causes, had lost no time moving in.

Inside the flat, Darcy glanced at the answerphone on the small Florentine table by the door. The green light winked steadily back. No one had called during the evening.

All was quiet and still and glowing with lamps whose pink shades were fitted with pink bulbs. Anna had been a reluctantly ageing beauty who believed rosy light was the most flattering for the face.

Darcy smiled, as she always did, at the enormous portrait of her grandmother in the entrance hall, resplendent in lemon-yellow chiffon, smiling faintly and beautifully, and holding a plate of her favourite indulgences, macaroons.

From her earliest childhood, macaroons and her grandmother had been associated in Darcy's mind. There had always been a white card box of them in the refrigerator, beribboned and stamped with the address of a smart baker in flowing gold letters. Darcy had been entranced with the colours of these strange, exotic confections, half cake and half biscuit, that came in exquisite, old-fashioned colours.

But Anna, even as she sank her small, white teeth into them and rolled her eyes in delight, would exclaim that even these, baked as they were by the best confectioner in London, were not to be compared with those she had tasted in France.

"But you know, my darling," she would say, "they are the hardest thing in the world to get exactly right, and no one makes them like they do in Paris."

Anna had travelled widely as an actress, and her stories of the great European cities, Paris and Rome especially, as they had been in the 1950s, entranced her granddaughter, but not as much as the macaroons did with their intense sweetness and intoxicating lightness. She could not imagine anyone making a better job of them.

She loved the fact that her grandmother had taken her passion for macaroons as the guiding inspiration for her apartment's decorative scheme. Each room was painted in a different pastel colour: lemon in the study, pink in the master bedroom, pistachio green in the dining room, lilac in the sitting room, and pale orange in the hall. It was one of the whimsical jokes that Darcy felt were entirely typical of her grandmother.

Darcy had kept the décor exactly as Anna had left it. It was as ornate and feminine as she remembered it from her childhood, all florals, silks, and delicate furniture with oval backs and slender gold legs. Small, round tables still held Anna's collection of bibelots and small antiques. In the master bedroom, muslin and toile de Jouy curtains still swept up into a crowned half-tester above the big, white, flounced bed Darcy remembered bouncing on. The rosy light on the white, oval-mirrored dressing table made small decorative boxes and silver-backed brushes glitter just as Darcy, as a child, remembered them glittering.

There was still a big, old-fashioned roll-top bath in the ornate bathroom, which was entered through a pair of white double doors picked out in gilt. Here the bather could lie back and contemplate under a pink Murano glass chandelier, although, these days, without the glass of champagne that Anna had always enjoyed whilst abluting and to which she unhesitatingly attributed her longevity. Darcy felt her own life was quite indulgent enough, and Niall, who scorned self-indulgence and any form of pretension, would have been dead against it too.

Darcy felt the whole place remained so redolent of her grandmother that it was almost as if the old lady, with her impish smile, twinkling eyes, and immaculate blue hair, might come tripping daintily in at any moment. But she was aware that Niall, who had never known Anna, felt rather differently about it. "Camper than a Boy Scout Jamboree" was how he had put it in his no-nonsense Scottish way.

When he had moved in some months ago, Niall had not only suggested giving the entire place a coat of white paint but had offered to do it. He had, he pointed out, trained as a builder, still had a part-time job on a construction site, and, therefore, possessed all the requisite skills. But Darcy had been appalled at the idea. She had been yet more horrified at Niall's next suggestion, that they sell it and move to more fashionably edgy Shoreditch. Accepting defeat, Niall had laughed good-naturedly, shrugged his broad shoulders, and never mentioned it again.

As she passed the hall mirror now, Darcy paused. Her wide face was pale with exhaustion. Two large dark eyes with purple shadows, their full-lashed lids dipping downwards, squinted tiredly back from beneath thick, straight brows.

The full, raspberry mouth was drawn downwards with tiredness, and her head lolled unsteadily on her slender neck. A few tendrils of long, dark hair had escaped from the bunch into which she had hastily shoved it before leaving the theatre. It needed a wash, Darcy realised. But not now. The only thing now was bed.

Darcy tiptoed through the sitting room. The lamps cast soft pink shadows on the lilac walls; Niall had left them on. The slither of newspapers on the lilac, cushion-scattered sofa, and the various remotes for the television scattered over the thick carpet, also lilac, gave the impression that her boyfriend had only just gone to bed. Rather regretting the fact he hadn't waited up for her, Darcy bent forward to inspect the papers on the sofa. As she had suspected, one was a book; a small, paperback copy of *Hamlet* left upside down with "To be or not to be" pressing against the petit-point cushions.

Preparing for a crucial audition, Niall had been studying the part for weeks, as well as videos (Anna's old TV lacked a DVD setting) of classic performances of the role. Video boxes, their contents spilt, were piled before the television. Niall admired Sir Alec Guinness's most, Darcy knew, and had not spared her with his opinion that he thought Sacheverell Prince's the worst. Darcy had not minded however. Niall's unflinching honesty was one of the things she loved about him most. He was authentic. Down to earth. Real.

She found it both admirable and intimidating that Niall had grown up on an estate in Glasgow, that his father was a butcher and his mother a cleaner. That he worked as a builder for several years before putting himself through drama school and, therefore, despite being the same age as her, had had a real—not to say a hard—life before entering the rarified world of acting.

And he was a wonderful actor too, as serious about the profession as she was. More so, if anything.

They had especially bonded over the importance of Shakespeare. He venerated her parents—if not her grandparents—as great actors, and they, in turn, had been excited and enchanted by his council-estate provenance.

"A butcher!" Angharad had breathed in delight when he had told her about his father's business. "A cleaner!" she had murmured ecstatically, when the subject of his mother came up.

And she had positively purred when he had finished telling her how he had walked round Muswell Hill all night, unable to speak, after seeing her performance on DVD as Nora in a celebrated seventies production of *A Doll's House* transposed to an S&M Amsterdam brothel.

"It said everything about the condition of women," he had told Angharad hotly, and she had pushed back her still-beautiful-but-greying wild, black hair from her still-exquisite high-cheekboned face and gazed at Niall with dark-eyed rapture.

Niall would get there, Darcy felt certain. He was just taking some time to break through, that was all. His Scottish looks, coupled with the fact he actually was Scottish, meant that TV drama offers of Scottish policemen, Scottish drug-dealers, Scottish pimps, Scottish alcoholics, Scottish wifebeaters, and, on one occasion, a Scottish corpse, regularly came his way. But these were hardly the parts he was looking for, and he was determined not to be pigeonholed. Or "Macpigeonholed," as he put it. Hopefully the Hamlet audition tomorrow—or today, Darcy realised, it being one in the morning—would bring him what he deserved.

Darcy now tiptoed into the bedroom where Niall lay sleeping. She smiled at how incongruously rugged and masculine he looked in Anna's enormous, rather princessy bed.

Absorbedly, Darcy stretched out a hand over the thick, dark-red curls that, when he was standing, flowed almost to Niall's shoulders and lightly touched the reddish-brown brow. She traced the jutting nose with its rounded end and brushed the red-gold stubble on the determined cleft chin. She half-wanted him to wake, to open the big, pale-blue eyes that she had, when they had first met, laughingly told him were the colour of boxes from Tiffany's. "Are they?" he had replied in his Glaswegian growl. "I wouldn't know."

But Niall slept on, his left arm bent under his head, his hand only just visible beneath the hair. Darcy smiled as she saw the scrolled silver tops of the Celtic rings he wore on every finger of this hand like a Caledonian knuckle-duster. The white-blonde lashes, each one tipped with a fleck of brownish-red, remained pressed against his white and freckled cheek. Even when she skimmed the flat of her hand over his pale, broad chest with its red-gold hair, he did not wake. Noticing the shiny, purple hollows just south of his closed eyelids, she decided to leave him alone. Working on the building site was, she knew, exhausting, and he had had *Hamlet* to learn on top of it.

He was sleeping in a particularly horrid and ancient T-shirt, she noticed indulgently, a dirty, white one with a St. Andrew's flag on it that she had nagged him many times to get rid of. But she loved the fact Niall utterly lacked vanity. Unlike some men she had known, he never blow-dried his hair, used fake tan, or visited a salon for any reason other than to meet her.

In a corner of the bedroom, Anna's little white-and-gold telephone suddenly shrilled. One in the morning, Darcy realised, glancing at the ornate ormolu clock on the bedroom mantelpiece. Who on earth could this be?

Had something happened to her mother? Her father? Panic seized Darcy's throat as she answered.

"We haven't spoken," came the booming voice of Mitch Masterson. "But I'm the agent representing you in Hollywood, and I'm calling with some very good news."

Darcy felt an uncharacteristic wave of annoyance. It was late, and she was tired. If this was someone's idea of a joke, it was not very funny. She had not even realised she was represented in Hollywood. Her London agents, a pair of exuberant, eccentric, and much-powdered old ladies who had been her parents' and, towards the end of Anna's career, her grandmother's agents before that, seemed to have enough problems representing her in London.

Darcy had stuck with them out of a sense of loyalty and history, but she had been sent to the wrong auditions too many times recently—the latest to be a singing grape in a wine commercial when she had expected to be testing for Miranda in *The Tempest*. The infuriating thing was that the woman who had been intended for the grape had landed the Miranda part and was now playing to great acclaim in Stratford.

"What good news?" Darcy said suspiciously, her voice low so as not to wake Niall.

At the L.A. end of the phone, Mitch Masterson, the receiver under his chin, rubbed his hands gleefully and prepared to tell her.

Chapter Ten

MITCH HAD EXPECTED ALMOST any type of reaction from this unknown British actress. Screams of disbelieving joy. Sobs of passionate delight. Even a thud and a crash as she collapsed in an ecstatic dead faint to the floor. But never, not even in a million years, had he expected an outright refusal.

"What do you mean you're not sure you're interested?" he exploded, after listening to her speak in her rather high, prim, very English voice. "It's one of the leading parts, for Chrissakes."

The woman was obviously insane—like most Brits, Mitch thought grimly—and clearly had no idea what she was saying. He was determined not to let her mess this chance up. Hers wasn't the only career on the line, after all. What sort of an agent would it make him look? What would Arlington Shorthouse think? Nor did he want to miss out on what that smug slimeball Greg Cucarachi would think when he realized he'd given Mitch a diamond amid all the dust. A side issue, admittedly, but potentially an extremely satisfying one.

"Do you realize what *Galaxia* is?" Mitch asked Darcy, in the tones he might have used if he was talking down a dangerous lunatic bent on leaping off a high roof to her death. Which, in a manner of speaking, he was. If Darcy turned this down, she would be through in Hollywood. And so would he. He was, Mitch recognised, fighting for his professional life here.

"It's gonna be the new *Star Wars*," Mitch said tremendously. Surely if anything was going to make this dame focus, that would.

As he waited for what she would say next, every hair inside

Mitch's large, hot ears strained erect. "I've never seen any of those, I'm afraid," Darcy added, evidently unmoved.

Mitch's eyes were bulging and seemed to be fizzing in his head. Never seen *Star Wars*? Was that possible? This chick was unreal.

He decided to cut to the chase. Subtlety had got him nowhere, after all. "Don't you want to be famous?" As he heard the question disappear down the line to London, part of him wondered if it had ever been asked in Hollywood before.

Darcy had a stubborn streak, and being rung at one o'clock in the morning—by someone she had never met, telling her to fly halfway across the world and test for some kids' space film in which she had absolutely no interest—brought it out.

"I'm a proper actress," she stated primly. "I do proper things. Theatre. Shakespeare."

Mitch took a deep breath and thought as best he could, given that his mind was a hot churn of frustration and disbelief. It was like moving a paddle through very thick, hot mud. But finally, in his darkest and most desperate moment, inspiration struck.

"Hey, don't write it off, baby," he urged Darcy. "Some of the greatest actors make these films. *Star Wars*, for example. Sir Alec Guinness, you know, he was in it, and he was one of he most famous Shakespeare actors ever, right? English too," Mitch added, striking home what he felt was his advantage.

He was right to feel this. Mention of the name of the great Shakespearean made Darcy pause. Part of what had driven her initial refusal was the knowledge that Niall, even more of a purist than she was, would be in equal parts amused and appalled by the *Galaxia* prospect. She had not even wanted to speculate about what her parents would think; for them, she knew, Hollywood symbolized all that was worst and crassest about the American capitalist machine. But the fact that Guinness had appeared in *Star Wars* films was something for both parties to consider.

Mitch sensed the tide had turned. Deftly, he increased the pressure. "Look, baby. You make this film, and you make enough money to do whatever you like afterwards. It'll make you free. You can do all the Shakespeare there is. Hell, you could get someone to write some more for you if you want."

Another good argument, Darcy recognised. And she was too honest with herself not to admit that, despite herself, she was curious about Hollywood. Who in the acting profession wasn't?

"If you've ever been interested in seeing Hollywood—just for interest, y'know—this is the best possible way," Mitch now breathed into her ear.

To his own amazement, he seemed to have developed a psychic understanding of what was required. He was obviously at his best in the afternoon. Late afternoon too, Mitch saw, looking at his watch and seeing it was 5 p.m. No wonder he'd never gone anywhere, given the Hollywood obsession with meetings at the crack of dawn.

"You'll breeze in as Tinseltown royalty, make a fortune, see everything and meet everyone, and just breeze out again. None of that coming in by Greyhound bus and working in a burger joint for years while trying to land a part in a bitcom," Mitch added, with what could have been a guilty glance in the direction of his filing cabinets.

"A bitcom?"

"A small sitcom. Kind of unsuccessful. As opposed to a hitcom," Mitch supplied helpfully.

She said nothing after this. He sensed that she was thinking. It wasn't a sense he often had. Most actresses he knew didn't think; they just shouted. Like Belle, who he had to ring next. The dreadful thought made him all the more determined to close down Darcy's objections and make this offer a done deal. Something good had to come out of his day.

"Darcy," he said, summoning his most serious, persuasive tones.

"The *Galaxia* series is gonna be the biggest thing since *Star Wars*. It'll send your career into the stratosphere. Quite literally," Mitch added, snorting at his own joke.

"But I want to be known for quality," Darcy objected, but less stridently than before.

"And you can be," Mitch reasoned. "You'll be in such a good position after this film that you'll be able to choose whatever part you want. In any bloody theatre you like."

Darcy darted an apprehensive look at the still-sleeping Niall. But a certain excitement was stealing over her as well. Mitch was offering a first-class flight to L.A. When was that ever likely to happen again? Her grandmother had been a film actress after all.

"OK," Darcy muttered. "I'll come and meet the director."

"You've made the right decision, baby," Mitch said as calmly as was possible while simultaneously pumping the air with exultation.

For five minutes after the phone call, he ran round his office, whooping in delight. The walls shook, and Greg Cucarachi, the agent in the next-door cubicle, who Mitch had not realised was in the building, suddenly poked his narrow, foxy face through the door.

"Good news?" Greg asked, his tone pleasant and interested but his eyes straining with competitive fear.

"Great," said Mitch smugly, slowing to a halt and breathing heavily after all the exertion. He passed a plump hand over his sweating brow.

A glint entered Greg's preternaturally shiny eyes. "I see from the gossip sites that Belle Murphy's had another great time on the town."

Mitch held his gaze steady, but his hands shook and he felt his heart sink like lead into the soft mush of jelly doughnut in his stomach.

"Yeah," Greg Cucarachi said. "Major bender, by the looks of it. At lunchtime too. Lots of nice, clear pictures." Satisfied that his dart had found its target, he grinned wolfishly and withdrew.

Slowly, Mitch sat down.

The telephone rang. He picked it up to find Arlington Shorthouse on the other line, and his foreboding became immediately colder. "Darcy will be here next week," Mitch blustered, in order to get the good news in first.

"Sure she will," Arlington snapped. "I'm not calling about her. I need a meeting with you and Belle," the studio head said, his chill voice a few degrees more frozen. "She's becoming a problem," he added ominously. "A big problem. We need a meeting. Next Monday at 7 a.m., okay?" Arlington rang off before Mitch could answer.

Mitch's heart plummeted. Another early-morning meeting. That it was now all over for Belle seemed inevitable. But she had no one but herself to blame. Apart from him, of course.

Chapter Eleven

As soon as he opened the front door, Richard sensed anticipation in the air.

"Ta da!" Georgie suddenly appeared in the hall in a white kaftan. "Like it?" she trilled. "It's one of my new ones!" Her rather anxious eyes sought his. "From the Countess of Minto's organic après-yoga collection." She was twirling so hard that she caught her heel in its hem, lost balance, and staggered, heels clattering, into the kitchen.

Richard followed her in and sniffed appreciatively. "What's for dinner, darling?"

Georgie turned on him, her eyes accusing. "You haven't forgotten that the Faughs are coming?"

Immediately, Richard tried to look as if, indeed, he hadn't; few things annoyed Georgie more than her social arrangements slipping his mind. Although in this case, it was less that something had slipped and more that Richard had been in denial that the dinner was happening from the moment it had first been discussed.

"You have forgotten!" Georgie wailed despairingly.

"I, um, well, no, absolutely, um…" Richard stammered helplessly. He was nothing if not truthful, which had never exactly been a boon to his career either.

The twins looked even worse than Orlando remembered. The new jeans with a stiffly ironed crease in the front and the pressed City shirts with cufflinks were all present and correct as they exited the family Range Rover—parked illegally in a disabled spot, Orlando noticed—and tripped confidently after their parents up the front steps into the hall of the house. Orlando, in his usual unlaced trainers and baggy, unbelted jeans, looked in disbelief at the Faugh footwear. Ivo and Jago wore identical shiny, black, clumpy-soled loafers exposing a lot of chunky white foot.

"Good evening, Mrs. Fitzmaurice," the twins chirped smoothly, clicking their solid heels together and making a great display of kissing Georgie on both of her wan cheeks, which rose with delighted colour.

"So lovely to see you," swooned Georgie. "You look marvellous, as always."

"Not as marvellous as you, Mrs. Fitzmaurice!" she was immediately assured.

Orlando, while wanting to retch at the sycophancy, was nonetheless transfixed by the twins' hair. It was flat, black, short, and with side-partings so straight they could have been done with a surveyor's theodolite. Shoved on top of each large head was a pair of Raybans, which Orlando felt would have been better employed worn on the twins' faces to cover up their goggling black eyes. Admittedly, not much could be done about their unattractive, big, and shiny red lips and huge, horsey teeth.

He watched as the twins' father now moved in on his mother. "Marvellous kaftan, Mrs. Fitzmaurice. You're just so fashion forward..." one of the twins was saying.

How could anyone be so cheesy, Orlando wondered, seeing Hugh reverently take Georgie's tiny, fragile hand and raise it to his plump, red lips, his eyes gazing fervently into hers all the while.

"Georgie! As beautiful and gracious as ever!" Hugh declared in his thick, rather sticky voice. As his mother quivered and squealed with flattered delight, Orlando wondered how she could possibly fall for it. Yet fall for it she obviously had. Along with the majority of Hugh's constituents, presumably. It was, Orlando thought, incredible.

"How's it going? A level results due soon, are they?" Orlando tore himself from contemplation of the father to find both pairs of the sons' goggling black eyes turned to him.

Beneath the curtain of his hair, Orlando's eyes narrowed with hate. Looking straight at Ivo, he saw that the goggling orbs were slitted in a similar fashion. Orlando felt a ripple of surprise. He had not realised until that moment that the Faugh brothers loathed him just as much as he loathed them.

Richard, as he busied himself taking Laura Faugh's pashmina, was battling with many of the same feelings. Passing down the hall in the direction of the cloakroom, his arms full of scented turquoise cashmere, Richard caught sight of the clock in the kitchen and estimated at least four hours would have to pass before he could retrieve the wrap and wave its wearer good-bye.

He had never liked Laura Faugh much, although, with his customary courteousness, he had done his best to disguise this. As opposed to her booming husband, Laura had always seemed rather repressed, although not a mousy sort of repressed. On the contrary, she gave Richard the impression of being inordinately pleased with herself.

She was tall, pale, and glacial, with a long neck, shoulder-length dark hair with a reddish sheen, and very straight shoulders. She had rather hooded eyes and lips—coloured in a dry-looking red lipstick—that seemed always to twist slightly with amusement or disdain.

How he preferred Georgie's warmth, immediacy, and excitability, even if she had her brittle and fragile moments and, at times, could seem rather unhinged. Unhinged, Richard knew, was how some of his colleagues saw her, and possibly this had been another brake on his progress. Laura, with her icy poise, had more of a power-wife air. On the other hand, she had also managed to produce the two Faugh boys, which Richard felt he would not wish on anyone, even Hugh.

Many of his young constituents in the housing estates were the sort that only a mother could love, and the fact that no mother ever had only deepened the problem. That such boys and girls were hard to like was no surprise, and Richard, knowing something of their history, treated them with the sympathy all but the hardest cases deserved. But Ivo and Jago's history was one of unremitting privilege, exposed as they had been and were being to the finest teaching and most beautiful environments. None of it seemed to have rubbed off on them however.

From outside, a tinkle of laughter (Georgie) followed by a cannon-like boom of mirth (Hugh) dragged Richard reluctantly back into the here and now. Georgie had ushered the guests out in the garden to enjoy the warm weather. She had spent some considerable time earlier arranging glasses, nuts, wine-chiller, and corkscrew at just the right angle on the white, cast-iron garden table, the sort, along with the rest of the furniture, that either scraped the patio or put his back out whenever Richard tried to move it.

Richard, having spun out for as long as possible hanging Laura's wrap in the cloakroom, now had no further excuse not to join them. He descended the steps slowly, sensing this would be his last chance to relax or enjoy anything.

It was a beautiful summer evening; the warm air was heavy with scent from Georgie's beloved wisteria, snaking along the wall dividing their garden from the neighbours in a discreet mass of lilac flowers and pale-green leaves. The unmown lawn—too late, Richard remembered this was supposed to have been his job—actually looked lush and lyrical in the lowering sunlight, whose yellow glow intensified the youthful green leaves of the old apple tree that stood towards the back of the garden and cast such a useful shadow in the summer over anyone lounging there with the Sunday papers.

As he crossed the lawn, Richard noted with dislike Faugh's big, tall form, clad, as indeed Richard himself was, in the standard upper-middle-class summer uniform of pale-blue shirt and light-fawn trousers, albeit a more expensive version than his own. This big Faugh form, one hand thrust into a pocket, but not so deeply so as to obscure an obviously expensive watch, was rocking back and forth in appreciation of one of its own jokes or observations.

"Ha, ha!" boomed Hugh, nodding his big head with its thick black hair. Next to him, Georgie in her white kaftan was evidently engaged in fanning his wonders to a blaze with which even he was satisfied.

Surging up within Richard came an urge he had not experienced for the last half century at least. The almost overwhelming desire to spit. Firmly suppressing the compulsion, he walked up to the group with a smile.

"Family Values!" Hugh was orating. "In the end of ends, it's what it all comes down to: Family Values!"

Richard joined in. "I couldn't agree more. The thing is, what does it mean?" He turned to Hugh. "How would your interpretation of family values be a solution to, say, the increasing problem of bad pupil behaviour in schools, particularly those in poor areas?"

Hugh swilled down half a glass of Frascati before answering. "Well, it's obvious. We must look to the mothers and fathers to take responsibility. Discipline questions are not something the schools can be expected to solve all by themselves."

"Yes, I'd agree with that," Richard said, nodding seriously.

"We must go back to the parents."

"Absolutely."

"And sterilise them."

Richard Fitzmaurice choked on his white wine. "What?"

"Just think about it." Hugh smiled calmly. "If all women of social classes C, D, and E were sterilised, they could screw whatever drug addicts and wastrels they fancied, and the country and community wouldn't have to tolerate the resulting destructive, disruptive, and invariably stupid offspring." He grabbed a handful of nuts from the table and shoved them in his mouth.

It was at this point that Georgie returned with another two bottles. "Sausages!" she hissed at Richard, her eyeballs rigid with meaning.

Torn from the argument, still churning with indignation, he looked at her uncomprehendingly. What did sausages have to do with anything?

"Sausages!" Georgie squealed, her grip tightening painfully on his forearm. "In the kitchen. Nibbles."

"Oh. Right. Er…yes. Okay." Still coursing with most unhostlike feelings, Richard fled to the kitchen for the honey-glazed sausages. He found them on the butcher's block in a gold-and-white Meissen bowl that struck him as rather too grand for mere bangers.

"Here comes my honourable friend!" Hugh declared loudly. "With the sausages, ha, ha! I'm peckish."

Georgie turned. Her welcoming smile was only half-formed before it disappeared into a worried frown. "You've forgotten the dip!" she hissed. "And the napkins! The ones with the fleur-de-lys pattern."

Richard fled back into the house, taking the bowl of sausages with him. "Hey!" Hugh called after him in alarm. "Leave the bangers, old chap." But Richard, pretending not to have heard, had gained the house by then.

The sausage victory, he now discovered, was a Pyrrhic one. He lingered over the napkin hunt as long as he decently could. Finally, with dips and the requested fleur-de-lys finger-wipers, he emerged to find Georgie waxing lyrical about the Tuscan farmhouse they had rented for the holidays. Richard instantly felt the tremor in his knees and feet that always meant danger, a feeling that increased as Hugh turned towards him, his large white teeth gaining a bloody-red flash from the sunset.

"Jolly decent of your wife to ask us to Italy with you, old chap. We'd love to come with you—as your guests," Hugh hastily added, with emphasis.

The sun chose this moment to finally sink behind the neighbours' wall, and the evening suddenly felt dark and cold. The aghast Richard hardly noticed, absorbing as he was the fact that Hugh had used the time he had spent looking for napkins to make further progress in his life's work of securing complimentaries. Far from demonstrating there was no such thing as a free lunch, Hugh had now abundantly illustrated the fact there was such a thing as a free holiday too.

Chapter Twelve

A FROWN CREASED ARLINGTON Shorthouse's tanned, lean, and strangely elastic face. Behind his thick lenses with their distinctive heavy black frames, the small grey eyes narrowed with annoyance. He shifted his short body irritably in his chair. As well as cross, Arlington felt tired. It was only seven in the morning, but it had already been a long day.

Arlington worked twenty-four seven, three-sixty-five. He was always open for business. Even, quite literally, on the operating table. He'd tried to take calls once while having his appendix removed, but the surgeon had snatched away his mobile. Arlington hadn't been back to that hospital since; the surgeon had obviously been in the pay of a rival studio.

Arlington cleared his throat and drummed his fingers irritably on his desk. He hated it when the studio made turkeys; they felt like a personal failure. And the people who were in them made him feel the same way. They made him feel small, a sensation he particularly hated as Arlington was indeed small. Very small. Short by name, short by nature. "Pocket rocket," the fourth of his six wives had called him, immediately before finding herself in the middle of one of the most acrimonious divorces in show-business history.

Arlington had tried to conquer his small height the way climbers try to conquer Everest. He had tried big hair, lifts in his shoes, even hats. Chairs, in the end, were the only satisfactory answer: while everyone else in his office had to sit on seats at a level normally associated with nursery schools, the throne-like construction behind Arlington's burr-walnut desk had special padded cushions to raise him to a comparatively towering height. As the effect was lost whenever he stood up, Arlington sat on this chair behind his desk for entire meetings. He was careful to drink little beforehand. Comfort breaks severely compromised his status.

From the summit of his chair, Arlington could look out across his meeting room like the commander of a tank. He did so now, and those present stiffened in response. There was about the room, with its grey carpet, grey smoked-glass walls, and framed maps of the world showing the cities in which NBS's films had opened and what the box office takings were, an air of the war cabinet. And this was appropriate, as to all intents and purposes, a war room was what it was. Arlington regarded himself as being in a permanent state of hostilities with all the other studio heads in the world and anyone else who dared to challenge him.

Mitch Masterson was among those present. He was at the boardroom table, his large, plump bottom crammed uncomfortably into one of the diminutive chrome chairs beneath the unusually low, black-ash table surface. He was trying hard not to look how he felt, like a dad at a kindergarten parents' evening. Mitch didn't have kids, thank God, nor did he want them. His clients were his children, although not in the nice way that sounded. They were like children in the sense that they were unreasonable, endlessly demanding, spoilt, violent, prone to screaming and tantrums, and could not be trusted to behave.

She had a meeting with the head of the studio, her ultimate boss, Mitch was thinking, and was she on time? Was she even in the building? The hell she was. Great start, he thought, trying to shove his fat and trapped legs into a more comfortable position below the tiny table. He looked at the other men doubled painfully up on the miniature furniture for support, but they stared back at him coldly. Arlington

Shorthouse's lieutenants, they clearly knew, like everyone else, that if you wanted to make it big at NBS, you had to think small.

"I'm so sorry Belle's late, Mr. Shorthouse," Mitch assured him, the pain in his voice in every way reflecting the pain he felt physically. His awkward sitting position meant that cramp was now paralysing his leg. It had also totally creased and screwed up the new Armani suit he had bought for the meeting, inside whose lined interior he felt great patches of nervous sweat spreading from beneath his armpits. He'd put a Hollywood-power-meeting level of deodorant on as well, but it hadn't seemed to make the slightest difference.

Arlington Shorthouse ground his veneered teeth and stared at his burr-walnut desk. He tried to still the panic that was rising within him at the thought of all the time he was losing: whole seconds, entire unfilled minutes that he would never get again, and which, no doubt, his rivals at other film companies were using to streak ahead.

The desk was no comfort however. It was grand, with its green leather top and scrolled gilt handles, and it was even historic, being the desk that all the presidents of the company had used before him. Legendary film stars had signed contracts here. Douglas Fairbanks had even scratched his name in the leather. Belle Murphy had signed here too, and a contract of historically huge proportions. Arlington felt sick at the memory.

He looked at his Breitling watch and scowled. She was fifteen minutes late now. No one was ever fifteen minutes late for Arlington Shorthouse. No one was ever one minute late for Arlington Shorthouse.

Something had to be done about Belle Murphy. And would be, today, here in this room, by these people. Arlington, skimming over the wretched Mitch with his cold grey eyes, appraised his henchmen.

Nearest to him, at the end of the black-ash conference table, sat a dark, handsome man in a red, striped shirt. Arlington's battleship-coloured gaze raked approvingly over Michael J. Seltzer, NBS's

Head of Creative. He was young, good-looking, smart, determined, undoubtedly gifted, and sitting ramrod-straight in his chair, completely focused on the moment. There was a lot about the Head of Creative that reminded the company president of himself at a similar age.

Next to him sat Chase McGiven: young, restless-looking, and thin-faced, with burning eyes and fashionably cropped dark hair. As NBS's CEO of global communications, he'd come up with some interesting thinking about Belle Murphy. Very interesting thinking indeed.

Yes, thought Arlington. There a lot about Chase, as well, that reminded him of himself at that age. Not wanting to waste a second, always some plan on the go, some scheme buzzing in his head.

The final member of the trio was Bob Ricardo, NBS's Head of Finance and the sharpest guy in the business. He looked sharp too, Arlington thought, with his pointy nose, bristly grey hair, surgical-looking rimmed glasses, and sharply cut grey suit. Bob sat upwards, stiff and alert. In front of him was a large calculator with oversize keys next to a floppy, white book open to display columns of figures. Yes, Arlington thought. Bob was ready. He had an eagerness about him that reminded the studio head of himself when younger, although that couldn't be right because Bob was more or less his age.

A sudden movement behind the smoked-glass walls dividing the inner sanctum from the outer area caught Arlington's eye. It was his PA, Miss van der Bree, her arms flying in the air as she tried to restrain something or someone. Someone now appearing at the doors of his office. Holy shit. Arlington's tanned hands flew to his chest to check that his bulletproof vest was in position. It was. His handgun was, as usual, in its holster under his arm. Physically as well as professionally, he was never less than prepared to withstand an attack from a rival studio.

The doors flew back, and in, rather to everyone's amazement, came Belle Murphy, her lavishly lipsticked mouth stretched in a dazzling smile the width of a watermelon.

❖ ❖ ❖

"Hi guys!" she trilled. The guys waited for a reference to her lateness, followed by an apology. They were disappointed on both counts.

Belle looked, Mitch thought, not only smaller than she appeared on screen—every star looked like that—but even smaller than when he had seen her last. Clearly her relationship with food had got that bit more distant in the meantime. For all the movement and vitality of her presence—the shining hair, the flashing sunglasses, the exposed and prominent rounded domes of her breasts rearing beneath a necklace of very big diamonds—Belle's body, Mitch estimated, was about the width and thickness of a copy of *Vogue*. And not a Christmas issue, either.

She looked pretty good, all the same. He noted with relief her clinging grey silk dress with plunging neckline, black high heels, enormous black sunglasses, and the way her cascade of white-blonde hair pushed back from her face and poured over her shoulders as far as her elbows. She was working the high-octane glamour look, as she should be. She was doing that bit right at least.

He shot a timid yet triumphant look at Arlington. Surely even Hollywood's chillest lizard, however angry, couldn't be immune to such a tasty piece of ass as this. He took heart when he saw that Arlington was apparently staring at Belle's breasts.

Arlington was, however, looking at the bag Belle had under her arm. It was huge, heavy with gilt and buckles, and almost as big as she was. He recognised the type without enthusiasm. His fifth wife had had one in every colour. They cost a minimum of two thousand dollars a pop. What was even less appealing to Arlington was the presence in one corner of the bag of a small, brown dog with a very big diamond collar.

It was one of those trembly, skinny, yappy ones, Arlington saw with dislike. It looked restlessly about with enormous and very prominent black eyes. They held a ruthless expression, a look that clearly warned it might go for the throat at any minute. Arlington recognised the expression; it was one he often used himself in business meetings.

Mitch's expression, meanwhile, was one of abject misery. That Arlington Shorthouse disliked dogs was common knowledge in Hollywood. NBS was the only studio that never put out movies with dogs in them, which were the sort that more or less kept all the other studios afloat.

"Darling!" breathed Belle in her trademark little-girl voice. Holding out her arms, she staggered across the carpet in her high heels towards the burr-walnut desk. "Arl! May I call you that, for short?"

The sound now filled the room of four strangled, horrified coughs. Four minds reverberated with one single thought. She had called him Arl, Mitch realised, cringing. No one called Arlington anything for short. No one ever said "short," and she had done that too. "Short" was not a word that was ever breathed in Arlington's presence.

Mitch, who knew how the studio head also loathed unscheduled physical interaction, now watched in horror as Belle seized Arlington's neck with a white hand on which a huge diamond ring glittered. "Mwah! Mwah!" Arlington gasped with pain as her razor cheekbones banged against his smooth and elastic cheeks.

It crossed the screeching, veering chaos of Mitch's mind that Belle might be drunk.

Belle, having smeared Arlington's tanned cheeks with red lipstick, now stood unsteadily erect in her five-inch stilettos. She held up the bag with the dog in.

"Gentlemen," she pouted breathily, batting her wide, blue eyes behind her sunglasses. "I'd like you all to meet Sugar. It's Sugar's fault we're a tiny weeny bit late. I had to take him to the dog beautician for a manicure."

The men in the room stared dumbly. Each and every one of them was familiar with star behaviour. But this woman wasn't even a star anymore. Mitch stared at the floor, wishing it would not only swallow him up but also mash him to a pulp. He felt he didn't want to live anymore.

"There you go, precious," Belle crooned to the dog as she put him on the floor. "You go run about, sweetie." As Sugar immediately shot beneath Arlington's desk, Belle beamed at the studio head. "See, look. He likes you."

"I don't like him," Arlington said ominously.

Belle's megawatt grin abruptly disappeared. Her big mouth, which was painted shiny and red, bunched disapprovingly, and her darkened eyebrows snapped angrily together. "How can you say that? Sugar's so sensitive. So easily hurt, poor baby." She bent under Arlington's desk and cooed some endearments. At least he gets to see her tits now, Mitch thought.

"Look, shall we get on with the business?" asked Bob Ricardo, looking at his boss and drumming his calculator with his fingers.

Arlington flexed his stubby hands and stared at his neatly clipped nails. "Look, baby. So you were huge last year. But a year's a long time in showbiz. You're losing it, and there are plenty of other girls out there just dying to take your place. Bob?"

"Basically, the bottom line is this. *Bloody Mary* cost two-hundred-and-fifty-million dollars to make, and so far it's grossed thirty."

"Thirty million?" Belle beamed. "Hey, it's only been out two weeks. Thirty million's pretty good."

Bob shook his bony, crop-haired head. "Not thirty million dollars. Thirty dollars. Three-oh."

Mitch gasped. He'd no idea it was this bad. This was historic.

"Thirty?" croaked Belle.

"Thirty," confirmed Bob in his grating tones.

"Thirty dollars! But that's impossible!" Belle shouted. "No one's

ever made…"—she screwed up her mouth to spit out the words—
"thirty freaking dollars on a two-hundred-fifty-million-dollar picture!
It's impossible, right?"

"Wrong," Bob said with relish, his lean fingers gently tapping
the white surface of his balance book. "Sure, it's made a few million,
but when you take away the taxes, the costs, and so on, well…" He
pulled a face. "Thirty's what you're left with. Which means," he
frowned and tapped the large buttons of his calculator, "a deficit
of two hundred forty-nine million, nine hundred ninety-nine thousand, nine hundred and seventy dollars."

Even though he had heard it before, the figure hit him just as
hard as it had the first time, right bang slap in the balls. Arlington
closed his watering eyes and swallowed. Forget calling this a turkey.
It was an outbreak of swine flu. An epidemic of H1N1 right through
their balance sheet.

The extent of the damage was still, in fact, coming in. There was
some confusion over whether *Bloody Mary* had been number six or
number nine in Moldovia. "It's the right number, all right," their
contact there had reported. "Right now, we're just establishing what
way up it is."

"You got your sums wrong!" Belle gasped, breasts heaving up
and down agitatedly. "The critics said my acting was great!"

Arlington pursed his lips. "No one gives a gnat's snatch about
the acting."

From under Arlington's desk, the dog growled.

"I always said we should make a sequel to *Marie*," Belle declared passionately. "But no one would listen to me." She thumped
a skinny fist heavy with diamonds so hard against the prominent
bones of her upper chest that it seemed to Mitch that she might
snap them.

"We couldn't do a sequel," Michael J. Seltzer said shortly. "She
got her head chopped off in the last one."

Belle glared indignantly at Seltzer. "We should have done Anne Boleyn instead. Or Elizabeth…whatever number she was. The one in the big ruffs. Or Henry the whatever. You know, that power-crazed psycho with the six wives." Belle rolled her eyes. "Six wives! How normal was he?"

The six-times-married Arlington looked predictably thunderous at this. The folly of *Bloody Mary* struck him anew. Burning desire. What the hell had the studio been thinking of to use that as the film's catchline?

Or, to be precise, Arlington thought, eyes slitting as he looked at his Creative Head, what had Michael been thinking of? It had been his idea to make the film in the first place; to make it, moreover, not straight and historical, but sex it up, make it like some sixteenth-century Catholic Playboy Mansion, with Philip of Spain running around pleasuring everyone from the lady's maids to the spit boy. He had even pushed for an alternative title, *Burn, Baby, Burn*, on the grounds that it was more commercial. It had been his decision to take out all the Protestant-versus-Catholic elements on the grounds it might offend people, meaning that nothing made any sense and the executions looked gratuitous.

Belle's sunglasses, which she had now replaced, flashed defiantly. "Anyway, *Bloody Mary* did very well in the Ukraine."

"Only because they thought it was about alcohol," replied Bob wearily.

Arlington slid another look at his watch. Shit. He had another fifty meetings scheduled today. This was taking far too long. He looked meaningfully at his head of PR.

Chase McGiven cleared his throat. He sat with one ankle raised to his knee, on which balanced a blue plastic folder he tapped restively with a fountain pen. "Miss Murphy. We've been doing some, ahem, qualitative personality research…"—he tapped the folder harder—"which I have right here."

"Some what?" Belle snapped rudely.

"Qualitative personality research is qualitative research concerning a personality," Chase informed Belle. "See what they think of you, in other words."

"Was this really necessary?" Mitch interjected, feeling he should say something, anything, to remind them all he was still here.

Chase ignored him. "According to our research, and, of course, this is confirmed by the figures from *Bloody Mary*, your popularity is, how can I put this?" He looked thoughtfully at Belle.

"Huge?" prompted Belle.

"Slipping," said Chase.

"Are you sure?" Mitch interjected desperately.

Chase leant back in his chair and put his arms behind his head. "Her popularity's at rock bottom."

"Like the takings," interjected Bob, with relish.

The dog began to yap under Arlington's desk.

"C'mon, Belle. You know it's true." Chase leant forward. "People are dropping you from projects left, right, and centre. No film will touch you at the moment. You've lost your cosmetics contract, the perfume launch has been decommissioned, and you're not even being considered for that Disney animation about a worm with issues any more. The part's gone to Scarlett Johansson."

Mitch's breakfast came shooting back up his windpipe in a sudden and unexpected manner. He pulled an apologetic face as Belle ripped off her sunglasses and whipped round to meet his eyes with blazing balls of blue fire.

"I was gonna tell you," Mitch murmured unhappily.

Chase ploughed on. "Specifically, what our qualitative personality research tells us is that your recent behaviour has played badly with the fans. You've misread the zeitgeist."

"I've never read the zeitgeist," Belle blustered.

Chase stared at her with such a bewildered expression on his face that Mitch almost felt sorry for him. He had clearly underestimated the scale of the task before him, but then, who hadn't?

"People don't want stars like that anymore," the studio PR continued. "Drunken, wild, dressed like hookers…"

"Hey," interjected Belle indignantly. "It takes a lot of money to look that cheap."

"You gotta calm down," Chase advised. "Get some respect from somewhere. Get yourself some gravitas."

"What sort of ass?"

Mitch wiped the napkin from this morning's purchase of jelly doughnuts over his perspiring brow. He felt a slight tightness form in the wake of the wipe; sugar crystals, he realised too late. He had frosted his own forehead. "What Chase means," he said to Belle, "is that you need people to take you more seriously."

Belle nodded sarcastically. "Whaddya want me to do, go play Hamlet at the Royal Freaking Shakespeare Company? Huh?"

"Shakespeare. It's a thought," Arlington admitted.

Belle gasped in angry disbelief. But Chase interrupted.

"Fans these days…" he continued smoothly, "want stars they can respect. Caring stars, loving stars. People who care about the big issues. Global poverty. Families. The environment."

Belle stared at him disbelievingly. "I'm a celebrity. I'm not running for president."

Chase grinned wolfishly. "Belle, let me tell you, you know what you are. Sort of. People expect their stars to have issues these days. Consciences. Just look around. There's Angelina and Brad there with their rainbow family, Madonna and that little African guy, Clooney and Darfur, Gwyneth Paltrow and, uh, her macrobiotic yoga…"

Belle's shiny red lips were twisted in a scornful sneer. "So what are you saying? That you want me to—she snorted with disgust— "adopt…"—her eyes rolled incredulously, and she tossed her white hair—"an African baby?"

There was a dead silence.

Arlington's eyes burned, and his mouth rushed with water. His groin felt suddenly tight, as in moments of extreme sexual excitement. This was the answer. The idea they had been looking for. If anything could turn round Belle's career and reputation—and she was, after all, one of his most expensive stars—it was this.

"That's exactly what we want you to do, Belle," he said. "And if you don't, you're dumped."

Chapter Thirteen

NIALL MADE NO BONES—well, his father was a butcher—about his disapproval of her going to L.A. "You're an artist, Darcy," he stormed, his freckled Scottish face pinked up with anger, his brows drawn together in one long, disapproving, fox-coloured line. "You're supposed to be serious about acting. And Hollywood isn't acting. It's crap. Money-spinning, commercial crap with no moral or artistic value whatsoever."

A huge, hot wave of unease and embarrassment almost overwhelmed Darcy as she tried to defend herself. Niall on the attack was a formidable opponent. She could imagine him, like the Highland ancestors he so often spoke about, like the one Hollywood film he did approve of, *Braveheart*, running, bellowing down some glen side, and brandishing his sword, his ragged tartan billowing behind him.

Niall drew himself up to argue. He was stocky and powerfully built, but not tall. "*Galaxia*," he growled. "It sounds bloody awful. Simple-minded, commercial space trash. How can you even consider it?"

Darcy twisted her fingers and shot him uncomfortable looks. What could she do? She had given her word to Mitch Masterson now. And she was still curious about Tinseltown. What was wrong with going to have a look?

"Because they'll suck you in," Neil thundered, reminding Darcy of some handsome but terrifying Calvinist preacher shouting from a lofty pulpit in a grey-stone Edinburgh kirk. "They'll corrupt your values. Twist your mind."

Darcy felt half-mortified, half-exasperated. It was an audition she was going to. Not the Moonies. He was over-reacting, surely. Perhaps even over-acting; the sense, with him, even with her parents, that she was participating in some scene from a play never quite went away. Of course, they were all four of them actors. But that impression of slight distance, of watching herself from the outside, had been with her for so long Darcy felt it was quite normal and that everyone experienced it.

"Look, I'm not planning to become a Scientologist," she told Niall doggedly. "It's only an audition. It might not come to anything. They don't always," she added, with meaningful emphasis. The fact that Niall's Hamlet at the National Theatre hadn't come off was still a raw subject.

She regretted such below-the-belt tactics immediately. Niall's entire face changed. He looked at her, his—whatever he said about it—Tiffany blue eyes large with childish bewilderment, appearing larger and more childish still because of his pale blond lashes. Her heart twisted; he looked like a five-year-old unable to understand why anyone would want to hurt him. Which she obviously had.

"Thanks," Niall said bitterly, the bewilderment changing to a resentful stare. "That's right. You swan off to Hollywood, and I'll carry on trying to land a part as third spear carrier somewhere. But if I don't, there's always a part as a Scottish pisshead to fall back on."

She flung herself at him at that, full of the urge to comfort and reassure. "You're a great actor," she soothed, stroking his turbulent dark-red curls. "One of the very best. And people will realise it. They will. You'll get the recognition you deserve—"

"When?" he ground into her slender shoulder, gripping her to him hard.

"Soon." She looked earnestly into his eyes, pushing back his russet hair with both hands to expose his face. "It's got to happen," she added rather desperately. "Probably before I even get back."

He broke into a grin at this, shook his hair back over his broad shoulders, and rolled his blue eyes ruefully. "So you're definitely going, then?"

Darcy smiled back, trying to keep the mood light. "Why not? It might be fun to have a look at the whole crazy place. See what we're not missing."

"But you're a serious actress," Niall repeated, although his expression remained indulgent and open, not bunched and thunderous as it had been before.

"Alec Guinness was in *Star Wars*," Darcy reminded him, displaying her trump card and deciding not to tell her what Angharad had said about this.

"He regretted it the rest of his life," Angharad had declared, when Darcy had got to this bit of her speech with her mother. "Serious actors always do. I remember when Larry…"—Olivier, Darcy knew—"made a film with Neil Diamond in the eighties. He said he was more embarrassed about it than anything he'd ever done and it made him sick to think about it. Still, it's up to you, darling." Angharad smiled brightly at her daughter, having launched this fusillade at the idea. "You're at liberty to make your own decisions. Unlike so many people in the world, which reminds me, I've got a Free Tibet meeting at lunchtime. Must dash, darling."

❖ ❖ ❖

Mitch, ramping up the glamour and excitement for all he was worth, had claimed that the Heathrow-LAX first class had, at any given time, almost more famous people on board than luggage. But Darcy arrived late at the airport, thanks to the Tube train she had taken as a sop to Niall and keeping it real. Now, on board, the possibility that she was surrounded by stars was tantalising. But a sort of shell surrounded each seat, from which protruded various crossed legs dressed in expensive-looking trousers and feet with shiny leather shoes. Impossible to tell if some belonged to George Clooney or Brad Pitt.

Her disappointment melted as the champagne came round, along with a supply of new glossy magazines. Darcy took one avidly. *HotStars America* was exactly the kind of publication she would never have dared touch with Niall about. She flicked through with a guilty speed; then, as her eye hooked on the more sensational headlines, her perusal slowed.

CELEBRITY GRILL
We meet an A-lister for lunch

Actress Belle Murphy, 25, shot to fame last year in *Marie*, a bosomy biopic about Mary Queen of Scots. Since then, she's rarely been out of the gossip columns. To celebrate the release of her latest film, *Bloody Mary*, we caught up with Belle and her inseparable companion, her Chihuahua, Sugar, in New York's hottest new restaurant, the pink-themed Rosie's…

There was a large, accompanying photograph of Belle Murphy sitting in a pink, fluffy armchair wearing what looked like a black latex bikini.

HS: Belle, you're looking great. That's an incredible outfit you're wearing.

BM: Thanks. I like to keep my style original, but I always dress for myself.

HS: Belle, how do you keep so slim?

BM: I don't weigh myself, but I guess I have a really fast mentabolism.

HS: You mean "metabolism"?

BM: Yeah. I just can't put on weight. It's just so bizarre. I mean, I try. Last week I had four MacDonalds in one sitting. And you should so see me on the set when the sandwiches come round. I'm so like, "Whoa, hey, over here with that big old tuna melt!"

HS: Talking of sets, how exactly is *Bloody Mary* doing at the box office, Belle? Is it true the figures are a little, how do we put this…?

BM: No! It's doing great. I mean, I don't have the exact figures, but it was the number five film in Serbia last week.

HS: Would it have helped if *Bloody Mary* had had more nude scenes, do you think? After all, these were a feature of *Marie*.

BM: I really believe that the nudity in *Marie* was integral to the character.

Darcy chuckled. She had seen *Marie*. Niall had lifted his usual Hollywood embargo on the grounds that it was a film about a former queen of Scotland. Although, in the end, Scotland had played the most minor of roles, far more minor than the two main ones played by Belle's bosoms.

HS: On a different subject, we were sorry to hear about your break-up with Christian Harlow…

BM: Yeah. You know, it was fun with Christian while it lasted. But he wanted serious commitment, and I don't want to be tied down. He's got over it now, and we've both moved on. It's been very amicable. We're still great friends and call each other all the time.

HS: But now there's a new man in your life, we understand. A baby! Called Morning? Congratulations!

BM: Thanks. Yeah, motherhood's just, like, awesome. It was like all of a sudden I knew the secret, I became a member of this tribe of mothers and felt, like, really interwoven with everything, you know?

HS: You adopted Morning, right?

BM: Yeah. He's African. From an orphanage. You know, I feel a great empathy with African people. Particularly ones in orphanages. They have, like, nothing, but they always seem so happy with their lot. It's kind of humbling, you know?

HS: Are you looking after him yourself?

BM: Yeah. I've got this great British nanny. Called Jacintha; Lady Jacintha, in fact. She's from some top nanny college where they wear special hats and badges. Used to work for a famous author. She's very cool. Her ancestors go back to the Mediaeval Ages.

HS: So you're enjoying family life?

BM: It's beautiful, just the greatest. The moment I first held Morning, I felt, you know, kinda so connected to the world. I didn't know I was capable of such love.

Darcy shoved the magazine in the plush seat pocket. The champagne suddenly seemed to be curdling with the truffles and foie gras in her stomach. The interview she had just read was everything her mother and Niall most despised. That she had once affected to despise herself. And yet Belle Murphy was a Hollywood star, and Darcy herself was about to enter the same machine. Perhaps she really was selling out, being sucked in, having her values twisted, after all. Perhaps she really was making the biggest mistake of her life.

"Another glass, Madam?" The male air hostess was beaming at her side. Darcy looked miserably up at him. As he proffered the bottle, the tightness inside her relaxed. She watched as the foaming, pale-gold liquid tumbled into her glass. On the other hand, all this might just be great fun.

Chapter Fourteen

THE AFRICAN ADOPTION SHOULD, Belle knew, have swung everything in her favour. It had not been an easy business and had involved a great many dull meetings with embassy officials, as well as even duller ones with the baby itself. Belle lacked a single maternal fibre in the whole of her emaciated body and had found pretending to be transported with delight whilst holding a child one of the most difficult acting jobs she had ever had to do. Especially after it possetted on her Zac Posen dress.

But what was especially infuriating was that her Zac had been ruined in vain. None of the effort had achieved the expected results. While there had been coverage—an interview in *Hot Stars* and a couple of others—and even a few photo shoots with Morning, the general effect on the press had been far from electrifying. The consensus seemed to be that everyone had seen it all before. Celebrity African adoptions were nothing new. Madonna and Angelina Jolie had got there first.

Damn them, thought Belle, with more venom even than when she usually damned them. Damn them to hell. Because now here she was, stuck with a baby she didn't want, who she wouldn't even be able to dump without a great deal of the wrong sort of press interest. It would be years before he could quietly be packed off to some boarding school somewhere and she need never set eyes on him again. The whole enterprise had been a disaster.

"Like, just what does a girl have to do to remake her image?" Belle had wailed at her agent.

"*Hamlet?*" he replied.

"Excuse me?"

He reminded her how Arlington, in the meeting, had seemed interested in the idea of her doing some Shakespeare. It was desperate, sure, but desperate times required desperate measures. Desperate *Measure for Measures*, even.

Two days after this conversation, Belle had found herself in London.

It was, Belle felt, a pretty depressing city. Quite apart from the rain. June it might be, but the gloomy, marbled-grey skies beyond the great penthouse windows gave, Belle thought, the impression that the whole city was on some great dimmer switch turned permanently down low. The trees in the park opposite were always bent under some windy blast. The pavements were always shiny with rain. How unlike the sunshine of California, as permanent and dazzling as everyone's grins.

Thank God, her stay here was going to be short. The idea was that, having trod the boards as Lady Macbeth or whatever in London for a couple of weeks, she would succumb to a sudden, convenient virus and go back to L.A. with prestigious, serious-Shakespeare credentials. Having got a few weeks of real stagework under her belt. And if that didn't silence her detractors and impress people, nothing would.

It was more difficult than it sounded, even so. This morning's audition had been a particular nightmare. Some actress who had played Cordelia in an avant-garde *King Lear* in a small Soho theatre had gone to L.A. apparently.

"Good luck to her," Belle had sniffed. "She'll need it."

"She's got it, lots of it," groaned the theatre director, which was not what Belle wanted to hear.

There was an understudy for the absent actress's part, but the maverick young hotshot had naturally jumped at the chance to cast a Hollywood name like Belle, even if Belle's name was rather faded and besmirched of late. Indeed, so enthusiastic had been the direc-tor—business at the box office had been less brisk than hoped—that Mitch had assured Belle that she was a shoo-in for the role, and all she had to do was turn up.

The phone at her bedside rang. Belle groped clumsily about for it.

"How'd it go?" Mitch asked.

"Gross. That nude stuff. You never warned me."

"You never mind being nude normally," Mitch bewilderedly pointed out.

"I don't, no," Belle snapped back. "It wasn't me I was worried about. I mean the guy playing Lear. He's about a thousand and has his dick out all through the performance."

Mitch, from his end, sighed. None of this was working out the way it should. First, there had been the disappointment about the baby; admittedly, the timing seemed to have been slightly out there. And now London was going tits up too.

She had sounded drunk just then, and possibly, Mitch suspected, he had overestimated Belle's ability to cope without a vast quantity of help. He had advised that the usual Hollywood entourage of bodyguards, a personal assistant, and press officer would adversely affect any efforts to give her image the realistic, authentic, down-to-earth edge the studio clearly felt it needed. He had reminded her that you never saw Dame Judi Dench mob-handed with stylists, security, personal trainers, and spokespeople.

But Belle had insisted on the Portchester, London's best and grandest hotel, and the penthouse suite to boot. She had also insisted on bringing Morning's nanny; it seemed she couldn't even pick her new adopted son up without help. Well, given the amount she seemed to be drinking, that was probably true, Mitch reflected gloomily.

Chapter Fifteen

FOR DARCY, THE PAMPERING of the plane proceeded seamlessly into the pampering of a limousine sent by Mitch to meet her at LAX. Whisked, with the rest of first class, off the aircraft before everybody else, Darcy whirled through Immigration and out of the baggage reclaim at a speed far faster than she imagined possible.

She spotted her driver in the arrivals hall. He was a peak-capped diminutive Puerto Rican holding a sign with "Mr. Darcy" written on it.

"It had what on it?" Mitch, calling her on the mobile once the limo was underway, did not see the joke.

"It doesn't matter," Darcy said, blinking with tired eyes through the tinted windows at L.A. Her first impression was that it was bright and hot and busy with shiny, unfamiliar-shaped cars, sunlit roads, low, magnolia-coloured buildings, dusty palm trees, cloudless blue sky. Seeing it through glass gave it a distance, as if she was watching it on the television. Actually, it looked like it always did on the television. Perhaps she was watching it on the television and this was all a dream.

"I thought it was funny actually," she added about the chauffeur. She wanted to comfort Mitch, who seemed upset about it for some reason.

She thought it was funny? The hell it was funny, Mitch fumed to himself. A bad start was what it was. That limo company with its caps cost a freaking fortune. It was supposed to impress clients, not make them—and him, more to the point—look stupid.

"Don't worry," he assured Darcy in a voice of grim determination. "Pretty soon you'll be so famous that no one could even think about making a mistake like that."

"I'm not worrying," Darcy assured him back. She wanted to add that she neither particularly believed the bit about being famous nor wanted it all that much. But she desisted; it seemed impolite, given how excited about the Jack Saint meeting Mitch was.

"How about dinner tonight?" Mitch asked. "Go to your hotel, have a siesta, and I'll come by and pick you up at about seven-thirty."

Darcy's hotel was a cream-painted palace whose staff all looked like supermodels and whose entrance was flanked with lawns as smooth and glossy as bright green velvet. There were ornate fountains, palm trees, and beds of almost painfully colourful flowers whose every petal seemed hand-tweaked into position. It occurred to Darcy, as she looked about, that the extra brightness could be due to the fact that everyone seemed to wear sunglasses; you had to overcompensate on the colour front as nothing was ever viewed with the naked eye. Or was it because any colour out there had to compete with the California sky, a powerful swimming-pool blue?

Inside the hotel, by contrast, all was muted and calm. Her room, which faced front over the zinging gardens, was vast and cream, with cream-coloured furniture. It was, she thought, a bit like being inside a meringue. The only non-cream aspects were striped white and yellow—the awnings on the enormous windows and the parasol and chair cushions of the table outside on the balcony. And, of course, when you combined white and yellow, cream was what you got.

"Can I get you a glass of champagne, Madam?" the chipper bellboy who had shown her up asked on leaving. Darcy shook her head. She didn't want to even think about champagne now. She felt that she had drunk her own weight in the stuff on the flight; her head throbbed and her mouth was dry. Apart from water, something comforting and sweet was what she wanted: something that would send her into an afternoon doze. Suddenly, she could see it, in a tall glass in a silver cradle, foamy, light, warm, wonderfully thick and sweet.

"Got any…um…hot chocolate?" she asked.

The bellboy looked thunderstruck, then collected himself and nodded. "Certainly, Madam."

Darcy wondered why he was so surprised. Surely it wasn't that unusual an order? It wasn't as if she'd asked for a whip and a black-peaked cap with a Nazi badge on it. And yet, he'd looked almost as shocked as if she had.

When the hot chocolate came, it exceeded all expectations. It was in the tall glass she had imagined, complete with the silver cradle, topped with cream and chocolate shavings, studded with marshmallows and with two chocolate-chip cookies on the side.

Afterwards, Darcy lay down on the big bed, sinking immediately into the airy, cool, linen-scented embrace of the duvet and padded mattress. It was still hard to imagine she was really here.

She burrowed into the billowing, cream bed linen feeling that her grandmother was smiling down on her. Alone of all her family, Darcy knew, her grandmother would have encouraged the L.A. visit. She was no stranger to the town herself, after all. She would, Darcy knew, also have appreciated the meringue décor. And she would certainly have appreciated all the champagne.

❖ ❖ ❖

When Mitch turned up at seven-thirty, Darcy's first impression was that he was most unlike her idea of a Hollywood agent. His voice on the phone had been urgent and persuasive, and she had pictured some hawk-eyed Hollywood machine. But Mitch was large—enormous, in fact, billowing and bulging in all directions—and had an apprehensive, chaotic air to him that, contrary to such airs in England, was obviously not something he was cultivating. Rather, it seemed to be something he was desperately trying to hide.

He looked at her, also approvingly. Darcy wore a vintage Dior sleeveless sheath dress she had been delighted to find in a Knightsbridge charity shop the very day before she had flown out to L.A. She had spotted it, gleaming darkly on the rail, and swooped with a gasp of delight. It was, Darcy had thought as she examined the dress, almost as if it had been waiting for her. It fitted her perfectly; its rich, inky-blue satin gave a velvety depth to her dark hair and a creaminess to her pale skin.

Immediately after buying it, she had, in an uncharacteristic seizure of extravagance, splashed out on a pair of Prada heels to match it, which cost far more than the budget she had mentally earmarked for her entire L.A. wardrobe. She had not told Niall about these; although, admittedly, he was so angry about the L.A. trip in general that a pair of shoes was hardly likely to make a difference.

"You look great, baby," Mitch assured her. He was relieved. The picture of Darcy on the website run by those mad old trouts in London who called themselves her agents had been the usual hideously unflattering monochrome headshot that British thespians for some reason preferred. It was incredible any of them ever got work.

The headshot gave no indication of how very pretty Darcy was in real life. Her skin was a pure, milky white, so white it almost glowed; only as he looked at it did Mitch realise how boring the uniform roast-chicken tans of L.A. could be. Her face was a pale oval with a touch of pink in the cheeks. Her thick, shiny black hair was unhighlighted. Mitch stared at it in awe as it slid about her white shoulders, probably the only undyed young female hair in the whole of the city.

She was taller than expected and not as thin as he had imagined. Slim, certainly, but no twig. She had breasts and a bottom. She filled that stunning dress beautifully, Mitch thought. People were staring at her as they left the hotel lobby—and no wonder.

She seemed both pleased and excited to be here too. That Brit reserve, all that hoity-toity stuff about the theatre she'd laid on him during that first phone call, seemed to have melted away like snow in June now she was here. As she greeted him in the hotel foyer, she was beaming. Those teeth looked natural too, although, being white and straight, entirely unlike the usual snaggly, yellow ones the British were famous for. She seemed positively bubbling with the excitement of it all.

It was hard to believe she had just that morning stepped off an eleven-hour flight, but this, Darcy told him, giggling, was due to the restorative properties of a huge hot chocolate she had ordered from room service. Mitch had almost fallen over at this.

"You're kidding." A hot chocolate! With cream and cookies on the side? "Hey! Young actress in Hollywood orders calorie shock," he grinned.

Her face flashed with surprise. Then she smiled. "Oh. Now I get it," she said.

"Get what?"

"Why the waiter was amazed. Oh!" Darcy covered her hand with her mouth. "And I ordered a hamburger when I woke up as well. He must think I'm such a pig!"

"Good for you," said Mitch approvingly. Like all fat people, he liked to encourage others to eat as much as possible. He led her to the limo waiting outside.

"Actually, can you believe it, but I'm hungry again," Darcy admitted, looking excitedly about her as they emerged from the hotel entrance into the scented early-summer evening. "Where are we going to eat?"

"Puccini's," Mitch announced, and confidently awaited the exclamations of surprise and delight. When they failed to come, he gave her a sideways look. "You heard of Puccini's, right?"

"Er…no," Darcy grinned.

"L.A.'s hottest Italian restaurant," Mitch told her, suddenly not minding that his great achievement in getting a table there meant nothing. There was something so infectiously open and unpretentious about this girl, her big black eyes everywhere, missing nothing, so obviously interested and amused. She was like a breeze blowing through the open window of a hot, noisy room, Mitch thought, as the limo drew up outside the hot and noisy room that was Puccini's.

Puccini's looked unexceptional to Darcy, a long, low building swathed in vines and with tables outside with cream shades. But then everything exploded in shouts, grinding and zooming noises, and blasts of white light.

Paparazzi, she swiftly realised as a sashaying waiter led them to a table. Not for her, thankfully, but for Jennifer Aniston just behind. Darcy was amazed both by the way the lights exploded—fast, furious, noisy, frightening—and the way the actress, far smaller and thinner even than she appeared in magazines, just smiled her way through it and walked to her table with her companion, seemingly undisturbed by the fuss.

"Like this place?" Mitch reached for a breadstick. The table they had been given was one of the worst; restaurants of this sort, he suspected, had a Fame Board like his agency's in the back somewhere too. He would be somewhere way down the bottom of it. Darcy, on the other hand, wouldn't yet be on it at all. But she would, Mitch was certain.

Darcy was examining the menu. It was enormous, although it had far few dishes than expected on it. None of which were as Italian as expected either.

The champagne arrived. Darcy picked hers up gingerly; her head still felt slightly tight and thick from that on the plane.

"To you!" Mitch declared, in a voice so loud that she cringed. She chinked back, reddening, desperate for people not to stare. Mitch, on the other hand, was desperate to attract as much attention to his client as possible.

The champagne having helped suffuse her embarrassment,

Darcy started to look about her again. Her wandering eye caught a well-known face. She leaned over to Mitch. "Is that…?"

"Drew Barrymore, yes,"

"And that…?"

"Is Cameron Diaz." Mitch grinned delightedly. This was fun.

A waiter glided to the table. "May I take your order?"

"Oh, yes. Sorry," Darcy beamed. She applied herself conscientiously to the vast menu, then raised her head. "This is an Italian restaurant?"

Mitch and the waiter affirmed that this was indeed the case.

"But there isn't any pasta on the menu."

The waiter's eyebrow arched upwards. The agent put a fat paw on Darcy's small, slim hand.

"This is Hollywood," he reminded her. "No one eats pasta here. Carbs are a no-no."

"Perhaps Madam would like the steamed fish with lemon," put in the waiter acidly.

Darcy scanned the menu again. Her face lit up suddenly. "Hey. I've found some pasta. Nude ravioli. What's that?" she asked, her voice dropping slightly. "What's, erm, nude about it?"

"It doesn't have any pasta." The waiter spoke with a touch of triumph. "It's just the stuffing."

"Which is?" Darcy asked hopefully, her hungry imagination conjuring up rich patties of red-wine ragu. Or something deliciously cheesy and herby…

"Steamed spinach balls," the waiter said flatly.

"I'll have the shark risotto," Mitch said. It was the standard power order. Shark—for sharks. The nearest Hollywood restaurants got to a joke.

As he handed the vast bill of fare over, Darcy watched, amused, as the waiter struggled to incorporate it about his person. There was nowhere to put it apart from under his arm.

"An Italian restaurant without pasta!" she exclaimed as the waiter disappeared.

"You don't get it," Mitch grinned at her. "Restaurants in Hollywood aren't for eating in. They're to avoid eating."

The black eyes staring into his widened in amazement. "But you eat."

"Yeah, but not in restaurants." Mitch thought guiltily of the jelly doughnuts and the doctor's advice he routinely ignored. He resolved to change the subject. "This meeting with Jack Saint," he began, deciding to get straight on to the important business, rather than waiting.

Darcy nodded, tilting her head slightly and attentively. Her eyes slid slightly to the right of Mitch's face. It was then that it happened.

The chat and buzz of the restaurant disappeared. Mitch's voice faded to nothing. The remains of her hangover vanished. Darcy was aware of nothing but a singing sensation in her every nerve-ending—and the eyes she was looking into. In which she felt caught, unable to move, almost unable to breathe.

They were ridiculous blue even from this distance, drilling into hers. He was, she managed to absorb, almost stupidly handsome, all cheekbones and lips and glossy, ruffled black hair. He looked like something from a perfume advert, one of those bulging crotches in white underwear that women crashed their cars into walls straining to look at. He ought to have made her laugh.

But Darcy had never felt less like laughing. Her heart leapt in mixed terror and excitement as he rose to his feet. Her scrambled senses realizing a few seconds later that he was leaving. The two people he was with led the way: a man·and a woman. The woman was thin and fiftysomething, not lover material, Darcy quickly noted. His agent, maybe? The man looked businesslike too, tanned, grey-haired, trim, sharp-eyed, the Hollywood player type she had imagined Mitch being. Her eyes followed him; his remained locked to hers. For all she was focused on his face, she could sense the power of his body: broad shoulders and a graceful animal muscularity, like some jungle big cat. She felt a pulsing in her groin.

"Hey, are you listening to me?" Mitch interrupted. His eyes followed Darcy's; he breathed a sharp inward breath. His small eyes narrowed in dislike. Oh no. Not that guy. Anyone but him.

Darcy glanced at him vaguely. "Yes, of course, I'm listening. Go on. But before you do," she leant over and hissed, "tell me who that man is."

Mitch's heart sank at the urgency in her voice. He had heard it before. He spoke stonily into the wooden table. "Christian Harlow."

"And who's he?" Darcy asked, her eyes following Christian through the restaurant, her heart steadily sinking because any moment now he would disappear through the door. Then, to her delight, he stopped, paused at the entrance, and, eyes still on her, raised two fingers to his lips and kissed them. Then he disappeared into a hail of flashbulbs.

Darcy whirled back to Mitch, her eyes blazing. "He's famous?"

"Famous for being an asshole," Mitch growled, his good mood severely dissipated. Famous too, he added to himself, for being the man who had caused all Belle Murphy's problems. Ruined her career, pretty much. And, to endear himself to Mitch ever further, Christian had just this week joined Greg Cucarachi at Associated Artists; Greg having pried Christian away from the agent he had been with since the beginning. Although given Christian's loyalty record, that was, Mitch imagined, probably as difficult as prying apart two halves of a cheese sandwich.

Darcy was still gawping at the door through which Harlow had just departed. Then something clicked in her head. She blinked and felt a strange sensation, as if released from a spell. She felt a wave of sickening guilt. Where was Niall in all this? Where was her loyalty?

She felt hot with self-disgust. How could one glimpse of a stranger wipe out so completely all thoughts of the man she loved?

She had called Niall repeatedly on landing, but he had not answered. He had an audition today, she knew—yet another. She desperately hoped it would go well. Or, at least, not as badly as the others. Sitting in the L.A. restaurant, sickened and ashamed, Darcy concentrated all her love and thoughts on her boyfriend and, from eight-thousand miles away, wished him luck from the bottom of her anguished heart.

Chapter Sixteen

"Cow!"

"Pig!"

The children's angry-sounding shouts were the first thing James heard as he opened the front door. He closed his eyes briefly. A wave of misery swept through him, followed by the reflection that perhaps it was only to be expected. The honeymoon period with the new nanny was over.

Hero and Cosmo were arguing. Chaos had come again. He'd known Emma was too good to be true, and now here was the proof—she'd lost control of the children, just like every other nanny before her. From now on, it would be the familiar downward spiral to her inevitable sacking. If she didn't walk first, that was. He'd seen it many times before.

Only this time, he wasn't going to.

Soaring into James's mood of glum acceptance now came a thunderbolt of determination. Usually he just watched the collapse of their childcare regimes from the sidelines, but this time he couldn't. The other nannies hadn't been much of a loss anyway, but Emma was different. The fact that she cared about the children, loved the job, and was brilliant at it meant that on no account was she to be let go.

He would talk to Vanessa about it as soon as she got back. But the fact that his wife seemed inexplicably irritated by Emma had not escaped James. The thought had flitted briefly across James's mind then that his wife suspected him of more than strictly professional interest in the new nanny, but he had dismissed it instantly. How could Vanessa imagine anything of the sort? He was, admittedly, scared of her, but he was also devoted to her and always would be.

It was with a clear conscience and pure motives, therefore, that had James consistently shored up Emma's position within the household, praising her to Vanessa whenever he could, and in the strongest terms.

"Pig!" Cosmo now screamed, derailing his father's train of thought.

"Cow!" yelled back Hero.

The situation was clearly deteriorating. James set a determined foot on the bottom-most stair.

"Dog!"

He couldn't hear Emma's voice at all, James realised. Panic seized him at the thought that she had gone already, before she was pushed. For if he himself, notoriously unobservant as he was, had picked up the vibes from Vanessa, it seemed likely Emma had too.

"Elephant!" screamed Cosmo.

James had gained the landing now. A great sense of relief flooded through him as he saw, on the sisal floor of the upstairs hall, his children in clean pyjamas—pink gingham for Hero, blue gingham for Cosmo, hair neatly brushed and no doubt teeth too, sitting opposite each other with great grins on their faces and their legs stretched out. Between those legs was a pile of cards with animals printed on the back.

At a movement behind him, James turned. Emma, drying her hands on a floral tea towel, was hurrying up the stairs behind him. She smiled apologetically. "Sorry, didn't hear you come in. I was in the kitchen." She looked happily at the children. "I've just taught them to play Snap, and they're having a quick game before bed. They love it. I didn't realise they didn't know how…"

James did not reply. There was, despite the private child care they had enjoyed—if that was the word—since birth, so much the children didn't know. Emma's methods, her constant engagement with the children, showed in sharp relief the extent to which the other nannies had not bothered at all, unless it was to dump them both in front of a DVD or shove Cosmo in the direction of his PlayStation.

Since Emma had come, the DVDs had largely been phased out, access to computer games rigidly controlled, and the children taught Snakes and Ladders and Tiddly Winks, both of which they had quickly taken to. In addition, besides teaching Hero and Cosmo the beginnings of reading and some rudimentary arithmetic, Emma had taken them out into the world and showed them how buses worked, the Tube, post offices, and shops.

It was, James said admiringly to Vanessa, nothing short of a miracle. She had sharply pointed out that Emma was not the first of their caregivers to take the children shopping. James remembered that one three nannies ago had, indeed, taken Hero and Cosmo to Oxford Street Topshop almost every other day. Only not, he suspected, for their benefit.

"Mouse!" shrieked Hero, slamming her card on the pile, on top of which Cosmo had just put down a mouse. "Sna-a-ap!"

As Cosmo groaned with the agony of losing, Emma bent down, gathered up the cards—"Yes, children, you help. We tidy up our playthings."—and shooed them off to bed.

"Come on, Hero," Emma urged the silver-haired three-year-old as she lingered over a card with a cat on it. Of all animals, cats were Hero's absolute favourite. "You need your sleep. It's a big day for you tomorrow. What day is it?" she enquired gently, dropping to her knees before the child and taking both white, chubby hands in her own.

Hero's big blue eyes looked shyly into Emma's pretty, ruddy, beaming face. "Birthday," she whispered, before collapsing with an excited squeal on Emma's white-cottoned chest.

A surge of horror possessed James. While he had not forgotten it was Hero's fourth birthday, he now remembered he had heard nothing about the arrangements for it. Usually, when the children's birthdays loomed, Vanessa was storming about the house in a blue funk as she and whatever nanny was resident at the time tried to secure the real-life Charlie and Lola, the cast of *High School Musical,* or whatever that year's must-have happened to be.

But there had been no such scenes recently. That Vanessa had forgotten was surely impossible, but James resolved to talk to Emma after bedtime nonetheless. If Hero's birthday party had somehow slipped through the net, perhaps they could come up with something together. Emma was a resourceful woman, and he had absolute faith in her.

"Bed!" Emma was commanding the children. There was a flurry of movement and laughter, a blur of blue and pink gingham, and almost before James realised, his children had pressed warm, flannel-covered, bath-scented little bodies to his, deposited hard wet kisses on his cheek, and tumbled into their room, from whence the comforting sound of Emma singing nursery rhymes now issued.

As James went back down the stairs, an unfamiliar smell surged round his nostrils. Making his way along the threadbare sisal of the passage into the kitchen, James now discovered the source of the mysterious, but by no means unpleasant, scent.

It was baking. The sweet, warm, rich smell of cakes cooking. He hadn't recognised it because cakes were so rarely cooked in their house. Whenever needed, they were bought in from whatever modish bakery enjoyed Vanessa's favour at the time.

James's stomach gave a mighty rumble. He loved homemade cakes, and the sight that greeted him now was not only a fantasy made reality, but as if someone had, in one fell swoop, sought to make up for the baking deficit of years in their particular kitchen.

Every available surface—the table, the units, the cooker itself, the top of the fridge—was covered in cupcakes in paper cases. Sixty at least, James swiftly calculated. All decorated, all in different ways. Some had the squodge of buttercream icing—a generous squodge too, James noted approvingly—and twin sponge wings of the traditional butterfly cake. Others were jam and cream splits. Some were covered in the sprinkles called hundreds and thousands, others with chocolate, still others with silver balls on top of icing that had a pinkish iridescent sparkle. James stared at the shining, glittering, glowing mass of sweet-scented cakes in childish wonder. It looked like heaven as a five-year-old might imagine it.

The cakes on the table, James now saw with a more adult appreciation, had been particularly beautifully iced. They had that thick, flat, smooth professional look, some the pale pink of sugar almonds, some white. And with something iced on top of that—cat's faces, James recognised with a stab of delight. The pink ones had an outline in white, lovingly hand done, of a cat's face with silver sugar balls for eyes. The white ones had the same outline in pink.

A tremor of pure joy now seized him as he noticed, at the back of the kitchen table, a large white cake in the shape of a cat's face, with eyes, nose, and whiskers in pink icing. Other details of fur and eyelashes had been added in the same iridescent pink sparkle—edible paint, James realised—he had spotted on top of the silver-ball cupcakes. Around the cake's edge was tied a fat, pale-pink satin ribbon, to which was attached a small silver bell. Four silver candles stood, two each side, among the whiskers.

Hero was going to erupt with excitement. Her father felt almost tearful at the prospect.

Hungry too. Everything looked so delicious. He hadn't had a homemade cake like this for years, and it seemed years, too, since the canteen bacon sandwich that had constituted today's scrappy office lunch. He reached for the nearest cake, which happened to be one of the butterfly ones, and quickly, furtively peeled off the wrapper.

When Emma entered the kitchen, seconds later, the cake had just entered James's mouth.

"Sorry," he floundered, his mouth full of crumbs. It was worth the shame however. The cupcake was delicious, every bit as sweet, fresh, and buttery as it looked. Substantial too, not like those cakes you bit into only to find your teeth instantly meeting, that seemed to contain nothing but gritty, sugary air.

"Don't worry," Emma assured him. "There's plenty to go round. I'm expecting ten children tomorrow…"

She moved to the sink.

"Ten?"

"Yes. For Hero's birthday. We're having a tea party." Emma looked up from stacking the dirty bowls on a small tray to transfer them to the dishwasher in the utility room. It wasn't the most convenient of washing-up arrangements, James knew, but alone of all the nannies he could remember, Emma hadn't complained about it.

"A tea party?" James was aware that all he was doing was repeating everything Emma said, but he could not help it nonetheless.

As she looked up, nodded, and smiled, a hank of reddish-brown hair dislodged from the rest and fell fetchingly across her face. "It seemed the easiest thing," Emma said, rather breathlessly. "From what I gather from Vanessa, birthdays had become a sort of torture for her…"

James raised an eyebrow. Many things were a sort of torture for his wife.

"And she hadn't got very far with organising Hero's. Obviously she's busy and everything," Emma added hastily. "But, of course, she was thinking about one of those expensive party places…" the nanny continued, her eyes wide and enthusiastic. "And I suggested that, really, that wasn't necessary. That she could save a fortune, and Hero would have a much nicer time if—well"—she shrugged and smiled—"we just had an afternoon birthday tea party at home for

Hero's friends. With a few games. Old-fashioned, I know, but nice. Back to basics."

James's eye flicked towards the glowing, glittering, pink-and-white display of cakes. There was nothing remotely basic about those. Or if there was, it was his sort of basic. But as he rushed to the kitchen door to hold it open for her, a hideous thought struck him.

"Who'll do the games?" He pictured himself standing, vainly shouting about Musical Chairs, in the middle of a pack of rioting children.

Emma was looking at him in surprise. "Well, me, of course. Musical chairs, pass the parcel, that sort of thing. All quite straightforward."

James stared at her. She was going up in his estimation all the time. Not only was she professionally super-competent and a marvellous cook, but she was possessed of astounding courage into the bargain.

"You're wonderful," he exploded passionately, ears thumping too hard with excitement to hear the rattle of the front door. Just in time to hear him say this, Vanessa walked in.

Chapter Seventeen

BELLE LAY ON THE vast bed in the Portchester Hotel penthouse, clutching a bottle of champagne to her like a teddy bear. She was wreathed in creased linen and gloomy thoughts. So much so that she didn't hear the phone shrilling at first.

"I'm ringing to remind you you've got an audition this morning," Mitch told Belle with a firmness that masked the worry he increasingly felt.

He had hoped that, in the absence of a PA for Belle, the Portchester Hotel, prompted by him, could organize alarm calls, limos, and so forth.

As indeed it could, in theory. And, according to the manager, actually had. The problem was that the hotel couldn't physically make Belle go to the auditions. From the sound of her voice during some of their phone conversations, Mitch suspected the limos just took Belle straight to the nearest bar.

"You haven't forgotten about this audition?" he added suspiciously, into the silence.

"No," Belle said in a tiny, sheepish voice that Mitch hardly recognised from the thundering complaints of old. "What is it?"

"*Titus Andronicus.*"

Mitch wanted to scream. She had forgotten, damn her. Meaning she wouldn't have learnt any of the lines. She'd have to get through the audition on star power alone, and her wattage was getting dimmer all the time.

"What's the part?" Belle said sullenly. She sounded utterly unrepentant, Mitch thought. Not to mention ungrateful. He'd had to pull some serious strings to get the director to agree to see her. Word about Belle and auditions had clearly been getting around. Didn't she want to save her career?

"A queen," he replied carefully. At least, he thought it was a queen. He had only had time to absorb the vaguest outline of the plot, which hadn't sounded too good. The high point of the part Belle was auditioning for was the character realising she has just eaten both her children in a pie. He decided not to draw this to his client's attention just now.

"There's a limo for you downstairs, " Mitch urged, his wheedling tones spiked with impatience. "And the paparazzi too. Make sure you look good, yeah?"

Belle took a final, resolve-stiffening swig of warm champagne, which went straight to her empty stomach. She could not remember the last time she had eaten—a proper meal, that was, instead of the skinny lattes and crackers which she normally got by on—any more than she could remember not having a hangover. Her head ached with one now. Low-level but persistent, like someone slowly levering her brain apart. She had a feeling they had become constant around the time that Christian left. But she could not be sure. She hadn't been sure of anything since then.

She set to work to get ready. But a full face of redone make-up was more than she could be bothered to do. She wiped off the worst smudges from yesterday's mascara, pressed a powder puff to the shiniest bits of her cheeks and forehead, and reapplied her lipstick.

She pulled unsteadily at the door of the walk-in wardrobe next to the vast and mirrored bathroom, staggered back as it flew unexpectedly open, and grabbed at the first thing which came to hand, a Diane von Furstenberg leopard-print wrap. She pulled her unwashed, unbrushed blonde mane into a ponytail with a black silk Chanel scarf and considered the effect in the dressing-room mirror.

Bed hair wasn't very Californian, but it was quite London, where everyone seemed pretty scruffy. Or "edgy," as they apparently thought of it. Edgy was about the size of it, thought Belle. She'd felt edgy ever since she'd been in this god-damn city. She peered into the further, gloomier recesses of the cupboard, looking for a bag big enough to hide the three-quarters-finished bottle of champagne in. She needed something to help her through the audition.

Her eye fell on the very thing. The new, shiny, orange leather Birkin she'd bought yesterday during her blitzkrieg on Bond Street. Various other purchases she had made stood elsewhere in the cupboard, still in their bags. Belle stared at them for a second or two, vainly trying to recall what any of them were.

With a blast of strong perfume to disguise any smell of alcohol, she was ready. Swinging her bag defiantly, she walked out of the bedroom into the penthouse sitting room where Jacintha sat with Morning. Jacintha wore her usual disapproving expression. Seeing her, Sugar leapt to his feet and started yapping frenziedly; Jacintha's frown deepened. There was, Belle knew, no love lost between Morning's nanny and Sugar. Possibly even less than between Morning's nanny and herself.

She bent, picked up Sugar, and, crooning softly to him, stuffed him in the Birkin along with the champagne bottle. Then she hurried out of the door, into the private penthouse lift, and down to the limo.

❖❖❖

Ken sat on the wall opposite the Portchester Hotel, his camera idle in his lap. It was a cold morning, although it was June, and the chill from the concrete entering his buttocks was an unpleasant feeling.

Madonna had just jogged by in the park across the road. He

hadn't bothered snapping her. As she was wearing the same black tracksuit and shades as always, there was no point. Madonna was no fool; she knew the name of the game. Or the clothes of the game, at least, which was why, when she was out and about, she'd had on the same outfit for the last three years. To make the pictures look the same as they had for the last three years and render the image unsellable. It was a clever trick, and one all these celebrities who moaned about invasion of privacy would use if they really didn't want to be photographed.

If they really wanted privacy, Ken thought, they'd stay in, like Liz Hurley and Charlotte Church did until they'd lost the weight after the baby. Or they'd disguise themselves. Properly, like David Bowie always did, travelling on the Tube wearing a pair of cheap sunglasses and reading a Turkish newspaper.

At least Belle Murphy, whatever else one may think about her, made no bones about the fact she wanted the publicity. She gave good pose too. No one who had never seen a celebrity in full facing-the-paps mode, Ken knew, had any idea how the pictures that appeared in the newspapers were achieved. They imagined they were just shots that were snatched in a second, and, of course, some were.

But the ones like Belle, the ones who really wanted it, left nothing to chance. Belle would stand there, absolutely still, for minutes on end. Then she would change position very carefully, very slowly, the dazzling smile held for an infinity, even as the flashes went off. And she never blinked when the lights flashed. She had built-in sunglasses in her eyes, that girl, Ken thought.

Actually, she probably had. From the look of her, she had built-in everything else. Although not built-in famousness, as it turned out. Hers was on the wane, and although it had received a spike upwards from the adoption of the baby—always a good trick, that one—she was hardly big-time any more. Still, she was bigger time than most of the celebs about in London at the moment, which was why Ken was here.

"Come on, Belle," he groaned now, shifting his buttocks on the cold wall. "Come outside and give us all a break. Preferably with the kid."

He glanced in desultory fashion around him at the other eight or so photographers present that morning. He knew most of them; they were freelancers like him. Some lounged on the wall as he did, flicking through YouTube on their laptops. Some bantered and joked with the hotel doormen, their eyes on every passing limo, scanning number plates for registrations they recognised.

Ken glanced at the cadaverous features of the man next to him. Keith, a long-time colleague and competitor, worked for rival agency Top Pictures. Keith's skin was flaky and grey—as, Ken knew, was his own—with the constant pap diet of crisps and coffee.

Keith looked preoccupied and was rustling through one of the London free sheets. As he stopped and sucked loudly through his teeth, Ken leant over to see at what. A large photograph of Tom Hanks shopping in Covent Garden dominated the page.

"Spent all day waitin' outside 'is 'otel yesterday," Keith complained. He shook his head resentfully. "That's great, that is. Bloody great. You spend all day sitting outside some hotel in Knightsbridge, and he's there in bloody Covent Garden. What kind of a job is this, eh?" He drove a fist into his forehead.

Ken nodded absently. His eye was on the double yellow line on which his car was parked. It was at least twenty minutes since the traffic warden had last appeared, and he would be back any moment. His car looked, Ken thought, particularly dirty and battered this morning, piled high with yellowing newspapers, scrunched crisp bags, and torn chocolate wrappers. It wasn't the line to be in, Ken thought morosely, if you wanted a decent car. It wasn't the line to be in if you wanted a decent anything: flat, life, relationship, you name it.

The hotel doors revolved, and a frisson swept the line of

photographers, but only a couple of grey-suited businessmen had come out. Tanned, smooth-skinned, and bouffant-haired, they regarded the line of snappers with supercilious amusement.

Beside him, Keith moaned on. "I blame digitalization. Mobile phone cameras. People think all they have to do is wait outside some celebrity's house and they'll make a fortune."

Ken looked at him. "Well, that is all they have to do. So long as the celeb turns up."

He knew what Keith meant however. He himself had entered the business peachy-keen and fired up, lens primed, all agog, convinced he was about to hit the big time, or at least photograph it. Now he knew better. The paparazzi life was a grindingly dull one. The last thing it was was glamorous.

It was also, he was increasingly beginning to feel, worthless.

But on the other hand, what else could he do? This, so far as Ken was concerned, was the most depressing aspect of all.

There was a frisson again as the hotel revolving doors spun and Belle stepped out, blinking in the bright sunshine, her half-tied dress rippling like a leopard-skin flag in the breeze and flying up to expose thin white legs in long brown boots. She carried an orange bag in which the head of her small dog could just be seen, its malicious black eyes swiveling about.

An electric ripple of excitement shot through the crowd of snappers. Ken, zooming and shooting away with the rest, noticed that Belle looked less groomed than usual; she had a hurried, thrown-together, rather sluttish appearance that rather suited her, he thought. Of course, it would be deliberate down to the last misplaced hair: a new, rumpled look, more Bardot than her usual varnished Barbie one. Yes, thought Ken with a leap of spirit in which excitement was mixed with relief. From Bardot to Barbie. It was a picture story. Everyone would buy it. So long as he got there first.

His fingers frantically switched the calibrations on his lenses, moving the infinitesimal distances back and forth with the pulsing muscles in his fingers, playing them with the practised skill of a clarinetist.

"Look over here, Belle. That's right, down the lens," he shouted. The difference between a face staring straight into camera and off to the left could be hundreds of pounds. Thousands, sometimes.

"Belle, over here!"

"Over here!" insisted Ken.

"Marry me, Belle," yelled another in the line of cameramen. Ken, as his finger pulsed the camera button, registered the tactic. Anything to stand out. A comic approach might get the celeb's attention and a better picture.

"Hey, Belle," called someone else. "Got a new man, yet?"

She laughed theatrically at this and shook her rumpled head. Her mussed hair flew around her like an aureole. Very fetching, thought the massed paps, snapping away. "I'm giving them up!" she shouted.

"Don't do that," one of the paps shouted back. "Get another one. Give us something to shoot."

"I'll do my best," Belle yelled, slipping her emaciated body into the car. You could hardly see her sideways on, Ken saw. As her limo slid away, he packed away his lenses.

He walked towards his battered car just in time; the traffic warden was coming round the corner, face grim, affixed-notice-dispensing machine poised.

But he'd be back tonight, Ken knew as he started up his knackered engine and drove away. Jennifer Lopez was supposed to be checking in, straight off the plane from L.A. He felt weary at the very thought of it.

Chapter Eighteen

NIALL HAD ALMOST NOT bothered coming to this audition, only there was sod all else on offer. His agent had begged him to try out for the Scottish serial-killer part currently on offer in *The Bill*, but Niall had refused it on the grounds that he didn't do cheap sensational murders. Although it had occurred to him on the way here that, as cheap sensational murders went, you would have to go a long way to beat *Titus Andronicus*.

He'd entered the theatre with the usual lack of expectation. Things were bad at the moment. Worse than he had imagined they could ever be. He had been turned down recently for Shakespeare parts he had not realised existed. At the moment, Niall knew, his self-confidence was taking the downward lift to the basement. As it had been ever since Darcy left for L.A. First class into the bargain, as if her stupendous success needed to be any further underlined.

He'd begged her not to go. In vain, he had pointed out the artistic and moral consequences of her getting on the plane and going to meet the big, famous director. Had she no self-respect? Respect for her art? Respect for him? She had wailed and clung to him, her big black eyes filled with fetching tears, her slim body pressed to his in supplication, her arms lovingly about him. But she had gone all the same.

He felt betrayed. Emasculated even. Not jealous, of course. His current resentful feelings were nothing to do with the money, the fame, the first-class flights, the celebrity friends, the fun, the glamour, the money, the fame. The money, the fame. No, it was because he and Darcy had dreamt the same dream. Believed in the same things. Or so he had imagined.

It was with boiling, resentful thoughts such as these that Niall had given his name to the box office and been waved through to the theatre to take his turn on the stage.

❖❖❖

The other auditionees swept Belle a surprised glance when she entered and trilled a champagne-fuelled "Hi!" at them. They were sitting slumped against the brickwork in their loose, black clothes, staring at battered copies of *Titus Andronicus* and mouthing the words to themselves.

It was difficult, Belle thought, to make out which of them, if any, was female; all had that rather Gothic, waxen-faced, consumptive, crinkly-haired look she had come to associate with British thespians.

"ITV's in the next building," one of them remarked in lofty tones.

Belle stared. She had no idea what ITV was. "Isn't this the National Theatre?"

"Yeah. You're in the wrong place. Chat shows are next door."

"Actually, I've come to audition for *Titus Andronicus*," Belle assured him brightly, thankful for the champagne she had swigged in the taxi and the swirling, light-headed courage it gave her.

This caused a sensation among the seated. "As who?" one of them asked.

Belle giggled. "The Queen," she said airily. She had tried to learn some lines in the car, but the print had just fuzzed and swum about before her eyes. She was vaguely thinking of doing a tap dance for the director. It had helped Catherine Zeta Jones interest Michael Douglas after all.

The thespians looked at each other, rather sneeringly, it seemed to Belle. "You mean Tamora?" one of them asked. "The one who eats her children in a pie?"

Belle blanched. "Are you kidding?" She shook her tousled blonde head in astonishment. "This Shakespeare guy was wasted being Shakespeare. He'd have been dynamite in horror movies."

Chapter Nineteen

VANESSA SAID NOTHING TO James about what she had heard pass between him and Emma in the kitchen. As a result, he imagined that she had not heard after all. But the extent of Vanessa's insecurity was something James underestimated. He had very little idea that, coursing not very far beneath Vanessa's brashly confident exterior was another, vulnerable Vanessa—one uncertain of her talents, social position, fitness to be a mother, and how to be happy. And that Emma, instead of being a miracle in human form, was a constant reminder to her of her shortcomings; that Vanessa was, in short, jealous was something he could likewise not imagine.

Vanessa, for her part, would have scorned the idea she was jealous of her nanny. She knew only that Emma made her angry.

And now an outlet for the anger had presented itself. Hearing James tell Emma she was wonderful only intensified Vanessa's former feeling, now her conviction, that Emma had to be got rid of. Before, Emma's main sin was to make Vanessa feel inadequate; now she had more or less concrete proof that the nanny would be content with nothing less than her husband.

Vanessa did not ask herself whether she really believed this was the case. A case could be made; that was the point. And the time to get rid of Emma was now, as Vanessa was about to book a holiday to Italy. Among the wine, the delicious food, the mellow villages, and the sunshine, romance could only thrive, or so Vanessa imagined.

For this reason, Emma had not yet been told about the vacation. Vanessa did not intend that the nanny should get ideas.

Emma, for her part, would have been staggered had she guessed what Vanessa suspected, or had convinced herself she suspected. Emma was as fond of James as any conscientious and dedicated nanny would be to the kindly and supportive father of her charges. It had never occurred to her to desire him however. While she liked him, she did not find him physically attractive; James was ancient—in his mid-forties, at least—and looked like a slipshod professor. As for the material benefits of snaring him, Emma intended to make her own money her own way.

On the afternoon following the James and Emma love-in, as she waspishly thought of it, Vanessa came back at teatime after a long lunch with the editor of her column to find the house transformed.

It took a few minutes to remember that it was her daughter's birthday and that this, presumably, was her party.

The sitting room was full of paper flowers and cardboard trees. The carpet was completely covered in a thick green mat of fake grass, the sort one sometimes saw in greengrocers. Dotted around the edge of it was a large variety of cats: some fluffy toy cats from Hero's own collection, some cut-out large pictures of cats mounted on cardboard, some hand-drawn or painted in bright colours and mounted the same way.

"It's a surprise for Hero. She hasn't seen it yet. A pussy-cat's picnic," Emma, in the middle of the room positioning the last of the animals, explained. "Like a teddy bear's picnic, but because Hero so loves cats I thought…"

"Yes, yes," snapped Vanessa, irritated at the suggestion that she was incapable of making the imaginative leap from teddies to pussies. It occurred to her to wonder when Emma had had the time to make all these cats. Surely she could not have stayed up late for nights on end to make them all? They must have, Vanessa persuaded herself, been manufactured during time with the children, when Emma ought to have been looking after them.

"It must have taken ages to make those cats," she remarked. Emma, catching the spiky note in her employer's voice, realised at once she had done something wrong, but she could not imagine what. Should she have made the cats faster or something?

"Not really. I've been doing them in the evenings, after the children were in bed and I'd finished my coursework."

"That green-grass thing looks expensive," Vanessa remarked next, starting to prowl around the room. Emma wondered whether Vanessa imagined landing her with an expenses bill for it.

"It didn't cost anything," Emma assured her. "The greengrocer on the high street let me have it. You know, the one I take the children to sometimes…" She stopped short of adding "…because I was so shocked when I realised Cosmo had no idea what a zucchini was; Hero had never seen an aubergine; and neither of them were entirely sure about tomatoes."

Vanessa was hardly listening. Her attention now was on the expected guests. Each cat, she saw, had a plate before it and a ribbon round its neck to which a bell and a label was attached. The ribbons were blue and pink: blue for the boy guests, pink for the girls.

"Each guest has their own cat," Emma started to tell her. "They use the plate for their cakes…"

"Hengist Westonbirt?" Vanessa was tweaking a blue ribbon. "As in Lord and Lady Westonbirt?"

Encouraged by the leap of interest, even approval, in her employer's voice, Emma nodded. It puzzled her why, for all the efforts she made with the children, Vanessa only seemed to get crosser. It was almost as if the more effort she made, the crosser Vanessa got.

Thank goodness, she had done something right there by inviting Hengist Westonbirt. She felt sorry for him; Hengist did, after all, have to suffer having the appalling Totty de Belvedere as his nanny.

Remembering the tall, sneering, superior blonde with the tigerish yellow eyes, who always wore unfeasibly tight trousers, breast-revealing tops, and too much make-up, Emma hoped with all her heart that Totty, who would no doubt be delivering Hengist to the party, would not stay. Hopefully, none of the other nannies would stay.

"I do hope Hengist's nanny stays," Vanessa observed as she sailed off upstairs for a lie-down. "I rather like that girl—Totty, is it? Great fun, I always think. Great style. And, of course, very grand. Her father's a duke, isn't that right?"

Emma, as she positioned the last of the cats, felt the fun had rather gone out of things.

❖❖❖

Belle had been poised to flee. After everyone had laughed—nastily—at her horror-movies remark, she had been about to turn on her medium-height Chanel heel and leave. Athough whether back to the hotel or simply to the nearest bar, she had not yet decided. Then the black-painted door at the end of the corridor had opened and someone had come in. At that point, Belle decided things were not quite so bad after all.

The newcomer held something thick and short in his hand. A rolled-up copy of *Titus Andronicus*, Belle saw. She felt excitement pulse powerfully between her thighs. There was such a thing as a sexy British actor after all. One hundred percent solid, muscled, masculine, red-headed, mouthwatering, nipple-stiffening, gasp-making, rootin' tootin' prime beefcake.

He was about the same build as Christian. Thick-necked, broad-chested, and powerfully muscular, if rather paler and with red hair that tumbled about his shoulders in a thrillingly wild sort of way. His blue eyes—much paler than Christian's but just as striking—looked assessingly about as he moved. There was even a touch of anger about him, a resentful flash to that blue glance, that struck her as very exciting. Belle felt a catch in her throat.

Niall too was finding it hard to believe what he saw. Among the drab and dreary drips in black—whom one found, for some reason, at every Shakespeare audition—was a woman in her early twenties in boots and a clingy leopard-skin dress. She had big blonde hair, big red lips, big black eyelashes, and tits, while not especially big, rammed up so high and hard they almost touched her chin.

Touching her chin in actuality was the head of a small and nasty-looking brown dog with twitchy triangular ears and big, black, protruding eyes. It poked from the neck of an expensive-looking handbag, the sort that, Niall imagined, cost more than he had earned during the whole of the last month.

"Hey," she said, in a husky voice directed straight at him, as if no one else in the room existed for her. Which, actually, they didn't. "Come and sit by me."

Now, with a paparazzi-type flash of memory, Niall recognised her. He realised that celebrity magazine covers were exactly where he had last seen her. Even if you didn't buy them, as he didn't, avoiding her was impossible as she was a fixture on every newsstand. This was Belle Murphy, the American film star. The ultimate Hollywood bimbette.

"Hi," she said, smiling at him. Between the forests of thickly mascara'd lashes, her pupils appeared a deep, unnatural green. "I'm Belle. Great to meet you."

Well, it wasn't great to meet her, Niall thought. This woman represented everything he loathed most about the acting profession. If you could call what she did acting.

"Hi," he grumbled.

"What's your name?" She dimpled suggestively.

"Niall." He gave her a hard stare.

"I didn't realise you were French."

"French?" It was hard not to burst out laughing at this, and Niall did not resist the urge to do so as contemptuously as possible. "I'm Scottish."

"Wow. That's so cool. Scottish. Like Mel Gibson."

"He's Australian, actually."

"Isn't Scotland near Australia?"

"No." This, crushingly. And, he hoped, finally.

"Where in Scotland do you come from?" Belle asked next, brightly. "I think I've got some ancestors in Scotland. The Murphys?" she added, looking at him hopefully. "Do you know them?"

"Glasgow," growled Niall, ignoring the last half of the question. Murphy, as everyone knew, was about as Irish a name as you could get. "I grew up on a council estate—a housing project to you," he added forcefully. "My father's a butcher and my mother's a cleaner."

"Wow. A butcher. A cleaner," she said in admiring tones. "That's so, like, authentic. Really real, ya know what I'm saying?"

Niall ignored her. He unrolled his copy of *Titus* and stared at it hard, hoping she would take the hint and go away.

"Auditioning for *Titus*, huh?" she asked brightly. She was jiggling up and down next to him. Did she want to go to the loo, he wondered irritably. "I'm cold," she added, snuggling up to his sheepskin-lined leather flying jacket. "Nice coat," she added.

"Thanks," Niall bit out. The jacket really was nice actually. It was vintage, possibly even a World War II original. Darcy had bought it for him from one of the Knightsbridge charity shops she haunted.

"What part are you going for?" Belle persisted.

"Lavinia," he said, ironically.

Belle looked at him. "Isn't that a female…?" She searched, in vain, for the proper term.

"Role?" Niall snapped. "Yes it is. I'm extending my range. Besides, all Shakespeare's female characters were originally played by men."

"Wow! Is that right?"

"What part are you going for?" Niall asked, a sneering tone to his voice.

Belle tossed back her uncombed hair, clasped her knees with both hands, and announced breathily that she had no idea.

"No idea?" Niall echoed.

The hair swished about in a negative. "I've forgotten. Someone who eats her children, I think," Belle sighed. "Gross." Her face seemed to slip. She looked suddenly doleful.

Up close, her make-up looked less immaculate, Niall registered. The mascara was crusty and the lashes bent. Her eyeliner was wobbly, like Amy Winehouse's, and there was, now, a car-crash air to her that also reminded him of the troubled chanteuse.

"I wish I wasn't here," Belle said passionately. The effects of the champagne were wearing off, and now she felt cold and depressed. The familiar boom of pain was beginning in her head. If only she could get out her champagne bottle. Her glance darted towards the Birkin that she had now put on the floor. Sugar was scratching about inside it, ruining it, no doubt. Or possibly relieving himself in it; this occasionally happened and, Belle knew, accounted for the enormous number of large and expensive bags women like herself got through.

"So why are you here?" Niall was asking. "If it's so awful," he added.

Belle felt suddenly reckless. All the careful speeches Mitch had prepared with her for the benefit of whatever directors and journalists she might encounter, speeches about loving Shakespeare, his genius at illustrating motives and basic human truths, and loving England and its theatre audiences, and wanting to go back to the basics of her craft, suddenly vanished from her mind. She felt bored and frustrated. She wanted champagne. To get out of here. She turned to Niall.

"Listen. I don't give a rat's ass about Shakespeare," she told him. "I don't even care about acting. But I need to look like a serious actor if I'm gonna be a star again in Hollywood."

The speech had a seismic effect on Niall, far more so than if Belle had declaimed Lady Macbeth word-perfect from start to finish. First there was the honesty, which was disarming. Then, more powerful still, the reminder that this woman had once had Hollywood at her feet. Whereas he, Niall was suddenly horribly aware, with a clarity he had never allowed himself before, that he hadn't got anything at his, apart from his shoes. What right did he have to despise her?

"You don't like acting?" he repeated.

The blonde hair whooshed about in an adamant negative. "Hate it. I'm no good at it." The green eyes filled suddenly with tears. "But I really liked being famous. Being a celebrity was great. And not being as famous is…horrible," she added, in a tragic whisper that had a sob at the end of it.

She was underselling herself, Niall found himself thinking. She was good at acting. He was almost moved.

"But I'm not giving up. I'm willing to do anything it takes to get it back, even act in this shit." She waved her copy of *Titus* at him.

Niall looked around himself at whoever else might be witnessing this heresy. There was no one but themselves now remaining in the corridor. Apart from the dog in her bag, whose hostile stare was fixed unblinkingly on him. Since Belle had started to cry, it seemed to be quivering with aggression, poised to attack at any moment. He tried not to look at it.

He tried, too, to remind himself of his principles. He reminded himself that this woman was loathsome, the industry she worked for was loathsome, the whole reason she was here was loathsome—to make herself appear, of all things, a serious actress by taking Shakespeare parts away from those, like him, who really needed them.

"I mean, I know it's pretty disgusting," Belle was sniffing. "Trying to make myself look good by taking parts away from people who really need them. But baby, I really need them. Things have kinda gone into freefall for me in L.A. I need them bad." There was, Niall recognised, real anguish in her face as she looked at him.

He felt, to his amazement, sympathy for her. Or, more precisely, recognition. Their situations were not so dissimilar after all. He needed a part badly as well, and he too was willing to do anything it took. He looked at Belle speculatively. Here was a famous actress. Not as famous as she had been, admittedly, but still a million times more so than him—or Darcy, at the moment, for that matter. Could she help him?

Belle's blast of honesty felt to Niall as if it had dislodged something fundamental in him. Something that had been blocking his progress. Tacitly, carefully, he now felt around the hideous possibility that what had lain behind the determination to stop Darcy from going to L.A. was jealousy.

"You must think I'm such a flake." Belle was weeping now. "Pretending to be a real actress when I'm not."

He leapt to reassure her. Something was now telling him it would pay dividends to be nice to her. "Of course you're a real actress. You're very successful. You were in that huge hit movie, the one everyone saw...*Marie*..."

"*Marie* wasn't acting," Belle wailed. "It was lap dancing in period costume."

As he searched for a reply to this, Niall felt his mouth twitching and a laugh welling up in his throat.

At the sound of his chuckle, Belle lifted her head. Two wet, green eyes regarded him from a tangle of messy blonde hair. Niall felt a clutch of concern. Was she angry? But then a long-nailed hand crept to her mouth, and Belle's entire skinny frame began shuddering. She was laughing too.

"Just listen to me." She pushed her hair back, sniffed, and gave him a rueful smile. "What a wreck. My career's in ruins, my boyfriend's left me…"

"My girlfriend's left me," Niall volunteered immediately, before he could stop himself or wonder why he had come out so unexpectedly with such an outrageous lie.

But was it such a lie? What relationship did he and Darcy have anyway? With a stark, unrelenting clarity that was entirely new to him, Niall could see he had lusted after her at first, had been excited by her lofty and famous connections. But had he ever felt love for her? Sympathy even? It seemed to him there had always been resentment on his part. Had his love for Darcy ever been more than love for what her family represented? For what being with her could do for him. Only it hadn't done anything.

So if something or someone better or more useful came along, he was available. He sensed now that, in Belle, someone had and that it was a chance that might not come again.

There was a movement beside him. Belle was diving to the orange bag that sat on the floor. She pulled out something big, green, and glassy. Something with a gold-foil neck and a label. A bottle of champagne. With the cork out. He watched as she took a deep swig, her eyes closed in apparent rapture.

"Have a drink?" Belle wiped her fizzing lips and proffered the bottle.

"Er, fine…thanks." As he grasped it, Niall registered that the bottle was room temperature. She carried around warm bottles of open champagne in her handbag? Jesus. This woman was a serious mess. Which, so far as he was concerned, might be a seriously good thing.

"You must think I'm such a worm," Belle was watching him drink with eager eyes. "Being so shallow, when you're really deep and authentic."

Perhaps it was the champagne, which always went straight to his head, but there was something about her absolute, unexpected honesty and his own recent self-revelations that made Niall now want to unburden too. "I'm not really that authentic," he confessed.

Belle giggled. "Sure you are. You're from a housing project in Glasgow, aren't you? Your daddy's a butcher?" Her green eyes stared questioningly into his.

Niall swallowed and took a deep breath. He had not even told Darcy what he was about to admit now. "Well, I am from Glasgow, yes. But my dad's not a butcher. Well, only in a manner of speaking. He owns a chain of meat-processing plants."

There was a burst of laughter from Belle. "You don't say." Her expression was radiant with delight. She began to laugh. "Hey. I really believed you, you know. You were very convincing."

Niall felt mirth rising unstoppably up his throat. "Well, I am an actor. In theory, anyway."

Belle exploded again. "Me too. I'm an actor, in theory." And off she went into peals again. "Here, have another drink," she gurgled, passing him the bottle. "Oh," she added, shaking it, "it's empty. Never mind. I got another." She dived into the orange bag again, emerged with another gold-foil-topped bottle, uncorked it with expert speed, and thrust it at Niall.

Niall took a long swig, wiped his mouth, and handed the bottle back.

"I'm not even called Niall. My name's actually Graham."

"Graham!" yelped Belle.

Niall could hardly get the words out now for laughing. "My mother's a ps-psy-psycho…"

"Psycho?" shrieked Belle, face suddenly blank with alarm.

This struck Niall as funnier still. "Psychologist. I grew up in a detached house in one of Glasgow's smartest suburbs. We had gardeners, a nanny, and a weekend cottage on Loch Lomond…"

"Hee hee…" She was shaking her messy blonde head in delight. "You'll be telling me next that you don't even like Shakespeare and, um, his genius for exposing motives and basic human truths…"

"I don't!" Niall shouted. "I don't! I don't! I don't!" The sense of lightness was almost as intoxicating as the drink. He felt crazy and reckless, fabulously irresponsible.

"To be or not to be," he declaimed in hollow tones, his eyes turned up and hands crossed, corpse-like, on his breast.

"Lend me your ears…" Belle added with gusto. She frowned. "Is that the same speech?"

"That is the question," Niall continued in a mournful bass. For some reason, his failures to land leading roles now seemed hilariously funny. He remembered the faces of some of the directors auditioning him, floppy-haired shorthouses to a man, and wanted to double up with laughter.

Then he stopped. He remembered that he and Belle were here in this theatre for a reason. She had to get a part to save her career, while his own career might, Niall now acknowledged to himself, depend on a rather more physical part he had in his possession.

"I can help you," he told her suddenly.

Belle, in mid-swig, flashed him a lecherous grin. "Sure you can, honey." The alcohol was reinflating her libido. In a sudden, lightning move, she was on one of his knees, facing him, grinding her crotch against his thigh, rubbing his penis beneath its layers of demin and cotton, pushing her breasts—naked and exposed in her suddenly open dress—into his face and gasping as if she were about to climax on the spot. She was, he found himself thinking, like a one-man band of sex. He had never imagined it was possible to do so much at once. No wonder she had the reputation she had.

He was surprised at how erotic he found her. She was so obvious-looking. "Not that sort of help," he protested, pushing her away.

"Aw! Spoilsport!" Belle pouted through her hair. Her hand was still on his penis. "Someone here wants to," she smirked, stroking her nails in a practised fashion up and down his ramrod-straight organ.

"Just ignore that, will you? I meant I could help you with your audition," Niall growled. He had to take control of this situation. The director could come at any moment. Any of them could.

"I can hear your lines, now," he groaned. "You'll be called in a minute. It's been ages since the last one went."

Belle looked miserably through her hair at him. "I haven't learnt any lines," she confessed.

The old Niall would have stared at her in frustration and contempt. The new Niall, however, thought quickly. "I could teach you a few of mine," he suggested. "It could catch the director's imagination if you gave it a go." Then, as Belle began to tie her dress back up, he added, "Don't tie that too tightly."

Belle's speech, after all, might not be the only thing about her to catch the director's imagination.

Chapter Twenty

FROM HIS USUAL POSITION on the wall opposite the hotel, Ken looked up at the white clifflike façade of the Portchester, with its ornate balconies and striped awnings fluttering agitatedly in the unseasonal breeze. He'd had a tip-off from Ignatio, one of the doormen, that Lanelle and Dizzi, newly minted reality TV stars, were about to storm out in a huff. There'd been some misunderstanding over a cocktail apparently. Ken had briefly wondered how you could misunderstand a cocktail. Unless they had misunderstood they had to pay for it, which wasn't impossible.

Keith was on the phone. He snapped it away. "One of my tippers. He says Jordan's in the Wolseley. Interested?"

Ken shook his head. "Nah. I'll wait for Lanelle and Dizzi."

It wasn't the most exciting of prospects, but it hadn't been the most exciting of afternoons. Lionel Blair had been in for dinner, but that was hardly going to make the front page of *The Sun*. The one possibility was Belle Murphy; she had not yet returned from wherever she had gone with her hair all over the place. And that had been ages ago.

Although even Belle was obviously fading fast on the picture-desk popularity index, the Barbie to Bardot pictures, which Ken had imagined were good for a couple of grand in *Heat* or *Hello*, had, in the end, not come out as well as he had expected and only fetched fifty pounds from *Woman's Weekly*. All the picture editors—apart from *Woman's Weekly*—had said the same thing, that the only pictures of Belle they would pay any serious money for were ones of her with a new man on her arm.

Twelve floors above them, in the penthouse of the Portchester Hotel, Jacintha the nanny was reaching the end of her tether. It wasn't just that Belle Murphy had no interest whatsoever in her adopted son. This was entirely to be expected. Plenty of people she worked for had no interest in their children; this was usually why they employed her.

Occasionally, admittedly, after too much champagne, Belle would be overcome by sentimentality, pluck Morning from his cradle when he was sleeping, and waltz theatrically round the room with him. Morning, however, rarely appreciated being yanked from his warm slumbers. Then, affronted by his crying, Belle would shove him bad-temperedly back at Jacintha.

The nanny was not concerned about the obvious fact Belle had adopted the baby only to generate positive publicity for herself, to appear to be a caring person. It was hardly unusual behaviour among celebrities, after all. Non-celebrities too, come to that. Plenty of people she knew of had had children for the murkiest of motives. To snare a husband here, an inheritance there, usually.

No, it was in other ways that Jacintha was finding Belle Murphy impossible. "Mind if I call you Jackie?" Belle had asked breathily when they first met. It was a suggestion that made Jacintha—the twentieth generation of her family to bear the name—cringe and squirm. But with, as she had imagined, all Hollywood before her, she had been unable to refuse Belle anything.

Hollywood had not, however, materialised for Jacintha, still less the Celebrity Supernanny-style programme she had imagined herself fronting. Instead, she had found that working for a film star could be extremely boring. There had been a confidentiality contract to sign, which had been thrilling. However, its promise that there was something to be confidential about proved groundless.

Where were all the parties, Jacintha would wonder. The weekends with celebrity friends? The jet-setting? Far from flying round the world from one glamorous location to another, they never even left London. And far from glittering at the centre of a sparkling circle of friends, her life a nonstop whirl of fabulous events, all Belle ever did was lie around and drink, occasionally rousing herself to stumble off to an audition. Or a bar, as Jacintha was beginning to suspect.

And, as neither Jacintha nor Morning were required at auditions, still less in bars, Jacintha had only, since the moment she had arrived in it, ever left the Portchester penthouse in order to go push Morning around the park opposite.

Not that this hadn't been exciting at first. It had been thrilling to run the gauntlet of the paparazzi, who had rushed up close to the buggy. As the flashes had gone off, Morning had began to scream.

"Can't help but feel sorry for it, can yer?" one of the photographers had remarked to Jacintha. "Sweet little thing. I hate to 'ear babies cry," he had gone on, "especially if I'm the one who's made 'em."

But before long, the prospect of snapping the same woman pushing the same buggy to the same park paled among the photographers, and it had now been some days since Jacintha had faced a lens wielded in anger. What happened now was that the paparazzi descended on the buggy as she passed them—as close as she possibly could—in order to coo at and pet Morning. An unphotographed Jacintha would then move off to push her charge endlessly round the crisscrossing paths among the tree-shaded, statue-studded green of the park.

Chapter Twenty-one

"OH, FOR FUCK'S SAKE, Hengist, just get out, can't you?" The blonde in the tight, white jeans tugged hard at the little boy in the back of the car. Hengist had rammed himself down in the rear passenger-seat footwell and was hunting about for something.

"I've lost my King Arthur," he wailed, raising the flat, pale, rather hopeless-looking face that always so irritated his nanny.

"Sod your King Arthur," Totty snapped viciously. Now that she was about to be sacked by the Westonbirts, there seemed no reason to hold back the dislike she had always felt for their son. Hengist was unbelievably boring, and his penchant for small plastic figures of knights, which constantly slipped down the back of the seats and threatened her manicures in extracting them, more boring still.

"I've lost the sheep he was riding on, as well," bleated Hengist, his voice muffled under the seats.

Totty wrinkled her short forehead. Sheep? She had picked up little at school, admittedly, despite her parents sending her to the best ones in the country. But surely King Arthur had ridden on a horse?

"I couldn't find a horse to fit him," Hengist explained. "So I used a sheep from my toy farm."

Totty glared at him. But her dislike of him was not exclusive. Totty disliked all children. She had only come into nannying because, after the police raid on a party she had held in her flat, during which cocaine with a street value of thousands had been discovered, her father had threatened to cut her off from her inheritance unless she got a proper job. Nannying, which was just driving kids about after all, had struck Totty as the easiest possible work. She had had no idea how boring children could be.

But getting sacked was especially boring. Lady Westonbirt, who had been so nice at first and so delighted to have someone of Totty's aristocratic descent looking after darling Hengist, had turned considerably less nice after Totty failed to report for morning duty three days in a row. That the cocktails at Boujis were to blame had not been accepted as a defence. Nor would it be by her father, Totty knew, which was why it was essential to land a new job as quickly as possible, before he found out and the prospect of lifelong penury became a reality.

Dragging Hengist violently out of the car, she pushed the shocked boy, clutching his plastic king, up the steps and banged on the door. As she waited for it to open, she looked with contempt at the hand-drawn cat's face stuck on it, with a speech balloon coming out saying, "Happy Birthday, Hero."

The door was opened by a medium-height blonde wearing what Totty, eyes everywhere behind her Chanel sunglasses, guessed was head-to-toe Boden. Or perhaps that skirt was MaxMara. And, at a pinch, those shoes could be Emma Hope but were more probably LK Bennett. Either way, none of it was the couture Lady Westonbirt preferred and which Totty often amused herself trying on in her Ladyship's bedroom when Hengist's parents were out. No more, however. Damn it. Where was she going to get another job?

"Totty, isn't it?" The woman was smiling at her. Totty recognised that smile. Lady Westonbirt had worn it at first. It was a smile of acknowledgement of her lineage as much as it was of herself personally. With the native cunning often gifted to those with no intelligence to speak of otherwise, Totty sensed possibility. She pushed her enormous sunglasses up on top of her head, swung her shining hair about, and beamed. "Hi there," she barked in her grandest, most gravelly tones.

"I'm Vanessa Bradstock, Hero's mother. You probably know me from my columns." Vanessa flashed her an expectant smile.

"Absolutely," Totty assured her, although she had no idea whether the columns referred to were of the newspaper sort or the sort that stood, eight strong, supporting the portico of the family stately home in Wiltshire. Vanessa nodded, gratified.

"And you must be Hengist," she mewed, bending over the snivelling boy Totty had been shoving roughly before her but who she now made a great display of stroking comfortingly on the shoulder.

As she followed Vanessa down the narrow hall, Totty heard the sound of singing and laughter from behind the sitting-room door. Vanessa pushed the door—whose white paint was rather battered, Totty noticed—open.

Totty stared in astonishment at the sight of twelve or so of London's most difficult, spoilt children all clapping and singing a nursery rhyme against a cat-collage background and amid a sea of evidently homemade cupcakes.

"You've been busy," she remarked to Vanessa in surprise. Hero's mother had never struck her as the homemaking sort, much less the cake-making.

"My nanny did it," Vanessa admitted. Totty caught the bitterness in her voice and filed it away for future reference.

Totty now recognised Emma. Of course, it was that fat, northern one. The one she'd been so rude to when she'd first met her. She sniggered at the memory.

Vanessa pounced on the snigger. "What's so funny?"

Totty's cunning ear caught encouragement. She guessed that criticism of this apparently perfect nanny would not be unwelcome. "Oh, just that when I first met her I asked her what part of Eastern Europe she was from," she tittered in an undertone.

"Ha, ha," guffawed Vanessa, unnecessarily loudly. Emma, hearing the laugh, looked up from pass the parcel to see her employer and Totty de Belvedere both looking at her with smirks on their faces.

She returned resentfully to the game in hand. As she comforted a hysterical Hengist Westonbirt, who had missed by one place the unwrapping of the prize in the parcel, Emma felt rather like wailing herself. Just what did one have to do to please Vanessa?

❖ ❖ ❖

"I mean, it's not as if there's any money in taking pictures anymore," Keith, alongside Ken on the wall, was lamenting the golden days that had passed. "I mean, it used to be good fun. A bit like hide-and-seek. But now there are too many muppets hanging around."

"Clampers!" someone yelled.

Ken, Keith, and the eight or so other photographers idling along the wall outside the hotel entrance suddenly snapped to attention.

"That's all I need," groaned Keith. "I've already been bleedin' ticketed today."

"You're joking!" yelped another pap into his mobile. He flipped it back together, shoved it into his pocket, and shared with the rest of the group the unwelcome news that Leonardo DiCaprio had been spotted going into one of the hotel's side entrances while they all monitored the front. There was a groan of disbelief.

"What a life, eh?" said Keith to Ken.

Ken nodded. "Wouldn't it be nice," he said, rather dreamily, as the thought occurred to him, "to do something more useful? Take some pictures that mattered for once? That meant something?"

Keith stared at his colleague. "You feelin' alright, mate?"

A few minutes later, Belle's limo pulled up. They all recognised its registration. Despite hers being a steadily sinking star, there still was, Ken noticed, as he always did with someone famous, that unmistakable change in the temperature.

But it wasn't until she got out that the mercury really soared. Belle was not alone. She was with a man. A young, handsome man. With red hair and jeans. There was no mistaking their relationship. Belle's dress was hanging open, exposing almost the whole of one breast, and the man's face was covered in red lipstick.

The pack, so passive and lethargic even a mere few seconds ago, were now leaping about, electrified, frenzied. "Belle, Belle. This way, Belle. Who's your friend?"

Not that it mattered that they didn't know. The journos found all that sort of thing out. Ken snapped away with the rest. Finally, some shots he could actually sell.

❖❖❖

Totty was in the kitchen with Vanessa. She had lost no time in driving her advantage home. The possibilities proved to be far more extensive than she had ever dreamed.

"You can't be serious," she was exclaiming in a low voice, her eyes wide over the rim of the champagne glass Vanessa was refilling. It wasn't often she had a duke's daughter in her kitchen. "She's really after your husband?"

Vanessa nodded. Her own eyes, with their fixed-bayonet lashes, were bulging with all the indignation she could summon, as well as with alcohol, which always loosened her tongue. Somewhere within herself, she rather wished it hadn't, but the cat was out of the bag now, and she had the satisfaction of holding an aristocrat in thrall with her conversation.

"I caught them in the kitchen," Vanessa confided. "He was telling her she was wonderful."

"Wonderful!" Totty's unusual yellow eyes were staring into hers with unadulterated fascination. "Slept with her yet, has he?"

"I—I don't think so." Something within Vanessa struck a vague note of warning, that the waters she was about to enter were deeper and more dangerous than any she had ever encountered before. But she ignored it.

"Well, it's only a matter of time, obviously," Totty said briskly. "Have you," she added in a voice of sweet solicitude, batting her thickly blackened eyelashes at Vanessa, "ever thought of getting rid of her? For your own sake," she emphasised. "Your own peace of mind…You need to be able to trust the person who looks after your most precious possessions, after all."

Vanessa looked back at her speculatively. "Ye-es. I'd need a new nanny though. We're going on holiday soon, and I won't be able to go immediately. The children and the nanny will have to be the advance party."

During the silence of some seconds that Totty now allowed, she wondered where the holiday destination was. Hopefully the Caribbean. Asking would be a distraction, however.

"A new nanny," she repeated eventually. "Well, what about me?"

Across the kitchen table, Vanessa gasped. "You!"

"Me."

"But you work for Lady Westonbirt!" Awe and excitement brimmed in Vanessa's voice. Totty de Belvedere, the smartest nanny in London, the daughter of a duke, no less, was offering to work for her!

"That could, um, change. With, ah, immediate effect, actually." Totty beamed at Vanessa.

"Aren't you on a month's notice?" Vanessa's words were galloping over each other.

Totty pursed her glossy-pink-painted lips. "Yah. In theory. But…"—her voice dropped confidingly—"to be really honest with you, I'm not very happy there at the moment. Actually, I might leave. There've been a few problems…"

"Problems?"

Totty looked carefully down at the table. "Drugs…that sort of thing. Parties."

"Drugs!" Vanessa almost shrieked. "Parties! Lady Westonbirt?"

It never occurred to her to doubt what she was hearing. Or what she thought she was hearing; Totty was careful to do no more than insinuate.

"Yah. Cocaine and parties…yup." Totty shrugged. "I'm not sure it's an environment I want to be in, you know what I mean, yah?"

"Oh, absolutely. Absolutely." Vanessa blinked, still absorbing the stunning news. Then she shook herself. "And of course I'd love to have you, Totty," she ardently assured the girl across from the table.

"Great. Perfecto. Start Monday, yah?"

Doubt shadowed Vanessa's face, "Well…the thing is, I've got Emma on a month's notice…"

But Totty, with her goal in sight, had no intention of letting anything block her path. "You can sack someone on the spot," she insisted.

"Are you sure?"

"There are certain situations when dismissal on the spot is entirely justified," Totty stated, adding, by way of bold invention, "I know a nanny who just got fired for having drugs in her handbag, in fact. She was sacked on the spot."

Drugs again. Vanessa had not appreciated how prevalent narcotics were in the childcare business. "I can't believe it. What sort of a nanny would do that?"

Totty did not answer. But she thought of the wrap of cocaine in her handbag at this minute and her yellow eyes gleamed. It was possible, just possible, that she could speed the process along a little. Given the right opportunity. "Perhaps," she smiled, "you should show me the nanny's room. Let me see where I'll be living."

Vanessa stood up hurriedly. She was eager to seal the deal before Totty changed her mind.

❖ ❖ ❖

Belle was triumphant. The audition had gone better than she had ever imagined it could; the director had actually looked impressed as she had parroted the few lines Niall had taught her. Then she had whipped off her dress for a grand finale. The director had looked even more impressed. He had hired her on the spot. She had yet to hear as what, exactly, but what did it matter? She'd play a dormouse if she had to. The point was she had a part in a proper play in London. Her career was saved.

Niall, too, had made an impression.

"The director was really taken with your joyous and loose interpretation of the part," Niall's agent now called to say.

"Jesus," said Niall. "I should go into auditions pissed more often. That's where I've been going wrong."

"What?"

"Oh, nothing. Thanks for letting me know," Niall yelped. "Ooof," he gasped.

"What's the matter? You sound as if you've hurt yourself."

Hardly, thought Niall, looking down at Belle, on her knees in the limo's footwell, busy about his fly zip with her wonderfully flexible tongue.

Jacintha was sitting in front of the penthouse widescreen television as Morning snored in his cot, when Belle and Niall burst in, shrieking with laughter. They were obviously drunk and had equally obviously just practically raped each other in the lift. Belle's dress was undone, leaving nothing to the imagination apart from to wonder what she would look like with more flesh and fewer implants. The man, whoever he was, meanwhile, was tugging up his fly zip. It was the final straw for Jacintha.

"I'm leaving," said Jacintha, her hands folded calmly over the silver buckle of her uniform belt. She turned on her heel and exited the room. As she packed her bags and wrote her letter of resignation, she was able to hear the noisy smacking of lips from two rooms away.

Chapter Twenty-two

"JACK SAINT'S A PRETTY tricky character," Mitch remarked to Darcy as they drove towards her meeting with the director. She looked, he thought, great. He'd advised her to wear another dress, and this one was fitted and yellow, which went well with the rather bleached landscape. She looked vivid and radiant against it, her black hair richly shining, her pale face now showing the faintest hint of rose.

"Tricky?" she murmured.

"Tricky, yeah. The one thing you musn't do is talk about the film. He hates that. He..."

"Not talk about *Galaxia*?"

"That's right. Talk about anything but that. He likes to get a feel for your personality, holistic casting, he calls it. Let him ask the questions. He likes to be in charge."

Darcy nodded. Only a third of her was concentrating on the meeting, which, as Mitch kept hammering into her, could change her life. She was wondering about Niall. She had called him many times now, both on his mobile and at the flat in Knightsbridge, but he had not answered.

Mixed with the sense of sickening worry she felt was an equally sickening sense of guilt, almost as if he had been there in the restaurant last night and seen her gawping at Christian Harlow. She crimsoned at the memory. Her face, neck, and chest burned with shame. What had she been thinking of?

Mitch was rattling on happily. "Yeah, holistic casting, kinda unusual, I know, but honey, a man with his track record can do what he damned well likes…"

Mitch hummed as he drove along. He felt unprecedentedly confident. The whole Darcy thing was going as well as he had hoped, possibly better. They had a great platform to build on. The showcase dinner with her at Puccini's had been a success; people had stared, and one or two of the paps had snapped her as they had left—a really good sign.

There had, of course, been the Christian Harlow incident, but there probably really wasn't any danger for Darcy from that department. Harlow was far too self-serving to try and land some obscure British actress, whatever the future for her might hold. And there was no reason to think Harlow knew anything about Darcy and *Galaxia*. Saint, in line with his controlling reputation, preferred to keep things under wraps until everyone was cast.

Besides, Harlow was, as everyone in town knew, currently squiring—as the euphemism went—a big A-list actress, slightly long in the tooth perhaps, but powerful and well-connected. Not someone whose bed he was likely to leave in a hurry.

No, there was nothing to worry about there, Mitch assured himself happily. Worry, at the moment, seemed a thing of the past in general. Take that incredible business with Belle. Her descent into alcoholism and self-pity in London had spectacularly reversed itself. Out of the blue had come the incredible news that not only had she succeeded in landing a part in a Shakespeare play, but she had found a new man, a rising young British actor too, not some drugged-up loser.

There were photos of Belle and the actor in the American tabloids this morning; he had skimmed them at his desk but planned to take a better look at them while Darcy met Saint. It was a whole new feeling for Mitch to see a newspaper and actually look forward to reading about Belle in it.

But in the back of the car, Darcy still fretted about Niall. Why didn't he answer her calls? Had he hurt himself? She visualised his body sprawled in the flat or knocked off the emphatically rusty, old bicycle he made a point of keeping in the glamorous entrance hall of the building, to the annoyance of many of its residents.

She wished with all her heart that she was back in London. L.A.'s glitter and glamour had conclusively faded. She'd been there, seen it, got the idea, been briefly seduced by it. Now she wanted to go home.

And to add to her other woes, she was hungry. She longed with all her heart for a bacon sandwich, the type in thick white bread that the grease soaked into, that was the speciality of certain London cafes.

"Here we are," Mitch announced, breaking into her bacon sandwich thoughts. "The beginning of the rest of your life!" he added gleefully.

"This is a house?" Darcy exclaimed. The drive they were going up led to a series of low, broad, round concrete pods painted silver and linked together with huge circular windows fronting every link. It spread across the front of the hill it was built on like some fat cartoon caterpillar, throwing a ferocious silver blaze back at the fierce L.A. sun. As they got out of the car, Darcy saw there was no garden, nothing green at all apart from a few dusty cacti and aloe vera plants on the pale, dry, dusty slopes at the side of the house. It all felt very exposed and dry and somehow unfinished.

To Darcy's surprise, her first impressions of the famous director were positive. He was casually dressed and had a neat, wiry figure that seemed to radiate suppressed energy. Shiny white hair had been brushed jauntily up from his tanned brow; he had a trim moustache and a small, pointed beard. His eyes were dark and lively beneath white brows still threaded with determined black.

Mitch billowed forward to salute the great man. "Mr. Saint!" he gasped as he narrowly avoided falling over his own ankles. "May I say what an absolute, unbelievable honour it is to meet you? I've been a fan of yours for many years, you're quite simply..."

Saint nodded briefly at him. It was clear that Mitch was not the one he was interested in. He seized Darcy in a firm handshake, looked closely into her face, ignored Mitch's continued genuflections completely, and swept her away with him into the house.

Mitch, his heart rate pounding, returned to his town car to wait. He pulled the papers on the passenger seat towards him, opened them to the articles about Belle and her new man, and prepared to enjoy himself. This was a great day for him, and he was going to savour every minute.

❖❖❖

The room in which Darcy sat with Jack Saint was a big, light one in the basement of the house. He had taken her down in the lift, and out they had stepped into this spacious, airy rectangle whose exterior walls were glass sliding doors leading out onto a patio with a wide view down over L.A. There it was, this mythic city, its hills studded with houses, crisscrossed by streets, rising and falling all the way to the sea. The view was misty in the morning fog and looked, Darcy thought, rather ethereal. Were she not in the fierce grip of homesickness, she might have been enchanted.

The room was dominated by a pair of big drawing desks covered in highly detailed, fantastical-looking illustrations. Large tables were covered in what looked like toys: little scenes with futuristic, sheer-sided, vaguely mediaeval buildings or desert-like sandy landscapes on which small human-looking figures were dwarfed by bizarre dinosaur-like monster shapes or contraptions that seemed to combine helicopters with ballistic missiles. Darcy guessed she was looking at prototype sets and characters for *Galaxia*, but, remembering Mitch's warning, resisted making any remark about them.

Jack Saint was opposite her in a director's chair, which was turned back to front so she could see his name on the back, white letters on black canvas. His legs lounged apart around the chair frame. He leant forward. "Enjoying L.A.?"

Darcy looked at him despairingly. His eyes, black and intent, seemed to drill into her. If she told a lie, he would know it. "No," she said.

Saint laughed at this—a Santa-like ho, she noticed, accompanied by a flash of white enamel. "Where do you like to be, then?" he asked her.

"London," Darcy said, finding it difficult to get the name out without a sob, she wanted to be there so badly.

Saint nodded. "Like acting?" he asked next.

Darcy hesitated. Acting was in her blood, in the sense that both her mother and father had done it. She had been expected to do it. Again the black eyes probed her, demanding complete frankness. "I don't really know," she answered, frowning. "Sometimes I think I'm only doing it because of my parents."

Saint did not seem overly surprised about this. His pleasant expression gave no hint of what he might be thinking. He carried on in measured tones with his questions. "You're not doing it to be famous? Rich? A celebrity?"

Darcy shook her head vehemently. "Can't think of anything I want less."

"Okay. What do you want? To do? With your life?" he asked her next. "Apart from to go home, that is," he added with a smile and a tug of his beard.

Darcy sighed. She had an idea that many people at this point would make speeches about using their art to change lives, easing the suffering of humanity and reversing climate change.

"What do you like?" Saint pressed.

Quite unexpectedly, the vision of the bacon sandwich she had longed for now came rushing back to her. "I like eating," she blurted, flushing the next second with red-hot, heart-beating shame. Of all the stupid answers.

Saint raised a black and white eyebrow and pulled his beard. "That's all," he said, rising to his feet.

❖ ❖ ❖

Jesus, thought Mitch, examining the newspapers closely. Belle wasn't holding back in any of these pictures. She was pretty much sucking this guy's face off. He was obviously enjoying it though. And he was good-looking, which helped, and looked pretty clean, which helped even more.

> ...the lucky man is Graham MacDonald, 24, actor son of top Glasgow psychologist Professor Eleanor MacDonald and processed foods tycoon Sir Humphrey MacDonald. He is to act alongside Murphy—star of last years's mega-blockbuster *Marie* and who recently showed her compassionate side by adopting an African orphan—as she makes her much-anticipated stage debut in the experimental Upside Down Theatre's new production of *Titus Andronicus* in London...

"Star of last years's blockbuster *Marie*...showed her compassionate side by adopting an African orphan..." Hey, that was good, Mitch thought. It was straight. None of the usual spiky, snide asides. Anyone reading about Belle for the first time might actually think she was both successful and had a conscience.

As a flash of yellow caught Mitch's eye, a ripple of surprise ran through him. Darcy was out already? Here she came, down the path, the fat, silver caterpillar house shining behind her.

He glanced at the watch on his broad, hairy wrist, trying to suppress his panic. She'd been in there barely fifteen minutes.

Darcy opened the car door, shoved aside the papers, and plonked herself down on the passenger seat. "Take me back to the airport," she said in a low voice, looking straight ahead at the tinted windscreen.

"Whaaa-aat?" Mitch gasped. "What's the matter? What happened? Didn't he like you?"

"No. I don't think he did," Darcy answered quietly.

Something inside Mitch started to scream. Something outside him was screaming too. He realised it was him. He was screaming.

"Tell me," Mitch growled, breathing heavily between words. "Tell me what happened in there. What he said. What you said. Tell me."

"I told him," she began reluctantly, "that I didn't like L.A. or acting, that I didn't want to be rich and famous, but that I liked eating."

Mitch frowned. He couldn't be hearing right. Every word she spoke went into his brain like a triangular-shaped object trying to fit a round hole.

"You said you didn't like L.A.?"

She nodded.

"Or acting?"

"Yes."

"And that you didn't want to be rich or famous?" His voice was a whisper now, scraping, or so it felt, along the side of his throat as he spoke.

"But that you liked eating?"

"Mmmm."

"Oh. My. God."

For a second, everything fizzed and went black.

"Look," Darcy was saying, when his vertical hold returned. "I'm sorry, okay? But I don't want to be a film star. I want to go home to Niall. I'm really worried about him, Mitch. I need to see my boyf…"

She stopped, suddenly. She was, Mitch realised, staring at the newspapers on the car floor. He heard her gasp sharply and watched as, with terrible deliberation, she picked one of them up.

"I don't believe it," Darcy said in a cold, slow voice Mitch had never heard before, not even when she was being her chilliest and most disdainful on the telephone from London.

Slowly she put the paper back down and picked up another. She read this one faster, her breath coming short and sharp now. "It can't be…" she muttered. "It says here he's called Graham and his mother's a psychologist, but no, it's definitely him…that red hair… he was going for *Titus*…oh, my God."

"The fucking bastard!" Darcy yelled. Mitch wondered if he had ever seen anyone do a mad scene so well. What a loss to acting in L.A. she was going to be.

Chapter Twenty-three

EMMA FELT SHE WOULD remember the scene as long as she lived: entering her room on a summons from Vanessa to find her employer standing there with burning eyes, a small fold of white paper on her violently outstretched hand with a scattering of white powder on it. James stood uncomfortably behind her, shifting from foot to foot, his face red and his expression a mixture of tragedy and disbelief.

"And what," Vanessa hissed, pointing at the outstretched hand with her other finger, "is this doing here?"

Emma had stared at it. "I don't know." She guessed it was drugs immediately. But what they were doing in her room she could not imagine. It was the most unexpected possible ending to the triumph that had been Hero's birthday party. She had imagined praise, a raise even. But sacking, never.

Emma was sure that James believed her when she protested that she had been set up. That the cocaine had been planted there by someone. But when Vanessa—with vicious scorn—had demanded who in the world would want to frame some obscure nanny from the north, she had been completely unable to provide an answer. There seemed no explanation whatever, and in the absence of one, she had had to accept that being fired was the only possible thing to do.

"But you must give me a reference," Emma summoned the courage to ask.

Vanessa practically exploded. "Are you joking? You've just been caught with drugs in your handbag."

Emma spoke with as steady a voice as she could manage. "I didn't put them there though. And one day, I'll find out who did. But until then, I need a job, and I'll need a reference to get one. I've been a good nanny, and you owe me that at least."

"Owe you? Owe you?" Vanessa blustered.

Here, finally, James stepped in. "I think we should do as she suggests, darling," he had murmured to his wife.

Vanessa rounded on him. "What? You believe her?"

James sighed and pushed up the glasses that were forever slipping down his nose. "I'm not sure what I believe," he had said quietly. "The law, after all, is that people are innocent until proven guilty."

"Court?" Vanessa exclaimed. "I don't want the police getting involved in this. The publicity would be dreadful. After all, I'm quite famous…"

Emma felt a tug of fear. She was, she realised, in agreement. Making the matter public would not only endanger her own future, but also increase the risk of her parents finding out about what had happened. No one in the family had been involved in anything like this before.

"But it's a criminal offence," James protested. "By someone," he added hastily. He turned his bewildered, bespectacled, above all, disappointed glance on Emma. "Personally, I would like to believe that she was innocent."

"Innocent!" screeched his wife. Her chest was heaving violently up and down.

"Yes," James said firmly. "And if Emma believes she can clear her name, I'd be delighted." His face fell then, however, and the flame within Emma died proportionately down. "But until such a time, I agree: in the absence of evidence that she isn't responsible, she has to go."

Emma had no idea how she could clear her name. Where the drugs had come from and who put them there was still a mystery, a horrible mystery. Could it have been someone at the children's party? But who and why?

Pushing at the back of Emma's mind was the possibility that Vanessa herself had put the piece of paper with its explosive contents in her handbag. But something—Emma hardly knew what it was—made her hesitate to blame her boss. Nasty and cruel Vanessa could certainly be, but once or twice Emma felt she had glimpsed something beneath the surface, something rather lost, helpless, and vulnerable, something touching, almost, that made her doubt, at the last minute, that it was her.

And so she tried not to think about the injustice of it all, about Vanessa's poisonousness, about James, who she could not help feeling slightly let down by whilst recognising there was little else he could have done.

And especially she tried not to think about Hero and Cosmo, who she had loved so much and yet who, from the moment the drugs had been discovered, she had not been allowed to see. But whose eyes, round with horror and red with weeping, she had seen briefly through their bedroom windows and felt following her down the street as she walked away from the house for the last time.

❖❖❖

After driving back with Mitch following the meeting with Jack Saint, Darcy had headed straight to her meringue burrow of a hotel bedroom and stayed there. Having completely lost her appetite—the mere thought of food made her feel queasy—she had ordered nothing from room service. When she was thirsty—if she noticed she was thirsty—she simply put her mouth under one of the gold taps in the vast marble-lined bathroom. Otherwise, she merely cried and raged.

It all felt like a house collapsing. Niall had left her for the type of Hollywood bimbo he most affected to despise. He was a lying hypocrite of the first order. He had tried to prevent her going to L.A., but only because, it appeared, he wanted to go there himself. His high principles had been jealousy, nothing more.

She had believed in Niall, his principles and his art, even more than her own. Far more than her own. But he had left her for Belle Murphy, a woman whose only interest in art, given her veneered teeth and obviously artificial breasts, was that of the plastic surgeon and cosmetic dentist. She had never suspected, never ever dreamt, that what Niall wanted was a woman like Belle.

Never had she dreamt, either, that he was anything other than working class and gritty. His interpretation of the angry Glaswegian butcher's boy had been practically Method. Perhaps that was why he had never landed a leading role—he had put so much of his acting energy into the part he played for her every day that there was nothing left for anyone else.

Had he ever really loved her? But she had loved him. Hadn't she? As well as being good-looking, he had been the image of everything she wanted to believe in most.

Were she and Niall, after all, both as bad as each other? Flitting across Darcy's mind now came the possibility that she too might have loved what Niall stood for more than the man himself. Otherwise, might she have not looked closer beneath the surface?

Only—and it was a big only—she had not two-timed him with some screen bimbo while he was away. Well, not exactly. With a surge of acid guilt, she remembered seeing Christian Harlow in the restaurant.

But that had been a moment's lapse; she had been drunk, tired, jet-lagged. And the moment Christian had gone, she had come to her senses, which, to judge from the pictures in the papers, it didn't look as if Niall was ever likely to do.

Anger rose within her again. Authenticity, art—he could stuff it. Although, of course, he had stuffed it. More so than his father had ever stuffed a chicken or rolled up a loin of lamb. She'd quite like to roll up Niall's loins, come to that, butcher-style with very tight string.

Chapter Twenty-four

EMMA'S SAVINGS MEANT THAT a long-term stay in the bed and breakfast she found near King's Cross station was out of the question, even if she had wanted to, which she didn't. Her room, all the same, was small and clean with a wardrobe to hang her one good suit. And the nearby library proved a warm place to write applications. It might be full of smelly tramps reading the papers, but it had a computer she could use if she booked times with the front desk.

Here Emma copied down details of nanny agencies all over London. Off went letters to Servants' Hall, Mrs. Poppins, Domestic Bliss, and You Rang, Madam? Emma felt both relieved and vindicated when, some ten days later, a reply arrived in a thick cream envelope.

"Looks posh, that," commented Mrs. Cupper as she handed it over. "Most o' the letters we get for folks 'ere are in brown window envelopes from the DSS. Or else white from the police," she added darkly.

The letter, on thick cream paper, contained the longed-for news that Mrs. Theodora Connelly-Carew of Domestic Bliss, office address 24 Sloane Mews SW1, would like to see her for an interview the following day.

❖❖❖

Mitch was chewing mournfully on a jelly doughnut and reflecting on the nadir his career had reached. He'd just taken a call from his absolute least favourite client—and that was a hotly contested distinction—a British rock singer whose pushiness was in inverse proportion to his success. He blamed this, naturally enough, on Mitch. "When I signed up with you, you were going to help me crack America, man," the singer had whined. "You haven't helped me crack the top of a bloody crème brulee."

What had made him agree to represent this guy, Mitch wondered. It had been a moment of madness. But then, his entire career seemed to consist of moments of madness, all linked together. His life was one long moment of madness.

Perhaps the maddest moment of all had been believing Darcy could land the part with Jack Saint. Although it hadn't seemed mad at the time; the whole thing, in fact, had seemed as near to a certainty as anything he had ever been certain about. Perhaps that should have told him something, Mitch sighed. Nothing was certain in L.A. Apart from sunshine, plastic surgery, and cosmetic dentistry. And things not working out, particularly for him. Mitch stared at the grey carpet tiles and wondered if he was sitting on some particularly inauspicious ley line. It was incredible, the bad luck he had.

While he thought these thoughts, his eyes were trained gloomily through the slatted blinds of his office window on a street cleaner working below. As the man toiled gently in the sunshine, pushing his barrow along and picking up papers with the aid of a long pincer, it seemed to Mitch that he was deriving more satisfaction from his job than Mitch ever had from his own. He too worked mostly with rubbish. But it rarely made him feel as serene as that old guy down there looked.

His phone rang. And when he put it down at the end of the conversation, Mitch wondered whether he had dreamt it all or whether he was dying and it was one of those wish-fulfilment scenarios people sometimes experienced on the point of expiring. Then he pinched himself, rotated a few times on his long-suffering office chair, and stabbed out Darcy's number. The call he had just finished had come just in time. She was still in L.A.

The phone at Darcy's hotel bedside shrilled.

"Hey there!"

"You sound pleased," Darcy said, rather crossly.

"Pleased? You bet I am."

Actually, thunderstruck was more the word.

"I'll cut to the chase, baby," Mitch said now. "I just got a call from Jack Saint. He liked you."

"Liked me? But…all those things I said…"

"He liked your answers. They were the right answers."

"But you said…"

"Yeah, yeah, well forget what I said," Mitch said hurriedly. "Point is, he thinks you're honest. Original. Authentic." Mitch paused for effect. Then, with tremendousness, he announced, "Congratulations, baby. He wants you in his picture."

Then, as Darcy did not react, he added. "Are you listening to me? You're the Grand Duchess of the Galaxy in *Galaxia*, honey. Shooting starts in Florence, two weeks from now."

Darcy sat up. All the weariness she had been feeling fell away from her. She felt numb, then excited, then numb again, then excited again. Into the vacuum that had been her life shot a large object, not unlike the missile-cum-helicopter objects she had seen on Saint's model table. Whether or not she actually wanted to act in the movie seemed less important than the fact that she now had a distraction and a direction in life. Moreover, one that would probably really annoy Niall. Or Graham, as she was trying hard to think of him.

"That's incredible," she managed to say to Mitch. "Amazing."

Miraculous more like, Mitch thought. He'd never heard of anyone saying what she had apparently said to Jack Saint and being cast. Cast out, more like. And yet Saint had seemed to dig it. "Makes a change not to have a bimbo," he had remarked to Mitch. "Got plenty of them already in this film, believe me."

Mitch wondered who. Due to the huge scale and fantastical nature of his productions, Saint generally started filming before the movie was entirely cast. The end was sometimes shot before the beginning, and any number of intermediate scenes were filmed as the sets were completed. Much was done at the editing stage, and there would be the computer graphics sequences, which the director was famous for putting in too.

To an outsider, and to many of the insiders, the process was all incredibly confusing. The only person who ever knew exactly what was going on was Saint; it was part of his legend that he and he alone had the whole apparently rambling edifice organised down to the last tiny detail in his head. For all their apparent complexity, his schedules ran like clockwork, and the end results were always spectacular. Those were the reasons, Mitch knew, for why Saint was so sought after as a director.

"Saint's people will be in touch about Florence. Sounds pretty nice," Mitch added enthusiastically. "All those canals."

"That's Venice."

"Oh…yeah. Right. Well, frankly, baby, if Saint wants canals in this film, Florence might well get 'em too."

He put the phone down. Below him, through the slatted blinds, the street sweeper continued to pick up litter with his pincers. Mitch no longer envied him, however. He had the rare feeling of wanting to be no one apart from himself.

As joy seized him again, he swung round on his office chair. When, shuddering, lurching, and creaking, the chair completed the circle and faced front again, Mitch found himself staring at the long, sly face of his least favourite colleague. Greg Cucarachi was staring at him with an expression of cool superiority on his long, sly face. Or more cool superiority even than usual, Mitch corrected himself.

"Lot of excitement in here," Cucarachi remarked in a voice as smooth as his black hair. He was wearing a well-cut, obviously expensive grey suit, pink checked shirt, and pink silk tie. Mitch envied his colleague his style and trim frame, although not the work he did to maintain it. Cucarachi honed his body hard. He jogged at lunchtimes; he worked out; he did marathons. While, Mitch knew, the only part of himself that raced was his heart.

He folded his plump arms and fixed Cucarachi's eye with his own. "Yeah. It's kind of an exciting morning. My client Darcy Prince has just landed the female lead in *Galaxia*."

Take that, asshole, he wanted to add, but didn't. There was no need. It was a body blow.

Relishing the moment, Mitch happily anticipated Cucarachi's response, confidently expecting that thin, handsome-if-that-was-your-idea-of-it face to spasm and contort with jealousy.

But instead, Mitch's most loathed co-worker simply smiled. "Hey, I'm glad for you, buddy," Cucarachi said.

Mitch wobbled on his chair. Glad? What was the guy talking about? No agent was ever pleased about another. Unless they were failing.

"Yeah, I'm real glad." Cucarachi was nodding. "And I know you're going to be just as happy for me when I tell you that I had a conversation with Jack Saint this morning as well. That I too have a client with a starring role in *Galaxia*."

"You do?" Mitch gasped.

"My client Christian Harlow has been contracted to play the Duke of Lilo." The words exploded like bombs in Mitch's disbelieving, red-hot ears.

"Christian…Harlow?"

"That's right," Greg beamed, showing his strong, square white teeth. "The Duke of Lilo. The Grand Duchess of the Galaxy's number-one enemy. At first, that is. They're lovers by the end." He winked at Mitch, smirked, and withdrew.

Chapter Twenty-five

SLOANE MEWS HAD GATEPOSTS with balls on either end, after which the actual houses were rather a disappointment. It was a small, quiet, cobbled road with a row of low, white-painted buildings on either side. Number 24, where Domestic Bliss was, looked just like all the others. Emma rang at the bell.

The white-painted door opened to reveal a middle-aged, care-worn Filipina wearing a white cap and apron over a black dress.

"I've got an interview with Mrs. Connelly-Carew," Emma smiled.

The maid did not smile back. She made a gesture inviting Emma to come in. Emma followed her into a tiny kitchen, which she was surprised to find already inhabited. A polished brunette with long, brown legs, which began in a denim miniskirt and ended in a pair of black ballerina flats, was propping up the sink and talking into a mobile. After rolling uninterested brown eyes over Emma, the brunette continued with her conversation amid much flicking of hair and inspection of perfect nails with the mobile-free hand.

"New job going well is it, Totty? Must be if you've got all this time to talk on the mobile…"

Emma, staring at the kitchen's rather grubby floor tiles, blinked. Totty? That Totty? She had a new job? Emma felt relieved for poor Hengist Westonbirt but pitied from the bottom of her heart whatever children Totty was looking after—in the loosest sense of the word—now.

"The kids are a nightmare? Poor you, Totty. God, you always get the difficult ones, don't you. The mother's mad? The house is horrible? Oh, Totster. But they're taking you to Italy? Well, that's good, isn't it? Pantelleria? Costa Smeralda? Oh…Tuscany." This in a tone of the utmost disgust. "Yawnorama. God, how boring. Poor you, Totty."

A thought struck Emma. If Hengist Westonbirt was no longer enduring Totty, might he not need someone else? Her, for example?

"Where am I?" the brunette barked in a gravelly, well-bred voice. She looked scornfully around the kitchen. "Waiting to be interviewed. Daddy's threatened to cut me off if…yeah. I know. You've had that too. Where am I? Theodora's, of course. She sorts us all out, doesn't she? Didn't you get a job here once? What did you say?" The brunette screwed up her face. "Signal's a bit weak…you didn't realise I had childcare training?" She let out a goose-like honk of laughter, so loud it made Emma jump. "Course I don't. Did you? Thought not. Oh, you gotta go? Yeah. OK. Bye, Totty."

The maid appeared. "Isabella Gough-Chumley-Fylingdales?"

The brunette gave a curt nod.

Emma watched them leave. Her mind was churning with what she had just heard. Isabella Gough-Chumley-Fylingdales had not only seemed to be saying that she had no childcare training herself, but Totty hadn't either. Surely that couldn't be true.

By the time the brunette reappeared, shuffled past with a smirk, and was shown out by the maid, Emma had convinced herself she had somehow misheard.

Now it was Emma's turn. She straightened her spine, cleared her throat, pulled down her jacket, and followed the maid through the kitchen door into Mrs. Connelly-Carew's inner sanctum.

This was a small dining room whose walls were crowded with paintings that seemed rather too big for them, and the furniture, while grand, seemed oversized as well. Emma edged past an oval dining room table that almost pressed against the walls.

A thin woman of about fifty-five was sitting at one end of the desk and looking at her keenly over a pair of gold-rimmed, half-moon glasses on chains. She wore caramel-frosted lipstick, and her brown hair rose in an iron wave from the freckled skin of her forehead.

"You must be Emma."

Emma forced herself to rally. What was she worried about? Unlike the last person, her experience and qualifications were excellent.

Theodora Connelly-Carew was rummaging in a plastic file. Emma watched as she drew from it her own letter. Theodora Connelly-Carew glanced down at it and cleared her throat. "Emma, er…"

"Sidebottom," supplied Emma, wondering why Mrs. Connelly-Carew was asking when the name was printed there on the paper right in front of her.

"Sidebottom, yes. Mmm." The caramel-frosted lips pursed.

"Your qualifications are impeccable," said Mrs. Connelly-Carew, her fingernails sweeping Emma's letter.

Emma nodded. Of course, they were.

"However, that is not the issue."

"It's not?"

"Not entirely. You're rather more…" The agency head cleared her throat delicately. "Rather more northern than I imagined."

"Northern?"

"Mmm." Mrs. Connelly-Crew took off her glasses, stood up, and strode the five paces or so to the small window where she stood with her hand in the small of her back looking thoughtful. Emma took in the elegant, brown-suede trousers and brown-leather ankle boots and the sharp profile against busily patterned pink and white curtains.

She jumped as Mrs. Connelly-Carew turned round suddenly, her beige layers whirling. "What would you say," Mrs. Connelly-Carew asked, "if I told you most of the nannies we employ are Hons?"

"Ons?" echoed Emma, completely at a loss. On what?

Mrs. Connelly-Carew sighed. "Hons. Honourables. Daughters

of the gentry. For example, I've just placed the girl before you, whose father is a marquis, with Lord and Lady Westonbirt."

Emma felt her heart sink. Bang went the job with Hengist then. But hadn't she heard Isabella say with her own ears that she had no qualifications?

"Well-connected girls are our speciality," Mrs. Connelly-Carew trilled on in her imperious voice. "It's what people come to us for. Our USP, if you like. If you know what that means."

"I do know what it means and mine is that I'm a good nanny," Emma said doggedly.

Mrs. Connelly-Carew drummed her café-au-lait-tipped fingers on her dining table. She passed a hand across her tanned brow as if all this was the most fearful bother. "Oh, well," she said eventually, with the air of one conferring a great favour. "Let's get on with it. I need to ask you some questions."

"Of course."

"About how you would deal with, um, certain situations."

Emma waited confidently. There could be no situations in the nought-to-five category that, over the years, she had not either learnt about or personally dealt with.

"Imagine the scenario," Mrs. Connelly-Carew invited her, "if, at a children's birthday party, the son of an earl went to the food table before the son of a duke. What would you do?"

"Make sure they'd both washed their hands."

"Actually," Mrs. Connelly-Carew flared her impressive nostrils, "it's a question of precedence. Dukes come before earls in the social order. So the earl's son should go in after the duke's." She leaned forward. "Have you never read Debrett's?"

"Not recently," Emma admitted.

Mrs. Connelly-Carew took off her glasses and stood up again. "Thank you so much for coming," she said in syrupy tones as she wafted to the entrance door in a caramel flow of woollens. "We'll be in touch."

Seconds later, Emma found herself outside in the cobbled mews, Mrs. Connelly-Carew's dry scent in her nostrils and a feeling of ashes in her mouth. Picking her way carefully across the cobbles, Emma passed the stone balls at the entrance. She briefly imagined wrenching one from its position and hurling it through Theodora Connelly-Carew's window.

Chapter Twenty-six

THE SUN WAS NOW high and hot, but the sky's dazzling blue seemed a mockery. It would have suited her mood better if a gale had been howling and cold fingers of rain were feeling her collar.

As she turned from the mews into the street, something shot between her legs. A brown dog, the smallest she had ever seen, was cringing against the front of one of the mews houses on the other side of the road. It was staring at her with enormous black eyes and making whimpering noises.

Emma's love of small things in general had found its main outlet in children, but there was plenty left over to be kind to little animals like this one. "Come here, boy," she cooed, clacking gingerly across the cobbles towards it.

The dog let her come close. It was trembling, and the expression in its huge black eyes was one of petrified fear.

"Hey, I won't hurt you," Emma crooned.

But something else might, she now realised. There was a blood-curdling snarl, a deep bark, a slide of claws, and suddenly, round the corner, skidded an enormous Alsatian. It was evidently in pursuit, ears erect and eyes blazing with intent to murder. Without stopping to think abut what she was doing, she snatched up the small dog, kicked out at the Alsatian, which stopped in surprise, and staggered away as quickly as her heels would permit her.

She looked back to see the Alsatian standing at the entrance to the mews, its brown eyes full of apology, its tail wagging amiably.

Emma put the dog she had rescued down to examine its collar. The collar was, she noticed, very ornate, covered in huge diamonds, in fact, which had to be fake. But there was no address on it, merely the word "Sugar" and a small silver disc with a mobile phone number engraved on it.

"Oi! You!"

Turning, she saw a ginger-haired man in jeans making his unsteady way towards her down the mews.

"Hey! You!" His accent was Scottish and aggressive. He was quite big, Emma saw too. Broad and powerful, with strong arms and a big chest.

"You stealing that dog or something?" He was squinting at her; the bright light seemed to be causing him some discomfort.

"Actually, I rescued him," Emma said. "I was just looking for somewhere to phone his owner from."

"Don't bother," the man snapped, hoisting his jeans up. "I'm his owner. Well, my girlfriend is. He's lost. I've been looking for him for the last hour." He looked at the dog with dislike.

The newcomer looked, she thought, vaguely familiar. She was sure she had seen him recently, as recently as the last couple of days. But surely that was impossible. Unless he was staying at the bed and breakfast or a regular user of Camden Library, that was.

"Let me put him down," she suggested, lowering Sugar gently to the ground.

"Be my guest," growled the other. "I'd like to put him down permanently."

As his claimant approached, Sugar immediately let out a terrified yelp and leapt back up into Emma's arms again, digging his claws into her skin.

"I thought you said you knew him," Emma said suspiciously. "You said he was your girlfriend's dog."

She wondered now if she believed in the girlfriend story. She glanced again at the dog's diamond collar. It was almost painfully dazzling to look at in the sunshine. Perhaps, incredible though it seemed, it was real, after all, and he was trying to steal it.

Emma suddenly resolved not to part with Sugar until she had returned him to his rightful owner. It was not an especially convenient decision for her; it could lead to any number of difficulties, not least persuading Mrs. Cupper, who had a No Dogs rule, to let it into the bed and breakfast. Nor was she particularly fond of the animal. She disliked his bony brown head, which felt horribly fragile, and found his big, round, prominent eyes very strange as they were entirely black and apparently consisting entirely of pupil.

But to surrender a small dog to someone whose designs on it might be nefarious was irresponsible in the least and might even be cruel. She held Sugar and looked challengingly at his claimant.

His would-be captor now abandoned all attempts at charm. "You…you…arsehole!" he hurled at Sugar in frustration. While feeling it was wrong to shout at an animal, Emma knew the claim was not inaccurate. The specified part of Sugar's anatomy, quivering upwards towards her beneath its tail, was indeed very prominent.

Meanwhile, she had better things to do than stay here. The rest of her life to sort out, not least. And as for the dog, there was only one possible option now. It was inconvenient, but anything else could be inhumane.

"Look," Emma said briskly. "I'm happy to come back with you and give it to your girlfriend. How about that?"

The man shrugged his shoulders. "Okay, then."

"Ever heard of please and thank you?" Emma rebuked, stung at this grudging acceptance of the sacrifice of her time.

His eyes flashed open with surprise. In the split second before they screwed up again, Emma could see they were an amazingly pale blue. "You sound like a nanny," he grumbled, scratching his red hair.

"I am a nanny."

"A nanny?" He sounded, for some reason, thunderstruck.

"Yes. A nanny."

"Working round here, are you?"

Emma shrugged. "Actually, I'm, um, between jobs at the moment."

"Between jobs!"

"Yes."

Before she quite knew what was happening, he had taken her arm and ushered her down the mews to where, at the bottom, a big silver car was slowly drawing up. He seemed to be very excited.

"Where are we going?" Emma bleated as she found herself propelled inside the pale leather interior.

"The Portchester Hotel."

Within a few minutes, they were getting out in front of an enormous building of golden stone with striped awnings and trees in pots. Two white-gloved doormen in green tailcoats with red facings and top hats scurried towards them.

One of them smiled at Sugar and held out a white-gloved hand to pat his head. He withdrew it hurriedly as the dog gave a vicious growl. "Nice doggy," he said, in an Italian accent. Sugar gave an earsplitting bark.

"Actually, he's not a nice doggy," Emma confided. "He's horrible. But he's not mine so it doesn't matter."

The doorman grinned and ushered her through the shiny brass-and-polished-wood revolving doors after Niall. She emerged into a huge, high lobby, gilded and glittering and hung with chandeliers so huge and heavy it seemed extraordinary they could stay up there. Emma glimpsed champagne glasses, heard the sound of a piano, and caught an atmosphere that was hard to define: slightly elegant, slightly bored, entirely expensive.

In the lift, the gold doors slid together. There was a brief whooshing sensation and, within seconds, the doors opened again into another marbled lobby, smaller than the one downstairs but no less grand. The walls were painted cream, picked out with gold, and had small scenes and figures painted on them. It reminded Emma of the backdrop of a theatre. The two vast beige urns mounted on pedestals either side of the lift door were filled with lilies, from which a wonderful smell wafted. The place seemed to breathe luxury and decadence.

"Belle!" shouted Niall. "Hey, Belle. Come here. I've got a surprise for you. Two surprises."

Emma heard the approaching cry of an infant. A woman holding a baby wrapped in white entered the lobby. Sugar immediately erupted into crazed barking. Not to be outdone, the baby doubled its yells.

The woman was very beautiful. She was tiny, about twenty-five, and very thin. Her face was almost completely hidden behind enormous sunglasses. Glossy, white-blonde hair tumbled over her slender shoulders as far as her elbows. On her skinny arms, she wore a great many large and ornate bracelets, which seemed impractical for one nursing a small baby, and dark denim jeans of a tightness beyond what Emma imagined bearable, especially if one was bending to pick up a child. Her look was finished with a flimsy, leopard-skin, short-sleeved blouse and high-heeled red sandals.

"Sugar!" The blonde spoke in a breathy, girlish American accent that Emma felt she recognised. "My little baby-waby," she crooned into the dog's bony head with its bulging black eyes and disproportionately huge black-tipped ears. "Where have you been, my naughty waughty little doggy woggy?"

The baby in her arms roared on. The blonde looked at it impatiently.

"I just can't shut him up," she complained. "He's been going crazy for hours."

Hunger, Emma knew. Those sharp, pulsing yells were unmistakeable. She was surprised that the mother did not know this herself.

"Well, our problems are over!" Niall announced. "This is Emma. She's a nanny."

Immediately, the blonde thrust the bawling baby into Emma's arms. "You know what to do with it. You're a nanny. So go on. Nanny."

Emma felt a mixture of indignation and uncertainty. What made these people so sure she wanted to work for them…but no. All this could wait. In her arms, the baby, which felt incredibly light and frail, bawled its pulsing, relentless, desperate bawl. It was clearly starving. Meanwhile, at the level of the parquet floor, the dog barked on. The din was so deafening that Emma felt she might scream too. Or bark.

"Look," she said in concern. "He really needs food."

"Sugar gets fed later," the blonde declared.

"I didn't mean the dog. I meant the baby."

She noticed that the blonde's tight leopard-skin top revealed disproportionately big breasts for one of her small frame.

"Are you breast-feeding?"

"With these?" The blonde gestured at her bosoms. "They're one hundred percent silicon, sweetie."

"Got any formula?" Emma demanded. The crisis in her arms was getting worse.

"Hey, whaddy think I am? Einstein?"

"Milk formula."

"Oh. Right. There's some, like, powdery stuff in the kitchen, if that's what you mean." The blonde wafted her hand vaguely behind her.

The suite kitchen was small, white, functional, and modern. Emma soon found powdered baby milk and a number of bottles and teats. To her great relief, the fridge was well stocked with still mineral water, as well as, she could not help noticing, a great many bottles of champagne. Hastily, Emma prepared the formula.

The bottle ready, she removed the material mostly draping the baby's face. She had not until now looked at it closely; the ear-splitting sound it made had been the focus of her attention. But now she noticed something so unexpected it made her almost drop the bottle with surprise.

The baby was black. Very black, with liquid brown eyes that looked desperately up into hers. While Niall and the woman—Belle, he had called her—were white.

It was the clue she needed. With a thrumming in her ears, Emma finally remembered what she had been straining to recall. The reason she recognised the man was because only yesterday he had been on the front of every tabloid newspaper with Belle Murphy eating his face off. The article accompanying it had mentioned that Belle Murphy had recently adopted an African orphan.

Belle burst into the suite's kitchen. She had taken her sunglasses off, revealing intensely green eyes that reminded Emma of the Go signal at traffic lights. Belle put Sugar on the floor, where his sharp claws skittered unpleasantly on the tiles, and got out one of the bottles of champagne.

The cork went with a violent explosion. Emma jerked in shock. The baby's tiny arms and legs flew out in the classic panic position; his eyes snapped open; and he began to roar. Sugar, meanwhile, began to bark hysterically.

Belle dropped immediately to her knees. "Sugar! Shug-shug-shug!" she crooned extravagantly. "My baby! My precious pet. Mommy's so sorry her naughty wine made her baby jump. Let Mommy hug you, there you are…"

Belle looked up from where she cradled the dog on the floor. "Thank God, he's shut up," she remarked ruefully.

"He's a pretty noisy dog," Emma remarked, looking down to where Sugar lay on his back, legs out wide, exposing himself in the crudest fashion to Belle's caresses.

She found herself being regarded with annoyed green eyes. "Not Sugar. I mean, thank God, Morning's shut up."

"Morning? That's his name? I was going to ask…"

"Morning, yeah," Belle took out two champagne flutes from a cupboard. "He's actually called something unpronounceable and African, but I can't even say it, let alone spell it. So I thought Morning would be just fine. It's such a beautiful time of day—or so I'm told." She tittered.

"He's an orphan, is that right?" Emma tried to remember what the paper had said.

"Sure as hell is," Belle said matter-of-factly as she slopped the foaming wine into the two glasses. "You should have seen the orphanage. Like, gross."

"It must have been very difficult to go there," Emma said sympathetically, surprised at this evidence that Belle was perhaps not so shallow after all.

Belle put the bottle on the counter and tossed back her shimmering mane of hair. "Yeah, it was, so I didn't. I got the orphanage people to send my people some shots of the kids they had available on JPEGs and chose one that way."

"You never went to Africa at all?"

The strange green eyes pierced hers. It seemed to Emma they held a hint of warning. "Hey. Don't get me wrong. I'm gonna go there. Sometime. Keep him in touch with his heritage."

Emma cradled the child, now finishing the bottle, infinitesimally tighter.

"Hey! Look at that! He's going to sleep," Belle breezed, picking up the two brimful champagne glasses. "You've obviously got a way with babies."

Yes, I feed them, Emma thought. She studied the child's contented face, tiny and dark brown against the white cotton wrap. He was snuggled up so trustingly in her elbow. She felt a powerful surge of affection for him.

"We'll talk contracts in the morning," Belle announced over her shoulder as she left the kitchen.

Emma stared after her. It was obviously taken for granted that she would be looking after the baby from now on. But did she want to? Neither Niall nor Belle seemed particularly...what was the word. Pleasant?

But did she really have a choice?

Chapter Twenty-seven

SAM SHERMAN, HEAD OF the Wild Modelling Agency, London, sat tapping her desk impatiently in her glass-walled office. Her round hazel eyes, ringed firmly with kohl as usual, blazed through her curtains of heavily highlighted beige hair. She was giving an interview, which she never enjoyed. Especially since all the stupid fuss about Size Zero, journalists were apt to ask difficult questions.

Sam assembled her slightly heavy but nonetheless still handsome features in as obliging an expression as she could manage and answered each query with smiling acquiescence and the phrases "I'm glad you asked me that" and "Good question!" in rotation. Flattering the journalist, Sam had learned over the years, led to better copy. It also made it harder for writers to be nasty and ask difficult questions. Anything about Size Zero, for example.

Eye contact was also important; it made you look sincere. Nonetheless, Sam could not help the occasional glance away from the beady scrutiny of the woman opposite and through the transparent walls of her goldfish-bowl office, where twenty-seven lissome twentysomethings, all dressed in skinny hipster jeans and clinging T-shirts in the agency's signature black, buzzed about the business of beauty. Something loud and fast boomed from the stereo as showcards were shoved in envelopes, tickets were booked, visas arranged, and details finalised on any number of contracts.

One of them, Sam noticed, was Irina, a fifteen-year-old Ukranian and the agency's most recent signing. Their last Russian, in fact, Sam had vowed. Irina was very now, with her wide-eyed feral face and its thick, wolfish brows. But she was also very naughty. She had a habit of going AWOL for days on end before phoning in from some hippy festival in Cornwall. Or Wales. Anywhere other than where she was supposed to be.

"Er…could you repeat that?" Sam smiled apologetically at the writer, having completely missed the last question. Hopefully it wasn't Size Zero-related.

The journalist, crop-haired, red-lipsticked, and wearing a figure-hugging, plum polo-neck, rearranged her long, bare legs beneath her grey, pleated miniskirt. They were good legs, Sam had noted, smooth, lightly tanned, and with no sign of thread veins or bruises. She guessed they were being displayed for her benefit.

Most young female journalists who came to see her were not, Sam knew, after a career-making scoop about the modelling industry at all. What they were longing to hear was something completely different—those six words that could tip them from the nine-to-five to a glittering, perfumed world of heady fame and untold riches: "Have you ever thought of modelling?"

The question she had missed, now repeated, confirmed Sam's hunch that this girl was as eager as the rest to make the jump from grind to glamour. "What are you looking for when you spot a new model?" the journalist asked.

Sam had, by now, decided that the legs being displayed for her benefit had no commercial value. They were slightly too thick at the ankle. The girl was too old too. But frankly, anything much over fourteen was old these days.

"That's a good question," Sam remarked as she prepared to trot out her stock response. "The difference is a lot of things. But mainly, it's what I like to call…" she took a deep breath and paused importantly.

The girl was rapt. Her eyes urged Sam on. "Skinniness?" she suggested, with a provocative smile.

Sam gave a deep stage laugh. And of course thinness wasn't the only issue. Girls were successful for other reasons too. A rock star father never hurt; a film-star mother, any other kind of celebrity or billionaire, come to that, and, of course, aristocratic backgrounds in particular seemed to breed a certain sort of strangely elongated waif. But, of course, what they all had in common was thinness. Extreme thinness in many cases.

How did they achieve it? Officially, it was due to high metabolisms and genetics. Unofficially, of course, was a different and rather murky matter, and one Sam had no intention of discussing with this woman.

"The difference is what I like to call atmosphere," finished the agency head.

"Atmosphere?"

Not for the first time, Sam congratulated herself at coming up with this one. The idea of atmosphere intrigued people, injecting an air of mystery and individuality into a business which frequently lacked both. "Yeah, atmosphere. The sort of feeling that surrounds a girl. All my most successful girls have had atmosphere. And boys."

Across Sam's mind scampered, as it often did, the ever-irritating thought of the beautiful boy who had escaped her in Covent Garden. She had never seen him again, and, despite her urging them to keep their eyes extra-peeled, none of her scouts had either. The only compensation was that, so far as she was aware, none of Sam's rival agencies had snapped him up. But she was prepared any minute for some new campaign to be announced by Gucci, Armani, or some such, featuring the Hunk Who Had Got Away.

The writer seemed to be making packing-up movements. Sam, wrenching her thoughts away from the long-lost god, cheered herself up by reflecting on the skill with which she had avoided the Size Zero quicksand.

Then the writer looked up. "One more thing." She smiled.

"Sure," muttered Sam, glancing at the BlackBerry at her elbow on which was displayed her schedule, updated every morning by one of her two assistants. A meeting with a Spanish photographer was slated next. Carlos Cojones had a hook nose, wild curls, and the usual bad-boy photographer reputation. As well as the usual hatred of waiting. He would, Sam knew, expect to sweep into her office the moment he arrived. Better get this wittering woman out as soon as possible.

"I'd just like to ask you, by way of winding up the interview, what you think about the Size Zero debate."

Sam, who had lifted a glass of water to her lips, stopped herself with difficulty from spluttering. "Good question," she muttered. "I'm glad you asked me that."

Eventually, and having parried the thrust, Sam saw the journalist off without having conceded ground. She felt exhausted but relieved.

With a mixture of satisfaction and dismay, she saw Carlos Cojones had arrived at reception. He was stamping from foot to foot like a flamenco dancer, his skin flushed dark with annoyance.

"Call for you, Miss Sherman." The light whisper of Xanthe, who had replaced the uppity Nia, came through.

"I can't take a call now," Sam thunderered. "Who is it?"

"Someone called Brooke Reed. She says it's important, but I can tell her to go away," Xanthe pleaded in her almost inaudible voice.

Sam groaned. Brooke Reed was the extremely forceful head of public relations for NBS Studios, Hollywood. Iron-haired, iron-willed, iron-clad, she was the original and, many maintained, the best Hollywood PR. She knew everyone and everything. Sam was scared of very few people; Brooke Reed, however, was one of them.

Her fingers worrying at the turquoise beads around her throat, Sam looked nervously over at Cojones, who was now circling the reception desk like a matador coming in for the kill. But even Cojones would have to wait if Brooke Reed was calling.

"Shall I tell Mr. Co-Jones to wait?" Xanthe fretted.

"Brooke. So nice to hear…"

"Yeah, sure," Brooke's rasping tones cut in. "I'm calling about *Galaxia*."

"Okay," said Sam, expectant beneath her businesslike manner. She knew about the impending Saint film. Everyone in the fashion and media industries did.

"I want R and P on some talent," Brooke informed her shortly.

Sam understood this code. R and P stood, in Brooke-speak, for repackaging and polishing. Talent meant an actor, presumably the female star of a new film. It was standard NBS procedure. Part of the studio's preparations for any big movie would be Brooke contacting the Wild agency to help launch the female star by arranging high-profile shoots with top photographers and leading glossy magazines.

Sam watched Cojones still pacing the reception area. Whereas before he had looked like the matador, now, with his powerful leather-covered shoulders and the horn-like twists of his unruly black hair, he resembled the bull, pawing the ground threateningly. She could almost see the steam coming out of his nostrils. But he could wait.

"Who's the girl?" Sam asked

"Completely unknown. British."

"British?"

"Yeah. And with the usual British sense of style. Second-hand clothes, no idea about make-up, hair like a friggin' rat's nest…" Brooke, for all her elegant appearance, could be very earthy.

"You mean vintage and unstructured," Sam corrected. She owned a model agency; she had to keep her end up.

"I mean," snapped Brooke, "that she looks a friggin' mess."

"Right," said Sam hurriedly. There weren't many people who could talk to her like this, but Brooke was definitely one of them.

"Get Lagerfeld," the studio PR instructed. "That should do it."

Sam's round eyes flexed in surprise. Karl Lagerfeld? The all-powerful German uber-designer and photographer? Brooke, as usual, wasn't asking much.

"Er…I know he's pretty busy right now," Sam hedged. She knew this because four glossy magazine editors in the last week alone had called and asked her to use her influence with him on their behalf. Unfortunately, her influence, while considerable, was not of the mountain-moving variety.

"What about Carlos Cojones?" Sam suggested, as inspiration struck. Talk about killing two birds with one stone. Cojones, certainly, looked about to kill something. Catching his dark, burning eye, Sam felt sufficiently heartened to flash him a grin.

"Popinjay," said Brooke, witheringly.

"He's very hot."

"Hot now, sure. Ten minutes from now he'll have icicles dangling off him."

"I could try Rumtopf," Sam suggested.

There was a considering pause from the other end. "Mmm," said Brooke. "Rumtopf's definitely a thought."

He was, Sam knew. Although not a legend on the Lagerfeld scale, the Swiss designer-photographer Rumtopf certainly had ambitions in that direction. He was a definite name and—Brooke, as ever, was right about this—definitely better than Cojones.

"I'll try Rumtopf then. What's this girl's name by the way?"

"Darcy Prince," rasped Brooke. "You heard it first here. See ya."

Sam's phone buzzed immediately. "Mr. Co-Jones has left the building," Xanthe whispered dolefully.

Chapter Twenty-eight

FOR ALL THE OBVIOUS glamour and wealth of her new employer, Emma found Belle utterly impossible to pin down about terms and conditions.

"Later!" the actress would snap whenever Emma attempted to ask about money, hours, and holidays. "I'm busy learning my lines, okay?"

"Learning my lines," Emma soon realised, was a euphemism for disappearing into the bedroom with Niall and having prolonged and very noisy sex, after which Belle, in particular, was given to parading about the penthouse naked.

Emma was beginning to despair of gaining an audience with Belle outside actually going to the one in the theatre when, one afternoon after the matinee, the actress returned, most unusually, alone. Realising there would be no sexual activity until Niall returned, Emma seized her chance.

Belle looked at her, her strangely coloured green eyes filled with irritation. "You want to talk? About your job? Now?"

"Now," said Emma, gently but firmly.

Tutting and tossing her head, conveying with every fibre of her body just how inconvenient this was, Belle led the way into the suite's drawing room. Here, she perched on a striped sofa and, directing a narrow-eyed smile at Emma, clasped small, bejewelled hands round knees in tight, white jeans.

"Okay, so you want to talk terms," she said ungraciously. "And here's the first one. You sign a confidentiality agreement, okay?"

Emma nodded.

"The agreement is as follows," Belle announced, holding Emma in her cold blue gaze. "You work for Mr. and Mrs. Smith."

"Oh. I thought I worked for you."

"We're Mr. and Mrs. Smith."

"Oh, I see."

"You never talk about us to anyone."

Emma nodded again. It was obvious that that would be a clause in a confidentiality contract.

"You call me Miss Murphy at all times."

"Not Mrs. Smith?"

"No! Not Mrs. Smith!" There was a crack as Belle drove her fist impatiently into her palm. "Mr. and Mrs. Smith is what you call us if you talk about us to anyone else."

"But…but…I thought I wasn't supposed to talk about you to anyone else."

They were interrupted by a buzz at the penthouse door. "Niall," Belle exclaimed, rather testily, to Emma's ear. Had they had a row, she wondered?

"Great," said Belle, as a handsome waiter entered with a bottle of champagne.

"Just the one glass," she instructed as the waiter placed a flute before Emma. "In front of me," she barked, as he failed to remove it.

As the waiter, with a shaking hand, filled her flute and then made his escape, Belle continued setting out the terms of the agreement. "There will, of course, be no salary."

Emma stared at Belle in shock. "Sorry?"

"It's an education, working for me," Belle cut in. "You're working for someone famous. You should be paying me, by rights. For broadening your horizons."

Emma took a deep, stiffening breath. "I can't accept not being paid." She willed her knees not to shake. "And if you insist on not paying me, I'm afraid I really can't take the job." She met Belle's angry gaze with a flintiness belying her nerves. There was deadlock.

The suite telephone now rang. Exclaiming crossly about Niall again, Belle reached for the nearest receiver. Just as she did so, Morning started wailing from the bedroom.

Her heart thumping at the recent drama, Emma walked swiftly to her bedroom to attend to what was, for the moment at least, her charge.

She bent over the side of the cot and looked down into Morning's liquid black pupils with their pure, glowing whites. He made a gurgling noise and smiled up at her.

She felt a surge of tremendous love as she picked him up. He snuggled contentedly in her arms, a small smile puckering his pink little mouth, a smell of warm, washed baby wafting up from him. Emma gazed down at him indulgently, tightened her arms round the baby's little body, and planted a kiss on his forehead.

Could she really leave this baby with Belle? On the other hand, could she really stay without a salary? Of course not. It was impossible. Belle was impossible…

❖ ❖ ❖

In his Los Angeles office, Mitch was, once again, feeling slightly stunned. There he'd been, asleep after that rare thing in Hollywood—a colossally indulgent lunch—and deep in a wonderful dream in which all four of the Oscars' Best Actress nominees were clients of his.

This was followed by an even better dream: a call from Jack Saint saying he'd heard good things about Belle's current turn in London as an evil, child-eating manipulator and would she be interested in being the Countess of Tyfoo, *Galaxia*'s evil, man-eating manipulator? Only, after Mitch had pinched himself a few times, this dream had turned out to be real.

He still could not quite believe what had happened in London. That the production of *Titus Andronicus* in which Belle appeared—naked for much of one scene, admittedly—had proved an unexpected triumph. Belle had even been singled out by one critic "for adding undisputed buoyancy to the production."

When the call was at an end—never long with Saint—Mitch spun himself round in his seat so hard the chair shot across the room and fell over with him in it. The resulting shattering noise was enough to draw Greg Cucarachi to the doorway.

"Celebrating are we?" Cucarachi enquired snidely.

"Sorta," Mitch said, defiant from beneath the avalanche of papers he had knocked from his desk. "My client Belle Murphy's got a part in *Galaxia*," he added, replacing his glasses with a flourish.

"Congratulations," Greg said smoothly, without missing a beat. "My client Christian Harlow's gonna be very interested to hear that."

Mitch stared back at the trim figure lounging elegantly in the doorway. An alarm bell was shrilling in his heart. Amidst all the excitement of finding Belle back on the Hollywood bandwagon, he had completely forgotten that this particular bandwagon had Harlow on it already.

"Your client can be as interested as he likes," Mitch said steadily, "but my client no longer is. Things between her and Graham MacDonald are both steady and serious," he extemporised, watching with satisfaction as Cucarachi tried and failed to reply to this. As his hated co-worker departed, Mitch picked up the phone to call Belle in London.

The penthouse phone rang just as Emma had settled Morning in his cot. Under strict instructions not to answer any calls, Emma ignored it. Happy after his bottle, the baby snuggled into his mattress. Now and then a warm brown eye flicked open; Emma sensed that he needed to reassure himself that she was still there. He often woke her in the night for the same reason, but one look into the liquid chocolate eyes so full of appreciation, and all tiredness would melt away.

Emma yawned. As ever, it was hot in the penthouse and, as ever, she was tired.

She was shocked wide awake by a loud and persistent shrieking from the next room. Such sounds, of course, routinely emitted from the bedroom, but there was a less orgiastic quality than usual to what Emma was hearing now. Seizing Morning, she leapt to her feet and ran to see what the matter was. It sounded, she thought, as if Belle was being murdered.

One could always hope.

Chapter Twenty-nine

THE CAMERA FLASHED AND whirred.

Darcy, her knees raised in their tattered fishnet tights, her naked back against the cold marble floor, and her head thrust into one of the none-too-clean corners of the ornate fireplace, wondered, not for the first time that morning, afternoon, or whatever time of day it had got to by now, what the hell she was doing here.

She reminded herself hurriedly that this was high-fashion photography of the most esoteric and artistic kind, under the direction of the style legend Rumtopf. And that she, an actress about to make the breakthrough into the big time, ought to be grateful for the opportunity.

Darcy knew this because her newly acquired model agency, Wild, had told her so. According to Sam, its fearsome head, the Rumtopf shoot was the first in a series of photographic sessions and features aimed at launching Darcy into the stratosphere ahead of *Galaxia*'s release. The fact that the film had not yet been made was immaterial; interest had to be created right from the start.

Whether Darcy actually wanted to be in the stratosphere was, she gathered, immaterial too. The studio making *Galaxia* wanted it, and fashion shoots were part of the contract NBS had sent her. It had been the size of a telephone directory—possibly two—and bristled with little, yellow plastic stickers marking where she was to sign.

Darcy squirmed on the hard studio floor, feeling her ribs press painfully against it. It was just as well she had lost so much weight following her break with Niall. Rumtopf, however, didn't seem to think she was thin enough. He had stood glowering in the back of the changing room as Darcy was tugged, rammed, and generally shoe-horned into a basque so full of rips it looked as if a lion had attacked it. This was, she discovered, one of Rumtopf's own designs. It did not make her warm to him, in any sense. The studio was ice cold, and the floor she sprawled on felt gritty, as if it could have done with a good sweep. The fact that everything was painted white didn't help.

Rumtopf himself wore white: white jeans, white cowboy boots, a white leather jacket, and white circular spectacles that did not appear to have lenses in them. His hair was white and cut extremely short. He had a mouth like a bouncy castle, and his nose looked as if it belonged to someone else. Perhaps it did. Or had.

He turned glittering, strangely slitted eyes on Darcy through his glassless frames and regarded her unsmilingly and at length. "Nein, nein," he stormed. "Spread ze legs more. Push out the chest more. Ja!"

The smell of hundreds of scented candles was making Darcy feel sick. Tuberose had never been her favourite. And she had recently read somewhere that a liking for very strong perfume signalled de-pression or madness.

The scenario Rumtopf had cast her in seemed to strongly support this theory. "The Master's vision," one of the acolytes had explained in awed tones, "is The Murder House." Darcy listened with disbe-lief. Every shot—or "tableau"—was to feature a different room and a different murder, with herself as all the victims.

The first "tableau" had been the bathroom; she had lain in the freestanding, claw-footed, candlelit tub in a satin ballgown in whose design Rumtopf's trademark rips and tears were generously represented. It was ripped particularly around the area of her breasts where a bloody, fake stab-wound appeared.

As the next "tableau," to feature her strangled in the bedroom, now got under way, Darcy's feeling that the shoot crossed the line from the artistic to the downright psychopathic increased. Perhaps, she now tried to convince herself, it was just as well that Rumtopf, an obvious homicidal misogynist, had an outlet for his fantasies. It may be humiliating and unpleasant for her as the model, but she was probably doing humankind a favour. What might have happened had the Master been obliged to bottle this sort of thing up hardly bore thinking about.

It was obvious that women weren't Rumtopf's thing. The white-blond, powerfully muscled figure in black who sat on the sidelines behind the snaking cables of the lights was, Darcy had gathered, the Master's current muse, Stefan. He wore a black baseball cap, which was turned back to front, and the piece of material attached to its reverse to shield the wearer's neck from the sun hung in front of his face. And these, Darcy thought despairingly, are the people telling everyone else what to wear.

The next "tableau" was The Grand Salon, and so she was lying under a table, her makeup smoothly immaculate apart from the fake bullet wound in her temple. A side-parted and pouting male model in boxer shorts and lenseless spectacles stood beside her, holding a toy pistol of green neon plastic. Darcy had noticed that, while his chest was waxed, the legs protruding from beneath the houndstooth-checked boxer shorts he had changed into were extremely hairy. As the Master prodded her again, Darcy felt a giggle rising irresistibly in her throat.

"Nein! Nein!" shrieked Rumtopf, the spurs on his cowboy boots ringing as he stamped his feet. "Think murder! Think Sweeney Todd! Think Jack the Ripper! Think Dr. Crippen! Think…"

"Yeah, okay," Darcy interjected hurriedly, anxious to be spared more of the grisly roll call that had evidently provided inspiration. What she was really thinking about was lunch, however. Her stomach was a storm-tossed sea of hunger. She had been rushed to the Rumtopf shoot directly after the plane from Los Angeles had touched down in Rome and had seen hardly anything of Italy. Least of all the leisurely-lunch-in-shady-vine-draped-taverna type of Italy she would so appreciate now. Where was the Florence where they'd film *Galaxia*?

Finally, the end came. Darcy, hurriedly gathering her small number of things together—her luggage, such as it was, waited outside in the car that had brought her from the airport—looked up to see Rumtopf's strangely diagonal eyes gazing assessingly at her.

"Rumtopf," he declared suddenly, in thrilling tones.

Darcy eyed him uncertainly, wondering what was coming next. Perhaps nothing was. Perhaps the mere iteration of his identity was meant to be sufficient, reminding the lesser mortals in the room like herself that one was in The Presence of Genius.

"Rumtopf will now make you a wonderful offer. The most wonderful thing a woman in your position could wish for."

Darcy glanced at the camera. Frankly, the most wonderful thing a woman in her position could wish for was the destruction of the images just taken.

"Rumtopf will make your dress for the Oscars."

Chapter Thirty

HIS RED BROWS KNOTTED, his pale-blue eyes narrowed and cold, Niall sat glumly in the back of the Mercedes conveying himself and Belle to the airport. But of the two of them, only Belle would be boarding the first-class flight to Florence. Only Belle would be taking a lead role in a guaranteed blockbuster movie.

As the car ground slowly through the London traffic, Niall raked a resentful hand through his dark-red hair. It was so bloody unfair. Just what was it about him? Why was it that every woman he went out with automatically got a part in *Galaxia*, tipped to be the biggest thing since Everest, while he remained treading the boards, a mere bit-part player?

Granted, he was a bit-part player in one of London's current hits, but now that Belle's own particular bit parts were leaving, it seemed unlikely the success would continue. Not even the most ardent Shakespeare loyalist in the cast was deluded enough to imagine that the audience came to hear the Bard's words alone. The chance to see a Hollywood celebrity bare all had had more than a little to do with it too.

The director, certainly, had been devastated to hear Belle had been struck down by a mystery bug and would be unable to continue with the run. Niall had been even more devastated to discover that the mystery bug was Jack Saint and that Belle was leaving for Italy to resume her career as a leading film star.

Granted, her behaviour had been imperious and difficult of late. There was now no trace of the blackly humorous, irreverent car-crash he had met at the audition. Belle had then been at rock bottom, but now success in *Titus* had re-inflated an ego whose titanic proportions Niall had not suspected but which had terrifyingly combined with the voracious sex drive of which he was all too aware. Performing for Belle twice a day, in addition to performing at the theatre, made for an exhausting ride in every sense of the word. In a nutshell—and shells were what they felt like these days—Niall felt used.

While he sat angrily upright, resentment emanating from every stiffened muscle, Belle lounged against the beige leather seat next to him in an exaggeratedly relaxed fashion. Her long white legs, dangling one over the other were exposed—from the top of her cowboy boots, at least—almost to the pubis in tiny denim shorts with frayed edges. From time to time, she swung her legs the other way; Niall, at her side, only narrowly missed—thanks to a well-judged dodge—being hit by the bootheels each time.

He threw several hurt and offended looks in her direction, but it was impossible to see whether they had hit their target. Belle's liquid-green eyes were hidden behind black sunglasses so huge they made her look like a fly, while her attention was completely focused on the silver mobile mostly hidden in her cascading platinum hair. Her inflated lips, slicked a glossy pink, chewed gum energetically, breaking off from their efforts occasionally to allow a loud and theatrical laugh to escape. "Tom Cruise said that? You're kidding me!"

Niall was sick of hearing how all her celebrity friends were taking Belle's calls once more. Or, rather, he was sick of hearing, in every word Belle said, how completely and utterly she discounted how much she owed to him, Niall, or rather Graham, MacDonald. It had been he, had it not, who helped her with her lines at the audition, which in turn had got her a part in *Titus*, which had led to all this?

"Harvey Weinstein did what? No-ooooo!"

But had she breathed one word of gratitude to him, let alone one word into the ear of the director that might get him a part too? Had she…hell. He had been right all along to loathe the commercial film industry, Niall brooded.

"Well, everyone knows Nicole can't stand her…" Belle cackled delightedly, swinging her legs about again. It was, Niall thought furiously, as if he simply didn't exist anymore. She hadn't even been especially keen that he see her off at the airport.

Niall watched jealously as Belle's jewelled hand dandled fondly on the brown, bony head of the animal that was, of all beasts in the world, his least favourite. Sugar was, as usual, under Belle's armpit, staring evilly at him out of the corner of a big, red, gold-chained handbag. There was, Niall saw, a hint of smugness in the evil, as if Sugar saw the future and it pleased him. It made Niall, despite himself, feel nervous.

Now that they were on the motorway going out to the airport, the car had picked up speed. The increase in velocity increased Niall's insecurity, as if events were moving more quickly than he was. He stared out of the window, swallowing hard. She was ignoring him, and she owed him so much. More than she owed that greedy bastard of an agent of hers, sitting over there in L.A. raking in the money. What was so difficult about that, Niall fulminated silently, his eyes pale slits of resentment as he watched the traffic flash past. Whereas he…he…

You just had to take the last few days. Having saved her career by getting her a part in *Titus*, he had gone on to save her reputation when, having got the nod from Saint, Belle was all for heading straight to the film set and dropping everything. Including the baby and the nanny, whom she was refusing to pay. It had taken him, Niall reminded himself, to point out that flouncing off to Italy while leaving an abandoned African orphan in a London hotel room might not play the press all that well. Especially when she was taking her goddamn dog with her.

"Well, the press didn't care when I adopted him," Belle sulked. "No one took any notice."

"They'll care a lot when you un-adopt him," Niall assured her. "They'll take plenty of notice if you just leave him by himself in London."

"Who says I was going to leave him by himself in London?" Belle swung her mass of brittle, perfumed, white hair back over her shoulder.

"Well, who else were you going to leave him w...?" Niall did not, however, finish the sentence. There was a purposeful glint in those liquid-green eyes. His heart hammered. She could not mean, surely...

"You, of course," Belle said breezily.

"Me? Me?"

He'd managed to persuade her not to sack the nanny only by adopting the lowest of tactics. "If you fire her, Emma will go to the papers," he had warned. "Remember how, um, hugely famous you are now, Belle."

"Famous again, you mean," corrected Belle. The tactic had worked, however. Belle had, with the utmost reluctance, agreed to pay Emma a minimal salary, and she and the baby gone ahead to Italy earlier that morning. Much earlier: their bargain flight had been scheduled to leave before six.

The Mercedes, Niall saw from the signs above the motorway, was now nearing Gatwick. The parting was imminent.

Seeing the crowd of photographers outside the glass doors at the terminal entrance, Belle gave a theatrical sigh. "Oh. My. God. Just look at those goddamn paps," she drawled, as if, Niall thought, these were not the very same men whose attentions, a mere few days ago, she would have tap-danced round a toilet seat to attract.

"I'll come with you," he offered eagerly. "See you on the plane. I'm strong. I can shove my way through..."

He stopped. Belle had held up a hand. "No."

Niall stared. "But why not? I mean, I've come with you all this way..."

"I didn't ask you to," Belle said with a curl of her pink glossy lip.

As, beside her, he caught the glint of Sugar's teeth, a sickening feeling now spread through Niall. The despicable animal was grinning. Ignoring it as best he could, Niall fought for a passage through his swirling emotions. "I came," he assured the dog's mistress with all the passion he could muster, "because I love you, Belle. We haven't been long together, but you've come to mean so much…"

Belle was texting. She wasn't, Niall saw despairingly, even looking at him.

"It's over," she said, frowning over the keys. "I was gonna text you when I got to Florence, but I guess I may as well tell you now. Eyeball to eyeball," she added, from the other side of her enormous sunglasses.

"Over?" Niall croaked. His mind whirled. Oh, God. Where was he going to sleep tonight?

"Over," Belle confirmed, pressing the send button on her text. She looked up and flashed him a megawatt smile. "I've gotta move on," she explained.

"Move on?" Niall exclaimed in a tragic croak. He was determined to give this one the works. The YMCA was beckoning otherwise. "Move on from me? But why? I thought you loved me." His voice broke on a sob.

"Loved you?" Belle's tone was astounded. "Baby, this is Hollywood."

The chauffeur opened the door, and she slid out. He watched her stalk past the paparazzi, sunglasses flashing disdainfully, and disappear inside the terminal. She didn't even look back.

What now? He could hardly go back to Darcy's Knightsbridge flat, not now that he had left her for someone else. Any hope that Darcy, from the distance of America, was unaware of the liason had been shattered by the widespread publicity it had received. Plus the venomous texts he had received from her on the subject. That their relationship was over was in no doubt.

He'd left his bicycle at her flat, Niall recalled gloomily. It would have been useful, now that the days of limos and chauffeurs had come to an emergency stop.

Chapter Thirty-one

ORLANDO FITZMAURICE SAT IN the airport, his legs in their cut-off jeans stuck out in front of him, his large, trainered feet subtly drumming the ground along to the iPod whose earphones were entirely hidden under his tangled, dark-gold hair.

The place seemed full of leggy teenage girls with long blonde hair. Well-heeled Jasmines and Elizas, he could tell, heading for Daddy's villa in Tuscany. As he was himself, even though Daddy, in his case, had rented it, shuddering at the price, and his mother twitteringly referred to it as the *aubergo*. And they were, of course, sharing it with the Faughs.

Although it had been some weeks since the invitation was issued, and he should probably be used to it by now, Orlando still found it hard to believe that his mother really had invited the world champions of freeloading on their summer holidays with them. Moreover, that the Faughs would be present when his A levels came through. The results were going to be terrible, and so was being with his parents when the dreaded fax arrived. The prospect of being with the twins as well was almost beyond bearing.

There was a rustle from the seats opposite. His mother had lowered her *Vogue* and was looking at him. Her mouth was moving up and down, but he heard nothing through the thunder from his earphones. She was making turn-it-down gestures. Orlando turned it down.

"Darling?" Georgie shrilled.

"I've turned it down, Mum," Orlando mumbled, shooting a self-conscious look at the people passing about them.

"Honestly, darling," Georgie said in a more normal voice. "You're supposed to be looking out for Laura and Hugh, and you're just staring at the floor from what I can see." Her thin face creased with exasperation.

"Sorry, Mum," Orlando grunted in the resonant baritone he had recently acquired. His voice had become deep and gruff in a way that seemed to catch even more female attention. Unwillingly, he raised his chin and cautiously, beneath his cliffs of brow, began to scan the airport for the Faughs.

"Look! Look! Over there!" Georgie yelped, her face ablaze with excitement.

Beside her, Richard lowered his newspaper in panic. Had the dreaded hour come?

"Look!" Georgie exclaimed again, pointing.

On the wide carpeted gangway that led through this departure hall into the next, a blonde woman was walking quickly through, gesturing angrily, surrounded by photographers. They were all yelling and letting off their flashes.

"Isn't that Belle Murphy?" Georgie gasped.

"Who?" asked Orlando. He had no interest in celebrities, apart from the distraction from himself that they afforded his mother.

There was a sharp, irritated, intake of breath from Georgie. "Honestly, darling. Don't you know who anyone is?"

"I'll go and see if I can find the Faughs," Orlando mumbled, untangling his legs to stand up to the whole of his six-foot-plus height. He had every intention of avoiding their guests if he saw them, but it got him out of the maternal firing line.

"Ow!" yelled Emma, as a colossal training shoe crushed down on her foot.

It had not been a good day. She had arrived at the airport and checked in what seemed like weeks ago, only to discover that the bargain flight she and Morning had been booked on had been delayed by up to four hours. She had walked around the heaving terminal more or less constantly since and now knew every single item in every single shop.

And now some clumsy oaf had walked slap-bang into her and crushed her foot. As well as, Emma saw, annoyed, made a dirty smudge with his sole over her white Converse.

"Sorry," Orlando blurted. He had not seen this woman until it was too late, and he had practically knocked her over. He saw in horror that she had a baby strapped to her front. "I'm really sorry," he grunted, in the new deep voice he still didn't feel entirely comfortable with.

Her assailant was very tall, Emma saw. About her age; maybe younger. He wore a pair of cut-off denim jeans and a sagging white T-shirt. His face was hidden beneath lots of blond hair, and there were iPod earphones curling around his neck. So far, so bog-standard, Emma thought.

He pushed his hair back to expose his face, and, instead of the spotty and misshapen bunch of bog-standard teenage features she had been expecting, Emma now found herself looking at a face of celestial beauty. He had the most extraordinary eyes, a brackish green ringed with yellow. She was immediately conscious of her predawn lack of make-up and the way her hair scraped back in an early-morning ponytail from which it was constantly escaping. Her exposed ears seemed to double tenfold in size, turn purple, and pulsate.

Of course, she thought he was an idiot, Orlando realised. You could tell by the way she was looking at him. She had a very direct gaze. Most girls he knew sort of squinted, giggled, and whooshed their hair about. This girl's cool and interested appraisal was something entirely different.

For a moment, the world around Emma had simply melted away. But now, against her front, Morning stirred. She hoped desperately that he wasn't about to scream.

But the only sound from directly south of her was a happy gurgle; looking down, Emma saw that the baby was smiling at the boy.

"Nice baby," said Orlando appreciatively. "What's his name?" He had not failed to notice, of course, that the baby was black. Very black, in fact, more so than one might expect if this girl was, as seemed likely, his mother.

"He's called Morning."

Orlando was intrigued. "Why did you call him that?"

"Oh, he's not my baby," Emma said hastily. "I'm his nanny."

But she was, even so, the nearest to a mother Morning had. Especially now that Belle, grudgingly agreeing to pay her after all, had made it abundantly clear that she wished to see as little of the baby as possible.

With this in mind, while she had seen Belle go through the airport just now, heading for the VIP lounge and followed by the paparazzi. Emma had kept her own head down.

Where this situation was ultimately leading to, Emma could not guess. But if current form was anything to go by, she would be spending the next twenty years following Belle, flying bucket class and on slave wages, until Morning was old enough to look after himself. Any hope of another, better job relied on keeping this one for a respectable number of months.

"His nanny," repeated Orlando, interested in her northern accent. Hardly anyone ever spoke to him in anything other than an English upper-class accent, or what they imagined was one.

Emma was getting more used to the boy's extraordinary appearance now, but looking directly at him was still a bit like looking directly into the sun.

"I'm Orlando, by the way…"

She smiled. "You look like an Orlando." Damn. Why had she said that?

"And you're…?"

"Emma."

He nodded. "Yeah, you look like an Emma."

She did look like an Emma, he thought. The simple grace of the name suited her. There was something very fresh and English about her face, which was open and clear, with large, brown, shining eyes. There were touches of pink in her cheeks that reminded him of roses. He liked her brown hair, too, which was falling out of its ponytail more and more all the time. Released, it looked glossy and weighty and incredibly healthy and was shot through with rich red threads. She had nice little ears too, tinged with pink.

She wore either none or very little make-up. She looked so clean she might squeak. She was not thin, but not fat either. She looked as unlike as it was possible to look from the rickety, kohl-eyed, blonde Elizas and Jasmines he knew from school and Facebook. One could not easily imagine any of them holding a baby with the confidence Emma was doing now, nor gaining such obvious pleasure from it. She was, Orlando sensed, very kind.

A force beyond his usual diffident self now impelled him. "How about a coffee?" he blurted, surprising himself and sending a violent charge through Emma's knees.

In the terminal Costa Coffee, Orlando flicked some torn sugar papers from the table. They had established in the coffee queue that they were both going to Italy, although on different flights. And for different reasons.

"I wish I was working, not just going on holiday," Orlando remarked longingly.

"Really?" she looked at him quizzically.

"You bet." Orlando longed to earn his own living, but at what he had no idea. He had never worked in his life, not because he hadn't wanted to, but because Georgie had not let him. During his entire time at school, she had ruled out holiday jobs in supermarkets or on building sites on the grounds he could be using the time studying.

In fact, he had used it to watch television. And now what career lay ahead? He had no idea what he was going to go into, apart from the local unemployment office.

Emma was surprised at this outburst. It was not what she had expected such a gilded youth to say.

There was, he thought, something really rather distractingly pretty about the way her hair kept falling out of its ponytail. And the shine of her lips and eyes when she looked at him.

"The holiday's going to be a nightmare," Orlando moaned. "I'm expecting my A level results, and they're going to be the worst ever recorded."

"Why are they going to be so bad? Was your school bad?"

He shook his blond hair. "No, the school was fine."

"Didn't study?"

Orlando shook his head. Of all his weak academic aspects, studying was his weakest. Until an exam was actually upon him, he could never believe it would actually happen. And then, of course, it was too late.

"Shame to miss the opportunity," Emma said tacitly. "After going through all those years at school."

Orlando considered this. He had trained himself to be deaf to anything his mother ever said about wasting his privileges. Coming from this girl, however, failing exams sounded like something other than failing to get on the next level of social achievement, as Georgie so obviously saw it. It just sounded like a waste of effort, which, he supposed, it was.

"I suppose you got lots of As," he said wistfully to Emma. "You look the clever sort."

Emma grinned. "No one's ever said that before. Most people think nannies look thick."

"You don't look thick."

"I never took A levels. I decided to leave and start work."

"Lucky you," Orlando said, again. "The only way my mum would've let me leave is if I'd passed all my exams and a degree freakishly early and become the youngest brain surgeon ever employed at University College Hospital."

Emma laughed. "Are you saying your mum's a bit pushy?"

He pulled a face. "I mean, she's nice. She means well. But…" He stopped. Where did he start, with the buts?

In the obvious place. He started with the Faughs. Describing their horrors made him feel strangely lighter of heart. As Orlando spoke, he forgot his awkwardness about his voice. He felt a new confidence blossom; he had not realised he was possessed of such eloquence, particularly before a girl. Or that anything he might have to be eloquent about would interest a girl.

As Emma listened, the urge rose to tell Orlando about the almost equally peculiar conditions of her own Italian trip. It felt a long time since she had had a ready and sympathetic ear, someone her own age, not an employer or other adversary, but someone who would understand. She felt for the first time how lonely she had been in London.

She stopped herself, however. Emma was unsure to what extent the confidentiality agreement was watertight, but she was certain that whatever water it held Belle would squeeze to the last drop if she breached it.

"How awful," she remarked, when Orlando's torrent of resentment had spent itself. "They obviously think they can do what they like just because their father's an MP."

"And he thinks he can do what he likes as well." Orlando told Emma about Hugh Faugh's views concerning hanging or sterilising single mothers in the lower social classes.

He was satisfied to see her expression was absolute amazement.

"But…this man. He represents people. In Parliament."

"Yes."

"People voted for him."

Orlando confirmed that, incredibly, this was so.

"He has power and influence. And that's what he thinks…" Her nostrils flared. "People trust him."

Orlando regarded her with blazing eyes, his heart surging with the joy of, at last, finding someone who really understood. "I know. It's unbelievable. If only his constituents knew…" He tore a packet open and began layering the top of his cooling cappuccino.

"Do you realise," Emma interrupted him, "that you're putting salt on your coffee?"

The next thing he knew, she was scrambling to her feet as quickly as Morning and his bottle made possible. "My flight's actually up there! Boarding now!" She paused, her eyes awkwardly flicking his. "Um, thanks for the coffee…"

She had gone, disappeared into the crowds, before he could even ask her where she was staying. Before he could get her mobile. If she was near him, they could have met. Had another coffee. Become friends.

Chapter Thirty-two

TWO MEN WERE WALKING despondently through Gatwick's main departure zone. One was tall and thin with a lugubrious grey face, a long nose, and greyish, thinning, long hair. His companion was short and pink, with reddish, thinning short hair. Otherwise, they were more or less identical in jeans, trainers, and black leather jackets, the front of which bristled with black camera equipment. Huge lenses, flashes, and various other black cylindrical objects, all hung suspended from their necks by broad black straps. In their hands, the men held take-away cappuccinos and croissants.

"Bleedin' 'ell," said Keith. "Hardly got a single shot there. Agency's gonna bang me nuts between two bricks."

The photographers sat down and stared moodily at their cappuccino cups. "Always the bloody same, ain't it?" Keith added. "These stars, they're desperate for us when they're struggling, but the minute they're back up there, it's—" he mimed someone throwing out a hand. "Oooh! No photographs! They get all bloody grand again. And there we were, taking pictures of Belle Murphy when she couldn't get bloody arrested in London, let alone a part in a big film."

Even though he had heard it all before, Ken gave a slight, despairing, disbelieving shake of his head in support.

Cappuccino foam shot out of Keith's nose, and he wiped it with one black leather sleeve. "No bloody gratitude, that's the problem."

"No. Yes." Not that Ken cared. He had long since stopped expecting gratitude. Why should the celebs be grateful? The paps made money off of them; they, in a less direct but probably more profitable way, made money off of the paps. It was a straightforward business arrangement. Gratitude—and the moral values associated with it—didn't come into it.

"Never thought Belle Murphy would be back up the greasy pole though. If anyone looked down and out, it was her."

"Yeah." Ken stuffed the rest of the croissant into his mouth and, chewing vigorously, screwed up the paper bag it had come in and lobbed it at a distant bin, which it missed.

"But then she gets a part in this new film, and she's off like a greyhound at Walthamstow."

"Yeah."

The two men sighed in unison and surveyed the scene around them.

Ken heard Keith grunt as a tall, lissome blonde in very tight white jeans undulated slowly past, her high red heels clacking sharply on the shiny floor, her rather close-together eyes, which had a yellow tinge, fixed on the two photographers all the while. She had obviously realised they were paparazzi. "Poor man's Paris Hilton," Keith, leaning over, rasped in a stage whisper to Ken.

The blonde, who had two young children in tow—and tow was the word; they dragged at the ends of her arms unwillingly— narrowed her yellow eyes. "Poor man's Mario Testino!" she spat viciously at Keith, before pulling the children after her so hard Ken feared their arms coming out of their sockets.

He looked after her in concern; the little party had stopped a few yards away, and the blonde was shouting. Ken gathered, with his quick ear, that the little boy, who was straining desperately to break free, had dropped something that had rolled away, a little red toy train. "Oh, for Christ's sake, Cosmo," the poor man's Paris was yelling in a harsh patrician voice. "Just stop messing about. If you've lost it, you've lost it. That'll teach you. If you must take those bloody trains everywhere, you've got to keep hold of them. No. No!" she shouted, dragging the child back as he made a break for freedom. "We've got a plane to catch, okay?"

"Please, Totty," the boy begged. "Please. It's over there. I can see it…"

His white-haired sister pleaded in his support, pulling hard on the arms determined to drag them away. "Totty," she cried. "I can see the train. It's just there…" She stabbed the air urgently with her other hand, which was holding a small, pink-striped toy cat.

It was true. Ken could see the little red train. It was just there. It had sped across the hard, shiny walkway and come to an abrupt stop against a white-painted plant pot housing a weeping fig. He could see it. The children, all too agonisingly obviously, could see it. The blonde could see it too, Ken knew. It was sheer sadism that was preventing her from allowing him to go the few steps to it and pick it up.

"Mummy would let me…Daddy would…" the boy pleaded, obviously intent on using every weapon in his arsenal.

"Well, Daddy's not here; he's had to go abroad again," the blonde retorted with what seemed to Ken an inappropriate sneer. "And Mummy's working. It's not her holidays yet; she's coming out next week. We're going ahead," she added savagely. "We're going to have a lovely time in Italy by ourselves…lots of your friends are out there already, like Hengist. He's in his villa…"

The boy was desperate now, Ken saw. He was sobbing and straining towards the plant pot with every muscle in his five-year-old body. "Please, Totty. I can't lose it. Emma gave it to me…"

"Emma!" exclaimed the blonde, swishing her hair about her like a whip. "If I hear that name one more time…" Her face contorted with angry contempt, she pulled him roughly away down the hall. The boy's desolate howls echoed after him and twisted Ken's soft heart. With terrifying suddenness, he leapt to his feet and ran to the weeping fig so fast he almost skidded into it. Swiping down, he seized the train and pelted off down the departures hall after the boy. He was just in time, he saw. The blonde and her two charges had reached the passport control.

The boy, mewing in despair, was still resisting every inch of the way and casting longing looks over his shoulder. As Ken dashed up, as fast as his short legs could carry him, wheezing and holding the small red object out in front of him, the boy's eyes widened in an expression of unadulterated joy. He gave a shout of delight. All of a sudden, quite unexpectedly, Ken had a powerful feeling of wanting to cry too. He wondered if he had ever brought such joy to anyone before.

"This yours, sonny?" he asked in a gruff voice, disguising his emotion. The boy grabbed the train and clasped it passionately to his breast. He nodded, and his eyes filled with tears again. Ken dropped to his hunkers and patted him on his dark-blond head.

"Hooray!" cheered his sister, jumping up and down. "Thank you, Mr. Man."

"No problem, little miss. What's your name then?"

"Hewo," she lisped. "And that's my bwother Cosmo," the child added, after a quick glance at her sibling confirmed that he was, as she apparently had anticipated, too overcome to speak.

"Well, nice to meet you, Hero." Ken tweaked the girl's pink cheek, straightened, and eyed the blonde, who was intensely occupied with the passports. She did not meet his gaze.

"Bit rough with them kids, aren't you?" he observed. "Reckon you ought to be more careful."

The yellow eyes narrowed and glittered as they met his. "Reckon you ought to eff off," she snarled, her accent mimicking his.

Ken shrugged and walked away. He'd done his best. He'd have told the parents, but they obviously weren't around. He shook his head. What was the point of having kids—especially nice kids like that—and handing them over to that blonde monster? Parents these days.

He returned to Keith, who was still grumbling about his spilt coffee.

"Nah, mate. I done you a favour," Ken told him.

"How'd you reckon that then?"

"Well look at you. You're grey from eating nothin' but crisps and drinkin' nothin' but coffee. It's not 'ealthy," Ken opined, still feeling strangely light after the encounter with the boy. It was as if, for the first time in his life, he had done something worthwhile. The child's face had been dazzling in its teary happiness; wish I'd taken a photo of it, thought Ken.

"'Ark at you, bleedin' Jamie Oliver," exclaimed his colleague in annoyed surprise.

Ken did not reply.

Keith fiddled with his focus. "You goin' to wait around for Angelina?" he asked conversationally. "Hear she's comin' through later."

"Ballerina or Jolie?" Ken asked facetiously. Dancing cartoon mouse or pillow-lipped, multi-fostering celebrity; suddenly, he didn't care.

Keith stared at him. "Jolie, of course. The mouse ain't real. 'Ere," he said, pushing his lugubrious grey features closer to Ken. "You feelin' alright?"

Ken did not answer. Actually, he wasn't feeling remotely alright. A strange sensation had possessed him. Quite suddenly, he felt not mildly bored at the prospect of famous people—this was not unusual—but almost violently antagonistic. He felt as if he didn't want to see another celebrity in the whole of his life. It was no mere skittering thought either; rather, a powerful, burning, almost acid antipathy that began in the depths of his stomach and radiated in every direction to the end of his every nerve.

"You alright?" Keith repeated. "You look a bit funny like."

"Might have been a dodgy curry last night," Ken murmured, rather alarmed by the powerful feelings now gripping him. Were all those takeaways taking their toll? It had been months since a fresh vegetable had entered Ken's house, and a thick layer of dust reclined atop his kitchen utensils. But what was the point of cooking for one?

He knew, even so, that the local Taj Mahal was in no way to blame for the sensations currently besieging him. Not directly anyway; the fact he relied on it so heavily—and was becoming so heavy as a result— was another matter, however. His scrappy, stressful, badly nourished, low-job-satisfaction, pointless, unhappy, and, most of all, lonely life now seemed to appear before Ken with a hideous and uncompromising starkness. He had one life—only one life. And what was he doing with it?

Keith was looking away now. He lifted his camera and squinted through it. "That's the woman from *Dragon's Den*, ain't it?" he was asking himself. "Nah…" he added, lowering his equipment. "Too thin. Looked like her though…"

Ken hardly heard. He was in the grip now of a strong urge to escape the airport, the people, the cameras round his neck, his job most of all. As if he had come, with a dead stop, to the end of his professional road. He felt as if he never wanted to take another picture in his life.

"I think I need a holiday," he said, uncertainly. He could hardly remember the last one he had taken. With no one to go with, there had never seemed much point.

Keith nodded. "Don't we all, mate?" he said briskly. "I've got me eye on the Maldives, meself. Where you thinking, then?"

Ken glanced up at the departures screen above them. The one at the top was a flight to Florence. "Italy," he found himself saying. Suddenly he had a vision of hot, sunny hills rolling away to a purple horizon and narrow, shadowy streets winding up through peaceful, ancient towns. He pictured himself at some rustic taverna, at a rough-hewn olivewood table drinking rich red wine from a thick, greenish glass and winding basil-scented spaghetti round his fork. Yes. Italy.

"Oh, yeah?" Keith's high-pitched Cockney voice drew him back to the unwelcome realities of Gatwick. "Nice, Italy," his colleague nodded. "When you thinking of, then? I was wondering about August for the Maldives, meself."

"Now," said Ken.

Chapter Thirty-three

DARCY WAS STARVING. ALL the way up the narrow, winding street of the village, she had been assaulted on all sides by tantalising smells of cooking issuing from the houses on either side. Powerful whiffs of garlic and onions, snatches of tomato, deep base notes of wine and beef, and sharp, grassy jabs of herb. She had not eaten since leaving the hotel in Florence that morning, when there had been only time to snatch a roll and a quick cappuccino.

Admittedly, until now she had hardly noticed the state of her stomach. She had spent the entire time she was driven down the motorway on the mobile. First, there had been a long call from Mitch about the fact principal photography was being delayed in starting— "They always are, and it's only to be expected, baby, on something so goddamn big and complicated as this one"—and then another from Sam at Wild about another forthcoming fashion shoot, this time for shoes. The prospect, after what she had endured at Rumtopf's hands, made Darcy's heart sink.

As Sam finally rang off, Darcy noticed, with a jolt of joy, that they were off the motorway and driving through some of the loveliest countryside she had ever seen.

So this was the famous Chianti. It was like the most beautiful garden. The countryside they were passing through, on winding grey roads that dived up and down, was full of gentle green hills packed with verdant, decorative detail: some hills fluffy with pines, others ridged neatly with vines, still others topped with the dark-green flames of cypress. Here and there, a glimpse of sun-warmed, golden stone, a hint of red-tiled roof, the occasional exciting turret even, denoted some dwelling.

It was so extraordinarily neat and ordered, Darcy thought, framing the tranquil scene in her fingers and thumbs. It glowed richly in the afternoon sun, below the hot purple-blue of the sky. She felt a warmth inside, a sense almost of recognition. For all the fact that the place was new to her, she felt immediately at home. She slid the window down, and a gust of hot, herby air sprang into the car.

A wave of energy and excitement seemed to spring in with it. Darcy felt suddenly refreshed. The vision came to her again, as it had during the Rumtopf shoot, of vine-shaded tavernas in ancient hilltop villages where dark, cool streets wound up to sunny main squares presided over by a barn-like churches with marble fronts. She thought of brilliant sunshine and cool shadows, of resonant flavours: thick-crusted breads, golden slicks of oil, and red wine that was almost black. In short, lunch could be delayed no longer.

She leant forward and asked the driver, Marcello, if there was anywhere good to eat in the area. She watched the back of his neatly trimmed black head nod enthusiastically. "Si, signora. Very good restaurant in Rocolo."

"Rocolo? That's a village?"

"Si. Ees over there."

They were passing a hill on which a village crouched in the sun. Houses in all shapes and sizes and all shades of the spectrum from cinnamon to apricot were crammed and piled one on top of the other, like a fantastical and ornate stone hat. On top, the yellow stone towers of what was presumably the church protruded like two yellow stone fingers.

"There's a good restaurant there?"

"The best. Marco's. On the bend as you reach the top."

Try as Darcy might to persuade Marcello to come with her, he refused. He seemed amazed by the offer. "My wife, she pack me lunch," he smiled as they drove into Rocolo's carpark. "I sit here. I read the paper. I fine."

The village was, Marcello explained, reached on foot. He seemed anxious about how she would receive this, but Darcy was delighted, glad to be out of the car and under this deep blue sky, relishing the heat. The climb up the cobbled street pulled enjoyably on her muscles as the gradient steepened and twisted. The clearly ancient buildings on each side rose sheer as cliffs, albeit cliffs covered in flaking plaster and romantically rioting creeper and vine and, via deep-silled windows, emitting delicious smells from their shadowy depths.

As she walked, Darcy, getting steadily hungrier, looked about her for the restaurant Marcello had mentioned. Ah, yes, that must be it. On the bend, with white sunshades and pretty pale-green chairs and tables. And that strange-looking, wild-haired man outside, who was staring at her for some reason.

❖❖❖

The chaotic-looking chef with the big sunken eyes stood outside his establishment in his creased whites, frowning in the bright sunshine. He was trying to look at the front of his restaurant dispassionately. As someone who didn't live, breathe, sleep, and, most of all, eat it might.

Rodolfo, his old schoolfriend, now a decorator, had painted the place. He had been doubtful about the colour. But I was right, Marco decided now. The sage did work. It was a cool, pretty colour that gave the place a contemporary lift and made the heat less oppressive on an intensely warm day like this one. Anyway, sage was one of his favourite herbs. The only herb Marco loved more than sage was basil, but basil green was not right for the restaurant: too dark. He had, however, planted basil in the two large terra-cotta pots that flanked the restaurant entrance.

His mind drifted back to sage. It perfumed and gave character to one of his favourite dishes, the saltimbocca of Rome, that combination of veal, proscuitto, and sage that, with a squeeze of lemon, jumped in the mouth, which was what the name meant.

Marco swallowed, just thinking about it. Was there anything better than a really good saltimbocca? Well, there was plenty that was just as good, he thought, an image of the perfect San Daniele ham leaping effortlessly to mind; the waxy, near-transparent, light red slices edged with white fat rippling over a heap of fresh arugula dressed with oil and shaved Parmigiano.

Parmesan cheese, now there was another thing, and a thing he often ate for supper, late at night after the restaurant closed. Just a lump of Parmesan: rocky, saltily pungent, pale yellow, and dressed with a little balsamic vinegar, nothing more. Except for a handful of peppery arugula, perhaps, the real stuff that blasted back down your nostrils. Sensational flavours. Italian flavours.

Flavours that were the reason why, after chef school, after honing his trade in some of the great kitchens of Europe, he had come back to focus on the country cuisine of his homeland and youth. The memories of the simple food he had eaten as a child, food that had its roots in necessity, resourcefulness, and whatever ingredients came to hand at the time, came to dominate his thinking and his cooking. Cucina povera, as the magazines liked to call it. Simple flavours that spoke for themselves.

Marco, while grateful for the praise, was always embarrassed by the descriptions of himself. "Rumpled charm" was a phrase that occurred frequently. Marco wasn't sure about the charm. He was hardly most women's idea of good-looking. First, there was his hair, dangling in curly clumps, chopped at with the kitchen scissors whenever it got too long. His face, with its great, wide eyes, long cheeks, and squashed nose, looked, even to him, as if someone had trodden on it.

His towering height, with long arms and big hands that seemed to wave about awkwardly and redundantly whenever—and admittedly, these occasions were rare—they found themselves without a knife or ingredient of some kind. His long legs, forever becoming tangled in things, and his large feet, forever stumbling over things. Outside the kitchen, he was clumsy and ill at ease. Only within it were his movements sure, fluid, and graceful.

But he was amused by the way the write-ups made it sound as if his décor was the result of months of agonising with a team of interior designers.

"Artfully simple" was the term most often used. But there had been nothing artful about it; simple had been the no-choice option. When he opened, money had been tight. He had not been able to afford carpets, or even particularly nice tiles, so the oak floors that had been there for centuries had been sanded and polished. He had done the sanding himself and now had those scars to add to various cut and burn injuries. The place had been filled with utilitarian wooden chairs and tables, bought secondhand.

Marco pushed back some of his rumpled dark hair from his forehead and pushed his big, clumsy-looking hands into his violet-circled eye sockets. The effect as he rubbed his closed lids produced, he noticed, a light red similar to that of a new Chianti.

He looked at his watch. Time to put the oxtail on. In six hours' time, it would be a thick, dark, silky sauce rich with meaty, winey, bone-marrow flavour. After that, he'd peel the peas. No other chef would bother, he knew, but getting the puree completely smooth was a point of pride.

He remembered how Rodolfo had laughed about his pea puree. "You've got it wrong," the decorator had declared.

"Have I?" Marco's heart had quickened. While he had never thought of Rodolfo as much of a cook, he had learnt over time that tips come from the most unexpected places.

Rodolfo grinned. "You're missing something."

"Yes? Yes?"

"It's obvious."

"What is it? What am I missing?" What did Rodolfo know about pea puree that he didn't?

"A life, amico mio." And with that, Rodolfo had plunged his brush into his pot and cheerfully carried on.

Rodolfo didn't understand, Marco mused, how much food meant to him, how much pleasure he got from the simplest of things. How the taste of a fresh carrot could bring tears to the eyes. He had said this to Rodolfo who had laughed and said that, personally, onions were the only vegetables that made him cry.

He looked at his restaurant again and felt a hot wave of love and pride. It was a former wine cellar, whose cave-like mouth stretched across the entire front of the building in a shallow arch. Inside was a long, wide space with a plain wooden floor and a brick barreled ceiling painted white. It was simple and intimate, as well as wonderfully cool on hot days, especially given the elderly but nonetheless vigorous vine that trailed around the doorway. At the top of the building, in the roof, were the tiny pair of low-ceilinged, whitewashed rooms—bathroom and bed-sitting room—in which Marco slept the few hours he was not in his restaurant. Or, as now, outside it in the cobbled, table-covered courtyard.

The building containing his restaurant and his home was one of a row—or rather a curve—of similarly ancient, mellow, and slightly crumbling structures that followed a winding, cobbled street rising from the bottom of the hill, on which the village was built, up to the main square at the top where the church and the shops were. Everyone in Rocolo passed it regularly—had to—as cars were not allowed.

As a result, there were few locals who didn't partake of a morning cappuccino, daytime espresso, or evening prosecco. At dinner and lunch, moreover, especially on Sundays, the courtyard was heaving with Rocolo families crowded under the big, white parasols shading tables piled with bread, wine, pasta, and whatever big-flavoured delicacy the popular local chef had produced that morning.

"Ciao!" Some coffee-drinkers were leaving, and he waved them off.

He watched approvingly as Daria, the waitress, came out and cleared away the coffee cups from some earlier breakfasters. Daria was pretty, certainly, with her doe-like face with its creamy skin and the shiny black ponytail that flopped down her back. But what Marco admired most about her was the speed with which she could chop a carrot and her neatness at table-setting. He had no time for women, for romance. The love of his life was his restaurant.

He looked over the courtyard once more before disappearing inside. And it was then that he saw her.

She was walking up the steep cobbled street towards him, flushed as even the fittest usually were by this point. She was about twenty-five and the hair that swished about her shoulders was as thick and shining as squid ink. Her wide, creamy face made him think instantly of panna cotta, and her pale arms and legs, the beautiful sheeny white of freshest leeks, were set off by a dress the bright yellow of saffron rice. As she got closer, he saw her pretty, full mouth was a rich, strawberry-semifreddo pink.

A hot wave of excitement washed suddenly over Marco. Rocolo, being one of the jewels of the Chianti tourist trail, attracted its fair share of beautiful women. Some of them even famous. But he had never looked at any of them the way he was looking at this woman now. She was enchanting.

Chapter Thirty-four

CHRISTIAN HARLOW WAS NOT having a good day. This boneheaded Italian cop's refusal to let him drive at top speed up the village street was merely the latest example of how events at the moment seemed to be conspiring against him. Why the hell couldn't he, anyway? The crumbling old heap of a village needed something fast and new in it. The place was a mess; you could see that from here.

"Whaddya mean I can't get my car up there?" he demanded, stabbing one of many beringed fingers at the small cobbled lane leading under the arch. "I'm starving. I need a burger, like, now, man. Hey. You don't know who you're dealing with here, yeah? Don't you know who I am?"

The cop was jealous, Christian decided. Sure he was; the Ferrari he'd had the film company hire for his entertainment while in Italy was a great car. He'd had a blast roaring up and down the country lanes in it this morning—Jesus, they made them small round here—but now he was hungry, and this shitty little village was the nearest place to where he was staying. He'd zoom in and stop at the burger bar.

"Walk?" he shouted angrily as the policeman mimed ambulatory movements. "Are you kidding?"

It was on the tip of Christian's foot, expensively shod in Versace sandals, to put the pedal to the metal and roar away. But where the hell would he get his burger then? Besides, he wanted to check out the scene—and the chicks. There was bound to be someone willing to have a little fun with a Hollywood superstar.

What was this freak of a cop saying to him? Christian frowned and tried to understand, not a process that came to him easily. "Bicycle?" he repeated disbelievingly.

The policeman was bending his legs, holding his arms out in front and jiggling. A crowd that had gathered, and was swelling, tittered. Thunder gathered in Christian's heart. He threw his arm across the low, black leather back of the driver's seat, flung the Ferrari violently into reverse, and screeched away. Grudgingly, he parked the car, and, once the crowd had dispersed, trudged across to the bridge to begin the ascent to the village on foot.

Bloody Italy, thought Christian. He'd never wanted to come here in the first place, had no interest in Europe whatsoever. Who did? As markets went, it was a million miles behind the only one that really mattered, his own native U.S. of A.

And now, of course, he was stuck here for weeks on end. One of the other reasons that this morning had been such an ass-pain was the call he had got from his agent, Greg Cucarachi. Cucarachi had informed him that principal photography on the film had been set back by a week or so while locations were finalised.

"Jesus," Christian had shouted. "Nothing on this goddamn film is finalised. Locations, actors, whatever. What is it with this guy Saint?"

"The fee he's paying you and the fact the film will be huge," Greg had replied immediately. "And as it happens, another actor has been finalised." Christian now learnt that Belle Murphy had been given a part in *Galaxia*. "You're kidding me!" Christian screeched.

"Don't you read the papers?" Greg asked.

"No, I fucking don't," he yelled. "I pay people like you to read them for me."

"In which case," Greg rejoined smoothly, "let me explain. Belle had a hit with some Shakespeare play in London. She's hot again—well, pretty warm."

"You say this movie's gonna take eight weeks to shoot once principal photography actually starts? Eight weeks with her?"

"Eight weeks in Italy, yes," Greg said. "But that's only the ceremonial space city bits—Saint wanted real palazzo interiors for them. There's about three months of shooting elsewhere, plus post-production…"

"I don't wanna see her!" Christian interrupted violently. "Saint's gotta drop her from the film!" Not least because his chances of bedding anyone else would be badly scuppered by having his banshee of an ex around.

"Not much chance of getting her dropped," Greg remarked. "But don't worry," he soothed. "There's a way round this. You don't have to see her. Or, rather, she doesn't have to see you."

"How d'ya figure that out?" Christian demanded hysterically. "We'll be on set together."

"Sure, but whenever you're on set, you're in disguise. You're the evil lord Jolyon Wooloo, half lizard and half man," Greg reminded his client, quite unable to believe that Christian was unaware of this central fact.

"That's the main part, yeah?" Christian said aggressively.

Greg confirmed that it was. "It's a great part. Your costume's gonna be incredible. You'll wear a lizard mask made of latex. It takes four hours of make-up every day…"

"What?"

"Hey, all this is in your contract. Didn't you read it?"

Christian fired hot air impatiently out of his nostrils. Of all the stupid questions. He hadn't read anything in the contract apart from how much he was getting paid. "I've got a latex mask on my head? In the middle of an Italian summer? I'm gonna cook, man."

"You get cooled between takes by air pumped through a tube."

"Big fucking deal," growled Christian. His big film break was looking less sexy all the time. Eight weeks in Italy with Belle Murphy, dressed as a lizard in a latex mask. Great.

"Remember, it's a big part," Greg reminded him. "It's gonna make you huge."

It had better, Christian thought as he stomped up the cobbles into Rocolo.

Chapter Thirty-five

"IT'S YOUR RESTAURANT?" DARCY was asking the wild-haired man in whites who had come out to take her order. He really was very tall for an Italian—over six feet, she estimated. But you obviously got tall Italians. There seemed no reason why not.

"Every inch," Marco declared proudly. "I am chef-patron."

She was lovelier than he had imagined, her long sweep of lashes like the tiny tentacles on the most delicious of sea urchins. Her perfect ears reminded him of the tiny, tasty clams he liked to use for spaghetti vongole. Her lips were not, as he had first imagined, the colour of the most perfect raspberry sorbet. No, they were redder, more like the tomato ice he had recently been experimenting with and which had actually turned out rather well.

"What sort of food do you do?"

He sighed happily. He was tongue-tied with women, and never more so than with this one, but this was the one subject in the world on which he could hold forth with the utmost confidence to anyone. "Country food, you know. Of the region. Traditional dishes, with perhaps a little modern twist here and there."

"Is that what I can smell?" Darcy was sniffing hard. The scent was strong, herby, and delicious.

"Si. Today we are doing a minestrone with beans and pesto. We make it with rice too, so much rice you can stand your spoon up in it and watch it fall slowly back down. Oh, and with a big glug of peppery, golden olive oil to finish…what is that noise?"

Marco asked suddenly, inclining his big shaggy head the better to listen.

Darcy did not answer. She had no intention of admitting it was her stomach.

Lunch started with aperitivo of crisp Prosecco with salami and olives, along with a dish of bright green beans, a speciality of the region, Marco explained. Then followed some sausage and pea risotto, and afterwards lemon ice cream. A succession of wonders, Darcy thought.

Never before had she tasted such food. Everything was so fresh, so colourful, so obviously full of goodness and flavour. It seemed to Darcy, as she absorbedly ate this lunch, that she had only ever fuelled herself at tables before. Only now, here under the cool shade outside this little but excellent restaurant, was she really eating for the first time.

From the kitchen window, above the main dining room and commanding a courtyard view, Marco watched her eat. At that exact moment, he knew, the nutty, creamy flavour of the rice was combining with the fresh sweetness of the peas. Her eyes were closed as she forked the risotto in. This, thought Marco, was a woman who really appreciated food. He had sensed this was so from the start, which was why he had arranged a handful of his prized green fava beans, the early, baby broad beans he so loved to eat raw, in a dish for her, a privilege he accorded normally to only his very favourite customers.

What was the matter with him? Beautiful women came to the restaurant all the time. Most of them left him cold. Mostly because they didn't eat, just poked salads about and crumbled the breadsticks, which Marco hated to see. They were taking up a place at his table a food lover could have had.

Darcy, lost in contemplation of how absolutely delicious that pea risotto had been, almost jumped when the white plate bearing two creamy scoops over which strips of candied lemon peel had been laid descended to the table in front of her. She looked up, startled, to find herself staring into the distracted eyes of the chaotic-looking chef.

"Lemon ricotta ice cream," Marco murmured. She watched his big brown hands—they were scarred, she noticed, yet had long and sensitive fingers—move in explication. "Made with Sicilian lemons. The best."

He saw her eyes glow at this; they had the burnish, he felt, of candlelight on a perfect chocolate-covered coffee bean. Then, out of the corner of his eye, Marco saw something move behind him.

He turned, and his heart sank. A man was making his way up the slope. A macho type, with the muscle-bound swagger Marco associated with the gym. He was obviously heading straight for the restaurant.

He wore a tight, white T-shirt on whose front, beneath the mass of gold chains, crosses, and pendants he wore, the glittering name Gucci flowed over undulating pectorals. His bare, brown, and powerfully muscled arms bristled with bracelets and an expensive-looking watch, and he wore a black-and-white knitted hat covered in interlinked Chanel Cs.

Marco sighed. The few minutes alone with the beautiful food-lover had been delicious, but they were all too obviously over. Not least because the muscle-bound swaggerer seemed to recognise her.

"Hey!" he said.

Darcy Prince, Christian was sure. His latest co-star in what had better be the greatest film of his career. Looking even better than she had in Puccini's. Christian's thick-cut, sensuous lips curved in triumph as he got closer. That dark hair, that pale skin, those very nice tits under that yellow dress.

Darcy, whose tastebuds were exploding like a firework display with intense lemonness, looked up, disconcerted. She did not immediately recognise the man standing at the edge of the parasol-shaded tables. But then he strode forward, dropped into the chair in front of her, and tore off his sunglasses. With a lift of her heart and a swoop in her stomach, Darcy found herself staring into the same pair of eyes that had hypnotised her in L.A. Christian Harlow. She never forgot a name, and his face was unforgettable anyway.

"Darcy," Christian repeated, pleased at the effect he had had. She would be putty in his hands; he could see that immediately. He fixed his eyes on her breasts. Jesus, they even looked real. That was an unexpected bonus.

Marco, pretending to push chairs in a few tables away, glowered from behind the sunshades. This muscle-bound beast of a man, all cheekbones and cock. He was staring at her breasts without even attempting to hide it. What was even worse was that she seemed to like it.

"Christian," Darcy breathed, all confusion. Her ability to appear normal deserted her. She blushed hot, went cold, and felt shaky and oddly light, as if she might float or fall of the chair. "What are you…I mean…what are you doing here?"

"*Galaxia*," Christian returned triumphantly.

"You're in *Galaxia*?"

He loved her voice. That prissy, high-end English, all repressed fire. You could just tell by looking at her that she'd never had a really good bang.

"You alone?" he asked her, pulling out a chair and sitting down. "No, like, boyfriend?"

She looked surprised at this, but Christian preferred to find out where he stood from the start. He was interested to see that a spasm of anger shot across her face as she shook her hair in a negative. The bust-up had been messy, Christian triumphantly deduced.

"He didn't realise what a good thing he was on top of…I mean onto," Christian hurriedly corrected himself.

"No." Darcy eyed him balefully. "He preferred to get on top of Belle Murphy instead."

Christian fought to conceal his horror. He was an actor, after all. The coincidence was appalling. His ex…her ex…together?

It wasn't, Christian realised, going to help his campaign if he now admitted he had been with Belle himself. Perhaps, later, he could gently slip it in. But—Jesus—that woman. She got everywhere. Still, he could control the situation; there had been plenty of similar ones before.

"What do you think I should have for lunch?" he asked, changing the subject abruptly.

"Well, everything's great. I almost had the lamb with aubergine myself…"

He nodded, even though his only interest in what she was saying was the way her full lips pouted and parted in speech. They were very kissable. He caught a tantalising glimpse of pink tongue.

Would it be tonight or tomorrow night, Christian wondered complacently.

She watched him admiring himself in the shiny bowl of a spoon. "You're rather vain, aren't you?" she teased.

Christian agreed readily. "Sure. You gotta look after yourself." His frankness was disarming; that he obviously saw vanity as a virtue, amusing. As Christian chatted on, Darcy noticed that he referred frequently, and in terms of the utmost approval, to his willy, but perhaps that too was refreshingly honest. Perhaps British men—or at least the ones she knew—didn't talk about their willies nearly enough. Perhaps bottling up all that angry sexuality was what, ultimately, had led Niall to Belle.

Christian was smouldering at her. "You're very flirty," she remarked.

He flashed her a grin. "I know. I can't help it. If I wasn't flirting with you, I'd be flirting with that fork over there." His grin broadened, and Darcy found herself smiling back. His candour was irresistible, as was the rest of him.

As the man and the woman laughed on the terrace, Marco,

inside, felt as seared as the salmon he was preparing. He had never felt this jealous before. At least, not of a man, about a woman. He'd felt something similar when tasting a particularly perfect dish in someone else's restaurant, but even that, now, seemed tame in comparison.

Marco felt disappointed. The woman had displayed such impeccable taste up until now.

Chapter Thirty-six

OF COURSE, SHE WAS going to sleep with him. If sleep was the word. She had known that as soon as she had seen him walk up to her at the restaurant.

She knew that now as he drove her off in his car. She could imagine what Sam would say about exposing her newly valuable features to the full force of mid-day Italian glare in an open-topped Ferrari. "Factor fifty sunblock at all times," the model agency head had warned. "And hats from eleven to three."

She had tried to protest. "They're expecting me at the villa," Darcy had gasped. "My car's down in the carpark; there's a driver..." She thought guiltily of Marcello.

"So what, baby," Christian had shrugged as he took a slug of sparkling wine. He had not been impressed by the fact Marco's did not stock champagne, only the Italian equivalent. "You're a star; you do what you like. What the hell does it matter about anybody else?"

"But they'll be waiting..."

"Baby, they're paid to wait. They expect to wait. So let 'em wait."

"It's a bit rude..."

Christian plonked his glass down hard and burst into incredulous laughter at this.

Darcy let herself be persuaded. Marcello was sent to her villa with the luggage. Christian, with his designer clothes, his flashing gold, his cheekbones, and most of all, his swaggering self-confidence, made fame look like such fun. He talked about *Galaxia* endlessly through lunchtime, hardly noticing the food, it seemed to Darcy, as he outlined just how seismic the effect of the film would be on both their careers.

"Just enjoy yourself, baby!" Christian shouted, grinning, as they raced along in the Ferrari. "You English chicks, you're so uptight!" His white teeth flashed in the sunshine almost as brightly as the car's chrome fittings.

He made her feel fast and reckless. The air rushing at her was exhilarating; she felt like a plane taking off. The speed was such that she felt they might.

"Where are we going?" she shouted excitedly.

"My place," he yelled back over the air screaming past them.

Darcy pushed caution firmly aside. She wanted some fun, after what seemed in retrospect years of deprivation. She had an alter ego now, a reckless, pleasure-seeking, beautiful young film star. And going to bed with your co-stars—especially if they looked like Christian—was the sort of thing film stars did.

He zoomed up a hill and skidded to a halt in front of a pair of huge gates.

A wide, gravelled path led through the middle of a garden to a large villa whose central door was surrounded by grandiose carving. There must, Darcy thought, be hundreds of bedrooms.

"You're staying here?" she asked Christian, in awe. "On your own? It's incredible."

Christian shrugged. Incredible was one way of describing it. Huge and creepy was another, and he didn't like the way the place was so old. Secondhand was bad enough; this place was probably hundredth-hand. Not for the first time, Christian rather regretted his insistence that the film company book him the biggest villa in the area, all for himself.

"You're so beautiful," he murmured, folding her into his arms.

Darcy felt her whole body thrum with anticipation. She traced his face, her eyes hungrily devouring his features. They had been together a mere few hours, but really, Darcy felt, her mind all excited in a alcohol-fused, pleasure-hungry whirl, they had known each other for ages. Ever since their eyes had met across a crowded, neck-craning restaurant in L.A., a defining moment. Maybe even the turning point of her life.

"We're gonna set that screen alight," he whispered to her, his eyes wide with excitement. "You an' me, we're gonna be the new Burton and Taylor."

She pressed herself against him. As he dipped his mouth to hers, she felt a stab of joy between her legs.

"The bedroom's up here," he muttered thickly, pulling her gently but firmly up the stairs.

It was a huge, high-ceilinged room with enormous shuttered windows. In the muted light, a tall bed with white curtains rose like a ship in full sail.

On the bed, in the cool shadows cast by the canopy, he pushed her gently back, his mouth locking hers down. Pushing up her dress to reveal her breasts, he kissed them reverently, flicking the tips with his tongue. She shuddered with delight.

He looked up, his eyes soft with surprise. "Hey. They're real!"

"What did you expect them to be?" Darcy asked laughing.

"Oh. You know. The usual silicon valleys," Christian grinned.

Afterwards she rose from the bed, flung open the shuttered windows so that the dazzling light poured in, and looked out over the sunny garden. It stood still in the singing heat. As she stood there, a gentle breeze sprang up and hurled soft balls of scent from the earth against her bare skin: rosemary, sage, pine. Darcy closed her eyes and breathed slowly, luxuriously in.

Chapter Thirty-seven

EMMA STOOD AT THE gate. The name chiselled in gold on the neat, white marble nameplate—"Villa Rosa"—was that of the address Belle had given her.

She felt relieved but exhausted. It was dazzlingly hot, and Morning, whose weight seemed to be doubling daily—he'd soon be out of the baby carrier altogether—hung like lead around her neck. Fortunately, he was quiet and content under his little white sun hat, looking about him with interest as he had throughout the journey on the bus from the airport. A taxi would have been better, but Emma's funds, as yet unswelled by Belle, did not stretch to one.

Would Belle be here, Emma wondered as she pressed the buzzer on the thick, stone gatepost. She had not seen her employer since Belle disappeared into the VIP area at Gatwick. And while travelling alone with the baby had had its hair-raising moments, being in charge had been enjoyable. Emma realised, with a clutch of regret, that her feeling of autonomy was about to end.

"Benvenuto!" someone called from the other side of the gate.

Emma peered through the wrought iron to see a middle-aged, beaming woman of wiry build and wiry cropped black hair that was tinged with grey. She wore a black skirt and white blouse.

"I'm Mara," the woman smiled as she punched a code into somewhere unseen on the other side of the gatepost and swung open the wrought-iron screen. "The housekeeper. I do housework, laundry, cooking...ah. Bello bambino!" She tickled Morning under the chin and beamed at Emma. "You have had a good journey, Signorina Murphy?"

"Actually, I'm not Signorina Murphy."

"Not Signorina Murphy?" For a moment, the housekeeper looked suspicious. Then she smiled again. "Ah. You Signorina Prince then."

"No."

"I am told," the housekeeper said, rather crossly, "that Signorina Prince and Signorina Murphy, they both arrive at lunchtime. I cook my special beef lasagne."

At the thought of Mara's special big lasagne, Emma's stomach growled. She was here. She was hungry. She hastened to explain herself. "I'm Signora Murphy's nanny. Signora Murphy's son's nanny, rather..."

Could it possibly be true that Belle had not given any advance warning? Had not told the housekeeper that her son and his nanny were expected?

"Ah. Si. I see." There was a flash of black eyes, a smile, and friendliness was restored. "I carry the baby?" Her voice was as much command as it was suggestion. Gratefully, Emma unbuckled the heavy child and handed him over. Morning's reaction was to open one eye and survey Mara sleepily before closing it again.

"Bello!" Mara deposited a loud and smacking kiss on the top of his head. "I am frustrated grandmother!" she explained, shaking her head and grinning ruefully. "I have no children, only nephew. And he never find right girl!"

"Oh dear," Emma muttered. She wasn't sure she was terribly interested. The full weight of the afternoon sun seemed to be pressing hard on her head. She longed to be somewhere cool.

The villa before her looked, she longingly noted, very cool. It was an attractive, mellow building, a long oblong of pale-yellow stone with a red tiled roof. There were windows everywhere, at all heights, of all periods, of all sizes, and in all places. It looked as if someone had picked them up in a fistful and just thrown them at the wall.

"He very nice. Very funny, very 'ardworking. He chef."

Mara, Emma realised, was evidently still talking about her nephew. "But Marco, 'e work too 'ard. No time to meet right girls."

She looked Emma up and down. Her lips pursed, and one black eyebrow raised speculatively.

Emma felt indignant as well as hot. Mara seemed very nice, but she'd only met the woman five minutes ago. What made her think she would be interested in her nephew? Besides...

An image of a handsome, blond boy rose and fell in her mind's eye. Briefly, Emma let herself dream, yet knowing there was no point. Orlando was in Italy, certainly, but it was a big place.

Mara was leading her down the middle of a sunny green lawn with a leaping, foaming, scented, gloriously colourful border of roses.

"What beautiful roses," Emma said in delight. "Do you do the garden?"

"Gino! Yes! He has been gardener here for long time. More than thirty years. He love just roses. He say they are the queen of the flowers. He no want to plant anything else."

Emma felt she could see Gino's point. There were brilliant roses of all colours, of pink, yellow, white, apricot, and red, and endless variations, rippling pink through purple, yellow through red. Some were classic Valentine's blooms, huge dark and velvety, each curl-edged petal distinct. Others were tumbling, old-fashioned, pink floribunda, petals tightly squished and gathered like the skirt of a ballgown. Still others, smaller and more businesslike, scurried along the ground. Others clambered the weathered stone walls, wrestling with honeysuckle. The scent, even in this hot part of the day, was powerful. Emma could imagine, in the cool of the evening, that it would be almost overwhelming.

The rose garden gave way to a big, flat, sunny terrace in which an enormous oblong of water sat like a bright blue jewel. There were chocolate-brown recliners beside the pool, trimmed with white, each with its own matching shade. It was, Emma thought, disbelievingly, like something from a magazine.

They had reached the villa now. Mara led the way into a big white-painted entrance hall hung with tapestries and large black paintings whose subjects were obscured by age. A flight of wide, shallow wooden steps led to a fatly railed upper landing.

"I take you to your room," Mara said. She paused and looked puzzled. "You share with baby, no?"

Emma nodded. "Is there a cot?"

Mara shook her head apologetically. "No one tell me about bambino." She brightened. "But you can get one from Florence tomorrow."

Emma swallowed. After the long trip she had just endured, a next-day journey to an unknown city for a large piece of furniture was all she needed. What the hell was the Italian for travel cot anyway?

❖❖❖

A couple of fields away from the Villa Rosa, Richard Fitzmaurice was trying hard to enjoy his holiday. He sat beneath the big green parasol, his spare frame in its white, short-sleeved shirt and old blue trousers hunched over the dining table, a bottle of Nastro Azzuro next to him, ostensibly buried in the *Daily Telegraph*.

His surroundings were gracious. Behind Richard was the farmhouse, the *aubergo* as Georgie preferred to call it, with its glamorous succession of double bedrooms decorated in the best contemporary rustic-luxe manner and with adjoining bathrooms featuring power-showers. Plus the impressive lounge with denim-blue suede furniture, satellite telly, and bright contemporary paintings.

The kitchen's highlights included a lifestyle-statement six-ring cooker, a butcher's-block-cum-champagne-bar. and a leatherbound *Visitor's Handbook* with recommendations of local eateries.

In front of him spread the patio, clean and brilliant in the sun. At its far end was a large, round-ended swimming pool whose blue water, enlivened by gushing pumps, danced and sparkled and sent spiky reflections over the white recliners at its edge. Around the patio was a garden that went as far as the wall bordering the main road. The intense green of the lawn had surprised Richard at first, until he had spotted the twisting sprinkler that jerked back and forth like a whirling dervish.

Yes, Richard reminded himself. He was in a beautiful house, in a beautiful country, with his wife and son, whom he loved. Even if Orlando had disappeared into his room immediately on arrival and had not emerged even for lunch. And now, thanks to the combined efforts of the Faugh males, nothing remained of the big spaghetti carbonara that Georgie, with her usual skill and resourcefulness, had whisked up. Richard tried not to give in to the sense of bitterness that swept him whenever he thought about how Hugh and Laura Faugh had hijacked his holiday.

If Richard raised his head a fraction and looked over to the pool, he could see a darkly sunglassed Hugh, big hair glossy in the sun, stretched out in a pair of well-packed electric blue trunks on a recliner. His sons lay next to him, one reading, Richard saw, a glossy called *FHM* and the other one called *Nuts*.

They had lost no time in making themselves comfortable; they had only been in the damned place an hour.

Hugh's big, long, trunk-like legs were slightly apart, and, like his huge, fleshy chest, covered with sun oil and black hair. He watched the shadow of Hugh's big, long arm, raised slightly in the air, juddering over the patio stone as he keyed into his BlackBerry. He was obsessed with the thing. He claimed it was full of messages from constituents, as well as, of course, those from the centre of Shadow power.

This Richard found puzzling. Hugh's constituency was quite similar to his own. His own comprised the tenants of an impoverished Gloucestershire housing estate as well as their near neighbours in one of the Cotswolds' wealthiest villages. Only very few of either group—uneducated and poor on the one hand, elderly and conservative on the other—had the faintest idea how to send an email. Certainly not enough to keep him as busy as Hugh seemed to be, his thumbs and forefingers in a blur of almost constant movement.

But perhaps such keenness had got Hugh where he was. If his constituents wanted to get in touch with Richard, they rang him on the telephone. Or on the mobile, as he was on holiday, but only in dire emergency would he expect any such calls now. In twenty-five years of representing his constituency, Richard could count on the finger of one hand the number of times he had been disturbed by a constituency emergency on summer holiday.

Hugh grunted, sat up, looked around, and waved at Richard. He ambled over to where he sat, stared at his Nastro Azzuro, and boomed, "Any chance of one of those beers you've got there, old boy?"

Richard's reply was drowned in the sudden chug-a-chug-a of a helicopter overhead. This was just as well.

❖ ❖ ❖

Emma had just put Morning to sleep in her own bed. There was nowhere else for him to go until she could get to Florence tomorrow. Lightening her burden slightly was the fact that Mara had offered to look after Morning while she made the journey. He, at least, would be spared a long stretch in a hot bus.

"You're sure you don't mind?" Emma had asked the housekeeper.

"I'll only mind if you come back early," was the twinkling reply.

Emma looked out of the window of her room. It had a view of the rose garden…

The colours of the flowers blazed in the rich evening light beneath the still-azure sky, and the scent was as heady as a boudoir.

It was a beautiful, blue and gold end to what had been a beautiful, blue and gold day. The air rang with competing birdsong, some of it surprisingly loud.

Chuga-chuga-chuga-chuga.

Very loud indeed. There was a thudding noise—a helicopter, Emma now realised as, suddenly and without warning, everything was plunged into sudden shadow and the black underside of some huge airborne beast suddenly appeared above the villa.

Emma shot down the stairs and dived out of the rose garden onto the pool patio and peered up at the menace roaring above, dark and heavy, slashing violently at the air. Surely—surely—it wasn't trying to land in the garden?

Mara appeared. She stared up at the approaching aircraft with an expression of utter incomprehension.

The helicopter was lower now. It filled the sky; Emma could no longer see the sun for it. Where there had been birdsong and an expanse of warm blue, there was now earsplitting noise and blackness.

Who was this idiot, who'd so spectacularly lost his way? She must stop this enormous, destructive, noisy thing from landing. She ran back on to the lawn of the rose garden, her arms waving wildly.

"It's not a helipad!" Emma screamed, leaping up and down, trying to spot a pilot, a passenger, someone behind the expanse of impassive black plastic covering the front of the helicopter. She couldn't see anyone; could they see her? Could they see anything?

"The rose garden!" Mara yelled, as the scented air was smashed and sliced by the deadly whipping blades. Emma ducked and ran towards the villa, not just her ears but her entire body full of the hideous screaming of the engine.

It was incredible, but it actually was happening. The helicopter really was landing in the rose garden. Right in the middle of the path. The heads of the blooms were being pulled into the air, sucked into the blades, mashed by slashing lengths of metal. And now the blades were slowing down, the machine subsiding—and not a single rosehead remained.

The silence that now flooded Emma's ears was as violent and absolute as the noise had been. Not a bird could be heard.

As for the garden, that beautiful rose garden, full of colour and scent and movement...

Shattered petals plastered the front of the helicopter. The grass beneath it was gouged and black: churned, torn, and crushed as the beast had juddered in landing. All that love, Emma thought, all that care and time, all the planting, weeding, spraying, watering, all the pride, joy, and knowledge that the unknown Gino had put into creating this beautiful garden. All destroyed in an instant.

Emma rarely got angry, but a terrible rage filled her now. Whoever was in that helicopter, whoever it was who had done this horrible thing, they were going to hear exactly what she thought of them.

The helicopter door now slid back. A woman emerged. Emma started forward, her anger hot on her lips, but then she fell back.

The woman was blonde and held a small dog. Her platinum mane blazed white in the sun as she shook it out. Shadowy caves shifted beneath her cheekbones. She wore a tight, short black dress, bright red lipstick, and huge black glasses.

"Well don't just stand there," Belle exclaimed angrily to Emma. "I've got a cockpit full of luggage here."

"You've ruined the rose garden," Emma stammered.

"Oh, did I?" Belle looked about her and surveyed the devastation. Not a muscle of her face moved. She looked back at Emma. "You're sure that was me?"

"Quite sure."

"Never mind," Belle beamed. "It'll grow back."

Chapter Thirty-eight

THE ITALIAN LANDSCAPE, IN which Darcy had so delighted before, now seemed to flash past her as in a dream. All she was conscious of was Christian. His watch, which was thick and large and had tiny diamonds round the face, flashed in the sun as his muscled arms changed position on the Ferrari's padded leather steering wheel.

They were driving to the villa where Darcy would be staying for the duration of the filming. A quick call to Mitch had pinpointed the location.

"You haven't checked in there yet?" The agent had sounded concerned.

"Not yet, no," Darcy confirmed gaily. "But we're on our way."

"We?"

"Me and, um, Christian."

"Christian!" Mitch yelped in horror.

He'd been right to fear the worst in Puccini's. The slimiest, most calculating asshole in Hollywood—and a hard-fought title that was—had struck again. Of course he had.

Mitch could have kicked himself. If only he was more of a calculating asshole himself. He'd been insane, hopelessly optimistic or just plain wrong to think that his latest protégée, dewy-eyed, new to Tinseltown, unaware of its ways, could in any way withstand Christian Harlow on a full-scale charm offensive.

He'd been even more insane to have hoped, as he had, that once Belle discovered Christian was in *Galaxia* too, they could somehow pick up where they had left off. Or vice versa; Belle, brought back from the career dead by her Shakespeare stint, was a more enticing prospect for Christian now, after all. But not as enticing as Darcy obviously.

Mitch clenched his fists with frustration. Darcy and Christian together was the worst possible scenario. Complicating it was the fact that his client still had no idea that Belle, the woman who had publicly stolen her boyfriend, was in the film. Mitch had been keeping the news from her in the hope that he would think of a way to break it acceptably. He was aided in this by the standard Jack Saint practice of keeping the cast of his films a mystery until the very last minute. Of course, there were rumours, but Darcy did not appear to have heard any. By the time she did, hopefully, she would be too far committed to *Galaxia* to withdraw when she finally found out.

Mitch moaned and clutched his head. Because this, messy though it was, was not all, of course. Not by a long way. The final piece of unexploded ordnance was the prospect of Belle's reaction on discovering Christian and Darcy together on set. Mitch winced; he could almost hear now the shrieks of both his clients shouting about each other down the phone.

"Well, you've got a shoot tomorrow, in Florence," he managed to grind out to Darcy from between clenched teeth. "Some kinda shoe thing."

At least that would keep her out of Harlow's way for a day, Mitch thought. The delay in principal photography, in Darcy's case, wasn't only irritating, it was downright dangerous. He could imagine Harlow oiling himself up and parading about by the swimming pool, flashing those persuasive teeth at his giggling client. Or Belle, pushing Darcy right in that pool and holding her under, or perhaps the other way round...

He took a big bite of jelly doughnut and swung his chair round to his window. Between the blinds, his eye caught the streetsweeper again, shuffling happily down the sunlit sidewalk. Mitch experienced a new surge of heartfelt envy. Who'd be a Hollywood agent?

Irritated in Italy, Darcy slipped her mobile back into her pocket. What right did Mitch have to spoil her party? If, at the very back of Darcy's mind was the niggling thought that she had given in too soon, slept with someone she hardly knew, and that such behaviour was not to her credit, Darcy forced it away. She deserved some fun, after all that had happened with Niall. She must grasp the moment, gather the rosebuds, enjoy herself. Live a little—or even a lot. She was a big star, after all, as Christian kept saying. Or about to be one.

"Everything okay, doll?" Christian beamed at her, knowing perfectly well that it wasn't. He could well imagine what that fat creep Mitch Masterson had said.

"Fine," Darcy beamed back. Christian looked, Darcy thought, like a young god. She felt a rush of sudden desire, even after all the desire she had just felt and which had been sated, over and over again. He had made love to her in positions she had not realised possible, raised her to heights of pleasure so intense they had almost been pain. As starburst followed starbust behind her eyes, she had become lost in sensation. Time, space, and even identity had melted away.

"Hey!" Christian shouted, taking a hand off the wheel. "Italy really suits you. Your hair looks great against that blue sky."

Delighted, Darcy shook the black mane that was whipping her rather painfully across the face.

"And the dark green of those trees really matches your eyes," Christian yelled, trotting out his second most useful endearment. You just changed the name of the place—Italy, New York, California, wherever. It worked every time, as it had here.

Perhaps too well. You could see in her eyes that she wanted more.

Christian was worn out, however. Darcy might look composed, but she had been a fireball in bed. It wasn't only her breasts that were real. Every other bit was too, and it had all needed attention. Clearly she had been making up for lost time.

"Are we anywhere near?" he called above the wind. He needed to deposit her at this villa, go home, and recover.

Darcy looked confused for a moment, then remembered the instructions. She crouched forward as they hurtled along, looking anxiously about her. The turn off to the villa should be coming up soon. Yes, here it was.

"There!" she pointed frantically, yelling over the scream of the wind. But Christian was still hurtling forward, certain, it seemed, to overshoot it. He flashed her a grin and, with a twist of his biceps, a jerk of the wheel, a mighty screech from the tyres, the car pivoted at full tilt on two wheels and hurtled up a lane along which a wall ran as far as a pair of gateposts. "Villa Rosa," Darcy read. "Here we are," she yelled to Christian, as they shot past.

A mighty pull of the brakes, again a screech of tyres, and then silence. A flood of birdsong entered the space where before there had been only the roar of an engine. Darcy, heart racing and head thumping from where it had just smashed back against the seat as they stopped dead, took a deep, relieved breath. Of course, Christian knew what he was doing. He was in control. But in any other hands, that speed, that turn…well…

The powerful, sweet scent of roses drove out the reek of petrol fumes in her nose. Surprised, Darcy realised it must be coming from the villa garden. How absolutely perfect. The Villa Rosa smelt of roses.

She unbuckled her seat, heaved herself out, and hurried to the black wrought-iron gate. But the beautiful garden, whose scent filled Darcy's nose and which suggested ordered rose-beds, fountains, and manicured lawns, was nowhere to be seen. She looked on horticultural carnage: a cut-up mess of flowers and leaves and a stretch of churned-up grass. Churned-up grass, mud, devastated bushes, and roseheads everywhere.

Darcy turned to Christian who, unrestricted by any seatbelt, had leapt out immediately to follow her. "What on earth do you think has happened? It looks as if someone's landed a helicopter on it."

Christian hardly heard her. He, too, was looking on a bone-chilling sight, albeit not the same one. Standing on the patio was a creature he recognised. And who recognised him, moreover. A tiny brown dog with big pointy ears began to run back and forth agitatedly, emitting as it did so a series of shattering barks. Its protruding black eyes were trained directly on him. The slightest element of doubt was removed by the fact it wore a collar so full of diamonds you could see them glittering from the gate.

"No one would land a helicopter in a rose garden…" mused Darcy.

Oh, no? Christian could think of someone with a dog like that, who was more than capable of landing a helicopter in a rose garden. Belle had never had green fingers. Gold fingers, more like.

"I, um, gotta go," Christian muttered, pushing hastily past her in his way back to the car.

She turned, her eyes wide with alarm. "You're not coming in?"

"Sorry. Gotta go home, look at the script again."

Christian had opened the trunk of the Ferrari and was almost throwing Darcy's few bags—still bearing their British Airways first-class tags—onto the road. He dived back into the driver's seat. There was a burst of thunder as the ignition struck up. "I'll call you," he yelled, reversing with a screech and hurtling down the road. Within a few seconds, he had turned the corner and was gone, leaving only a blue cloud of exhaust fumes hanging over the sunny road.

Darcy, blinking after him, noticed a yapping noise. She looked round to see that a small, brown, big-eared dog with a glittering collar and a loud, irritating yap was racing over the mangled rose garden towards the gate, a murderous expression in its horribly protruding black eyes.

"Sugar! Baby!" A thin woman in a short black dress with long blonde hair, red lipstick, and enormous sunglasses was picking her way in high black heels over the shattered bushes after it. "There, there," she was calling, exclaiming in annoyance as her sharp spike heels sank in the mud. "Come back to Mommy! What's the problem, sweetie…?"

Mommy spoke, Darcy registered, in a babyish voice with an American accent. Suddenly, all her scattered thoughts and senses came rushing together.

She knew this woman. She had seen this hair, these sunglasses before. She might even have seen this dog. Pored over them for hours, in fact. On the front page of several newspapers.

This was Belle Murphy. Belle Murphy. The plastic doll. The woman who had stolen Niall while she had been away in L.A. Who had precipitated a personal and professional crisis.

For a second, Darcy pictured herself either punching Belle in the face or turning on her own, flat, flipflop-shod heel and striding away in a magnificent gesture of contempt and rejection.

A pointless gesture, however, in both cases. Belle's face looked so thin and sharp she might cut herself in the first instance and in the second she had no transport; the main road at the bottom was long, hot, and dusty and, moreover, she had nowhere else to stay. This was the villa which had been booked for her by the film company.

But she had not realised she was sharing it with Belle Murphy; that Belle Murphy was in Galaxia too. Mitch had not mentioned it. On purpose? Darcy wondered darkly now. Particularly after what he had said about Christian, she was beginning to wonder if Mitch really did have her best interests at heart. Perhaps, like Christian, she should change agents annually. "Keeps 'em on their evil, grasping toes," he had laughed.

For a second, Darcy teetered on the edge of abandoning Mitch, the film, Jack Saint, and incipient stardom, and returning to London. Only the knowledge that this inevitably meant abandoning Christian too drew her back. She then reflected that there was nothing to return home for anyway. Largely thanks to the woman in front of her.

Belle had gained the gate by now and retrieved her pet. It was of course annoying and uncomfortable to have to walk this far in heels only ever intended for the few steps between limo and lobby. But Sugar would obviously respond to no one else. And now she had got this far in pursuit of him she would have to answer the gate too.

Of course, strictly speaking, that miserable old bat of a house-keeper was there to perform any menial tasks, but she'd disappeared in a sulk some time ago. OK, Belle admitted to herself, so she'd messed up a few plants, but the garden would grow again, what was the problem? That's what gardens did.

A cross-looking dark-haired girl was staring through the ironwork, right at her. Belle met the hostile look with an equally hostile one of her own and looked her up and down, unimpressed. Ordinary-looking, tall with black hair that lacked a single highlight, and wore a yellow dress of no recognisable designer, unless it was some years-ago Roland Mouret number. She was also very pale and not particularly thin. And that, of course, was the telling detail. Not thin, so not someone important. Very obviously none of the people rumoured to be acting with her in *Galaxia*. Not Cate Blanchett or Nicole Kidman. Definitely not Jack Black, Brad Pitt, George Clooney, Russells Brand or Crowe.

There had been so many rumours about her co-stars, none of which had been confirmed. Mitch had been particularly pathetic on this score, pleading endlessly the iron control Jack Saint exercised over every aspect of his films. "No one really knows. They won't until he wants to tell them."

"But you're a goddam agent, you're supposed to be on the inside track," Belle had stormed. "Is it true that Christian's in *Galaxia*?"

"I really have no idea," Mitch had replied carefully.

"Christ," she exploded. "The only inside you know anything about is the inside of your goddam refrigerator."

❖ ❖ ❖

"Can I help you?" Belle now asked Darcy disdainfully. "Are you a housemaid or something?"

She was taken aback when the other snapped. "I'm not a housemaid, thank you very much. I'm an actress."

English accent, Belle thought. But she wasn't Kiera Knightley, Kate Winslet, or Helen Mirren. And what other English actresses were there?

"My name's Darcy Prince."

Belle recognised there was something expectant about the silence that followed. She fixed a disdainful stare on the girl the other side of the gate. Was she supposed to have heard of her or something?

"If my name doesn't ring a bell," the other said steadily, "then my boyfriend's might. Niall MacDonald?"

Belle stared for a moment, then gave a peal of laughter. "Oh, Niall. I'm so glad to hear he's moved on. I hope you'll be very happy together."

Darcy's mouth dropped open. "You mean...you're not with him anymore?"

"No, sweetie," trilled Belle. "It was never gonna work. We just weren't on the same page."

"Same...page?"

Belle giggled. "You see, it's kind of like this. I'm on the successful page and he's in more of a failures type of scene. That's showbiz, honey."

Sheer surprise had stolen away much of Darcy's outrage. She

frowned at this strange-looking blonde with a body like a thin stick on which two brown balloons were hanging. She tried to think of some shattering rejoinder, but nothing came to mind.

"I've never been crazy about redheads anyway," Belle now remarked with an airy trill. "But, you know, like I say, I'm just so glad to hear he's moved on. I hope you'll be very happy together."

"We're not together," Darcy managed to grind out, furiously. "Thanks to you."

"Me?" Belle blinked.

"You slept with him in London. While I was in L.A.," Darcy hurled at her in a shaking, uncertain voice. "You broke us up."

"I so did not," Belle exclaimed indignantly. "He said he was single."

Anger flashed through Darcy. Of course Niall had said he was single. "I bet," she said heavily, "that he told you his father was a butcher as well."

Belle looked back at her with eyes of a curiously artificial green and shook her white-blonde hair. "Yeah. He did."

"He was lying," Darcy said flatly. "His father owns a chain of meat processing plants."

"Yeah. He told me that too."

"He told you that too? And you didn't mind? That he wasn't telling the truth about the butcher?"

Belle grinned. "Baby, why should I care about the truth? It wasn't the truth I was trying to sleep with." She shrugged her skeletal brown shoulders. "Hey. I did you a favour, honey. What's the point of being with Niall? That guy's going nowhere, baby."

None of the mud she was flinging was sticking. Darcy gave the woman on the other side of the gate a hot, resentful stare. "You don't get it, do you?"

Anger flashed across the thin face of the other. "You don't get it, you mean. You're an actress, did you say? In *Galaxia*?"

"Yes."

"Well, you're at the wrong place, okay? I guess there'll be a hostel in town for all you crowd scene guys. This villa's for those with major roles. I," announced Belle, drawing herself up proudly, "am the Countess of Tyfoo. "

"And I'm the Grand Duchess of the Galaxy," Darcy snapped. "Let me in, will you?"

Chapter Thirty-nine

MARCO, SETTLING SOME DINERS into their courtyard table, looked up at a loud, agitated, female voice. He smiled politely at the girl who passed by with two subdued blond toddlers attached to each of her hands. She wore, it seemed to Marco, high-heeled shoes inadvisable for the scaling of Rocolo's hill, as well as a pair of extremely tight white jeans even less suited to the purpose.

The blonde stared haughtily back at him and continued talking in a loud and honking voice into the mobile phone to which she was attached by earphones. "Nightmare, honestly," she was complaining. "Bloody kids running riot. Just ghastly. Cosmo!" she screeched, as if to underline the point, even though the blond little boy she was addressing didn't seem to Marco to be doing anything particularly offensive. Apart from looking unhappy, that was. Both he and the silver-haired girl, presumably his sister, looked miserable. As well as tired—shouldn't they be in bed at this hour? What were the parents thinking? It was obvious this woman was not their mother.

Marco guessed the tight-trousered blonde was British and a nanny, no doubt to that type of wealthy, pushy British couple that flocked to Tuscany in droves in the summer. Many of them ate in his restaurant. That was the only problem with running a successful restaurant. You attracted successful people who seemed to think that being successful was all about treating other people badly.

Marco took the order from the just-settled table—Daria and the other waitress were busy elsewhere—and was about to go into the kitchen when another group loomed up.

The dominant figure in it was a tall, solid man with red cheeks, thick black hair, and an air of staggering self-satisfaction. He wore the standard-issue middle-class-Brit-male-on-holiday uniform, Marco saw: pale blue shirt, beige chinos, white Panama trimmed with dark band.

The rest of the group comprised a frazzled, skinny, fiftysomething woman in a yellow and cerise clinging scrap of dress, a couple of smug-looking young men with identical big hair and bigger bottoms, and another downbeat man, presumably the frazzled woman's husband. The well-preserved, rather sly-looking brunette was unquestionably the wife of the big dark-haired man.

"Table for seven," he boomed in one of those loud, fruity, bullying English accents Marco knew from experience meant trouble.

"I'm sorry," he said apologetically. "We're completely full tonight." Two, he might have managed. Three at a pinch. But seven? In a restaurant the size of his? Wasn't it obvious that would have to be booked?

The frazzled woman stepped forward. "What do you mean you don't have a table?" she demanded hysterically, clacking her matching pink shoes on the cobbles in agitation. "We have two members of Parliament in our party."

Marco considered them calmly. So what? You got MPs round here all the time. "I'm sorry," he repeated, with another shrug.

The man's eyes, big and black beneath thick shiny brows, widened with annoyance. He was obviously outraged to discover he and his party could not just walk in off the street and sit down. "I want to speak to the owner," he boomed.

Marco sensed a stir at the tables about him at this. Many were filled with regular customers, all waiting for the trump card to be played.

"Actually," Marco said gently, "I am the owner."

The man's red face flushed redder. He stared at Marco in disbelieving fury. "You? But you're taking the orders…"

"Yes." Marco regarded him levelly. He would not trouble to point out to this man that, besides the best food possible, his restaurant was all about treating people fairly, with respect. There were no tantrums in his kitchen. No one was more important than anyone else, only, in some cases, more experienced. Marco sensed this would mean little to a man like this.

"But I'm Her Majesty's Shadow Secretary of State," the big man bleated, clearly unable to believe his large, red-tipped ears.

Secretary of State for shadows? Marco raised his hands in a gesture of helpless defiance. He was determinedly avoiding the amused gaze of the large table nearest to him, which was filled with Rodolfo the painter and his family.

The black eyebrows snapped together. "You say we need to book?"

"That's right. Yes."

"Even if we were God Almighty, presumably."

Marco smiled tightly. "I could possibly make an exception for Him. But He would be the only one."

Hearing Rodolfo chuckle softly at this, Marco flashed him an irritated look. He saw Rodolfo now rise to his feet, his eyes bright with laughter, passing a napkin over his mouth in a gesture of finality.

Marco watched apprehensively. Oh, no. Rodolfo liked to tease, but this was going too far. Surely Rodolfo wasn't going to…

But he was. "Finito!" Rodolfo announced, clattering his espresso cup back into its saucer. The rest of the table was rising in a muddle of chatter, laughter, reaching for bags, and wiping the mouths of toddlers. Turning to Her Majesty's Secretary of State, Rodolfo added. "We have finished. You can have our table."

"Grazie, amico mio," Marco bent and hissed furiously into Rodolfo's ear on the pretext of picking up a napkin that had fallen on to the cobbles.

"Prego," Rodolfo beamed.

The group, in that British way, rushed to sit themselves down in the seats before the vacating party had finished its manoeuvres. It was now that Marco noticed the boy, the last to sit down, at the back of the group and plainly wishing he was anywhere but here. A tall boy with a transportingly beautiful face that he seemed to be trying to hide under his hair. Marco shook his head faintly in wonder. He looked like a saint from a Raphael fresco.

The beautiful boy looked up as he slid into his place. He seemed to slide him a glance of mute apology. Marco gave him a sympathetic smile with more than a hint of conspiracy about it.

❖ ❖ ❖

At the Villa Rosa, a brilliant disk of sun, thin and bright as a beaten penny, was slipping down from a sky entirely saffron yellow. Thin scraps of gold cloud reflected the vanishing furnace. Below, the darkened hills rose and fell like waves. The air was sweet and still and warm.

Upstairs, Emma was checking on Morning. He was asleep. She crossed to the window, where, avoiding looking at the devastated rose garden, she saw, on the patio below, that the table had been set for dinner by Mara.

It looked beautiful and very inviting. The parasol had been dismantled, and the silver of the cutlery gleamed in the rich, but much milder, evening sun. The wine glasses flashed, and the snow-white napkins glowed.

Emma gave a start as, immediately below her, Darcy now appeared. She was frowning over her mobile phone, as if she expected a text from someone. Then the scent of food seemed to hit her; she sniffed the air appreciatively and went immediately to the table, which she proceeded to inspect with relish. From the vantage point of her room, Emma smiled as, first checking to see that no one was looking, Darcy tugged the thick and crispy end off a piece of bread, took the oil phial, and poured some of the bright yellow contents on it. As she chewed, her face assumed an expression of ecstasy.

Darcy had, Emma thought, turned out to be something of a surprise. As she was also an actress, and in the same film as Belle, Emma had expected another tantrum-prone diva, but Darcy seemed good-natured and to have no airs at all. She had cooed over Morning and had been especially polite to Mara. Most endearingly of all, she seemed anything but fond of Belle. Her expression when Belle had airily explained what the helicopter had done to the garden had been one of mixed disgust and horror.

Emma watched Darcy chewing. She had finished the whole of her first piece of bread by now and was launched on the second. The level in the oil phial was dropping drastically. Emma reflected that Darcy had eaten more in the last few minutes than she had ever seen Belle eat the whole time she had known her.

She felt herself warm further to the dark-haired actress. She had a certain distance and dignity—especially with that cut-glass voice—but was the complete opposite of Belle. While Emma readily acknowledged her employer was beautiful, it was a hard, artificial kind of beauty. But there was something altogether lovely about Darcy; she had a pretty, fresh face with what looked like the original features. Her body, compared to Belle's, looked almost normal. She was slim, certainly, much thinner than me, Emma thought. But at the same time, nothing on the emaciated, artificially inflated scale of Belle.

There was a clattering sound now, and Belle herself clacked onto the patio in a very short, figure-hugging dress of some stretchy, black, glittery material. Her white hair streamed over her shoulders, and her red mouth glistened from beneath the black sunglasses.

In her skinny brown arms, Sugar looked about him with his habitual ill-natured stare. In the candlelight, the diamonds on his collar flashed brilliantly, almost rivalling those on Belle's fingers and wrists.

She had, Emma thought, made a considerable effort for dinner at home with the nanny.

Or perhaps she wanted to outshine Darcy, a competition Darcy, simply dressed in jeans, a white shirt, and black glittery flip-flops, seemed uninterested in taking part in.

Emma began to back away from the window. It was time she went down herself now. Dinner was evidently about to start.

There came the sharp clacking sound of spike heels on ancient stone as Belle went to the table and sloshed some wine into a glass. "Hey," she exclaimed. "She's set the table for dinner."

"Yes!" Darcy agreed delightedly. "Isn't that great?"

Belle swirled her hair. "No, it isn't. Who asked her to do that? I've asked the driver to come at eight. I wanna check out the local scene, see what's going down…"

"Er…" Darcy began.

Just at this minute, Mara appeared with a large plate of what looked like sliced meat. Sugar, in Belle's arms, immediately started to strain and snap.

"Oooh!" Darcy exclaimed. "That looks amazing, Mara!"

Mara smiled. "Is antipasto. Local specialities," she said proudly. "Salamis, proscuitto, air-dried ham, sliced smoked sausage, and chorizo."

Using one of the forks on the side of the plate, Darcy, eyes sparkling, peeled off a dark red layer of ham.

"No, thanks," Belle snapped as Mara offered her the plate. "I never eat anything with a face." Sugar, who most definitely did, snapped at a row of salami at the edge. Mara tugged the plate away in disgust. "You are vegetarian?" she asked Belle. "Okay, fine. I bring some grilled vegetables."

Belle eyed the housekeeper. "Like I said," she retorted rudely as Sugar dragged off a pile of ham. "I don't eat anything with a face."

"Vegetables don't have faces," Darcy remarked.

"Sure they do," Belle snapped. "Have you ever looked really closely—I mean really closely—at an onion?"

Mara's lips had tightened angrily. "I go get secundo piatti," she muttered, stomping off with the dog-licked antipasto, which she now held at arm's length.

"Don't bother!" Belle shouted rudely after her. "We're going out."

Mara, who had turned at the villa entrance, looked stony. Darcy, indigant at being roped into whatever Belle was planning, was about to assure her that she wasn't going anywhere and that secundo piatti would be most welcome, when there came the loud bleep of a text message being delivered. Darcy whipped out her phone and flicked it open.

From above, Emma saw, instantly, her entire demeanour change.

"I'm terribly sorry," she gasped apologetically to Mara. "But actually, I have to go out myself. Can't the main course keep?" she added pleadingly.

"Or feed it to my nanny," Belle suggested in a sneering tone. "She needs to keep her weight up." As the listening Emma gasped with fury, Belle grabbed Darcy's arm. "Let's go."

❖ ❖ ❖

At the table occupied by the seven Britons at the Italian restaurant, a discussion about corporal punishment was in, as it were, full swing.

"I don't believe in hanging," Hugh declared.

"I don't believe in hanging either," Richard agreed.

"Quite right," Hugh said heartily. "Hanging's too good for them. Bring back the drawing and quartering, that's what I say." He dug his fork into his spaghetti with relish.

The twins Ivo and Jago, meanwhile, were trying to prise from Orlando what he intended to do during the ritual year off before university. "If, that is, you're actually going to university, Orlando," Ivo taunted.

"He is," confirmed Georgie grimly from where she picked over lobster linguine at the end of the table.

Orlando drained his bottle of Italian lager crossly. Did he have no say in the matter? Were his opinions irrelevant? Actually, he wanted to go on a gap year even less than he wanted to go to university. He had no desire to save pygmy elephants in Borneo or teach English to villagers on the slopes of Kilimanjaro. He didn't want to do film-making in Paris or surf skills in South Africa.

What he really wanted to do was get a job, any job, and actually have some money of his own. Like that nanny, Emma, he had met in the airport.

He wished he had her mobile phone number. She kept slipping into his head, and whenever she did, he had a sensation like a fresh breeze on a close and humid day. He remembered her unaffected smile, her scrubbed and shining cleanliness, her keen and searching gaze, her air of independence and of being absolutely frank. It would, he thought, be good to see her again. More than good.

"You'd never last a gap year anyway," Ivo was scoffing as pudding arrived on the table.

"Better bugger off and do Surf Science at Mousehole University or something," mocked Jago, tucking into a large portion of tiramisu.

Orlando stared with loathing at his persecutors, with their stupid stiff Eurotrash clothes and Raybans stuck on the top of their ridiculous big hair. Who did they think they were? Hugh bloody Grant?

He resented the fact he had never worked in his life. Especially as the time he'd meant to spend studying he'd actually used to watch television.

Seeing Orlando's miserable face, Richard was about to come to his son's defence when he realised his leg was trembling in a disconcerting manner. It took some time to work out that, unexpectedly, he was receiving a call on his mobile phone.

He cleared his throat. "Excuse me," he said softly as he stood up. "I seem to be required by one of my constituents."

"Good man!" roared Hugh from the other end of the table, unsteadily holding aloft at least half a bottle of Chianti in an extremely large glass.

"I know what Orlando should do in his year off." It was Laura who had spoken, lounging at the other end of the table from Georgie, eyes glittering in the candles that had now been lit, one hand playing with her long black-red hair which, combined with her white face, reminded Orlando of evil queens in Disney films.

"What?" asked Georgie eagerly, while Orlando met Laura's teasing gaze apprehensively from under his brows. He had no idea what was coming but had every idea that he wasn't going to like it.

"Ensnaring," Laura said, in tones of nasal triumph, "some plain and dumpy heiress with his looks.'"

Everyone turned to look at Laura.

"Why not? He's marvellous breeding stock," Laura drawled, looking Orlando up and down in a way that made him blush and burn.

Hugh, who prided himself on intimate acquaintanceship with the ways of the gentry, now joined in. "Absolutely," he boomed, his sharp, wet teeth flashing in the candlelight. "A thoroughbred stallion that any landowning family with a suitable mare would be thrilled to get into stud. Eh, Orlando?"

Orlando pressed back into his chair and stared stonily at the table, but his heart hammered beneath, his guts twisting with embarrassment that he had been spoken about, in public, in such sexual terms. Beneath the hair he tried to shake protectively over his face, his cheeks burned. He looked helplessly at his father. But Richard, pacing the table-crammed courtyard with his mobile pressed to his ear, clearly had other matters on his mind.

❖❖❖

"Mr. Fitzmaurice! Theodora Greatorex here."

"Mrs. Greatorex. What can I do for you?" Richard forced a pleasant tone into his voice. If one of his constituents chose to call him on holiday, then so be it. Representation of the people was a noble calling—or so he persisted in trying to believe, despite the contradicting presence of Hugh Faugh.

"Have you any idea what, ahem," Mrs. Greatorex, in Wellover, took a deep, dramatic breath, "doggering is?"

Richard started so fiercely he almost fell over. "Doggering?"

"You don't mean," Richard hissed, bending slightly and heading instinctively for the shadows cast by the houses, "dogging, do you, Mrs. Greatorex? The practice of, ahem, how exactly shall I put this…"

"Casual sex with strangers in the open air? I most certainly do, Mr. Fitzmaurice," thundered his interlocutor from her converted chantry in Gloucestershire as Richard, hundreds of miles away in Italy, reeled across the village street. "We all do in Wellover, let me assure you. Every Friday night, without fail."

Richard's jaw fell slackly open. Was he hearing properly? Had the heat done something to his head? Wellover? Mrs. Greatorex?

It could not be possible. Dogging was something footballers did in pub carparks in Essex. Wellover was as far from such a scenario as could be imagined. It was the archetypal English village. Its doorways rioted with roses; its gardens nodded with gladioli; its windows were mullioned; and its inn, a muzak-free zone, was full of polished brass and quiet bonhomie. Its church was well attended and adhered to the King James Version; its village green was clean and kempt; its inhabitants, all white and mostly fifty-plus, subscribed to the *Telegraph* en masse and had stockbrokers.

Wellover was in the *Domesday Book* and regularly and effortlessly saw off all comers in Best-Kept Village Competitions. Period dramas were regularly filmed there. Keira Knightley had been in the village shop and Colin Firth in the post office. The only dogging

Richard had ever associated with Wellover were ladies in tweed briskly striding the local leafy lanes in the company of brushed and glossy spaniels.

"I didn't realise," he said faintly, wondering nonetheless why he was being selected for this extraordinary confession. Was Mrs. Greatorex suggesting he joined them? He waited for her to speak again. He had to be sure of what was being discussed here, whether the practice was being condoned or condemned. Fools not only rushed in where angels feared to tread but also ran the risk of losing their seats.

Mrs. Greatorex spoke. "It appears," she said in stately tones, "it appears…"—the stately tones shook a little—"it seems…" she added, with an audible sniff, "that Wellover, our beautiful Wellover, is…"—there was a shuddering sound as Mrs. Greatorex seemed to fight for self-control—"the dogging capital of Europe!"

"Oh dear," said Richard, staring hard at the tarmac.

"Russell's Leap—you know Russell's Leap, of course…"

Richard confirmed that he did. The landmark referred to was a well-known beauty spot in the woods not far from Wellover.

"Well, it's there they go. Every Friday night." Mrs. Greatorex's voice was shaking again.

It was the "they" that clinched it. Mrs. Greatorex was ringing to complain then. Richard felt oddly relieved. The thought of the Parish Council Chair bent backwards over a car bonnet, tweed culottes round her ankles, had been a disturbing one.

"And what I'm ringing to ask, Mr. Fitzmaurice, is…"

"Yes?" Richard whispered shakily.

"…what exactly you're going to do about it."

Chapter Forty

"WHADDYA MEAN WE GOTTA walk?" Belle screeched as the car drew up in the carpark at the foot of the village.

"It's a historic site," Darcy explained agitatedly, anxious to get Belle out of the car as soon as possible. Her heart was pumping double-speed; her very nerve-ends were tingling at the thought of seeing Christian.

Of course, it would have been better if he had texted earlier to suggest they met in Rocolo. Then she could have given poor Mara more notice. But when, finally, Christian's call had come, it had been unignorable. And Darcy's main regret, as they bowled along in the limo, was that she had not had more time to prepare herself. Jeans, T-shirt, and no make-up didn't seem much of an ensemble. But none of this would matter to Christian. He was always telling her she was the most beautiful woman he had ever seen.

"I don't do walking," Belle snarled as the driver opened the rear door.

Hardly surprising, in those. Darcy glanced at Belle's shoes. Seven inches and counting, and with soles that looked as thin as ballet slippers. She would feel every cigarette butt on Rocolo's cobbled main street.

Nine o'clock at Marco's, Christian had said. Darcy stole a glance at the heavily jewelled timepiece on the thin arm clutching the dog. Five minutes to. Darcy's heart skipped. Get Belle up the hill in those shoes in five minutes?

At the restaurant, Richard had returned to the table. "Sorry," he muttered in his wife's ear. "Can you excuse me again just a sec? I've just got to make a phone call. It's rather important…"

Excitement flashed across Georgie's face. "Ooh. *The Leader*, is it?"

Richard shook his head. Georgie, for some reason, persisted in believing he was only ever one phone call away from the promotion of a lifetime. He had long since stopped trying to persuade her otherwise. In fact, he had to speak to Guy, his constituency agent; the man on the spot in Wellover. Find out what the real story was

As Richard punched out his constituency agent's number, he felt something of his old campaigning spirit stir. But Guy, with whom he planned to campaign, did not answer.

As Richard dejectedly returned to the table, he noticed that everyone in the restaurant seemed to be looking at something. Some were even holding up their mobile phones to take pictures. There was nudging and gasping and exclamations. The subject of all the excitement seemed to be a blonde woman in huge sunglasses, a very tiny dress, and huge heels, who was holding a small and ridiculous dog. "Who is it?" Richard asked Georgie blankly.

"Belle Murphy!" Georgie gasped. "The film star. We saw her at the airport, remember."

It was like a bad dream, Darcy thought. First, there had been the ascent of the hill. She'd actually had to push Belle up the steeper bits.

As, finally, they arrived at Marco's, the bells chimed the quarter hour. Quarter past! Fifteen minutes late! The panic this plunged Darcy into was deepened when she looked searchingly round the crowded tables full of moving, eating, laughing, talking faces. But nowhere among them was the face she longed to see. Christian had not yet arrived. Or, worse, he had arrived and, seeing she was not there, had left again.

As it happened, Christian had not yet arrived. He had got lost in the darkening lanes in the Ferrari. The ancient peasant he had asked for directions—almost giving the old guy a heart attack as he roared unexpectedly up beside him in the sports car—had for some dumb reason given him the wrong ones.

It was nine fifteen by the time he nosed the gleaming red roadster into the carpark at the foot of the village. He was late. Christian, however, had no fear that Darcy would not be there when he got to the restaurant. Of course she would be. Women always waited for Christian Harlow.

He locked the car from the inside and swung himself out of the open top in one fluid, athletic movement.

He pushed a hand through his oiled black hair, quiffed up for the evening. Cramped from the car seat, he shook his muscled thighs in their white linen trousers and shrugged his gym-honed arms in the black leather waistcoat.

The waistcoat was all he wore on his oiled torso apart from a hip-hop thick layer of silver crosses, diamond initials, shark's teeth on leather thongs, and gold medallions. Most of them had been given by women over the years: the shark's tooth by his first conquest and the diamond initial by his most recent. Belle had provided one of the silver crosses. Christian thought of them as his trophies. His war medals, gained on the campaign route to stardom.

He walked away from the powerful vehicle, pinging in the heat of its recent exertions, deliberately not looking back at it as he strode with unhurried confidence through the carpark.

❖❖❖

Belle was milking every minute. She preened and posed, tossing her hair about, soaking up the attention. Darcy could hardly believe how excited people seemed to be about seeing her, not least because after just one minute of her company, it was hard to imagine why anyone could possibly admire her. Having been at close quarters with her for some hours now, and finding her anything but impressive, Darcy had almost forgotten Belle was famous.

It was with relief that Darcy saw Marco the chef now appear from his kitchen. She could ask him if he had seen the actor; hopefully, he would remember Christian from earlier.

This possibility was scotched by Sugar's immediately exploding into barks. The dog was straining in Belle's arms, trying to snap at Marco. The chef backed away, annoyed.

"You've upset him," Belle accused. "Upset my little baby-waby!"

"I'm very sorry to hear that," rejoined Marco pleasantly.

Behind Belle, Darcy tried to catch his eye.

"We need a table for three," Belle barked.

Marco suppressed a sigh. Did he have a table for three? No, he did not. Did this shouty, American, plastic-looking woman not realise that booking was essential on busy nights like this?

"I'm sorry, signora," he started to say, intending to include her companion in the apology. He glanced at the dark-haired, white-shirted woman who seemed to be with the blonde, albeit some distance behind her.

Her. His nerves jangled; his palms moistened; his breath felt suddenly constricted. It was...her.

She looked less coiffed than before, more casual in her jeans, and her black hair was damp and twisted as if she had just jumped out of the bath. The bath. Her in it. Marco paused, fleetingly, at the thought.

"Whaddya mean, you're sorry?" Belle blustered. "You've got no tables? Don't you know who I am?"

She was looking at him so intensely, the beautiful girl with dark hair. Marco felt suddenly light and unanchored and giddy. He looked wildly around. There had to be a space somewhere. If not, he would make one. Out of thin air, with his bare hands...

As it happened, a table for two had just become free. And Daria, wonderful Daria, with her usual efficiency, was already clearing it.

"Should think so too," Belle huffed over her shoulder to Darcy. Darcy ignored her. She was concentrating on asking Marco about Christian at the first opportunity. "Have you seen my friend?" she murmured to Marco as he pulled over a third chair. "My friend from lunchtime," she added, in a voice too low for Belle to hear.

So that was the third guest, Marco thought. He wouldn't have bothered had he known. The muscle-bound swaggerer. The one who had asked for ketchup with his spaghetti. What did this woman—who obviously so appreciated food—see in such a bonehead?

"He likes his steak rare," the blonde interrupted. "And he'll have foie gras to start with. Okay?"

Marco almost lost his footing on an awkwardly placed cobble, as it dawned on him that the dog, not the bonehead—or, at least, a different type of bonehead—was intended as the third diner at the table.

"I'm sorry." He collected himself swiftly. "Animals are not allowed in the restaurant."

"Not allowed?" Belle turned on him in shrill fury. "You're saying that my dog—my dog—is not allowed? I'm a VIP, okay?"

Marco felt, behind and around him, the ringing silence from the rest of the diners, all of whom were following the drama with bated breath. Even the ones eating inside, in the brick-vaulted room, had crowded out round the entrance, below the vine with its fairy lights.

"Animals are not allowed to eat at table," Marco maintained doggedly.

Belle drew herself up to her full height, which was impressive, given the extra seven inches. Her back was arched, and it seemed to Darcy that her very breasts were bristling. "Sugar," Belle said icily, "is not an animal."

Marco looked at the skinny scrap of brown fur in her arms. "That isn't an animal?" It looked like a dog to him. A nasty sort of dog too.

Belle shoved her sunglasses close to Marco's face and hissed. "Sugar isn't an animal; he's a VVID. A Very, Very Important Dog." The creature in her arms gave a rolling, affirmative growl.

Beetroot-faced behind her co-star, Darcy wished the cobbles would open up beneath her. Poor Marco. The only upside to this toe-curling scene was that Christian, at least, was not present to witness it.

Did Darcy but know it, this was not the case. Christian was, at that very moment, climbing the steep village street, fists thrust in his white linen pockets, returning with interest the admiring glances the promenading female youth of Rocolo were bestowing on him. But as he approached the lights and bustle signalling the restaurant, some instinct within urged him to slow down. Softly, quietly, stealthily, Christian approached the outer ring of spectators and inserted himself into the crowd.

The centre of the attention was a blonde in jet-black sunglasses and a very short black dress, with white-blonde hair spilling over her shoulders. Good legs, Christian thought. And her tits were impressive, if so obviously fake you could park a Harley between them. She was holding a small, nasty-looking brown dog whose diamond collar picked up the candlelight and threw it back with ten times the force.

That dog. He'd seen that dog before, Christian thought. Most recently, a mere few hours ago. It was Belle's dog, Sugar. Which must mean...

He looked at the blonde again. That...was Belle? It couldn't be. She looked so different. So confident, so polished, so utterly unlike the crushed wreck who had begged him not to leave her back in L.A., whose career was as broken as her spirit. That woman, Christian saw, had disappeared completely. The Belle he now saw before him, buoyed up by her new starring role in a big film and her success in Shakespeare in London, was a total glamazon. She stood proud and tall—very tall in those heels—radiating attitude.

She was gesticulating, shaking her hair about, in the apparent middle of an argument with that great, shambling loser of a restaurant owner who'd given him all those snooty looks earlier in the day. Well, go, girl, Christian found himself thinking. He liked that red lipstick. He liked the way everyone in the restaurant was staring. Belle was the centre of attention, and he liked that in a woman.

Christian's scrutiny travelled approvingly again over her erect breasts—more erect than he remembered them, tiny hips, and long brown legs. He felt a stir of lust in his white linen trousers.

Christian was about to step forward to attract her attention when he spotted, in the shadows behind his former girlfriend, the woman he was auditioning for the role of the present one. Darcy Prince. Actually, Christian thought, his eyes behind his wraparounds sweeping critically over the creased, white shirt and battered jeans, Darcy wasn't looking so great tonight. Her hair was a mess; she looked as if she'd just got out of the bath. She wasn't even wearing shades, for Chrissakes; no Hollywood stars went out without them, especially if they weren't wearing make-up.

He returned his gaze to Belle. She was looking good; there was no doubt about it. So good that Christian was starting to wonder if he'd thrown her over too soon. Now that she was going to be a big star again, it was beginning to look like a mistake.

But what could he do about it? What passed for his brain wrestled with the problem. If he stepped out now, he ran the risk of being claimed by Darcy, which would ruin his chances with Belle. Belle might even be mad at him. She was pretty pissed at him when he'd left her, and that hadn't been so long ago.

Either way, it was now clear to Christian, making himself known to these two actresses was a high-risk strategy. Too bad if Darcy was expecting him, and he could tell she was from the way she stared around from time to time, a desperate expression in her eyes. He'd have to go away and think about this. After all, he'd be seeing them both on set in the next couple of days, when principal photography started. Which might have its tricky moments. He needed a strategy, Christian realised.

Stepping softly out of the crowd in the courtyard, he gained the street and melted swiftly away, a flash of diamond and white linen in the shadows.

Meanwhile, in the restaurant, the dog drama had reached doglock.

"Sugar is a Very Important Dog," his owner was insisting.

Marco's eyes held Belle's—or the area where he imagined Belle's were. It was difficult to tell behind the sunglasses. "Having a dog eat at your table in your home is your business, signora. But a restaurant is a public place."

"Okay." Belle tossed her hair impatiently. "I'm willing to compromise with you."

"Signora?"

"It's a public place, right? So get rid of the public. Empty the restaurant. We'll eat on our own."

Chapter Forty-one

His guide book had been spot on about this place, Ken thought. Rocolo was a peach, no question. Crumbling houses, narrow passages, an ancient church, and a tiny main square at the top with funny little shops full of ham and cheese and suchlike. Straight out of Italian village central casting it was.

Not much space in his room, but he was pleased with it nonetheless. Above a bar right at the very top of the village and behind the barn-like church in the square. Took five flights of stairs to get to it, but worth the effort: white walled, simply furnished with the bathroom in the room, behind a little wall. Loo, shower, and basin, but what else did you need? At the other end of the room, the other side of the slightly saggy but otherwise perfectly comfortable double bed, were a pair of French windows. They afforded a spectacular view of the village below, the roofs spinning out below him, the ridged dips in the tiles making it look like a flamenco skirt made of terra-cotta instead of frills.

Directly below his balcony was the children's playground by the church. It had been a bit noisy when Ken arrived. It was teatime, and the kiddies had been having their last runabout. Probably some people might have objected; their Italian village idyll ruined by screaming brats and all that, but Ken didn't mind it at all. Who could possibly mind the sound of children playing? He liked kiddies. Had always imagined at some stage that he'd have a few of the little blighters himself. Hadn't happened though, but that was another story.

Dinnertime, Ken told himself, patting his stomach. There'd been a restaurant he'd spotted on the winding hill up through the village: nice little place on a corner, set on a courtyard with white parasols. It had been crowded even then, but hopefully they'd have room for one.

Ken proceeded in leisurely fashion down the winding main street towards where he remembered seeing the restaurant. The contrast with what he would have routinely been doing in London—what Keith was no doubt doing that minute—struck him forcefully. Sitting on the wall opposite the Portchester, most likely, waiting for some self-regarding celebrity to emerge. But now, here, without the long lenses permanently slung round his neck, Ken felt lighter in more ways than one.

His practised eye had not shut down however, and Ken found a certain pleasure in spotting all the shots that, normally, it would have been second nature to take and sell to the photo libraries. There were subjects aplenty. At the turn of every street, and particularly the winding main street that twisted up like a snake from the bottom of Rocolo to the top, there was something picturesque: a faded icon in a niche; an ornate fountain; an ancient, sunny windowsill ablaze with geraniums; the dark glint of red wine bottles in the depths of a cool shop; a child large-eyed under a mop of dark curls.

And the smells! Winding with the warmth and aftershave in the evening air was the scent of a hundred individual cooking dinners from the houses he was passing; the sharp spike of garlic, the mouth-watering surge of tomato, the dry burst of herbs, the nose-nipping rush of onion. He was starving now, Ken realised. And for proper food. After all those years of crisps and nasty coffee, ready meals and dodgy takeaways, he longed with his soul as much as his stomach for something real to eat.

He had been right to come here, Ken felt, spotting gratefully, as the road bent round, the lights of the restaurant on the next corner.

For a refugee like him, a casualty from the front line of a world obsessed with fame, what better place than somewhere so old, so peaceful, a place that must have seen it all in its time and that cared nothing for the vicissitudes of stardom—was barely aware of them, in fact.

The church clock chimed, a thin, foreign sound most unlike the more full-throated bells of home. London seemed so far away. Lurking for hours outside hotels waiting for celebrities seemed even further.

"Scuse me," Ken exclaimed, skipping deftly aside to avoid banging into someone.

"Hey, watch it, willya?" snapped the other in an American accent, irritably shaking a shiny black shoe that Ken had not been entirely able to avoid all contact with.

"Sorry." Ken repeated his apology to the disdainful youth, who was, he noted, flashily dressed in wraparound shades and with a great many necklaces draped about him. He had jet-black hair, wore nothing but a waistcoat on his top half, was muscularly built, and rather reminded him, Ken thought, of an actor called Christian Harlow.

The reminder was not pleasant. Harlow's dogged and seemingly unstoppable ascent up the Hollywood greasy pole had been greeted with dismay by every paparazzo Ken knew, all of whom loathed the actor to his fingertips. Even in a world where paps were in general immune to the diva strops thrown by stars, where egos were rampant and brattish behaviour expected and even encouraged, Harlow had distinguished himself.

Ken paused and turned as the Harlow look-a-like continued on his way downhill, his muscular legs in their white linen trousers flashing in and out. The engine of recognition that had started up within him was urging him to look again. The Rolodex in his mind whirred. Ken had not spent years as a successful paparazzo for nothing. Hardwired into his memory were millions of images of well-known people.

He knew most famous faces so well that he could identify a celebrity from the tiniest of clues: a pair of lips, a nose, a way of walking even. And all these clues, as he stared after the man in white trousers, were telling him that this, incredible that it seemed, wasn't just someone who looked like Christian Harlow. It actually was Christian Harlow.

Ken felt that all the magic had been drained from the evening. With a heavy heart, he continued toward the restaurant.

His spirits rallied a little as he neared Marco's, however. It was a nice little place, bright, optimistic, and stylish with all those little tables set out on the courtyard, all those candles and those fairy lights twinkling in the vine behind. It was obviously very popular. Every table was crammed with people laughing and talking; it seemed very vivacious. Excited, almost. And the food looked and smelt just the ticket, Ken thought, watching strands of spaghetti winding round forks and remembering how hungry he was.

Just as he was about to step into the courtyard, someone knocked him out of their way. "Don't they know who I freaking well am?" a woman, apparently exiting, was complaining in an American accent to her companion.

Ken froze. His Rolodex whirred again, but for a split second only. There was no doubting the identity of the sunglassed blonde hobbling out of the restaurant in shoes so high they were, strictly speaking, stilts. Just as there was no doubting the identity of that nasty-looking dog she clutched in her skinny arms. Belle Murphy.

❖ ❖ ❖

"Did you hear that? She told him to empty the restaurant!" Georgie gasped to Richard.

Richard nodded distractedly. His mobile phone was ringing again. Please God, not Mrs. Greatorex again. He still hadn't got hold of his man on the ground. Except that Richard now saw that the number on his display panel was that of Guy, after all.

He got up from his chair and hurried hastily out to the relative privacy of the street.

"Guy! At last!"

"Oh. Richard. Hello," came Guy's light and vaguely sardonic tone. "To what do I owe this pleasure? I thought you were on holiday."

"Yes, I am. But I've been called."

"Called? By"—Guy took a deep breath—"the Leader?"

"By Mrs. Greatorex."

"Oh." Guy sounded disappointed.

"About the, um, dogging in Wellover. Is it really happening like she says?"

Guy snorted. "They're calling it Legover now, apparently." He snorted again.

Richard felt Guy's attitude lacked something. But then again, Guy's attitude always had. He affected a lofty, patrician amusement with the world and its doings that sat oddly on a supposed servant of democracy.

"Well, it's a bit shocking, isn't it?" Richard demanded. "Mrs. Greatorex says Russell's Leap is heaving with people at it every Friday night."

"So I hear," Guy confirmed with a snigger.

"Well, shouldn't we be doing something about it? It sounds one hell of a mess, Guy." Richard assumed his best Battle of Britain tones.

Guy sniffed. "Yes, well, now it's all out in the open, as it were, they rather seem to expect us to sort it out at the double. Bend over backwards as it were, ha, ha."

"Ha, ha," said Richard mirthlessly. "But has anything been done? Have the police been informed, even?"

"Yes, but from what I can gather, some of them are worse than the punters."

"You don't sound very worried," Richard remarked heatedly. "This beautiful village is being defaced."

"From *Domesday Book* to dogging websites, you mean?" Guy chuckled.

No wonder, Richard thought, Guy had never made it as a candidate and was reduced to running the constituency office. "There are all these confused old people—outraged, disgusted, and possibly even frightened by these lewd acts being committed on their own doorsteps." Richard's voice rose as his conviction mounted. "They're our constituents, Guy. They're turning to us for help. They need our protection…"

He was interrupted by a guffaw from the agent. "Need our protection? Mrs. Greatorex? Come off it, Richard. She could tear a burglar's head off with her bare hands."

"But she sounded very disturbed, Guy," Richard protested.

"All that's scaring Greatorex is that the value of her house will be affected. She wants us to protect the price of her property. That's the only reason any of them care."

Richard felt rather punctured. "But…"

"Believe me. Morality's got nothing to do with it."

Richard subsided. He suspected, miserably, that Guy was right. He had worked himself up into a righteous and defensive lather only to be told he was being used as an adjunct to the local estate agent. Was this all democracy now meant?

"We have to do something about it, nonetheless," he maintained stoutly. "Though God knows what I can do from here."

"Well, you need evidence of what's going on, for a start," Guy advised, his manner switching, to Richard's relief, from the satirical to the more-or-less sensible.

"Yes. Yes. But how?" Richard asked sharply. "I'm not breaking off my holiday to go sneaking through the woods to watch…well… whatever there is to watch."

"Not necessary, old chap. You just need to look at the websites."

"There isn't a computer here."

"Well, are you near any big towns?"

"Florence."

"Bob's your uncle then," Guy said comfortably. "An Internet café's what you need. I'll give you the website addresses. On second thoughts, ring me up when you're sitting in front of a screen. You're hopeless on the Internet and finding these dogging websites can be complicated. Knowing you, you'd end up sitting in front of the Kennel Club site all afternoon."

Chapter Forty-two

"Brooke Reed on the line for you," whispered Xanthe.

Sam snatched up the receiver eagerly. Brooke was no doubt calling to congratulate her on the Rumtopf shoot.

"Brooke! Hi, great to…"

"That Rumtopf shoot with Darcy Prince?" The NBS PA cut in. "I've just been sent the images on JPEG."

"Great, wasn't it?" Sam purred complacently.

"No," said Brooke uncompromisingly, cutting straight to the chase as usual. "I'll be straight with you, Samantha."

At the other end, Sam twisted her fleshy, beige-painted lips in disapproval. If there was one thing she disliked more than being called Samantha, it was people being straight with her. It always meant that they were about to say something unpleasant. She knew this because she herself was often straight with people.

"Well, what's wrong with it?" she blustered. "Getting Rumtopf was a serious coup. He was booked up until 2012…"

"Yeah, yeah, yeah," Brooke interrupted. "Thing is, she looks fat. She's bursting out all over. This is not the image we wanted."

Rattled by Brooke's lack of appreciation, Sam fought to retain her self-control. She'd got Rumtopf for the studio, for Pete's sake. And the pictures had been fine. Darcy had looked a little rounded in some of them, but so what?

"Darcy's a woman," she pointed out. "She's got a few curves, but so what? Curves are where it's at, you know," she added, gaining confidence as the hit on a theme. "You know, after Size Zero and all that trouble about being too skinny…"

"Screw that," Brooke thundered. "Darcy's a long way off being even slightly skinny, let alone too skinny. She's seriously huge. Belle Murphy's in this picture, remember. She's a zero. Next to her, Darcy's gonna look like Nellie the goddamn elephant."

"Now just hang on. Just wait a minute…"

"We can't have a fat star in this picture. You gotta do something."

"Like what?" Sam snapped. "Go and trim some flesh off her or something?"

"Whatever. She's your client."

"She's Mitch Masterson's client too," Sam sulked. Why did she have to sort everything out?

"He does acting. You do looks. Just do something. Now. Or Jack's gonna start principal photography without her."

Sam put down the phone with a hand so shaking that it rattled all her bracelets. Then she raised her beringed fingers to her throbbing temples and thought hard. Darcy, she knew, was scheduled for another magazine shoot tomorrow, in Florence, with Carlos Cojones. It should have been the triumphant second salvo in the campaign; the publicity that conclusively launched the actress as the hottest and most beautiful new star around.

She needed to be at it, Sam realised. If she was there herself—supervising, suggesting, styling, whatever Carlos said, she might be able to prevent complete disaster. Because it wasn't only Darcy's career on the line here. If this next shoot went wrong, Sam knew, Brooke was unlikely to be picking up the telephone to her again.

She pressed the intercom to Xanthe. "Get me on the next flight to Florence."

Chapter Forty-three

EMMA LOOKED OUT OF the bus window and felt a surge of optimism. It was a beautiful, bright, blue, and gold day. The vehicle, with its throaty roar of engine, moved briskly along the near-empty roads through the sunny countryside. The brown hills with their thin, green stripes of vineyard looked, Emma thought, exactly like neatly combed green hair.

She was going to Florence in search of a travel cot. Or rather, she and Morning both were. Mara, at the last minute, had been unable to babysit after all, and Emma did her best to disguise her disappointment at losing a morning's solo shopping. It wasn't as if she had any money anyway.

They were passing the Rocolo carpark now. Emma looked up, enjoying the fantastical sight of the old village hanging on the top of the hill, shining bright in the morning sun. The buildings crowded together, no shape the same, all shades from terra-cotta to apricot, and bristled with towers, gables, aerials, and satellite dishes.

In the carpark below, some children were being unloaded from a car. The boy, only visible from the back, was Cosmo's age, while the little girl had white hair. Just like Hero.

Emma's happy mood disintegrated instantly. A sick, anxious feeling possessed her, and she wondered miserably, as she often did in tired or weak moments, where the children were now, what they were doing, whether they were happy, whether they ever thought of her.

Her anxiety was followed by the usual burning sense of injustice. Who had put those drugs in her bag? And why? Would she ever find out? It seemed increasingly unlikely.

Amazingly, within half an hour of her arrival, a travel cot was hers. Florence, Emma gratefully realised, might look all towers and flags and winding cobbled streets between canyons of ancient brown buildings, but it was no slouch when it came to twenty-first-century tourism and the needs of twenty-first-century tourists like Morning.

Two minutes after entering the tourist information office, she was outside again clutching a map on which a helpful and extremely efficient Italian tourist official had ringed not one possible cot shop but three. Ten minutes after that, she had ordered a cot and arranged for it to be delivered to the villa; that very afternoon, the salesman had promised. "Bello bambino!" he had added, tickling Morning's cheek. "You sleep well now, you hear?"

And now, Emma decided, for some fun. She had checked the bus return times. She and Morning had, she calculated, an hour free to explore the ancient city.

"Where first?" she beamed at him. "You choose."

❖ ❖ ❖

Orlando slid a sidelong glance at his father, who was driving along towards Florence, his forehead creased in thought. Richard was never exactly chatty, Orlando reflected, but the only thing he had said on this trip so far was to ask him whether he knew what an Internet café was. It seemed a strange question.

Orlando rubbed his eyes, heavy after a sleepless night of worry. It was hot by the window with the morning sun pouring through, but the only burning Orlando was aware of was the shame that would not go away.

He pushed his long fingers through his corn-coloured locks, squeezing his eyelids to try to excise the memory. But the inside of his own head, Orlando was finding, was not somewhere he could escape from easily.

He was in shock. He had no idea she had thought of him that way. Laura was a friend of his parents', for God's sake. The wife of a Tory Member of Parliament. And unbelievably ancient—over forty at least.

The irony was, he had been relieved when the restaurant visit was over, imagining it to be the end of the day's trials. When they got back to the villa, he'd made himself scarce at the first opportunity.

It had been dark when he opened the door of his room. But when he had felt for the light switch and pressed it, nothing had happened. Orlando had shuffled forward, trying to see in the darkness. But this wasn't London, with its permanently orange-tinged gloom; it was the middle of the Italian countryside, and, therefore, as black as ink.

Then, to his surprise, the lamp by his bed was switched on. To reveal, lying on the bed, his parents' friend, Laura Faugh.

"Oh. Sorry," Orlando had muttered, turning away in horrified embarrassment. He had strayed into the wrong room. Into Laura's room. Somehow, he had gone completely the wrong way.

Then his eyes dropped to the floor and he frowned. Hang on a minute, those were his trainers down there. His CDs and screwed-up T-shirt. This was his room.

"Don't be sorry." Her deep, gravelly voice came from just behind his shoulder. A hand with red fingernails crept round his front and placed itself over his crotch. Paralysed, he stared down at where it clenched over his balls like a large white spider with red shoes on. The hand began gently to rub.

Orlando sprang to escape, got his feet tangled in sheets, and fell backwards onto the bed. "Mrs. Faugh!" he squeaked, terrified.

She had unbuttoned her fitted, herringbone-patterned blouse. Beneath her demure double rope of pearls he glimpsed a neat black bra with small, white polka dots on it, trimmed with a small white ribbon. "Call me Laura," she said, smiling as she shrugged off the shirt. Her eyes under their hoods glittered blackly as they travelled him slowly up and down. The dry red lips twisted in amusement.

"You're married," Orlando, still tangled in the sheets, reminded her desperately.

He heard her gravelly chuckle. "Yes, but Hugh and I have a very open marriage."

He watched transfixed, as she peeled her bra off. Her breasts, larger than Orlando had expected, sprang out. They looked hard and pointy, with jabby little nipples on the end. Rather like a pair of missiles, he thought, nonetheless feeling a jolt of desire that horrified him. He wrenched his gaze away.

She was unzipping her black skirt now. Frozen to the spot, he watched her step out of it. Bells clanged chaotically in his head. Laura wore no knickers, and her pubic hair was neatly trimmed and demure, black against her milk-white flesh, as the straps of the garters were black. Orlando had never seen the full rigout in real life before, had never believed anyone besides Jordan and possibly Russell Brand actually wore it.

"What's the matter?" she asked huskily, kneeling up so her breasts pushed into his face. "Don't you like girls?"

Orlando swallowed heavily, the newly arrived equipment in his throat ratcheting noisily as he did so. He had no idea whether he liked girls. They had changed from rejecting him to wanting him virtually overnight, and he was completely confused about them. And, in any case, no way could Laura Faugh be described as a girl. She was forty-five at least. The friend of his parents, just feet away down the corridor. The wife of her husband, also feet away. The mother of her children, who were there as well. All this Orlando knew, and yet the insistence in his trousers was swelling, pressing, throbbing. He felt as if he might explode if he did not give way to it.

"Come on, Orlando. You know you want to." Laura was sitting on the edge of the bed, naked apart from her garter belt. Her smile was sly, mocking.

As she opened her long white legs in their black garters, Orlando saw the hoods over her eyes flick upwards to reveal a glittering, predatory expression, that of a snake hypnotising a rabbit. He knew he should resist and yet felt pulled helplessly towards her by the magnet in his crotch.

He stared about him in panic.

On the bed, Laura cupped her missile breasts in her hands and caressed the nipples with her thumb. "I've just had them done. They cost the equivalent of a year's school fees."

The mention of school fees, the bane of his life, brought Orlando to his senses. His more practical senses, that was. He realised that, contrary to what his examiners always said about him, he could think ahead. He did have an idea of consequences after all. He leapt to his feet. He opened the bedroom door and fled out into the dark corridor.

Should he tell his parents? Laura and Hugh's long-standing friends? He had concluded that probably he should, but he couldn't. He was physically incapable of telling it, and Georgie, in particular, highly strung as she was, was probably incapable of being told it. Even now, side by side with his father in the intimate atmosphere of the car, Orlando's jaw still remained clamped shut on the subject.

❖ ❖ ❖

In Florence's famous Piazza della Signoria, Emma felt awed at the great, brown mediaeval Signoria palace rearing up before her, the row of painted shields along its front shining in the sun and its long, thin, central tower pointing into the bright blue sky.

And just over there, looking rather smaller than she had imagined, but nonetheless instantly recognisable, was Michelangelo's statue of David. Emma crossed the wide, paved square towards him, weaving between knots of tourists.

A couple of children reached the statue before she did.

"It's Daddy!" announced the smaller of the children, an adorable pink-cheeked moppet with dark curls who Emma guessed, with a pang, to be Hero's age. The parents, harassed and obviously English, came panting up and swooped on their brood.

"Look, Daddy, it's you," repeated the smaller child, pointing at the naked statue.

Daddy, who Emma guessed walked around the house unclothed a lot, flushed a deep red.

❖❖❖

"There you are, Dad." Orlando stood before the silver, purple, and red logo'd door of the first Internet café his father had ever visited.

"Er, Orlando…" Richard cleared his throat and searched for an excuse. "Thanks for your help. But I, um, I'll be fine now. I can manage. In there." He stabbed a finger through the hot air at the shop doorway.

Orlando pushed back his locks in surprise. "Manage? You? In an Internet café?"

"I'll be fine. Really." Richard grinned a rictus grin. There was no question of Orlando coming with him and seeing what he had come to see. It would be embarrassing beyond belief. "You go and do some sightseeing," He rummaged in his pocket for his wallet. "Here. Buy yourself a drink."

"Oh. Okay. Thanks."

"I'll give you a ring on your mobile when I've, um, finished." And with that, Richard disappeared into the Internet café.

Chapter Forty-four

THE SHOOT WAS TAKING part in a smart Florence shoe store. Cubbyholes in the red velvet walls held variations on the stiletto-heeled, sparkling, skinny-strapped look that had made this particular designer a household name.

His latest creation was what Darcy was to be photographed in: shoes of brilliant black patent with a peep toe, silver spike heel, and two-inch-thick black platform. The look fell, Darcy thought, somewhere between the porn star and the vaguely orthopaedic and horribly similar to what Belle had been wearing last night when she pushed her up the hill. She was also to wear a short, black leather trench coat and what seemed to Darcy some very strange make-up.

"Something so appalling happened to me last week," the make-up artist painting Darcy's lips metallic blue told her in tones of horror.

"What?" Darcy asked as best she could without moving the lips that were being painted. Like dentists, make-up people always chatted as if one could respond quite normally.

The make-up artist, whose name was Skye, did not inspire confidence. She had frizzy yellow hair and layers of smocks; a billowing, white-cheesecloth, lace-trimmed one rode on top of a nylon clinging one patterned in swirling yellow-and-purple Pucci print. She also wore black leggings and clumpy Mary Jane shoes in bright red patent.

"I drank a can of Diet Coke," Skye gasped. "But guess what? It was fat Coke, and I never realised. Can you imagine?"

The assistant, who huddled on the floor rubbing baby oil into Darcy's bare legs to produce a suitably gleaming look for the camera, exclaimed at the make-up artist in horror. "Omigod! What did you do?"

"Rang my personal trainer in hysterics, of course." Skye shuddered at the memory. "He told me to calm down and get on the treadmill for two hours…"

"Two hours!"

"Yeah, which wasn't bad, considering."

Darcy's thoughts drifted away, pulled like iron filings to the great magnet that was Christian. Since his no-show at the restaurant, he had texted occasionally, but only at the rate of one short answer to five or so long messages from her end.

Still, principal photography on the film started the next day. She would be on set with him then; she would see him then. Darcy cheered up.

"O-kaaaayyyy!" Carlos called now, tossing his mane of un-combed black hair.

Carlos was the photographer. He was a piratical, wild-haired Spaniard, black-leather-jacketed and full of attitude. Darcy hadn't terribly liked the way he looked at her with more than a touch of droit du seigneur.

"You look red 'ot, baby," he told Darcy.

Probably because I am, Darcy thought. Carlos's Japanese assistant was positioning her, wobbling in her perilous heels, before five brilliant spotlights. She was sweating in her leather coat.

The in-store stereo started to boom out Sister Sledge. Darcy tried hard to give Carlos what he wanted. "Chin down!" he yelled, throwing his hair about behind the camera. "Bottom out! Smile!"

Darcy had heard that saying "sex" produced a great camera smile, but she didn't want to encourage Carlos, who obviously felt entitled enough as it was.

"Okayyyyyy!" Carlos roared. "Eyes, go." Darcy widened her eyes obediently. "Teeth, go." She forced her aching lips yet further apart. "Hair, go." She tossed it wildly. "Aaaaah."

Afterwards, they broke for lunch. Darcy lined up in her leather coat and agonising heels at the crew buffet, which had been set up on a white-draped trestle table in front of the ribbon-wrapped mirrors.

Eagerly, Darcy dived in. Her haul comprised of one large slice of juicy quiche and a great square of pizza sprawling with mozzarella, tomato, and herbs. She was biting into the pizza just as a short woman with thick beige hair, heavily eyelined eyes, tight ginger trousers, and a lot of jewellery burst into the room. "Stop!" shrieked Sam.

❖ ❖ ❖

Orlando wandered through Florence. He had been following for some time the line of a winding and obviously ancient street that now opened into a huge and sunlit square.

The square was full of colour and movement. People in T-shirts and trainers sat everywhere: on walls, on the bases of the statues that seemed to be everywhere, at the bars with their colourful sunshades and scurrying waiters. This square was obviously a major hanging-out place of the sort you didn't get in London.

Florence was pretty impressive, Orlando decided. He stuck his hands in his pockets and strode off. Might as well see what else there was to look at. Spotting a sign saying "Duomo" and remembering that his father had said something about it, Orlando followed the direction the arrow was pointing.

Emma was looking at the Duomo. Morning had, most thoughtfully, dozed off under his sun hat, and she was able to concentrate fully on the magnificent structure. She gazed, quite lost in admiration, at the massive and complex white marble mountain, alive with arches and pointy bits and round windows and all sorts of other architectural devices she wished she knew the name of.

"Um, Emma?"

At the voice, she froze. Slowly she turned and found herself looking up into a pair of smiling grey-green eyes with a ring of yellow at the centre. A large hand went up to uncertainly push back tumbling light-brown hair in which gleamed strands of pure gold. A violent flash of electric excitement passed through her knees and stomach. "Orlando!"

"Hi," he muttered, in a voice husky with awkwardness. His entire inside had leapt with excitement to see her, but now he felt shy.

"Hi," Emma muttered back, aware of his broad shoulders and brown arms beneath his T-shirt sleeves. She tried to rein in her excitement. No doubt he would say in a moment that he had come to meet somebody else. Some beautiful, lissome Italian girl, any number of which were sashaying past all the time.

"I had to come and get a travel cot for Morning," she said in a nervous rush. "The villa we're staying in doesn't have one…"

"Oh, right. Erm, I'm here with my dad. He's gone to an Internet café."

"Trendy dad."

Orlando snorted. Emma smiled.

"It's his first visit," Orlando confessed, more easily now. "Something to do with his work, I think. He didn't want me around, anyway."

She nodded.

"I was such an idiot not to get your address in the airport." Orlando rushed the words out. "I've been kicking myself ever since."

It was a big admission, and he instantly regretted making it.

Emma looked down, breathing quickly.

"Let's go and have a cup of coffee," she said.

"Er…Okay."

Emma looked challengingly at Orlando. "Sure you haven't got better things to do?"

He shook his head ardently. "Sounds like a really good idea."

❖❖❖

"Guy? I'm ready."

As Richard, in the back row of terminals in the Internet café, keyed in the address, he looked furtively around him. No one was looking. No one had the least interest in what he was doing. Everyone was busy with their own worlds. On the screen immediately before him, one crazed-looking youth with a black beard, who Richard had on entry thought a dead ringer for some terrorist of the smoking-shoes variety, was typing in a message that read: "Darling Mumsy, having a simply ripping time in Florence. It's a marvellous city, and I've met some awfully nice young people. I hope you're looking after my guinea pigs, lots of love, Bobsy."

"You've got there?" Guy asked a few minutes later.

"I think so," Richard whispered in horror, unable to tear his eyes away from the image on his screen.

"You've got a big, hairy bottom, right?" Guy asked, matter of factly. "Well, not you personally, of course, ha, ha, but…"

"Yes!" Richard hissed, shakily. He was in no mood for Guy's sallies.

"Well, click right in the middle of it, where the buttock cheeks…"

"Yes, yes," snapped Richard, louder than he had intended to.

He was aware of a movement in front of him, of someone very big suddenly rising up and looming over him. In vain and too late did Richard spread his skinny arms over the screen.

"Well, well, well," said the voice of Hugh Faugh.

Richard felt the colour drain from his face. He gulped dryly at his Parliamentary colleague, his head empty of all words, and in particular any that might explain and excuse him.

Hugh leaned heavily on Richard's desk and smiled. It was not a nice smile: sideways, cunning, and delivered with a cocked black eyebrow. It was, Richard recognised, a smile that said "'Aha! Got you!'"

"Rather spotty, isn't it?" the Shadow Education Secretary re-marked, scrutinizing the bottom shown on the screen.

Richard had finally located his vocabulary and hauled it out from where it was hiding. "Hugh," he gasped. "I can explain. It's not what you think."

Hugh regarded him pityingly with his large, bright black eyes. "Don't worry," he said conspiratorially. "I can keep your little secret. I'm only in here myself because my BlackBerry is bust and I need to email Fanny."

"Fanny?" stammered Richard. "Who's Fanny?"

"Well, it's not so much who, as what." Hugh grinned. "I call them all Fanny. But I have to say that this one definitely puts the tit in constituency."

"Oh, I see," said Richard, feeling disgusted. A mistress. The latest of many, by the sound of it. He felt he disliked Hugh more than ever. He gestured at the bottom on the screen. "I'm looking at this on behalf of one of my constituents."

Hugh gave him a "They all say that" grin. "Don't worry. I won't tell Georgie. Not if you don't tell Laura."

"There's nothing not to tell," Richard insisted as Hugh, winking with one of his fleshy, sheeny, thickly lashed eyelids, went back to his seat.

Nonetheless, he felt implicated. Horribly compromised. Dirty even. Looking at hairy bottoms so some old toffs in Gloucestershire could keep their house prices up? Where was the nobility in that?

He stared at the hairy, white buttocks on the screen. They struck him as a succinct representation, not only of what was going on in Wellover, but of his political career in general.

Chapter Forty-five

ORLANDO, SITTING IN THE café, was thinking that it must be wonderful to be a baby, so warm, cosy, looked after. All that was required of one was to sleep and smile, no responsibilities or expectations beyond that. And to be looked after by Emma, not least. To be cuddled up against her breast. He swallowed and felt a sudden glow sting his cheeks.

She was, he thought, as pretty as he remembered, if not more so. So many times since their airport encounter, he had recalled the soft shine of her brown hair, the sparkle in her eyes, the white of her teeth, and the red of her lips against her creamy skin.

"Got your exam results?" Emma asked eventually. She had been trying but could think of absolutely nothing else to say.

He shook his golden head unhappily. "I don't know which is worse," he groaned, addressing his huge feet. "Not having them and thinking they'll be bad or having them and knowing that they are."

A provocatively dressed woman was slinking past with swishing, dark hair and a long neck. Her lips, Emma noticed with awe, were even bigger than Belle's and possibly even more natural. Emma had been aware for some time that sidling girls with short skirts revealing long brown thighs were stepping closer to where she sat with Orlando than was strictly necessary.

The obvious centre of their attention was, Emma saw, clearly doing his level best to ignore it. His big hands uncertainly raked his unbrushed golden hair, and his long brown legs stretched defensively out in front of him.

Emma felt she could not blame the women, even if some of them were giving her less than friendly looks. Orlando's brooding, discouraging stare—eyes narrowed under level brows, full mouth set in a line—made him look more intensely handsome than ever. His haphazard clothes—battered beige shorts, raggy red T-shirt, and huge, scruffy trainers with no socks—contributed even more to his air of casual, even reluctant beauty.

He shrugged, then smiled at her, and again she felt that electric flash. She looked away hurriedly.

❖❖❖

After the Cojones shoot, Sam was exhausted but triumphant. The fiery Spaniard had been reluctant at first, but once Sam had explained that if this shoot went wrong, they all went wrong, Cojones had suddenly seen reason. He had used a lot of shadow on Darcy to slim her down as much as possible. The test shots had looked good. Sam was fairly confident that Brooke, who had demanded to see the results immediately, would be satisfied.

Darcy had been less keen. "I look pretty skinny," she had said, squinting critically at the test shots. "Sort of thin and ill."

"Oh, get real," Sam had snapped, frustrated. "Times are thin, okay? Thin, thin, thin. There's a racehorse vibe, a legs spilling everywhere thing, kind of newborn colt, y'know?"

Darcy had giggled. "You make modelling sound like a farmyard."

"Yeah, well that isn't so far from the truth," Sam snapped. "It's full of shit; you deal with a lot of pigs and a helluva lot of cows. And the figure on the bottom line," the agent added, as inspiration struck her, "is usually zero. Or double zero."

"Well, I'm a long way from that," Darcy returned, comfortably.

Sam shot her an exasperated look. You said it, baby.

Darcy had now gone to an art gallery, and Sam needed to get back to London. She decided to walk back to the hotel. She had no intention of waiting around for a taxi, and, besides, her London habit of spotting talent on the hoof could just as easily apply here. As she walked along, she looked closely at the people passing her. Returning to her agency with a new face in the bag would more than make up for the trouble she was having with one of her most recent.

❖ ❖ ❖

Orlando was holding Morning now. It made a touching sight, Emma thought: the gangling, broad-shouldered, god-like youth cradling the small dark child. "Lovely baby!" Orlando crooned now, peering down at the infant, who chose that moment to stir, open his big eyes with their liquid chocolate pupils, and give Orlando a huge pink smile.

"You've got a way with babies," Emma observed. "You must have held lots of them before."

Orlando, who had, in fact, never held a baby before Morning, was secretly staggered that he wasn't crying. He had thought all babies did that as soon as you picked them up. But holding one was far easier than he had imagined; they snuggled into you, their warm little heads tucked against your chest. He was surprised at how enjoyable it felt.

"You know," Emma said consideringly. "You could easily be a nanny. You're really great with children."

He looked at her in astonishment. "A nanny?"

She raised a wry eyebrow. "Try not to sound so, like, disgusted. It's what I do, after all."

"I'm sorry, I didn't mean…"

"So what did you mean?"

"I meant, you know, that…men don't…I mean, they aren't…"

"Yes, they are," Emma said firmly. "Male nannies are trendy. They're called mannies."

"Mannies!" He gave a shout of laughter. Then the amusement died from his expression. "But I can't…I mean, who would give me a job?"

"I would, like a shot," Emma assured him.

"But you haven't got a nursery."

"Not yet." She was thinking aloud again. "But I might one day. I just might."

A nanny, Orlando thought. It was a thought, definitely. It was true he liked children. And now he came to think of it, it would be great—really great—to work with them.

His mother wouldn't think so, of course. Georgie was determined he would be something impressive, preferably famous and definitely rich. He sighed heavily, raised his eyebrows, and looked up at the sunny, blue sky.

"Oops," said Emma now, as Morning's bottle rolled off the table and fell to the cobbled floor.

"I'll get it," Orlando offered, holding Morning carefully as he reached downwards. His hand crossed Emma's. He felt her begin to jerk it away and caught it.

Her lips, Orlando saw, were very close. His heart began to thunder, and his mouth felt as if a very strong magnet were pulling it forward. Before he knew it, he was kissing her. As Emma's lips parted, he felt a flicker of surprise. Gently, he touched her soft, warm tongue with his. A judder went through his entire body, followed by a spreading sense of wonder. So this was what it felt like.

❖❖❖

In the depths of her Luella tote, Sam's mobile phone was ringing. She dragged it out.

"Brooke Reed," came the piercing nasal voice of the NBS studio PR. "These pictures, I got 'em."

She was entering a large, sunny square, Sam saw. She pointed herself towards the nearest bar. A celebration drink would, after all, be in order within minutes.

"And?"

"She looks like a sumo wrestler."

"Sumo wrestler!"

"You heard me," Brooke replied crisply. "It's a bad angle to start with—who is this photographer guy?"

"Carlos Cojones. We talked about him," Sam said tightly, feeling her professional integrity was being called seriously into question. "He's up and coming."

"Not anymore he ain't. He's down and gone. He's obviously photoshopped these shots a bit, but Darcy's still got a double chin. Not to mention pork roast."

Sam groaned. Pork roast was not good news.

"Those tight, strappy sandals, with flesh bulging out between the straps?"

"I know what pork roast is," Sam grumbled.

"Well it looks like Sunday lunch here. I haven't even shown 'em to Jack. I daren't. And I can't begin to imagine what Arlington will say."

Arlington Shorthouse. The studio head. This was big-time stuff, Sam knew, for him to get involved.

"She's gotta start a diet and exercise regime now," Brooke ordered. "Otherwise she's out of the picture."

"Right," muttered Sam, feeling rather stunned by the machine-gun rattle of words from L.A.

"Jack can hold her scenes for a week. Luckily, we'd already talked about this."

"You had?" There didn't seem anything too lucky about it to Sam.

"It was the worst-case scenario," Brooke drawled. "We had to plan for it. Hit emergency mode. You know, I was seriously thinking about sending her off to a hard-core juicing camp in Thailand that I know. But I guess a thinstructor would be better."

"A thinstructor," repeated Sam. Hollywoodese, she knew, for a personal trainer. She would have liked to object, put some ideas forward at any rate; Darcy was her client, after all. But there was no stopping Brooke in full, determined, emergency-mode flow.

"There's one guy," the L.A. end rasped. "'He's actually known as the Hero of Zero. I've used him before. He gets people down from size six into something you can barely see side-on in time for the awards season."

"Right." A diet and exercise regime, Sam thought glumly. How the hell was she going to get this one past Darcy? She loved food—had been stuffing her face with pizza at the shoot when Sam had arrived, in fact. And Sam had a feeling that she wasn't big on exercise.

"Saw him at an industry awards ceremony just the other night," Brooke was saying of the thinstructor. "He's pretty busy, though. Said he had four lots of A-list batwings and some Golden Globe-nominated cellulite to deal with, plus some thunder thighs in Pacific Palisades that might be up for Best Actor. But I can call in some favours. Get him out to you."

"Great," Sam said heavily, as Brooke's end went dead.

"Signora?" A waiter had appeared.

"Double Jamesons," Sam snapped.

She pulled out her mobile and dialled Mitch Masterson. "Houston? We got a problem."

"Tell me about it," Mitch groaned. "I've just had Arlington Shorthouse on to me. If Darcy doesn't drop two dress sizes by the end of next week, she's out of the picture. Brooke's sending in some crack personal trainer."

"That's right. So when are you going to tell her?"

"Me tell her?" exclaimed Mitch. "I thought you…"

"You're her agent," Sam said firmly.

"Yeah, and you're her model agent. It falls within your remit."

"No it doesn't."

"Yes it does."

"Doesn't."

"Does."

"Okay," Mitch sighed. "Let's toss for it."

"Over the phone?" gasped Sam. "Where I can't see it?"

"Don't you trust me?" Mitch's tone was indignant.

"No. You're an agent."

"So are you."

"Exactly."

"Okay. I'll tell her." He'd known he would have to all along. Domineering women always got their way with him. It was, he supposed, a sort of fetish.

Sam's drink now arrived. She took a great swig; the fiery liquid blazed a trail to her stomach, and she felt immediately better.

Now more in control, she started to look around her, assessing the clientele. There were some pretty good-looking people in this bar. Take that boy over there.

Sam narrowed her eyes. He really was handsome. She watched the hollows beneath his cheekbones catch the sun as he pushed back his gold-flecked hair. He was laughing, his full lips parted, his long eyes sparkling beneath his brows.

Excitement gripped Sam, as it rarely did. As it only did, in fact, when she received vast checks or came across someone truly exceptional who could result in vast checks. And this boy was exceptional. Every nerve in her body was shrieking the fact. She was panting. She felt hot. She hadn't felt this excited since she had spotted The Hunk That Got Away in Covent Garden.

Suddenly, Sam gasped, a tearing gasp that felt more like a choke. Could it be? Hurriedly, she scrambled in her bag, fishing for her mobile again. She grabbed it—it fell from her frantic, fumbling grip—then pinged it open. Within seconds, she had found the picture of the boy she had taken. Her eyes ricocheted back and forth, from the fuzzy image to the living young man some tables away, gathering the evidence. She felt almost sick with excitement. My God. It really looked like…it really could be…

It was. It was him. She had no doubt at all. The face that had, to her eternal regret, got away. But it wasn't going to get away again. The hell it was.

Stealthily, as one stalking a butterfly might, Sam drained her whisky glass and raised her ginger-suede bottom from her chair.

❖❖❖

Up until the point Orlando's lips actually touched hers, Emma had not really believed that it was actually going to happen. And when it did, and she had melted into it, the kiss had been altogether deeper, more protracted, more tender than she had imagined possible.

And then, obeying a shy, yet joyful impulse, he bent over and kissed her nose. As his lips moved down her face to her mouth again, a great plunge of desire swept through Orlando.

She felt she were drowning in the green of his eyes.

Then something looming over them made them both look up.

Orlando stiffened in horror. He recognised her instantly. That awful pushy model-agent woman from Covent Garden. Oh, no. Not in front of Emma. The embarrassment would be excruciating.

He leapt to his feet. "Look, I've got to go…I'll be back…"

"Hey!" cried the woman. "Wait!"

"I can't!" Emma cried after him. Her hand clasped Morning. "We have to go too…"

She watched helplessly as the tall, blond figure rushed off across the square and disappeared into the crowd.

Chapter Forty-six

SO VIOLENTLY HAD DARCY opposed the idea of a personal trainer from America that her agents had eventually given in. Running alone was no fun, but preferable at least to the prospect of sprinting through Rocolo accompanied by someone calling himself the Hero of Zero.

Her victory was not absolute, however. Within days, a pair of DVDs addressed to Darcy arrived from L.A. via a courier. Apprehensively, she took them into the villa's large, light, stone-walled sitting room and slipped them into the gleaming, state-of-the-art player. Immediately the enormous, gleaming, state-of-the-art plasma screen was filled with some gleaming, white, obviously state-of-the-art teeth. The camera panned back to reveal a maniacally grinning man with big hair, a pink mesh vest, and a glistening caramel tan.

"Hello, Darcy!" he exclaimed with showbizzy emphasis. "I'm Rupert. Otherwise known as the Hero of Zero."

Darcy stared, stunned, at the shining, black, swept-back hair, unlined forehead, and superhero jaw. He was extremely thin. His legs reminded her of pipe cleaners, very brown ones.

"Otherwise known," the dazzling teeth on the screen continued, "as the Captain of Thindustry and the Queen of Lean. The guy the stylists to the stars all have on speed dial." He made a little exuberant, skipping movement. "And why? Because, dear, I can make you thin. I'm the man the model agencies call in times of crisis. And you're one lucky lady to have me make an exclusive and tailor-made programme just for you!" He rubbed his hands together gleefully.

There was a tinny, ringing sound. Rupert rolled his eyes. "Hold on, dear. My Thighphone. It's going crazy."

Darcy stared as Rupert lifted his bright-pink mesh vest to reveal a row of slender mobiles slipped into holders strapped along a belt. "All on vibrate, for emergency use only. It's a service I offer ultra-triple-A-list clients—people like you, Darcy," he added triumphantly, "when they have a problem. All part of my very special service," he explained to the camera with a smile like a flashgun.

"Each of these phones relates to a different part of the body," the Captain of Thindustry now revealed. "Clients ring the number relating to their particular body issue zone. This," he pointed to the first pocket, "is the Batphone. That's for batwings and bingo wings. This,"—the second pocket—"is the Buttphone—self-explanatory, obviously. Then the Bellyphone—my little joke, dear, rhymes with telephone. And, last, but by no means least, the Thighphone and the Pork Roast Hotline," he added, indicating the others. "Hold on, hold on, I'm coming," he exclaimed, pulling out the Thighphone and frowning at the number. "Yes, Nicole?"

He listened for a few minutes, his face grave. "Okay, Nicole. Not a problem."

He put the phone away, flashed another grin, and proceeded to bound about the screen like a young gazelle. "We'll do some cardiovascular every day, of course," he told Darcy brightly. "Tricep dips to streamline those upper arms. My special Butt Blaster lunges—you'll enjoy those, dear. Everyone does. And running, of course. A good brisk jog with some uphill for an hour a day at least…"

Running! Pure aversion seized Darcy. She hated running. Anything but that. It was painful, hot, and boring. Whenever, in the past, she had done it—usually in pursuit of an about-to-depart train—her chest had heaved violently; painful cramps had stabbed her sides; and her lungs had gulped agonisingly for air. She had always felt amazement that anyone could run for fun—could run at all—without a gun being pointed to his or her head. Running for her life was the only sort she could envisage.

"...the quickest and most effective way to shed those naughty unwanted pounds..."

Darcy lunged for the DVD player and switched him off.

She slipped the other disc in. This one was about food and featured the Hero of Zero in a bright, white kitchen with a white apron over his pink mesh vest. The horror that had gripped Darcy during the first disc started to subside. If it was about food, it could not be all bad, surely.

"Pasta's off, dear," Rupert beamed. "Ditto bread. It's all about low carb, low cholesterol, low fat..."

Low fun, thought Darcy in dismay. She strained to listen. Had he really just said egg white omelette, poached chicken fillet, steamed broccoli, and as much undressed salad as she wanted to eat? How much undressed salad did anyone want to eat?

"Seaweed protein shakes and tree syrup are an option..." Rupert was beaming. "And if you've got any food allergies, now's the time to really let them rip. Or else develop some. Food allergies can be very useful..."

Crouched on the cool stone floor, Darcy groaned. It was bad enough from her point of view, but what the proud cook Mara was going to make of it hardly bore thinking about.

The voice from the plasma screen trilled blithely on. "Finally, let me tell you something about diet food. Which is that nothing, absolutely nothing, tastes as good as..."

He paused. Darcy, eyes riveted on the screen, held her breath. Was some stomach-filling, acceptably tasty low-fat wonderfood about to be mentioned?

"Nothing tastes as good as thin feels," Rupert finished triumphantly.

Darcy switched him off and sat gazing, unseeing, into the sitting room's great empty fireplace with its carved canopy.

Never had the ridiculousness of Hollywood seemed quite so

ridiculous. Nor was the Hero of Zero the only example of it; Darcy had now read the script and discovered that bidding other equally unlikely sounding characters to "Come forth, loyal servant of my late father" seemed to be the main function of her role as the Grand Duchess of the Galaxy. It was not a part to get excited about in any artistic sense or in any sense, it was increasingly beginning to seem.

"Lose the weight, or lose the part," Mitch had warned her. He could talk, Darcy thought.

The situation was simple enough. The sooner she reached the requisite point on the scales, the sooner she would be allowed to go on set in Florence and film her scenes. And see Christian. If she'd do it for nothing else, she'd do it for him.

She missed him. Not spiritually or companionably, but physically. They had met only briefly, but searingly. Christian had lit her blue touchpaper, and now she wanted more. He was passionate and skilled. Was there a better lover in the world? No. Did she believe in love at first sight? Well, she hadn't, not before. But now everything seemed different.

❖❖❖

It had taken Emma some minutes to work out, amid the confusion, that the bossy blonde with the doggy bangs, fishy lips, and uncomfortably tight ginger-suede trousers was a model agent. She had, apparently, spotted Orlando in London, and he had run away then.

Emma, while aghast at his sudden departure, could nonetheless see why he might. But when, after the agent finally stomped off, Orlando failed to return before she had to leave for her bus, Emma's sympathy turned to despair. She had no address and no phone number for him—a fact the exasperated agent clearly had not believed.

The night that subsequently passed was one of the most miserable and joyous Emma had ever known, as alternately she recalled the kiss and the probability the kisser was lost to her forever.

"You're in love," Mara teased in the kitchen the next morning.

"Of course I'm not," Emma riposted. "Don't be silly."

"So if you not in love, why you leave the milk to boil over all the time?" Mara chided, snatching the pan off the stove. "Why you put Morning's clothes on back to front and walk around in a daze?"

"I don't!"

"And your face!" Mara teased. "You are glowing!"

"I'm just hot."

"And you are not eating!" the housekeeper accused. "Last night, I serve you some of my cannelloni, you not eat a thing."

Emma reddened further at the memory. It had been particularly embarrassing as poor Darcy, who had been condemned to some sort of diet and was eating broccoli, had stared at the steaming dish of pasta with eyes like saucers.

Chapter Forty-seven

"NOTHING TASTES AS GOOD as thin feels." Darcy tried to recall Rupert's words. But it wasn't true. Just about anything tasted better. She'd only been on the diet a day, and already, with the right sauce and seasoning, she felt she could eat the tablecloth.

And now Mara had just gone back into the kitchen after having carefully put down a dish of pork fillet with cannellini beans at the table under the parasol. It was the same dish whose sumptuous sweet-savoury scent had been drifting around the villa all morning and driving Darcy mad as she performed her star jumps.

Her own scheduled lunch was poached chicken and steamed broccoli, prepared by a Mara still tight-lipped after the experience of having to watch the Queen of Lean's dietary instructions on the DVD. She had agreed in the end to make what the Hero of Zero instructed—but her own dishes at the same time.

To see, now, the two side by side on the table—what she had to eat and what she wanted to—was torture for Darcy. Only the thought of Christian made it worthwhile.

It was intensely frustrating, communicating only by text. But as Darcy found herself effectively banned from the set, Christian seemed more or less permanently on it, and texts were the only form of mobile communication Saint apparently allowed, it was the only way. Until she was thin enough, that was.

It was ridiculous. She, who adored food, was in an Italian palace equipped with a wondrous cook. And yet she was on a diet of steamed broccoli and undressed salad.

No one had yet emerged from the villa for dinner. Meaning, thought Darcy, tiptoeing towards the table, the mice could play. Or at least taste what everyone else was having for supper.

As a great stab of hunger pierced her, Darcy picked up a shining silver fork from where it lay on a crisply folded white linen napkin. She reached over towards the pork and bean dish. Her mouth watered as she anticipated the taste of bean, crunchy on the outside, giving in the middle, soaked in all the juices of the sage-infused meat.

"Hoo, hoo, hoo! Hey, hey, hey! Whoa, there!"

There was a flash of pink. Something whooshed across the terrace and grabbed her fork.

"Thank God," panted Belle, with the air of James Bond having saved the world. "Darcy, you should be thanking me. I've just saved your career."

"Thanks," muttered Darcy heavily, trying not to notice how Belle's rake-thin body looked thinner than ever in her hot-pink wrap dress. Was she dressing skinnier on purpose? To make a point?

Belle shook her shining hair mock-sorrowfully. "I sympathise, Darcy. I really do," she breathed.

"You're very kind," Darcy said shortly.

"I mean, it's just so hard to stay thin," Belle added in syrupy tones. "For people like you, that is."

"Sorry?"

Belle smiled. "Personally, I don't know my BMI, and I have no idea what I weigh. I'm just made like this, I guess." She smoothed her tiny hands over the hipbones jutting through her pink wraparound dress and gave another of her tinkling laughs.

"Oh, c'mon Darcy, cheer up," she urged. "At least you're eating off a whole side-plate. Some actresses I know had to eat from a saucer for months. Or a teacup," she added with another tinkling laugh.

"I'm going running," Darcy growled. Anything rather than stay near that pork dish another second.

❖ ❖ ❖

Marco sighed happily as he munched the chocolate that had, along with a croissant fresh from the restaurant oven, made up his late breakfast. As the last bitter-sweet grains melted from his tongue, the chef paused, his dark brow creased in thought. It was splendid chocolate, the best he had ever tasted, and from a new supplier, someone who dealt with the oldest, most traditional chocolate houses in Italy. Just an old man and his brother had made this; they made very little, apparently. But what they made was good. Excellent.

Marco picked up another piece of chocolate and slipped it into his mouth. It really was the best. He knew because of the way, like all wonderful ingredients, it fired his brain with ideas.

He closed his eyes and savoured. Real, pure chocolate, using genuine Venezuelan criollo, the Ferraris or Lamborghinis of cocoa beans, complex and sophisticated like no other and producing a rich, fruity flavour of amazing power. Virtuoso chocolate you could do anything you liked with. Nougatine, parfait, mousse...the only question was which.

On the other hand, Marco asked himself, why choose at all? You could do all those things—mousse, nougatine, parfait—but on the same plate. A tasting plate, with little pieces of everything. What fun that would be for the customers as well as the chefs; they could show off their skills and the many ways in which such a perfect ingredient could be used.

Marco stretched. His mind was, suddenly, full of chocolate tart. A small slice, with the nougatine and parfait on the tasting plate. What could be better?

Something moving rapidly up the cobbled hill now caught his eye. Marco looked; speed of motion was not something usually associated with Rocolo's main street. People tended to struggle up it, panting and straining, red-faced and pop-eyed with the effort.

As the figure came nearer, Marco saw that it was a woman. She really was a beauty, he thought, admiring the long, pale thighs, the high bottom, the pert and deliciously unanchored breasts, the black hair flashing in the sun.

Before his rational brain could register it, something deeper and more visceral within him had produced a swell of excitement, a racing of the heart, a certain breathlessness.

It was her. The food-loving brunette who had come to lunch the other day. The one with the ridiculous swaggering boyfriend in the tight white trousers. Who had appeared in his restaurant later that day with that ridiculous blonde and her ridiculous dog.

Excitement gripped Marco. His new chocolate. This woman would love it. She had a boyfriend; she had no interest in him; but what Marco now wanted to offer went beyond flirtation, beyond romance, into the blessed realm where one food lover reached out to another.

"Hey," Marco called, as she staggered past. He raised his plate of chocolate. "Come and try this!"

He was unprepared for her response. Darcy looked at him in horror and sped off.

What on earth, Marco wondered, had he said?

❖❖❖

"Mr. Saint is ten minutes from the set." The information boomed through the studio PA system.

The great marble hall of the palazzo was a swarm of activity. Great wheelborne cameras rolled about along lines of tape on the floor; cables snaked; lights rose, fell, and were twisted into position amid shouts and arm-waving from the assistants. There were people everywhere, some dressed as aliens, some as space mercenaries, and some, the technicians, in black T-shirts and baseball caps with the *Galaxia* logo on them.

Belle, sitting in a director's chair, the script on her knee, felt a thrill of triumph. She was back. Back among her people. Even if most of them were wearing helmets and white plastic armour and some of them had three eyes.

Her own costume looked like some kind of satellite, all great silver cylinders and intersecting tinfoil ruffs. You could probably pick up Sky on it, maybe even NASA. She had a silver face too, looked like the goddamn Tin Man, frankly. Still, she should complain, Belle told herself. Look at that guy over there with a lizard's head. A red, black, and white lizard's head.

The guy with the lizard's head kept looking at her. But he could forget it. Belle shot the lizard a disdainful look. Reptiles weren't her thing.

Speaking of reptiles, Christian was supposed to be in this film too. Belle was insufficiently familiar with the script to be sure in what scenes he appeared—in what scenes she herself appeared, come to that. But she was curious about seeing him again, for the first time since he had walked out on her in L.A. How would he react, she wondered. Defiant? Ashamed? Ashamed, had to be, especially after the way he treated her.

Never had she imagined then that her star would rise in so unexpected a fashion and they would find themselves on the same cast list. It was pretty obvious Christian hadn't imagined it either. But Belle's sense of triumph, of relief, was such that she almost felt warmth towards him. When you were successful, you could forgive people almost anything. Especially people as good-looking as Christian.

"Mr. Saint is five minutes from the set," announced the PA.

Belle's gaze returned to the lizard. He was closer to her now and was walking up and down, flicking through his script in a concentrated fashion that she, who had no concentration whatever, found rather sexy. He had a pretty good figure too, which his black rubber-effect costume was hugging tightly. Broad shoulders. Neat, tight tush. Strong thighs. And it was abundantly obvious he was well hung. Looked like he had a salami down there.

Belle shifted in her director's chair and parted her thighs slightly under her cumbersome dress. There was a familiar ache there, an ache that demanded satisfaction. She was burningly aware of her nakedness beneath the costume. Behind the hot plastic bodice, her sweaty breasts, artificial as they mostly were, nonetheless yearned to be touched. What was it about that lizard? Who was it, come to that?

Beneath his reptile mask, Christian smiled. He could feel from afar that she was hot for him again. Just as he had hoped. Had she been able to see his face, there could have been trouble. She might have wanted to settle a few scores. But now all he had to do was give her the ride of her life and reveal himself afterwards. She could hardly argue then.

Everything was going his way, Christian reflected as he walked slowly, purposefully towards a Belle squirming and preening in her chair. The set had been alive with the news that Darcy Prince had been banned until she dropped a few pounds. If Christian thought about it at all, it was to vaguely regret the condemnation of those splendid curves, which hadn't been all that big, for Chrissakes. But if Hollywood dictated otherwise, so be it. Just as well he'd decided to move on from her. Once again, his instincts had been unerring. He wished she would stop texting him though. It was embarrassing.

"Mr. Saint is now on the set," announced the speakers. Christian turned to see the spry director with his check shirt, jeans, and neat white beard walking energetically into the midst of the cameras and cables, followed by a retinue bristling with clipboards and clapperboards.

Belle had bobbed up to her feet on hearing the director was now among them. Christian rushed to her side. "You're not needed yet," he growled at her. "Not by Jack Saint anyway."

Belle peered into the lizard's face. It was completely covered in latex and red, black, and white paint. Something about it reminded her of someone—the guy out of Kiss maybe. She smiled. "Hey. You're cute. For a lizard."

She thrust her hands seductively upwards, expecting to push them through her hair, remembering too late that her hair had been plaited, gel-sprayed and now stuck up out of her head as if she had suffered an electric shock.

The lizard seized her round the waist and, in a deft, bold movement, pulled her into the darkness under a nearby flight of balustraded marble stairs. Belle found herself being devoured in an urgent kiss; kissing him passionately back, she felt herself being slowly pushed down to the marble floor of the terrace. Above the rustling of her plastic dress, as, gasping, she pulled it up, Belle heard the squeaking and snapping of snaps as he eased himself out of his rubber suit.

"Oh, God," gasped Belle, from somewhere deep in her throat, deep within herself, as he entered her. "Oh, God," she repeated, rolling her head from side to side, stretching her arms above her head as he began to slowly thrust in and out. "I've never been screwed by a lizard before," she squealed. "I didn't realise what I was missing. You're incredible. Oh! Do that again! Ohhhh! The last fuck I had that was this good was Christian Harlow…oh…oh…ohhhhh!"

"Funny you should say that…" Christian breathed into her convulsing, silver-painted neck. "Because…"

Chapter Forty-eight

DARCY GROANED AS SHE pulled on her trainers. She had not thought it possible to be so hungry. She thought about food all day and had even started dreaming about it, a recurring dream about a castle made of chocolate cake. The hill on which the castle sat was made of profiteroles, and above it, in the blue sky, were great summer clouds of whipped cream. She would climb up this hill and reach the castle, but then a portcullis made of chocolate bars would fall, blocking her entrance.

Still, better get the hated run over with. She summoned all her willpower, pulled her baseball cap down hard, and made a move across the patio. Then, at the prospect of the torture ahead, she emitted a loud wail and retreated to the shade of the parasol.

Emma, by the pool and dangling Morning's legs in the water, could not help noticing this little show. She made no remark but sensed that Darcy, having staged her little tableau of resentment, was looking for sympathy.

"Apparently even after I've been running for half an hour, I've only worked off the equivalent of two slices of toast," Darcy wailed. "And you know what?"

"Er…what?"

"I'd so much rather have had the toast!" Darcy buried her head in her arms on the table. She looked up again, the picture of despair. "You know, dripping with butter. Like that pile Toad eats in *The Wind in the Willows*." The image glowed in her imagination, and her head pounded with longing.

"Oh yes!" Emma exclaimed. *The Wind in the Willows* was one of her favourites. "When poor old Toad's in prison…" She stopped, remembering with a pang how Hero and Cosmo had loved it too.

"What's the matter?" Darcy asked, seeing the nanny's expression fall.

"Nothing." But as the actress's dark eyes remained on her, Emma found herself continuing. "Some children I used to look after. They loved that book as well."

Darcy waited, half-sensing a story, but as nothing more was forthcoming, she embarked on her warm-up, bending and stretching. Her muscles resisted and protested. "Ouch." She stopped and groaned. "God, I don't want to be doing this. I want to be sitting in the shade with a drink. But alcohol's off. Ouch. Ouch!" Darcy jerked energetically up and down, trying to ignore the pain. "One glass would be two hundred sit-ups."

"Really? Two hundred?" It sounded extreme to Emma.

"A minute in the glass, a month on the ass," Darcy grinned. "This DVD I've been sent from L.A., it's got these useful little tips all over it. A couple of sips, hey presto, big hips…oh God. Can you believe it?"

Her smile faded. Beyond the edge of the sunshade, the blue air was full of birdsong and that fizzing, cricket rasp that is the sound of still, hot weather. Beyond, the green and brown hills baked under the summer sky. Did she want to go running? No, she did not. What she wanted to do more than anything was to sit there, or perhaps lie by the pool, flicking through some of Mara's recipe books until lunch was ready.

"Still, it'll all be worth it," Emma said encouragingly. "You'll be really famous when this film comes out."

"I'm not doing it to become famous," Darcy frowned. "Who'd want to be famous? I mean, I thought I did for about five minutes, but I can see now that it's a nightmare. Look at Belle. Who'd want to be like that…oh, sorry. Shouldn't be nasty about her. You work for her after all."

But why, it now occurred to Darcy to wonder. Emma did not seem a particularly Belle-like person. You could tell from the set of her jaw, her intelligent eyes, her kind and sympathetic smile, that she had strength and character. Pretty, too, with her thick, glossy hair, shining eyes, rosy cheeks. She looked extremely clean, glowingly well-scrubbed. There was something about her, Darcy felt, that was both comforting and utterly trustworthy. How Belle had landed herself a gem like this, had persuaded this obviously good person to come and work for her, seemed hard to explain.

"I suppose," Emma said, "that you must love acting."

"Acting!" Darcy chucked. "There's not a lot of art to *Galaxia*, I can tell you. Well, there may be in the special effects, the fight sequences, and the rest of it. But the acting's just a case of standing around in silly costumes saying, 'Welcome, my trusted counsellor,' and things like that." She sighed. "But even if that wasn't the case, if you really had to act well in it, then I really don't know whether I'd enjoy it anymore." She looked sadly at Emma. "I mean, I bet you always wanted to be a nanny, didn't you?"

Emma nodded. "I always knew I wanted to work with children."

"Sometimes," Darcy said after a silence, "I wonder if I ever really knew. My parents were actors, you see. Are actors. Quite famous ones. The theatre was sort of the family business. I was expected to go into it, and I did."

"It sounds very glamorous," Emma remarked.

"Not really. Either my parents were away acting, or they were at home obsessing over their causes. Family meals were always shared with hundreds of people—an entire Indian village once. My mother was a dreadful cook. I think that's why I so love food myself," Darcy was saying, a dreamy, wondering note in her voice. "Perhaps it represents everything I never had at home. Mummy could only make spaghetti bolognese. And often she didn't even bother doing that. It'd be fish and chips all round from the local chippy. The Indian village really loved that," Darcy added, a grin momentarily illuminating her face.

Emma smiled. She sensed she was not required to comment.

"But look where liking food's got me!" Darcy grimaced. "I'm too fat to save the galaxy at the moment." She began running on the spot. "And frankly, if it wasn't for the sex, I don't think I'd bother trying."

"Sex!" Emma was startled into an exclamation.

"There's someone on the film set," Darcy revealed. "He's called Christian. Christian Harlow."

Christian Harlow. Emma knew the name. She could even see the face; it was a staple of celebrity magazines. "I've seen him," she said. "He's very handsome."

"Gorgeous," Darcy corrected.

Orlando, in all his unkempt, golden beauty flashed before Emma. She could almost feel his face close to hers. That, in her book, was gorgeous.

"Yeah, Christian's gorgeous," Darcy was saying in besotted tones. "But I can't see him unless I get on set."

Which meant running, of course. She cringed at the thought of the torture to come. Much more fun to stay here and chat with Belle's nanny.

"But what about you?" Darcy gave Emma a broad smile. "Any romantic attachments?"

Emma shook her head. But the picture, never far away, rushed back: a tall, blond boy with green eyes and a deep, nervous voice that made her stomach turn over. A lingering, passionate kiss.

"Ah!" Darcy saw the shadow cross Emma's face. "There is someone." Her voice was teasing.

Emma heaved Morning up into her arms and hugged him. "There's this one. I'm in love with Morning."

"Don't change the subject," giggled Darcy. "I've told you about mine. So tell me about yours."

"He isn't mine…" Emma insisted.

"Who isn't yours?"

Emma sighed. There was no way out. "Well, there is this boy…"

❖ ❖ ❖

"Such excitement!" George greeted Orlando as he shuffled into the kitchen. It was just before lunch; she was uncorking some wine—to pour down the ever-ready throat of Hugh, Orlando guessed—and her habitually anxious eyes were shining. "Ivo and Jago have made a marvellous new friend in the village."

Georgie was still struggling with the cork.

"I'll do it." Orlando took the bottle from his mother.

"Terribly grand, a wonderful contact." He realised she was still talking about whatever unfortunate it was that had fallen into the twins' clutches.

Orlando concentrated on liberating the Pinot Grigio. He was not interested in Ivo and Jago's contacts. He was not, come to that, interested in anything anymore. He no longer cared, even, that his A level results were surely about to arrive at any moment. He'd met Emma again, and straightaway he'd run away from her. Had been given another chance and ruined it. Or, rather, that fearsome hag from the model agency had ruined it for him.

"Yes," gushed Georgie as she shook some crackers on a rustic plate. "She's called Titty de Belvedere."

"What a stupid name," Orlando remarked.

"Her father's titled!" Georgie exclaimed, as if this explained or excused it. Orlando looked up to see his mother's eyes glowing nuclear with excitement. "According to the twins, Titty's very attractive. Hot, they said." Georgie giggled, savouring this piece of contemporary slang that, as always with his mother, Orlando recognised, was a bit less contemporary than she believed it to be. "They're out somewhere with her now," Georgie added.

Orlando shrugged and returned to his room. Here he would sip cold beer and stare at the ceiling, or otherwise stare at Italian television. None of this got him any closer to seeing Emma again, although it did have the advantage of keeping him out of the way of Laura.

He never dared venture by the pool these days because it was shielded from the house by some large lavender clumps and anything could happen there. Even the garage, where he had discovered a battered, orange-neon foam football he sometimes liked to kick around, was haunted by the possibility of Laura suddenly apprehending him.

Of course, he could not speak to his mother about it. And what hopes he had harboured about talking to his father were now fading, as Richard seemed so distant. Orlando had no idea, could not imagine, what had happened during the trip to Florence. But something evidently had. Richard had set off on the trip as a man of few words and had returned as a man of no words at all.

As it happened, Richard would have told Georgie, Orlando, Laura, and anyone else who insisted on knowing the whats and whys of his visit to the Internet café. But to do so inevitably brought up the question of what Hugh was doing there too. And even though Freebie Faugh was the holiday guest from hell, it struck Richard as unhostlike in the extreme to expose the adultery of someone staying under his roof. As with Mrs. Greatorex, he was left feeling that his principles were being exploited.

He also had to bear constant innuendo. Since the Internet café incident, Hugh, having evidently decided Richard was a sexual adventurer like himself, never passed up an opportunity to act lewdly. Hugh Faugh, Richard thought, would be more accurately called Hugh Phwoarrr.

Last night he had pranced around with a large salami stuck down his trousers during pre-dinner drinks. This had not only been criminally unfunny, but a criminal waste of a good sausage.

The idea that he was colluding with such a reptile was sickening, and yet it was not his own activities Richard wished to conceal.

The fact that his father was obviously, if for reasons he could not quite guess, having almost as bad a time as himself with the Faughs was comfort of a sort, Orlando supposed. Another reason to be cheerful was that his loathing of the twins seemed to have penetrated even the ten-foot-thick social hide of Georgie, who had finally stopped suggesting brightly every morning that "you boys probably want to do something together." But otherwise, all was black, black, black.

Chapter Forty-nine

DARCY STRAINED AND PANTED up the hill into Rocolo. She was struggling for breath. The boiling sun pressed heavily down on her like a giant, invisible hand. She clutched the bottle of water hard, as if this would somehow transfer intravenously the liquid she had not stopped to drink. She had felt that if she stopped she would never start again.

Her heart was thudding in her chest, and she felt as if she were about to die. The Hero of Zero had waxed lyrical about the ketosis stage of exercising, the sought-after nirvana when the body stops burning fat and starts burning muscle. Perhaps this was what was happening now. The emptiness in her stomach had spread. Even her arms felt empty; the very tips of her fingers felt hollow.

As she heaved up the hill, snatched smells of savoury lunches hit her on the nose and in the stomach with the force of a punch. The merest hint of garlic or tomato brought a surge of saliva into her mouth and the sight of bread—especially the thick-crusted country bread that seemed a speciality of the area—made her want to weep. Running past Marco's brought the most delicious smells of all wafting into her nostrils, which was usually why she tried to get past it as swiftly as possible. Today, however, her lungs bursting with effort, her whole body wilting beneath the sun, she felt herself slow down as she approached it.

Marco sat outside the restaurant, enjoying a mid-morning snack. He had forgotten to have breakfast, as he often did if particularly excited about something. He was very excited this morning. His mind was full of fish. A magnificent consignment of trout had just been delivered, with eyes so fresh and bright they looked, for all they were dead, more vital and alive than many of the people who would eventually eat them. The rainbow glimmer of the scales had sent Marco into raptures. Such beauty. Such nobility.

A case of magnificent lobsters had also arrived, also absolutely perfect. The question was how to serve them the absolute best way. Grilled, probably. Yes, grilled, so their sweet, fresh meat could be savoured with as little adulteration as possible. Apart from, of course, a spot of butter and a touch of lemon.

He shook his shaggy hair, which felt hot. It was indeed a hot day, hotter even than usual; the sky above was brilliantly blue and had no clouds whatsoever. It would get even hotter this afternoon.

It was, Marco knew, time he returned to the kitchen. But before he did that, he'd just sit out here a second longer, under this deep blue sky, enjoying the sunshine. He lit another cigarette, took another bite of bread and tomato, and waved his hand at a passing mother and child. "Ciao, Marco!" they chirped in unison. He smiled happily.

His heart gave a sudden, violent leap. It was her. Darcy. Struggling up the road towards him. She did not look happy at all; her big, dark eyes glaring, that rosebud mouth of hers in a flat, cross line. It was obvious she was hating every minute of her run. She was almost bent double with the effort. It could not, Marco thought, rising hurriedly, be good for her to run in this heat.

"Hey! Hello!" he called to her. "Come and have a rest. You look as if you need one." He waved his big hands at the table he sat at.

Darcy paused at the entrance to his courtyard. "I can't," she gasped, hands on hips, bent double as she drew great lungfuls of hot, garlic-and-herb-scented air.

She was shaking, he saw. "You really have to sit down," he said, concerned. "Have some water…some coffee…"

Darcy felt her every nerve end agree with him. At that moment, nothing else on earth seemed more attractive than a rest in that pretty courtyard. Apart from Christian, that was. He had not been in touch for a whole day now. She was beginning to feel panicky. "I can't," Darcy growled.

She caught sight of the table behind him and what was on it. A great hunk of crusty bread, a jar of green oil, some tomatoes as plump, red, and audacious as Carmen's smile...

She swallowed. Her stomach erupted in a thunderclap of hunger. Marco heard it and scented victory.

Seconds later, she was sitting down in the shade with, in her hand, a hunk of the freshest, chewiest bread she had ever eaten, with a fresh, sweet tomato pushed into it, slicked with green olive oil and ground over with salt and pepper.

"The simplest sandwich in the world," Marco grinned. "The tomatoes came in this morning. They are perfect. From the south of Italy and full of flavour. You have never had a tomato like this one before."

Darcy nodded, her mouth full. Nothing had ever tasted so delicious. The tomatoey, oily bread rocketed her back to the land of taste after what seemed years of deprivation in the steamed-broccoli wilderness. The flavours exploded in her mouth with an eye-watering intensity. She felt as if she were coming back to life. Her legs and arms had stopped shaking; the dizziness had faded; her heart had stopped rattling and resumed its usual smooth beat.

Marco had stretched back in his chair again and was looking at the sky. The call of the trout and lobster, which had been so loud, was now fainter. Daria could take care of them. She was good with fish.

"You know what I think?" he said softly. "That the very best things in life are the simplest. Take that tomato. Could there be anything more perfect and luxurious? It tastes of itself, of having ripened in the sun slowly and lazily over the weeks and months. You know?"

Her jaws crashing over the crust, Darcy could only nod.

"True luxury's nothing to do with spending, you see. It's not about showing the world you've got the flashest car or whatever..."

Christian's car flashed into Darcy's mind. Was this a criticism? She shot a sharp, defensive look at Marco, but he was still staring into space, musing.

"Real luxury's about"—Marco inhaled dreamily—"salad leaves with the dew still on them, a day like today, a walk in the woods, the singing birds, the light on the new leaves, the smell of the earth. You know?"

Darcy nodded. The bread and tomato was finished. She had eaten every mouthful.

"Well, you're a really great eater," Marco said appreciatively. "A true gastronome."

"You mean a great, guzzling pig," Darcy wailed, thinking of the weighing scales.

He rushed to reassure her. "No. It was obvious you appreciated every mouthful. You've got a great palate."

Darcy giggled. She'd been admired for many things. But this was the first time her palate had got a mention.

She settled back in her chair and closed her eyes. "I expect you always wanted to be a chef," she remarked enviously. Someone else, like Emma, who had a vocation.

Marco looked at her. "Not at all," he said unexpectedly.

Darcy, eyes closed, listened carefully as he explained that, while he had always eaten it with relish, the ingenuity and tradition of the cooking of his region, of his family, had for years just passed him by. He had not noticed or been interested in how his mother and grandmother could coax rich flavour and sumptuousness out of a few scrag ends, how the fact that nothing was wasted became a culinary art form in itself. The risotto that had not been eaten at dinner was formed into small balls in the palm, stuffed with ragu and fried as a snack which, eaten after school, tasted even more delicious than the original dish.

All this, however, Marco had taken for granted. His main interest in life, after football, had been natural history. He loved nothing more than to pack up a satchel with a lump of cheese and some rough-crusted, homemade bread and set off into the rough, hot, stony, herb-scented summer hills with his binoculars and magnifying glass to spy on the insects and birdlife.

And then, as a boy of eight, he had gone to Paris on a trip with his mother and aunt. And after that, his attitude to food was never the same. And all because of a biscuit.

"A biscuit!" Darcy smiled, almost asleep now.

"Yes, a biscuit!"

And because of his mother too, Marco explained. She had been ill for some time and had been sent to visit a special doctor in Paris. Woven in with the experience of visiting the beautiful city had been the suspicion—for the facts of her cancer had not then been explained to Marco—that something was terribly wrong.

"Cancer," Darcy groaned. Her eyes shut harder, remembering Anna, her beloved grandmother.

"Yes. Cancer." His voice was softer now. "I knew something was wrong in Paris, but I didn't know what it was then."

Nor did he know later, he told her, during that terrible time when they had returned and his mother was ill upstairs at home, when doctors with concerned faces and hushed footsteps padded softly up and down to see her. And afterwards, when she went to the hospital and never came back, those few happy days in the domed, gilded, triumphal-arched and wide-boulevarded city would seem to Marco almost a dream.

"Oh, Marco!" Darcy whispered through the lump in her throat. With her eyes closed, she could see it all so clearly; the intense, curly-haired little boy, his dark eyes wide and puzzled, understanding nothing but the one central fact, the one thing that mattered, that his mother wasn't there anymore.

He said nothing for a few minutes, looking away so she could not quite see his expression. But then he seemed to shake himself and began talking about Paris again. For the days there, he said, had been happy; his mother, despite the reason for her visit, and very possibly because of it, was determined to enjoy herself in the city where, Marco now learnt for the first time, she had spent part of her youth.

His grandmother, who had died long since, had had ambitions in fashion and had worked for a time at one of the Parisian couture houses, meeting his Italian grandfather in a café in the city. They had returned to his native Tuscany when his mother was quite small, Marco now learnt, but not without planting in her the sweetest of memories.

Marco's voice was lifting now, as he explained excitedly how his mother had taken him and her sister Mara, Marco's aunt, to the rue Royale, where stood, she smilingly explained, one of her favourite shops in the world. Laduree, the home of the most wonderful macaroons. Marco had stared entranced at the polished, plate-glass window and the tiny pastel-coloured cream-filled biscuits, which seemed to fill the space behind it in a riot of pale yellow, rose pink, soft orange, pale coffee brown, darker chocolate brown, and delicate green.

Darcy's eyes snapped open in shocked delight. She sat up abruptly and stared at him with shining eyes. "Laduree! My grandmother was obsessed with their macaroons!" The coincidence was astounding. She felt quite winded with astonishment. "She decorated her whole apartment in macaroon colours."

"Great idea!" Marco laughed. "I'd love to have seen it."

"Well, maybe you will," Darcy assured him. "It still looks like that. It's my flat now, and I haven't changed a thing." She tried not to remember that Niall had wanted to and that he thought the décor anything but great.

"I'll hold you to that," Marco grinned. "Next time I'm in London."

"Do! Now carry on your story," Darcy urged.

"You're sure?" Marco raised a heavy dark eyebrow. "I'm not boring you?"

She shook her head with more energy than she had realised she had.

He went on to describe how he had stared and stared at the shop. He had never seen anything like these graceful fairy biscuits with their stripe of filling the exact same colour as their shells. The equivalent at home, the strongly flavoured amaretti with their scattering of sugar, were either hard and crunchy or soft and dry. They were delicious but had none of the delicacy of this pretty pastel riot of patisserie.

The macaroons seemed to him to be the essence of femininity; small wonder that he connected them, immediately and forever, with his beloved mother. The rose-pink one, anyway, was the exact colour of his mother's blouse that day. The chocolate brown, meanwhile, was like her hair.

"She sounds lovely," Darcy sighed.

"She was. But whose mother isn't?"

Darcy did not reply.

He had, Marco explained, watched his mother through the shop's plate-glass window, smiling and gesticulating at the assistants. Then she had come out, obviously delighted, with a large beribboned box of the precious macaroons. Giggling naughtily, the three of them went straightaway to sit on a bench and eat the whole lot at one wonderful, greedy sitting.

Listening to his mother and aunt excitedly exclaiming, watching them close their eyes with rapture as they bit into the biscuits, Marco felt something surge within him that was nothing to do with the almighty hit of sugar rioting round his system. He was seeing, as if the first time, the intense pleasure that food can give.

"These," his mother had smiled at him, holding a pink biscuit, "are about the most difficult things that a chef can make. They're almost impossible to do properly."

"That's what my grandmother always said," Darcy told him, wondering again at the coincidence.

Marco went on. For his mother, a consummate cook, to say such a thing made an impression on the eight-year-old boy. He liked the biscuits, and he liked a challenge. He also wanted to help his mother. Might the macaroons make her better?

And so the obsession began. Marco, now sitting in the sun over thirty years later, smiled ruefully as he described his eight-year-old self to Darcy, sieving and mixing with fierce concentration and then piping, breath held, on to a baking sheet. He could see himself, as clearly as if it were yesterday, bent over, bottom aloft, peering into the oven to see if the shells were rising.

Try as he might to follow the recipes—as many different ones as he could get his hands on; none seemed quite right, somehow—his macaroons were always too flat, too soggy, or too stiff and dry. They cracked; they stuck; they failed to rise and merged with the ones next to them in a flat, hard pool. Never once did they appear round and perfect with the shiny, shell-like dome on the top and the yielding softness beneath.

Darcy listened, touched beyond measure. Her eyes were closed even harder than before, so he couldn't see the tears that welled there.

Marco's voice was warm with laughter now. His family, he told Darcy, were amazed at his efforts. He had never shown the smallest interest in cooking before. Why now, all of a sudden, try to make the most difficult thing of all? But Marco took no notice. He was a boy on a mission. A child with a challenge.

The battle with the biscuits had begun to seize him; he was determined to get the better of them. It became an epic struggle made possible only by the fact that the family had hens laying plenty of eggs for him to endlessly separate and weigh, and almonds, which grew in the area, were also readily available and cheap, as was marscapone for the filling. But for months all Marco's pocket money, earned from paper rounds and odd jobs, went on food colouring and icing sugar.

And so, as his friends kicked balls about the park, working out their team formation, he worked out how to beat the eggs to perfection, how to sieve the almonds to fairy dust, how to make sure no air remained in the piping bag so a steady stream of glossy gloop emerged on to the baking tray.

"Good for you!" Darcy smiled, risking opening her eyes at last. She was just in time to see the remembered triumph in Marco's fade, to be replaced by a terrible sadness.

"Good for me," he said in a whisper. "But not good for Mama." The boy Marco, Darcy heard, now learnt that macaroons, however perfect, do not save lives. His mother had died.

But what a legacy she had left him, Marco explained, his voice strengthening. Nothing less than his restaurant. From experimenting with macaroons, he had gone on to develop an interest in cooking generally, and ultimately a pungent, earthy, full-tasting branch of his national cuisine that could not have been further removed from the insubstantial pastel confections in Laduree's window. "I don't know what Mama would think," Marco confessed, grinning.

Darcy did not care now that her eyes were red and full of tears. "I'm sure she would be enormously proud," she told him through the rock in her throat.

"You think so?" He smiled gently, a beautiful smile, Darcy noticed. She felt herself held in his gaze.

"Come by the restaurant again some time. Come by tomorrow. I've got some great new cheese I'd like you to taste."

Interest blazed in her eyes. "Cheese. I love cheese…" She seemed to check herself. "I have to go," she said hurriedly.

Then she walked away, down the hill. He watched her slight figure retreating until it passed round the next bend.

For the next few hours, after she had gone, Marco tasted, advised, planned, even tolerated the good-natured ribbing of his brigade—but had no idea he was doing any of it. His cooking senses were all present and correct, but every other part of his mind was somewhere else altogether. He replayed, up close, Darcy's passionate face—such a pretty name too—the way she had closed her eyes when tasting, her brows contracting as if it almost hurt.

That skin: soft and pink-flushed, with its dusting of faint freckles, like strawberry-infused cream with a scattering of chocolate powder. Those coffee bean–dark eyes. That hair, as black as liquorice from a few paces away, but up close, tumbled from its ponytail, not just black but with threads of brown and even gold and orange. Hints of carrot, cinnamon, Parmesan, saffron, and, glinting here and there, sheet of gold leaf.

Was he in love? Already? But why not? He was an expert judge of whether a dish was right, knew in an instant whether it looked right, was composed of the right things, had been made properly, whether its heart was right. So why should not be the same of a woman?

Chapter Fifty

KEN HAD ENJOYED A late breakfast on his terrace and was now taking a gentle constitutional round the environs of Rocolo's church. The building amazed him; the ancient, round-arched door opened to a flight of descending steps as wide as the building, leading down into the body of the church. There was a notice as you went in: a camera with a line through it. No photographs. A joy to obey.

All was cool, dark, and quiet; the rows of chairs—no pews here—stretched away towards the gloomy, gaudy altar. You got the sense, Ken thought, of something very old, of people having worshipped here for century upon century. People must have married here knowing that they would have their funeral services here, had their children baptized here knowing that they, in turn, would have their weddings here. The certainty of it all astounded him.

He emerged like a mole, blinking in the light and warmth, and a surge of deep joy for the beauty of the day assailed him, as perhaps the designers of the church had meant it to. The sensation was powerful enough to drive away everything else in Ken's mind, including his sighting of celebrities, the very people he was fleeing, in the very place he had imagined he was safe from them.

Spotting Christian Harlow and Belle Murphy had only been the start of it too. Halfway through his appetizer, Ken had realised who the big, dark-haired man with the booming voice at the table opposite was and why he had looked familiar.

Politicians weren't Ken's usual beat, but Hugh Faugh was

colourful, high profile, and self-publicising enough to stray into his patch from time to time. Were those two startlingly unpleasant-looking boys with big hair and huge teeth his sons? Bad enough to get one like that, Ken thought. But two?

And that vampire-like woman was Faugh's wife, presumably the boys' mother. Ken did not recognise the other man and woman, who looked harmless enough, if slightly crushed, or the other boy, who was quite amazingly good looking. Ken stared for a good few minutes. Was he a model? Ought to be if he wasn't. Film star, even. Oh, listen to me, Ken thought, half indulgent. You can take the boy away from the paparazzi, but you couldn't take the paparazzo out of the boy.

Leaving the church behind, Ken found himself opposite the entrance to the children's playground over which the balcony from his room looked.

Nice playground, Ken thought, with those cypresses all around it stretching up into the pure blue sky, a soft breeze ruffling the leaves and making them glitter in the light. He stood at the edge, outside the gate, watching for a while.

He had already gathered, from his balcony, that the playground was a rallying point for nannies in charge of holidaying British infants from miles around.

Now, between the plants and bushes that the playground was plentifully supplied with, he could see glimpses of the children. Yes, definitely British, definitely upmarket; he knew the look. He had, until recently, seen it several times a day with its wealthy parents disappearing through the revolving door of various five-star hotels.

The nannies, too, were of the typical smart-family kind: more or less alike with long, glossy hair all shades from blonde to black, vast sunglasses, and miniskirts exposing long thin brown legs and feet in glittery flip-flops. They were, Ken noticed, all standing together, smoking, talking, gesturing, shrieking with laughter, answering their mobiles. The children they were nominally in charge of seemed more or less forgotten, although from time to time one of them would turn round to yell at their charges in throaty upmarket voices. "Don't do that, Cosmo!" and "No, Hero! No!"

He recognised that voice, Ken thought as he turned away. The Rolodex in his head whirred. Where had he heard it before? Those names too. Hero and Cosmo. Somewhere very recently.

He turned back round, frowning. His eye caught a small blond boy and a white-blonde girl, about four and three respectively, charging about after each other. Of course. That boy from the airport. The one with the train. And, Ken remembered, the horrid nanny.

Yes, there she was. In the midst of the chattering nannies, that long-legged, heavily highlighted, thoroughly unpleasant blonde. What had the kids called her? Titty? Totty?

Ken lingered protectively, watching the children for some minutes. He felt strangely reluctant to leave them with her. Totty, Ken now noticed, seemed to be looking for someone. Not the kids though. They were walking up one of the slides now, a strategy certain to end in an accident of some sort. Totty was oblivious, however. She kept casting glances towards the gate, where he stood himself, as if someone was expected there. Not wishing to be seen by her, Ken slowly, reluctantly, moved away.

In doing so, he narrowly avoided bumping into two grubby-looking men in baseball caps and leather jackets who seemed to be heading for the playground. Fathers going for their children, Ken supposed. As they passed him, Ken felt the strong, hard pull of a scent he recognised tugging at his nose. Strong tobacco. A few minutes later, back in the square, he realised it was cannabis.

❖❖❖

Darcy had gone to bed for the first time in days without her stomach feeling like a robbed bank. The bread and tomato at Marco's, topped with the grilled chicken fillet and broccoli reluctantly served by Mara, had kept her going all day.

Now, the next morning, she was starving again. The egg-white omelette Mara had banged down before her for breakfast had not even taken the edge off it.

But, of course, they could not continue, these little gastronomic stop-offs at Marco's. He had mentioned cheese, which would be death to her diet. Today she would have to scurry past and hope he didn't see her.

She must concentrate on other things, such as the text that had come late last night from Christian, a mere two sentences in which the actor explained that he was involved in a complicated scene at the moment but would see her soon.

Darcy, now heading towards the gate for her run, felt almost cheerful as walked past Emma and Morning on the terrace.

"I'll see you later," she called gaily.

She reached over to chuck Morning under the chin. He really was sweet. She had not, until now, realised babies could be such fun, so well-behaved and so responsive. Morning was also so appreciative of her every effort to entertain, from waggling her fingers over his face to tickling him. He always smelt delicious, powdery, warm, and with a slight milky undertone. Emma kept him wonderfully clean and happy.

Especially now, after talking to her, it seemed to Darcy more and more mysterious why such a woman worked for Belle. It couldn't be that she was dazzled by celebrity; Emma just did not seem the type. Belle, however, hadn't been back to the villa for days, nor had she even been in touch. Perhaps Emma just felt sorry for the child. But surely she could not put her life and career on hold because of someone else's selfishness. There would be other nannies for Morning.

"You know," said Darcy, watching Emma using the sugar lumps

on the table to play a counting game with the baby, "you're really good. You could get a much better job. Why bother with the Evil One?"

Emma looked at her in alarm. "Evil One?"

"Belle's name in the film," Darcy assured her, smiling. "What all the good characters, like mine, call her. Belle's character is a beautiful but evil man-eating female monster who wants to destroy the universe. Typecasting or what?" She raised her eyebrows and snorted.

"You can't like working for her," Darcy pressed. Suddenly, she felt determined to get to the bottom of the mystery.

Emma looked down. She longed to unburden herself. She could imagine how she must seem in Darcy's eyes: Belle's slave and vassal, tolerating the routine contempt with which the actress treated almost everyone, when she bothered to notice them at all. But she could not possibly tell the actress the circumstances in which she had arrived in Belle's employment. Once made, such a confession could not be retracted and, if it got out, could be disastrous. Ending up penniless and unemployed in Italy was not something she could risk.

"But wouldn't you rather do something else? Like—I don't know—run your own place. Your own nursery. Be your own boss?"

As it happened, Emma had thought often since, and longingly, of the idea she had aired in the Florence square with Orlando.

"Former nanny to the stars," Darcy teased. "You could put that on your sign as well. Might as well get something out of your time slaving for the Evil One. You'll be turning people away."

Emma smiled.

"You could even have a Mediterranean menu," Darcy suggested excitedly. "Loads of pasta and olive oil. That'd get the aspirational parents beating down your door!"

Emma agreed that it would, indeed.

"So what's stopping you?" Darcy urged. "If it's money, I've got some. You set up a business, I'll invest in it!"

She was disappointed to see Emma looked doubtful. She had credited her with more get up and go.

"I really think you ought to look into it, you know, like now," Darcy enthused. "Strike while the iron's hot, find out what you need to do, what certificates you need and all that…"

Certificates. Official approval. That, in a nutshell, was the issue, Emma knew. She had all the skills, all the qualifications, all the energy required for the nursery project. She longed to tell Darcy the truth, that there was nothing she would like more. But then Darcy would obviously ask what the problem was, and that was something Emma could not tell her.

The problem was that she lacked a clear name. Should Vanessa ever find out about her plans—and it was unlikely she wouldn't if the nursery was, as Emma intended, in London—there was no doubt that the relevant authorities would be informed in short order about the cocaine in the handbag. And that would be that.

"Oh well. Let me know if you change your mind," Darcy said, disappointed that her grand gesture had unexpectedly missed its mark. Reluctantly, she set out finally on her run.

Chapter Fifty-one

ORLANDO WAS DAWDLING THROUGH Rocolo. He had no particular reason for going there, apart from the wish to get away from the aubergo. The Faughs had gone up another level on the smug-o-meter, and his father had descended even further into depression while his mother, distracted at having lost her precious pink Gucci wallet, was turning the villa upside down in search of it. It had, apparently, vanished without trace. The imminent arrival, into this volatile situation, of his A-level results would be, Orlando felt, like tossing a match into a barrel of petrol.

It was a sunny day and, despite his circumstances, the picturesque Italian village, its golden stone shining in the sun, lifted his spirits. He had walked up past the restaurant and was entering the arcaded square at the top when something made him stop. Right in front of him, on the cobbled surface of the square, a small, blond boy of about five years of age lay on the ground, unmoving.

Orlando looked about him. There seemed no one around who was in charge of this child at all.

Orlando bent over him. The boy was breathing—a relief—but very still. Had he fainted? Fallen and broken something? "Are you alright?" he asked. "What are you doing?" He felt instinctively that the boy was British.

To Orlando's great relief, the child lifted his tousled, sandy-blond head and looked round with unconcerned blue eyes. "Looking at a caterpillar," he said in a matter-of-fact treble, sticking a small plump digit out in front of him to where a small, plump grub slowly progressed up and over one of the cobblestones.

"That's quite a nice one." Orlando squatted on his haunches. "Fat and furry." He grinned at the child. "What's his name?"

Still lying on the ground, the boy propped himself up on his elbows. He frowned at Orlando. "Don't be silly. He's a caterpillar. Caterpillars don't have names."

"Who are you?"

At the imperious little voice behind him, Orlando turned to find a pair of solemn blue eyes beneath a fringe of perfect white blondeness. A girl of about four, dressed identically to the boy, had materialised apparently from nowhere and was looking at him with an unnerving stare. She was, he thought, an enchanting little thing, silver fair, with white skin and flaxen hair and naughty, dancing blue eyes.

"I'm Hero."

"How do you do, Hero," said Orlando gravely.

"And I'm Cosmo." The blond boy had scrambled to his feet, red impressions on his small knees from the cobblestones. "Do you know Thomas?" he asked.

"Thomas who?"

"The Tank Engine," expostulated the boy, as if the question were ridiculous, which, Orlando realised, it probably was when you were five.

He folded his arms and put a finger to his lips. "Now let me see," Orlando said, in comic-pompous tones that had their origins in Hugh. "That's the one with Percy in, isn't it?"

"And Harvey the Breakdown Train," Cosmo returned eagerly.

"Harvey the Breakdown Train?" Orlando raised his eyebrows. "I see you like the most obscure ones."

"Cranky, Mavis, Troublesome Trucks, Sir Handel," chanted Cosmo, in a tone Orlando realised was a challenge.

He picked up the gauntlet unhesitatingly. "Rheneas, Skarloey, Lady, Neville…"

"Salty, Bulstrode, Culdee…" hit back Cosmo.

"Catherine the Mountain Coach…" Orlando continued with ease. He hadn't watched Thomas the Tank Engine every morning on Nickleodeon for nothing. He could go on for ever if Cosmo wanted.

Looking down, he saw Cosmo's small, serious face was flushed with pleasure. "You know a lot about Thomas," he admitted.

"Doesn't everyone?" Orlando sounded mock-shocked.

"Totty doesn't," the children chorused.

"Who's Totty?"

"Our nanny."

Orlando was so relieved to hear there was a nanny that the tone of gloom in their voices almost passed him by. "Where is she then?" he asked. Totty. Totty. It sounded familiar.

The children looked blankly at him from their large blue eyes. "We don't know. She left us here. She sometimes does."

"Your nanny leaves you by…yourselves?" Orlando repeated. "You mean…she's just gone into a shop or something?"

They looked blankly back at him. "Totty didn't say," Cosmo said eventually. "She just…"—he shook his head and shrugged— "went off."

Totty. Where had he heard that name before? Orlando furrowed his brow in thought, to no avail, however. He had no memory for names; admittedly, as his A-level results were abundantly about to illustrate, he had no memory for anything.

"I'm hungry," Hero announced now suddenly. "Can you take us for something to eat?"

Eleven o'clock, Orlando saw from his watch. Some way from lunchtime, but, having been unable to face the communal breakfast—the great Faugh jaws and the twins' tumble-drier mouths—he was hungry himself. A panini and a beer at that restaurant on the hill would be perfect. And he'd be happy to take Hero and Cosmo too, but one couldn't just take children one had only just met. What if their nanny, this mysterious, obviously stupid, and incompetent Totty, returned? He could be accused of abduction, anything. Arrested, thrown into jail.

"Please," said the little girl, her eyes round and appealing. "I'm really, really hungry."

"So am I," added the little boy plaintively.

"Totty gave us hardly any breakfast…" Hero said, sighing tragically.

"She never does…" agreed her brother.

"She's awful…"

"Horrid…"

"But what about your parents?" Orlando broke in. "Can't they give you some more breakfast? Can't you talk to them?"

Two pairs of eyes now fixed themselves on his. "Mummy's always busy." Hero stared baldly.

"And Daddy's always away," Cosmo assured him, eagerly.

"Yes, but aren't they here now? You're on holiday, aren't you?" It was a guess, but it seemed likely.

Hero nodded. "But Mummy and Daddy aren't," she solemnly informed him. "They're coming soon though."

"It might be today," Cosmo added, hopefully.

Orlando regarded them. A wave of sympathy broke over him. It all sounded so miserably familiar. Mother too busy, father away. Holidaying with the nanny. Fourteen, fifteen years ago, this could have been him. Except that, of the many nannies who had cared for him, none were exactly criminally negligent, unlike the absent Totty.

"Well—can we get in touch with your parents? I mean, where do they live?" The hope that it was some tiny hamlet with only two houses that was easily traceable flared wildly within him.

"London."

"Oh." That was that then.

"There's a nice restaurant just round the corner…" Cosmo remarked longingly, returning to the food theme.

"But what about Totty?" Orlando objected.

"She won't care," the children chorused in unison.

❖❖❖

Marco walked among his tables, repositioning a chair here, brushing off a crumb there, taking deep breaths of satisfaction as he surveyed his kingdom. It was almost lunchtime, and all these tables would be completely full. The bookings diary said so, and there were regulars who just turned up, scorning bookings diaries. But as they came every day, he put them in the bookings diary anyway; not that they knew.

He glanced at his watch, the watch he had been given for his eighteenth birthday and whose glass was split after a bullying chef in a top London restaurant had hurled a pan at him in fury. He had not had it repaired. It would remain as a reminder never to abuse staff; a reminder, too, of the boiling hatred underlings such as himself had felt for their oppressors. He never wanted any of his staff to feel that way about him.

And how did he want people to feel about him? One person, in particular?

He looked at his watch again. Where was she? He'd got the cheese out and everything. It sat beside him on its board, warming in the sun; he fretted it was losing its flavour.

He had estimated she would arrive here around this time, but his calculations had all gone wrong. It was annoying. He was skilled at time estimates; his job and his dishes depended on split-second timing. But women, of course, were not soufflés or stock reductions.

"An espresso, Chef?" Daria was at his elbow. Marco looked gloomily up at her through the tangles of his hair. He felt guilty and rather silly. Here he was, messing about outside, when they had full covers for lunchtime, both early and late sittings.

"Grazie, Daria, but I'm coming in now."

Daria dimpled. Her almond-shaped brown eyes shone naughtily. "Are you sure, Chef? Your friend is here."

"What?" Marco gasped, his head and hair flying up. Excitedly, he saw that Daria was right. There she was, finally, a small figure among all the other milling shoppers, tourists, or mere loiterers, but a figure he had come nonetheless to recognise in an instant.

"You might want to stay outside a little longer, possibly?" the waitress smiled. "I can take care of the scallops," she added.

She glided off, leaving Marco staring after her, confounded. How on earth did Daria know? He had said nothing about the girl to his staff. They must have watched him, have worked it out for themselves. On the other hand, that his staff cared was wonderful. It showed concern for his happiness and well-being, which in itself showed he was achieving at least some of his goals as a restaurant owner. The only person he could imagine wanting to set any of his own former bosses up with was Cruella de Vil.

❖ ❖ ❖

She hadn't meant to. But Darcy couldn't resist. She had set out for the run that morning determined to pass the restaurant by. But she had slowed down, almost immediately, when out of eyeshot of the villa.

The lovely countryside looked much better when you weren't belting through it at full tilt, feeling that at any second your heart might give out. You had the chance to appreciate it. In the woodland outside the village, Darcy slowed down still further, admiring the sun-dappled shade on the stippled, slender trunks of the trees.

When she struggled up the hill into the village, Marco was waiting for her, as he had said he would be, with a large piece of pale, crumbly cheese. "It's made for us by one very small-scale producer in Italy. I'd like to know what you think of it." He placed the plate before her with a flourish and watched her expectantly.

Before she could stop herself, she had chiselled out a small lump from the cheese's golden crumbly side and put it in her mouth. The result was a terrific explosion of creamy, nutty saltiness that left her senses in free fall. She listened to Marco explain where it came from, by whom and how it was made, and that one of the best ways of enjoying it was with a ripe sliced pear with some good olive oil drizzled over. She should try it; he would go and get it.

As he headed back into the restaurant, she looked round happily at the pretty, pale-green tables with their creamy shades with, here and there, a few coffee drinkers under them. She felt warm and alive. That tight, scraping feeling of hunger had gone. It was like a car alarm that had shrieked for days being suddenly turned off.

Marco returned with a sky-blue plate on which a peeled, fresh, opalescent pear lay arranged in beautiful concentric circles, scattered with pepper and drizzled with golden oil. It seemed impossible he had done it in the time. Had he prepared it in advance, especially for her? Savouring the perfumed flavour of the fruit combined with the sharp cheese, she flicked a glance at Marco, who grinned, squinting in the bright morning sun that lit up the brown depths of his eyes. They were, she suddenly thought, rather beautiful.

"Good?" He cocked an eyebrow in her direction.

"Very good."

"Oh, and try these olives too…" He produced some, seemingly from nowhere.

"You're a magician," she laughed.

"Not me. Nature is the magician. A beautiful olive, it looks like a simple thing, but it is a great luxury," Marco said.

She smiled at him. "What's the greatest luxury of all?"

She had meant food and was surprised when he said, "Love. Of course. Love is the greatest luxury of all."

She noticed his intense and faraway expression. Was he thinking about someone in particular? Who, she wondered, suddenly interested.

"Beauty and love, they are both very simple," Marco expanded suddenly.

"Are they?" Neither seemed particularly so to her. Beauty—the Hollywood variety at least—could only be attained after starvation and painful marathons. And love? Christian hadn't been in touch after the last text. He had not replied to any of hers.

"Very simple," Marco asserted gently. He was careful to keep his gaze trained on the two old ladies talking animatedly in the middle of the square. If Darcy saw his expression now, she would guess.

A pair of small children suddenly wheeled off the main street and came clattering into the restaurant.

"Excuse me," Marco said, smiling, to Darcy. "I seem to have some customers."

The small girl ran up to him. Marco found himself looking into a pair of grave blue eyes beneath a silver-fair fringe. "Have you," Hero asked him earnestly, "got any spaghetti?"

Marco chuckled. "Plenty," he assured her, as Darcy, nearby, giggled.

Cosmo, catching up, folded his small white arms. "Tinned spaghetti?"

The gasp of horror from the coffee drinkers could, Darcy thought, be heard all round Rocolo.

❖ ❖ ❖

By the time Orlando arrived, it was a fait accompli. Cosmo and Hero stood in the doorway of the restaurant, their faces split in huge beams. When they saw him, they ran towards him, waving little fists clutching tall, pale breadsticks.

The chef now emerged. Orlando regarded him cagily. His mother and the Faughs had not exactly distinguished themselves the night they all dined here; it seemed impossible Marco would not remember.

But he seemed to have other things on his mind. "These children are yours?"

"No," said Orlando, horrified. "I'm looking after them…sort of."

"They asked me for tinned spaghetti," Marco exclaimed.

Orlando blushed, imagining what an insult this must be in Italy. The land of fresh pasta. "I'm so sorry…" he began.

"Woo woo!"

Cosmo, Orlando now saw, was busily lining up, one after the other, about ten chairs from all the surrounding tables and was sitting at the head of the line, revolving his arms at the sides.

"'Choo choo!"

"Cosmo!" exclaimed Orlando. "Sorry again," he added to Marco.

"Is fine," the chef reassured him. "Has given me an idea, in fact." He strode over to the little boy, dropped to his muscular hunkers, and tickled Cosmo under the chin. "You like trains, huh?"

Cosmo nodded.

"Well, what you say I cook you train wheels pasta?"

"Train wheels?" Cosmo's blue eyes glowed.

"Come with me." Marco crooked his finger.

Darcy, nibbling the last of the cheese, watched the two men and the children and felt rather choked. The big, awkward chef was so gentle with them. As was the blond boy, who seemed to handle the toddlers extremely well. He was, Darcy noticed—indeed, it was impossible not to notice—extraordinarily good-looking.

She thought involuntarily of Emma; her description of her lost Orlando could almost fit this boy.

She was distracted in her musings by a small explosion from the restaurant. "Train wheels, Orlando!" Cosmo yelped.

Orlando! Darcy stared, electrified, at the blond boy. Could it be? She reached for a napkin and dabbed her mouth as she hurriedly stood up. She needed to get back to Emma at once.

Cosmo rushing towards Orlando, unclenching his hand and

spilling about fifteen small, round, spoked pieces of dry pasta out onto the small, square, sage-painted table.

Marco appeared from the doorway. "Rotolline. That's Italian for wheels. I keep this pasta in the restaurant for when families come. Children usually like my menu, but sometimes we have…"—he rolled his brown eyes hugely at Cosmo and Hero—"children who prefer tinned pasta. Can you imagine that?"

They looked guiltily back at him.

"But even tinned-pasta eaters like train wheels with homemade tomato sauce," Marco told them.

"I'd like them!" Cosmo gasped.

But Hero shook her silver-fair head. Her pale brow was knotted, and there was a steely glint in her narrowed blue eyes. "Not me," she insisted. "I still like tinned best."

Orlando, Darcy saw, looked tense. She felt tense herself. Her eyes slid to Marco. How would the impassioned chef, the champion of all things authentically Italian, take this philistine attack, albeit from a child who looked some distance under five?

Marco's face, she saw, was expressionless. Then, as he continued to regard the indomitable, fair little figure, it became thoughtful. "Maybe I can do something," he said at last in a quiet voice. "Maybe, at the back of a cupboard in my kitchen, I have a tin of spaghetti… just maybe," he warned, raising a scarred finger as Hero began to exclaim and jump about in excitement.

Darcy rose from the table. "Marco. I've got to go." There were other matters afoot than tinned pasta, after all. The excitement of being able to give Emma the good news about Orlando was enough to obliterate completely the thought of the painful run back to the villa. She moved off across the courtyard.

"Come back tomorrow," Marco called after her. "I'm expecting some truffles."

"Truffles!" Darcy exclaimed. "I've never had those!"

"Then you haven't lived," Marco said easily. "I'll see you tomorrow."

Darcy did not move fast. It was obviously unwise on a full stomach. She floated, rather than walked, down the steep hill.

Her mobile beeped. A text? From Christian? She dragged it out of her shorts pocket, feeling the cheese she had just eaten rising up her throat in sick excitement.

> **R U horny? Wish I cd be scrwng U now.
> Tmorrow night?**

Darcy raised her eyebrows. It wasn't exactly Romeo. But it had a certain visceral directness that gave her a charge. Besides, her interest in Christian wasn't in his abilities at literary composition anyway. It was much less complicated than that.

❖ ❖ ❖

You shouldn't, Ken knew, judge a book by its cover. Nonetheless, he found it hard to shake from his memory the sighting of the two men near the playground. He had had enough experience of undesirables to recognise them when he saw them, and he felt increasingly strongly that the proximity of such people to small children was worrying. Drugs—albeit soft ones like cannabis—and kiddies were never a good combination.

Particularly if, as had seemed likely, the men were going to the playground to meet one of the nannies. And not just any of the nannies either, but the nasty blonde in charge of the two children who had made such a strong impression on Ken at the airport. Who were, in fact—and the boy especially—the entire reason he was here.

But what could he do about it, Ken asked himself. It was all very well having his suspicions, but he could hardly hang around the playground himself and order the men to stay away. Nor did there seem much point alerting the local police—wherever they were—as there was no evidence of any wrongdoing. Ken's hunch that, nonetheless, something was wrong, continued to preoccupy him.

Eventually, in a flashbulb-like flash of inspiration, he realised that the answer lay in a combination of the balcony in his room, which overlooked the playground, and also in his own baggage. To be precise, in the black, padded zip case under a heap of creased clothes in the corner of the room. This contained the Leica and long lenses he had hoped never again to use, but which, as they were actually around his neck when he made the spur-of-the-moment decision to fly to Italy, he had been unable to avoid bringing with him.

And thank God he had, Ken thought now. He could use them to survey the playground from his balcony. Because, while his roster of skills numbered neither cooking, nor dancing, nor playing the piano, nor even—he dolefully suspected—being a particularly nice or useful person, one thing Ken was supremely good at was watching—sometimes for hours or even days—other people's movements through the end of a long-lensed camera.

Surviving as a paparazzo had demanded that he was, and, while Ken, in turning his back on his former business, now regretted the years he had spent hiding in people's bushes or crouching down by their cars, he could now see a way to turn those questionable abilities to good use. Possibly even atone for the sins of the past.

Stealthily, swiftly, he set up his camera in the corner of the balcony where it would least likely be noticed by those from below. He pulled the rickety chair from the bedroom outside and positioned it behind the lens. He sat down, twisted the lens, and got the playground gate in focus. He was immediately filled with a sense of satisfaction. Whatever happened now, if those men turned up, if they met one of the nannies and nefarious business was afoot, he would capture it all on film.

Ken was, in accordance with general paparazzi law, expecting to have to wait some time before anything occurred. There was also the possibility that it never would, that the men he had seen had been a one-off. His instincts, however, which were rarely wrong, told him otherwise.

Having armed himself with some bottles of ice-cold lager from one of the shops in the square and a salami sandwich the length and breadth of his forearm, he settled down and prepared to wait.

Chapter Fifty-two

MITCH MASTERSON, IN HIS L.A. office, was chewing anxiously on his third jelly doughnut of the morning. But the sweet, chewy dough, while it plugged the ever-present hole in his stomach, could do nothing about the gap in his soul. That his spirits were lower than they had been when he was the least successful agent on the company's books seemed ironic as now, along with Greg Cucarachi, he was almost at the top of the pecking order with two of his actresses in the new Jack Saint movie.

As Mitch finished his doughnut, he saw, out of the corner of his eye, Cucarachi trying the door of his office. He had started to close it, even contemplated locking it, to avoid the daily torture from his co-worker that he knew was coming now.

Greg rattled the door open with a flourish. "Good morning, Mitchell!" he exclaimed. "And how are you today on this bright and beautiful Hollywood morning?"

"I'm fine," Mitch grunted.

"Belle learnt her lines yet?" Cucarachi asked in mock-concern. "I do hope so. I hear Jack's getting pretty pissed at her. Some of the cast are asking whether she can actually read…"

"She can read alright," Mitch snapped. No one who had seen Belle grab her contract and devour it with her eyes could doubt that. That she hadn't shown the same alacrity in learning her part for the film was, Mitch knew from Saint's frequent irate phone calls, becoming almost as much of an on-set issue as Darcy's weight.

"Arlington Shorthouse isn't very happy," Greg added gleefully.

"Yeah." He'd had Arlington on to him all the previous afternoon. It had not been a pleasant conversation, and, together with those from Jack Saint, had made Mitch almost long for the days when the only phone calls he received were from producer's assistants on obscure Latino soap operas.

"You know," Mitch said now, as inspiration struck him, "I'm kinda wondering if Belle's, um, issues haven't got something to do with your client Christian Harlow. Whether the influence he's exerting on my client, Belle Murphy is, shall we say…"—Mitch put his head mock-questioningly on one side and drummed his fat fingers lightly on his desk—"entirely a good one."

Ha! Take that, Cucarachi.

Greg, however, was ready. "Interesting," he mused, stroking his long nose. "An interesting thought." He looked up and smiled. "Perhaps you'd prefer it if my client Christian Harlow—who, incidentally, knows all his lines backwards—transferred his interest back to your client Darcy Prince?"

A pang of murderous fury went through Mitch. The bastard.

"Catch you later!" Greg sang, swinging Mitch's door shut with a bang that made the walls rattle.

❖ ❖ ❖

"I mean, Jack's, like, just so unreasonable," Belle stormed as they climbed into the Ferrari at Christian's villa. "He's bullying me. He's a mistletoe…no, misanthrope—that's hatred of women, isn't it?"

"I wouldn't know," Christian said wearily, fumbling for the ignition. But while he did not know the word Belle was searching for, he knew the sentiment behind it. Getting back with this particular woman had been one big mistake.

Jesus, had he got it wrong. He'd jumped back into bed with Belle believing her star to be once more on the rise, only to find her addled by self-importance and, Christian suspected, whatever drink she could get hold of. He felt he almost preferred her on the skids; she'd been clingy, sure, but at least she hadn't imagined she was Nicole Kidman, Cate Blanchett, and Elizabeth Taylor all rolled into one.

The fact she couldn't be bothered to learn her lines was the most dangerous aspect, however; the entire set knew she and he were together, and Christian found himself obliged to mount a charm offensive of spectacular proportions on the director to avoid becoming tarred with the same brush.

He'd even bought Saint a present the other day: one of those little, red Vespa scooters. There'd been a discussion about Italian scooters during a break in filming; Saint had described them as design classics. Christian, whose idea of a design classic was a yacht with two helicopters and a submarine and felt scooters were for losers, nonetheless wasted no time moving heaven and earth to get one for Saint—or obliging his agent, from the distance of America—to move heaven and earth to save him the trouble.

"That bastard Saint's making my life a misery," Belle butted in. "He's victimizing me. He hates women."

"No, he doesn't," Christian snapped. "He just doesn't like people who turn up six hours late on set without knowing their part. It costs money, that sort of thing. The schedule's pretty tight."

Belle's clinging top was even tighter. The swirling pattern made her breasts look bigger than ever, whereas her shorts were so tiny they looked like denim panties. Had he known what an imagination was, Christian might well have reflected that Belle left little to it.

A vision of Darcy in her floaty yellow dress swam before him. He'd texted her before they left and now felt a warm rush of anticipation in his groin. From her reply, she was more than on for it. And screwing Darcy was much more fun than Belle. Less painful, in every sense.

It might be a little complicated, but Belle probably wouldn't be around much longer. He'd heard Saint was calling agents left, right, and centre to get a replacement for her, although he still seemed to be holding out hope that Darcy would return to the set. "A rare talent," was how he had described her, in Christian's hearing. He'd felt a little sick at that. Darcy had been the better horse to back, all along.

Whereas Belle was a sinking ship, or as sinking as a ship could be with assets as inflated as hers. Maybe he'd dump her after this lunch.

He started the Ferrari with a roar that, as had been intended, sent Sugar diving for the depths of Belle's handbag.

"Shit!" she exclaimed, peering in after him.

"He's died?" Christian asked hopefully.

"No. He's shat all over the script."

❖❖❖

It was twelve o'clock now; the sun was high and hot in the sky. The shouts of the children in the playground were borne upwards to Ken on the lunch-scented breeze. It was very warm on the balcony; he had followed the shadow round, lugging his chairs and camera to the shade, but now it threatened to disappear altogether. Neither Totty nor the suspicious men had shown yet, and if they didn't soon, Ken knew he faced the prospect of having to await them under the full heat of the blazing sun.

He was beginning to lose heart. Perhaps they were all having lunch. Perhaps he ought to follow their example and have some too.

Ken stood up and stretched. And, as soon as he took his eye from the camera, he saw Totty. She was rounding the corner from the church end of the square.

Ken drew a swift breath in and sat hurriedly back down again at his chair, knocking the carefully set-up camera as he did so. His hands shook as he fumbled to refocus the lens.

Totty slowed down as she approached the entrance to the playground. Ken watched her pass it and walk down the encircling pathway directly below his balcony. Apprehension began to clutch him—was she headed somewhere else altogether?—and then relaxed its grip as she stopped just beneath where he sat.

Right next to where she had paused was a bench, half-hidden from the pathway running past by the bushes. As Ken followed her movements down his lens, Totty, after looking about her for a few seconds, slipped behind the bushes and sat down in the concealed area behind. She took out her mobile and began to talk agitatedly into it. Ken strained his ears, but, for all she was directly underneath him and the air was still, it was impossible to make out what she was saying.

Almost immediately, the two men he had seen before appeared. They walked with heads bent and hands shoved into their pockets, quickly, purposefully. And looking, Ken thought, lining up the first shot, if anything, more undesirable than before. They were loping along in battered jeans, tanned in a dry, dirty sort of way, their features mostly hidden in the shadows under their baseball caps. One held a mobile in a scarred and tattooed hand. Ken guessed he was talking to Totty.

Taking shot after shot, he now watched, excitement and amazement bunching in his throat, as the two men slid behind the bushes where Totty waited.

The encounter was businesslike. Little seemed to be said. Action was all: quick as a flash, dirty hands went into grubby pockets, and a slew of small plastic bags containing white powder suddenly appeared on the bench besides the nanny. Ken zoomed in and fired again and again, his brow dark and furrowed with disgust.

He kept the lens unwaveringly on her. Snap! Snap! Totty, taking the packets. Snap! Snap! Totty, slipping them into her handbag. Snap! Snap! Totty, getting out a crocodile-skin wallet, opening it, handing over a wad of notes. Snap! Snap! The two men, taking them. Snap! Snap! The two men, getting up and leaving, loping away as swiftly as they had come, down the shadowy pathway until they turned the corner into the sunlit square.

Carefully, Ken detached his face from the camera. He had pressed his eye and forehead to it so hard in excitement that it was now almost stuck. He rubbed his sweating forehead and blinked, feeling rather drained now with the drama of it all. Still, he'd got them now.

Glancing below, he saw that Totty had not yet moved. He guessed immediately that she was waiting. There was another act of this unsavoury drama to come. Someone else was expected.

He put his eye to his camera again. It could be quick; he had to be ready. Ken recognised but could not, at first, place the two young men with big hair and teeth who now hurried up the path by the playground. He got them in focus and fired away, his mental Rolodex spinning all the while. He'd seen them recently…

Oh yes! He'd got it now. The restaurant. They'd been part of a group, with that good-looking boy. And, more to the point, with a certain big, booming, colourful, well-known, and, Ken had always felt, particularly unpleasant Member of Parliament. Striding up the path now, looking inordinately pleased with themselves in their striped shirts, pressed jeans, and snaffled loafers, were the sons of Hugh Faugh.

As the boys slipped behind the bushes, Ken's camera whirred away. Snap! Snap! Kissing Totty on both cheeks as if they were meeting at a drinks party. Snap! Snap! One of them reaching into his pocket and producing an oddly feminine pink wallet that looked as if it might belong to their mother. Snap! Snap! Drawing out a handful of notes and being given a handful of plastic packets in return. Snap! Snap! Totty laughing. Snap! The boys laughing. Snap! Snap! The three of them getting up and leaving together, arm in arm. This was, Ken realised, his insides tight with excitement, shaping up to be quite a story.

Chapter Fifty-three

With a boom like thunder, the red Ferrari roared into the Rocolo carpark. Christian scanned wildly about him for a parking space, threw the car into one, and wrenched up the hand brake.

Belle's annoyance about Saint had, somewhere along the way, metamorphosed into raging lust. She had kept reaching over and stroking his penis as he drove, and with such a practised hand that, despite himself, he had found himself stiffening.

Christian looked up. Was the tree hanging over the space enough to hide them? It was lunchtime, and the carpark was sizzling in the heat, car bonnets blazing, empty of people. He could probably get away with a quick one; it would be the last one, after all. She was clawing at his fly zip now. Grunting, Christian unbuckled his belt.

❖❖❖

Full of excitement at having spotted the lost Orlando, Darcy pelted down the cobbled hill out of Rocolo. Slowing down to avoid some people crossing the bridge over the stream, she flicked a glance into the carpark and saw the red Ferrari under the tree.

Christian!

Skipping between the shining bonnets of the red-hot cars in the carpark, Darcy dashed across.

As she approached, she recognised the dark, oily quiff of Christian's head, his tanned and handsome brow facing downwards, bobbing up and down. She could hear a grunt. Were there problems with the car? Was he fixing something?

"Christian!"

The word hung in the air, in the bright, hot sunshine. Darcy could now see that he was indeed fixing something. Someone. Christian, a climactic cry breaking from his throat, looked up and met Darcy's horrified eyes.

For a second, she was stunned. Then her eyes rolled from his face to the woman writhing below him; her breasts jutting upwards, her bare thighs wound round his muscular buttocks like the tentacles of a tanned octopus, snakes of platinum hair shaking across the car seat like Medusa's own.

Belle!

"Darcy!" Belle's tousled blonde head now emerged. "Fancy running into you! It seems like ages!" She flashed a brilliant smile through extravagantly smeared lipstick. "Hope you don't mind me saying, sweetie. But I'm not sure it's working."

The woolly feeling was still enveloping Darcy. She moved her tongue, but it felt as dry and heavy as a block of wood. Her eyes rolled over Christian, who seemed similarly lost for words, stuttering in his sunglasses above his lipstick-smeared torso.

"Of course," Belle added smugly, "some people just have to face the fact that exercise doesn't work for them. I'm so lucky, of course, not having to do anything to keep my shape. But—and I'm saying this as a friend," she added, batting her somewhat bent eyelashes, "I gotta say, Darcy, that you've actually gotten bigger since you started running."

Christian, meanwhile, was following his instincts. Self-preservation, which dictated his every move, was dictating now that he started the engine and got the hell out. There was nothing to be gained from hanging around and trying to explain himself to both of the women at the same time. Even if he could have done.

"Hey, c'mon," Belle was calling to Darcy. "Don't get mad. You win some; you lose some. Although, to be honest, sweetie, you haven't lost any."

Christian screeched the car into reverse and roared around the carpark to the exit, heedless of anything or anyone that might have been in his way. Belle's hair streamed out like a white flag. "But don't take it personally," she was shouting. "It's not you, it's your metabolism."

As the cloud of blue smoke from the Ferrari's exhaust enveloped her, Darcy felt light-headed and nauseous. There was a buzzing sensation around the edge of her vision. The trees looked blurred; the shining vehicles in the carpark wobbled violently. She took a step back and stumbled. Oh, God, Darcy thought, I'm going to faint.

Christian roared off down the road. Belle's shrieks in his ear and the scream of the wind merged into one. She was clutching at her clothes, and her hair whipped around her face like a lash.

Rounding a bend, Christian saw too late the red Vespa scooter coming towards him. He slammed on the brake, clung to the steering wheel, battling for control as the heavy, blood-red car screamed, skidded, and convulsed into a great sliding side arc that crashed violently into the shoulder of the road, taking the motorbike and its bearded, cowboy-booted rider with it.

❖ ❖ ❖

A couple were walking up through Rocolo village. The man was tall, thin, and pale, with sparse, sandy hair and wonky glasses that slipped down his nose, no matter how often he pushed them up. He looked worried and cross and was striding some distance ahead of the woman, a trim blonde in a red flowered dress and with red-rimmed blue eyes.

Vanessa had cried all the way from the airport. She had never thought it was possible for James to be so angry. He had been stonily furious throughout the flight, but it was only when they were alone in the rental car that he had really let rip. "You let the children go by themselves to Italy? I just can't believe it." His knuckles, clenching the steering wheel in fury, were bone-white. His neck was thrust forward, and his eyes strained through the windscreen.

"They're not on their own. They're with Totty…" Vanessa bleated, for what seemed the hundredth time.

"Totty!" James snorted, with a depth of loathing Vanessa had never heard before. "Totty! You know I never liked her. Never trusted her. But you let her take the children. The most precious things we have. And now we can't get hold of her, we don't know what's going on…" His voice rose to a desperate wail, a cry of fearful misery that Vanessa found more terrifying than his anger. "What possessed you?" he hurled at her, his usually mild blue eyes now turned to balls of aquamarine fire as he glared through his spectacles.

"I've told you," Vanessa wailed, her fingers on her lap tearing at each other in terror. "It was a last-minute work thing. A feature I couldn't turn down…"

"You mean a free couple of days at a luxury spa run by some duchess," James screamed. "You've lost our children—all for the sake of a free back rub and a complimentary pedicure and tea with some fucking aristo."

"I thought it would be okay," Vanessa wept, trying weakly to defend herself even though she felt like a mouse in the claws of a huge and pitiless eagle. "I thought Hengist's parents were there, in their villa, to keep an eye on things. I didn't realise it would only be Hengist's nanny. I thought Lord and Lady Westonbirt were there…"

"Lord and Lady Westonbirt," James spat. "That's you all over," he snarled, hurling the blue fireballs at her again. "You'll believe anything, accept anything, give anyone anything, even our children, if you think they're upmarket. And now you've ruined both our lives with your fucking pointless, ridiculous, contemptible snobbery…"

"Don't!" cried Vanessa. As the car hurtled along, she stared at the blurred scenery, pressing away the realisation that any of this was really happening. That she had called Totty several times now, and there was no reply. That the children had been in Italy for several days without her, and she had no idea where they were. That she was the worst mother who had ever lived, the worst wife, the worst person.

Chapter Fifty-four

HERO NUDGED ORLANDO AGAIN. Realising she wanted his chocolate-sprinkled cappuccino foam, he obediently began to dispense spoonfuls with his huge, brown hands.

Hero and Cosmo had eaten their lunch now, in two seconds flat it had seemed. His own planned beer and panini had transmogrified into a bowl of the most delicious minestrone he had ever eaten, with a glass of light red wine. He had been reluctant to order this at first, wine, in his mind, being strongly associated with the horrible Hugh Faugh. But Marco had insisted, and the combination was, Orlando had had to admit, a good one.

The benefits of the lunch had gone beyond mere flavour, it seemed to him. Perhaps, he thought ruefully, a bowlful of minestrone before each exam might have considerably improved his A-level results. Certainly, it had affected his brain for the better.

The evidence of this was that Orlando had had a good idea. A feasible way forward had finally suggested itself with regard to the children. He was still certain that Totty could not be far away, but, in her continued absence, the most obvious thing to do was return to the playground. If Totty was not there, surely one of the other so-called nannies would know where the children were staying. And if that route failed, then the police were the obvious next stage.

❖❖❖

Marco looked lovingly at the chicken stock reduction boiling away in the pan. It was almost ready now, mere minutes from reaching its perfect state of being a shallow pool of unctuous, gloopy, dark, silky flavour, almost like chocolate sauce but with a taste at the opposite end of the spectrum: savoury, deep, intense, essential.

Yes, just a minute or so more now. Some chefs, he knew, would have taken the stock off at this point, but he liked to take it to the brink, to risk it, to literally play with fire, reach the moment when the reduction nearly burnt, then just scoop it off in time, caramelly, thick, rich, and brown. Like Darcy's hair.

He thought about the truffles he had promised her, for when she came next.

Truffles!

Exciting, mysterious, expensive, pungent, powerfully earth scented; vital, sweaty, and yes…sexy. Very sexy.

He could hardly wait to introduce her to real Italian truffles. He could see her face as she tasted them, her eyes closing, her mouth falling open…

His felt his heart rate increase. He began to breathe deeply. Steam was almost coming out of his nostrils, smoke even. But no, not out of his nostrils. The brown and billowing acrid clouds were coming from somewhere below him, in the pan.

Damn. He had burnt the reduction.

❖ ❖ ❖

Emma struggled up the steep, cobbled incline to the village. Even without Morning round her neck, it was a struggle. How Darcy managed to get up here every day was incredible.

Everything seemed a struggle this morning, however. She had struggled with her mood after Darcy had left for her run, sitting on the terrace lost in gloomy contemplation of the subject they had talked about—the nursery she longed to start but probably never would. Eventually Mara had appeared.

"Why you sit here sulking?" the housekeeper had demanded.

"You waste your time. You should go out. Go into Rocolo. I look after the baby here." She had looked at her watch. "If you go now, you will catch the bus. Go on. It will do you good."

Was it doing her good, Emma wondered. Now, ahead of her, was the restaurant, with its pretty white shades shining in the sun over its pretty green tables. When she got that far up, she'd treat herself to a cappuccino.

"Emma!" Children's voices.

Emma blinked. She knew those voices. She peered into the dazzlingly sunny courtyard.

The boy in his navy shorts and striped T-shirt, his blonde fringe shimmering in the sun, scampered excitedly towards her. His sister, an eager, pale little face under a mop of white hair, scampered after him. Her spoon, so recently an essential accomplice in the all-important matter of eating Orlando's coffee foam, clattered, unwanted, to the cobbles.

"Hero?" Emma whispered. "Cosmo…oof!" The child had cannoned into her and thrown his arms tightly round her knees.

She placed a trembling hand on the familiar, small sandy head. Through her blurry vision, she now saw someone tall come towards her. He shook his hair awkwardly, an unmistakeable gesture.

"Emma!" There was a strange, fizzing sensation in Orlando's feet. A warm feeling spread within him until it glowed in his throat and in his stomach at the same time. He felt light and wobbly, as if he could sing, dance, or even fly.

"Orlando?" A flock of butterflies so big that they could actually have been seagulls swerved through her stomach.

"Choo choo!" Cosmo steamed up. "You're blocking the line," he said sternly to Orlando.

❖ ❖ ❖

"You never told me you were going to let her take them," James growled, as he and Vanessa struggled up the cobbled hill into the village.

There were tears on his cheeks, she saw. Her heart twisted and tore within her. "The last thing you told me was that you and Totty were going together. And then I come back from this trip, ring you on your mobile from the airport to find you're still in London and they're... they're...God knows where," he added, his voice a broken whisper.

"I couldn't get hold of you," she said weakly, more as a statement of fact than any attempt to defend herself. That was obviously impossible. "The spa thing came up suddenly. And like I said, I thought it would be alright..."

"You knew I was going to the Congo," James stormed, his voice rising so that passersby stared at him in surprise. "You knew the FO was sending me out there again. All the more reason for you to take full responsibility for once, I'd have thought. But, oh, no. Oh, no."

There was such contempt, such hatred in his voice. This was not James. This was not her mild, hardworking husband. Not the man she had routinely put down, overruled, shouted at, bullied. This was a father who had returned from a work trip to find his wife had sent their children away with someone he neither trusted nor liked. And who Vanessa, were she able to admit it to herself, increasingly neither trusted nor liked either.

There had been many incidents with Totty—small but significant. The way she never made the children wash their hands before and after meals. The way she frequently put them to bed without bathing them or insisting they cleaned their teeth. The way in which, at every opportunity, she parked them in front of the television, Hero with a pacifier in her mouth. A pacifier!

Vanessa reserved particular unease for the memory, which she tried hard to suppress, of the way Totty had lingered in Emma's room when she had showed her it at Hero's party. Vanessa had gone to the loo and had expected to find Totty back in the kitchen, but instead she had appeared there some minutes after Vanessa and with the dramatic news that there was something up there she must see.

Vanessa could see herself now, leaping upstairs, seeing the handbag with the tiny, incriminating piece of folded white paper in it, calling Emma up, sacking her on the spot…

Oh, God. She had asked no questions at the time. Getting rid of Emma was all she had wanted. She had never admitted the true circumstances to James about her conversation in the kitchen with Totty and had vigorously beaten off all his suggestions that it could not possibly be true about Emma. Of course, it was true. It had to be, because if it wasn't, then where had that wrap of cocaine come from? How had Totty, in the less than five minutes she was up there, known where to look for it?

As the ascent tugged painfully on her calf muscles and the sun beat mercilessly down, Vanessa went hot and cold as she thought again of the clues she had not so much missed, as wilfully ignored.

It seemed incredible now that she had been willing to overlook all of this on the grounds that Totty's father was a member of the aristocracy. Oh, God, what a fool she had been. Please, God, forgive her; let the children be alright. Please, let them be here.

Vanessa felt a huge, desperate sob tear her chest. Her life was over. Her children were gone, and her husband hated her.

She watched him striding contemptuously ahead, almost shoving people out of his way. James, gentle James, who had never shoved anyone in his life. His idea was to get as fast as possible to the police station, which was apparently in the square at the top. This village was the last place she had had live contact with the children. They hadn't sounded very happy. "When are you coming, Mummy?" Cosmo had whispered, as if someone was listening to him.

James's back blurred as the tears rose. But she could still see how it radiated loathing. Loathing of her. And he had loved her so much. Devotedly and absolutely, Vanessa knew, stung by the additional knowledge that she had never really appreciated it. Had not only taken it utterly for granted but had occasionally affected to doubt it, as when she had toyed with the idea his interest in Emma went beyond the strictly professional.

As if! James's interest in Emma, Vanessa now knew—had always known, in fact—was gratitude for the effort and enthusiasm she brought to the job of looking after their children. Their children! The children he obviously adored, but which she had never really allowed him to spend any time with, so desperate was she to force him, against his will, up the greasy Foreign Office pole. And yet, even despite all this, James had never wanted another woman. He had adored her. And she had treated him like a dog.

He was a gentleman to the backbone. He had borne her tempers, her spite, her unfairness without complaint. He had never judged her, try as he might sometimes to discourage her.

Vanessa had never known pain in her heart like this. Guilt, regret, self-loathing were infinitely more agonising than anything physical she had ever suffered, the births of the children included. The children! As she crossed the bridge, the formerly proud Vanessa, broken and pathetic, all her former fire gone, contemplated throwing herself over it. Had the water below been anything more than a tricklesome stream, she would have.

If only she had listened to James about Emma. If only, Vanessa thought in silent anguish as they walked up into the village their children were last known to have been in, she had never let Emma go.

❖❖❖

"Emma! Emma! Where have you been?" Hero and Cosmo were chanting as they choo-chooed round the tables.

"We've missed you."

"We've had no one to play trains with. No one to play Snakes and Ladders with…"

She glanced at the children and back at Orlando, puzzled and delighted, her eyes framing the question.

"I found them in the square," he explained. "No one was with them."

"No one…?" Emma gasped. "They had no nanny?"

"Well, there is a nanny, but…"

"We've had no one to play Uno with," Hero was complaining. "Totty doesn't know how to play Uno…"

"Totty?" Emma was gripped immediately by a terrible force. "Totty…?"

It was, Emma thought afterwards, as if merely speaking the name had summoned an evil spirit. For, at that very moment, Totty rounded the corner and stormed through the restaurant, blonde hair streaming in her wake, legs flashing vengefully in a tiny miniskirt, scrappy breasts heaving behind a barely there black top.

Orlando stared at the long-legged blonde. He didn't recognise her, but he knew the people with her horribly well. Swaggering between the tables, laughing hysterically, came two stunningly unattractive youths in jeans and loafers with big bouncy hair and enormous teeth. Orlando now remembered where he had heard the name Totty before.

Totty, it seemed, was in nowhere near as good a mood as her companions. She ripped off her sunglasses to reveal eyes flashing in fury. "What are you two doing here?" she roared at the children. They backed away, frightened.

Orlando felt sick. He had absolutely no idea what to do. His instinct was to fell Totty to the ground, but obviously that was out of the question, especially with the children present. He realised miserably that his extensive and expensive education may have included balloon debates and school parliaments, but it had conclusively failed to teach him how to handle an occasion of this nature.

Emma's, however, had been more successful in this respect. "Don't speak to the children like that!" she growled, controlling with only the greatest of difficulties the urge to clamp her hands round Totty's long, brown neck and squeeze hard. She struggled to comprehend the unbelievable yet apparent fact that Totty Belvedere had succeeded her as Cosmo and Hero's nanny. What had possessed Vanessa? And James, who had always seemed so kind and sensible…

Totty looked at Emma. There was, the other girl felt, something of the hypnotizing snake in the eviscerating stare. She watched Totty's face twist with contemptuous recognition. "Just fuck off, okay?" she snarled. "This is my job now. Not yours."

"Not anymore, damn you," shouted the shaking voice of James as he hurtled through the tables, a shattered, weeping Vanessa stumbling behind him.

❖❖❖

"News picture desk, please, darlin'," said Ken. "Tell 'em it's Ken from Mega."

"Okay," came the disembodied, nasal tones of the receptionist.

There was a scrape and a scramble at the other end as the call was put through.

"Yeah?"

Ken recognised the graceless voice of the news picture editor. Dick "'Dastardly'" Richardson. "Wotcha doin' comin' through to me, mate?" Dastardly demanded, irritated. "It's Showbiz you want, innit?"

"Not this time," said Ken lightly, flicking through the images at the back of his digital camera. "These pictures are news."

Chapter Fifty-five

HER FACE WAS SO beautiful; the long sweep of lashes like the hairs on sea urchins, the tiny ears that actually really were shell-like, reminding him of the tiny, tasty clams he liked to use for vongole, the ones the French called palourdes. But this was no time to stand staring at her. She had fainted. She needed help.

"Fast work, Chef!" grinned Nino, the commis chef and the latest, youngest recruit, his naughty dark eyes full of laughter as Marco entered with Darcy in his arms. Rodolfo had brought her up from the carpark. "Mad dogs and Englishmen," Rodolfo had remarked as he handed her over, shaking his head.

She was so light Marco could have carried her however her limbs were arranged. But he had no intention of missing the opportunity of making her embrace him. As she now dutifully draped her long, white arms where he requested, he felt not the triumph he had expected, but something rather more tender. She was so beautiful, so light, so pale, so helpless, like a child.

He walked through the restaurant ignoring the winking brigade of chefs. He was, in fact, barely aware of them or of the excitement outside in the restaurant courtyard, where something between a fight and a reunion seemed to be taking place. For him, as he took her upstairs, the only thing that mattered was the beautiful burden he held.

The wonderful dream was continuing, Darcy thought. She was lying on something yielding and squashy in a cool, shady room. Someone with kind, dark eyes was very close. She felt safe, loved. She smiled.

Her eyes flew open. Recognising Marco, she gasped, jerking herself up into a sitting position and glancing round the simple, white room in alarm. "Where am I? What am I doing here?"

"Relax. You just fainted."

"Fainted?"

Tumbling into her brain now came a clatter of recollections: the red car beneath the trees, Christian's muscular bottom, Belle's tousled head. She closed her eyes. The dream was a nightmare after all.

"You've been running a bit too much," he said. "It's hot out there."

"I have to run," Darcy said miserably. "My thinstructor says so."

"Your thinstructor?"

"The man who's helping me get thin."

"'Helping you get thin? You have a beautiful body. Why do you want to get thinner?"

Darcy sighed. "I don't know," she said, staring at the worn, yet clean floorboards. "I don't know about anything anymore," she added in a whisper. "I've made such a mess of everything."

He did not break her silence. He sensed there was more to come. And indeed it almost was: Darcy breathed in, gathering her strength to launch into the whole sorry saga of the film, Christian, Niall, and Belle. But her shoulders slumped and her eyelids drooped. The effort seemed too much, the subject too long-winded and irrelevant now. Up here, with Marco, none of it seemed to matter. Even Christian. She felt above it and strangely distant.

It occurred to Darcy that the only real, lasting joy she had experienced in recent weeks, perhaps even recent months or years, was here in this very place. She had loved sitting outside Marco's, listening to him rhapsodising over perfect razor clams or the ultimate arugula, or whatever was exciting him that morning, as she sipped coffee and watched the people going by in the square. And even better than the listening was the tasting. The cheese, the olives, the bread…

His work was so creative. He made so many decisions every day, every hour. He was in complete control of what he did and had a clear view of what he wanted to achieve. A degree of self-expression she had always felt denied herself. It seemed to Darcy now that she had spent her life first being ordered about by her parents, then by Niall, then by directors, few of whose vision she had ever understood. She recalled the half-naked Lear and winced.

Oh, what had she done with her life? What had been the point of it all? She had never been in control. Chance and the desires of other people had plotted her path, never her.

She finished speaking and shot him a shamefaced look. She must have been talking for hours, banging on about herself, making him miss the lunchtime service altogether, probably.

But there was no censure in the eyes that steadily held hers. They were so kind. It seemed to Darcy that no one had ever looked at her with quite such understanding.

A warm glow spread through her, to her very finger ends. She wiped her eyes and smiled back.

Chapter Fifty-six

MITCH LOOKED AT GREG Cucarachi sorrowfully. "It's unfucking-believable."

"Tell me about it," replied the other.

Mitch squeezed his eyes together. "Just…" Failing to find a word big enough to express all he felt, he put a plump, perspiring hand to his sweating forehead and let the gesture do it for him. "Your client Christian Harlow…"

"And your client Belle Murphy…" put in Cucarachi, quickly.

"Were driving somewhere in your client Christian Harlow's Ferrari, but your client Christian Harlow was going too fast to be able to stop when he saw…"

"The scooter, yeah…" Cucarachi confirmed.

"The scooter…the scooter…" Mitch could hardly get the words out. "But not, like, any old scooter. The scooter with Jack Saint on it. And not any old Jack Saint. Jack Saint the famous director…"

"You got it," Cucarachi confirmed wearily. He was in Mitch's office, right opposite him, slumped despairingly in one of the chairs facing his desk. There was to be no goading today. The two agents were, for once—for the first time, in fact—united. United in a tragedy affecting both of them.

"All that lost money." Cucarachi groaned. "All we'll get is the signing-on fee."

"But that's a lot," Mitch pointed out encouragingly.

Greg flicked him a look. "For you, sure. You had two stars in this movie. I just had Christian Harlow." Mitch said nothing. He knew it was best not to intrude on private grief.

"This picture was gonna make Christian a big star. It was his big break," Greg wailed, suddenly impassioned.

"Yeah, and it was," Mitch returned dryly. "He's in a hospital in Florence with both his legs in plaster. And it was an even bigger break for Belle. Both arms and several ribs. She's gonna have to be entirely reconstructed."

"Again," pointed out Cucarachi.

"Darcy seems pretty relaxed about the whole thing," Mitch remarked. "Sorry about the accidents, sure. But much less worried than I thought about the film being written off."

"That's crazy," Greg opined. "That's gotta be an act. She's an actress, after all," he reminded Mitch.

"Yeah, but a British one, remember. You know what they're like."

"Crazy."

"Really crazy," Mitch rejoined. He frowned. "You know, I could have sworn she was almost relieved about it."

"You're kidding."

"No, really. All she seemed to care about was the money."

"That figures," Greg said, nodding. "Not that crazy after all, then."

"Except that she said she wanted to put it into a nursery."

Greg blinked. "She said a nursery? Not 'up her nose'?"

"A nursery. Like, you know, for kids."

There was a silence. Mitch reached for a jelly doughnut from the bag on the desk. "Want one?" he offered.

His lean, trim co-worker looked at the fistful of sugar-encrusted fried dough being brandished at him. He looked about to refuse, then his trim eyebrows raised themselves in resignation. He reached for it. "Hey," he said, chewing. "They're not half bad."

Mitch, eyeing his colleague, was starting to think that perhaps Greg wasn't so bad either.

"They say Saint's got no idea about anything," Greg mused morosely as he chewed. "That knock from the accident's completely changed his personality. He's got no recollection he's a filmmaker at all. He thinks he's a cat now." Cucarachi shook his wire wool hair. "Like—what's that about?"

Mitch shook his head. "What a business. Who'd be an agent?"

"You said it, buddy."

The two agents looked at each other in sorrowful complicity.

❖❖❖

In the aubergo, Hugh Faugh was slamming his meaty fists against the newspaper spread out on the table.

The picture that formed the centre spread of the newspaper was of Ivo and Jago laughing on a park bench with a blonde in a miniskirt who was placing small sachets of white powder in their hands. "Peer's daughter Totty de Belvedere (right)," read the caption, "passes the drugs to MP's sons Ivo and Jago Faugh."

"Oh, Christ. How could you. How bloody could you?" Hugh groaned to his sons, his fingers over his eyes so as not to see, yet again, the headline "'Family Values?" in massive fat black type. "How could you be so stupid?"

Family values indeed, Orlando thought sardonically. Hugh's anger seemed directed less at what had been done than at the fact the twins had been caught doing it. He almost felt a stir of pity for Ivo and Jago. With a father like this, what chance had either of them ever had?

"You're a pair of fucking idiots!" Hugh roared at his sons. "Not only have you been kicked out of Oxford, you've probably cost me my job."

Alerted by some party factotum in London that the pictures had appeared, Hugh had rushed straight out to the Rocolo news agent and then spent an agonized hour waiting for the British papers to arrive. But that agony had been sweet relief compared to his anguish when he had finally seen what the papers contained. From the blizzard of phone calls he then proceeded to field, and the loud protestations and pleadings he was heard to make, it was clear that Hugh was determinedly fighting for his political life and that his political masters were equally determined to switch off his life support.

It couldn't have happened to a nicer family, Orlando tried to make himself think. He dredged up every miserable memory of their stay he could remember to force himself to rejoice in the Faughs' downfall. What had happened was, after all, a sweeter and more agonising revenge on his tormentors than he could ever have planned, even in his wildest flights of retaliatory fantasy. Odd then, that he felt far from exultant. If anything, he felt rather sorry for them.

It turned out that Totty de Belvedere had something of a talent for destroying careers. Orlando had learnt with outraged bewilderment what she had tried to do to Emma's, although there had been a happy ending. As Totty and the Faugh twins were led away by the local police, there had been tears, apologies, and heartfelt hugs from the couple who had arrived so suddenly and turned out to be Cosmo and Hero's parents. The reunion had been so dramatic that he had left Emma to it in the end; it seemed to have nothing to do with him.

A sharp cry had stopped him in his tracks as he reached the edge of the courtyard. "Hey!" cried Emma, dashing after him. "Phone number, please. And address, and mobile, and NHS number, and blood group, and…"

And then, yet more drama. As he had left the restaurant, his A-level results had been texted through. He had got a D and an E, better than he had expected. Two whole passes. Enough, even, to take some sort of course.

He was no longer a failure. On the contrary, it was the gilded youth of Oxford that had fallen.

Chapter Fifty-seven

ORLANDO PUSHED HIS MOTHER'S trolley across the smooth marble surface of the airport floor. There was so much marble around; part of being in Italy, he supposed.

Georgie's luggage was heavy. He found himself wondering vaguely how so many flimsy bits of material came to weigh so much. And how Georgie could bear to spend so much time in the airport shops, which seemed universally boring to Orlando. Still, they probably kept her mind off things.

"Orlando!"

"Orlando!"

Someone in blue and white. Jeans and a polo top. Emma, standing there, exactly where they had arranged to meet, smiling at him.

"Great!" he exclaimed, wheeling Georgie's heap over at such speed he could hardly stop it. "You made it."

He held her close. She held her face up to his. It was fresh and glowing, like a new pink rose, he thought. He longed to kiss it but felt shy in such a public place. Then, as she continued to look at him, he decided that he didn't feel so shy after all. When he had finished, her eyes were still closed. Encouraged, he bent his neck and kissed her again.

"Guess what," he whispered into her clean-smelling hair. "I got two A levels!"

"Orlando! You didn't!" The air was filled with her delighted shriek.

"It's especially fantastic," Emma added into his chest, which was as far as the top of her head reached, "because I was going to offer you a job."

"A job!" he squawked.

She nodded. "I'd have offered you it anyway, but now that you've got the A levels, you can train properly."

He blinked. Training? What was she talking about?

"I'm opening my nursery," Emma explained. "Darcy's given me the start-up money. I want you to join it."

"What—as a nanny?" He screwed up his eyes in disbelief.

"A manny," Emma corrected him. "A male nanny. Men make great nannies, I told you. And I'm planning to recruit a lot of them."

A great surge of excitement possessed Orlando. Along with a great clench of fear. His beam faded. His mother had been dealt many blows of late. Could she bear what might be the bitterest of all, that her son was about to be a nursemaid?

"I'll pay you plenty, don't worry," Emma added chuckling. "Enough to make your mother realise it's a proper career with proper rewards. And don't worry, there'll be rewards. It's going to be a massive success."

Orlando felt more cheerful. If Emma said it, it would happen. "That would be great." He shook his head in a puzzled way. "Fantastic. Really cool. Wow!"

"It's a deal then," Emma exulted, hugging him again and pulling his face down towards her. Her insides were popping with joy.

"Cosmo and Hero will be there too," she told him. "James and Vanessa are desperate for me to look after them again." She permitted herself a small, triumphant smile. "Oh, and Morning will be coming too. He'll be in the baby room."

"Morning?" Orlando looked Emma up and down, as if she had hidden the child who so evidently was not hanging from her front somewhere else about her person.

"I've been given temporary custody of him. Belle's in no state to look after him—not that she was when she wasn't in traction in a hospital," Emma added, rolling her eyes.

Orlando looked puzzled. He knew nothing about Belle, Emma remembered. Oh well. Perhaps she would tell him. Then again, perhaps she wouldn't. It was all water under the bridge now. "If all goes well, it'll be full adoption," she added. "I'm adopting him. Going through all the official channels that Belle ignored."

"Adoption!" Orlando exclaimed. "That's quite...a responsibility," he added, as she gave him a rather defiant look.

Emma shrugged. "So what? No change from what I've been doing for him so far really. Just on a slightly more permanent basis. And at least at the nursery there'll be other people besides me to look after him. You, for instance," she grinned.

Orlando nodded, a slow smile spreading across his face. Yes. That sounded like a good idea. Looking after Morning. He would like that. "Where is he now?" he asked.

"With Mara somewhere. She's giving him his bottle."

"Mara?"

"The housekeeper at the villa," Emma told him, only now realising how closely she had stuck to the terms of the confidentiality agreement. There was a whole side of her life about which Orlando had no idea at all. "She's coming to advise on the food. She wanted a change of scene, and she's got family in London."

"Wow." Orlando nodded. "That sounds...cool." He felt rather bewildered by it all.

"Your parents recovered from the awful pictures in the paper?" Emma asked, her joyous beam giving way to an expression of concern. "It must have been really embarrassing, as that family were staying with them and everything."

Orlando looked surprised. His present happiness so filled his vision that the miseries of the very recent past seemed like years ago.

"What about your father and Parliament?" Emma probed worriedly.
Orlando brightened. "Actually, he's decided to step down."

"Oh, no!"

"It's good news," Orlando countered. "Some think tank specialising in the regeneration of inner cities has asked him to join. It's always what Dad's been most interested in. He's been fed up with Parliament for ages, to be honest. He doesn't do backbiting and sleaze, and I don't think the Faugh business helped, apart from finally convincing my mother that it's not worth herding Dad through it all anymore. She's finally accepted he's never going to be Prime Minister. Funnily enough, she seems happier for it."

It was a long speech, and he felt rather exhausted at the end of it. It reminded him of how much had happened in so short a time. All for the better. He spotted Georgie, waving frantically from across a bank of seating.

"Better go and get the plane," he grinned, taking her hand. "I'll see you in London," he added, giving her a final tight squeeze. "Boss," he added.

❖❖❖

The day seemed to Darcy not quite so sunny as usual, and so the road up through Rocolo seemed to wear a more sullen aspect than normal. At the restaurant, all the chairs were set out as usual, and it had its vine, its sage paintwork, and its sunshades. Only one crucial element was missing.

Marco was nowhere to be seen, and a terrible fear now gripped her heart. During all the rehearsals she had held in her mind for this moment, the possibility that Marco would not be there had never occurred to her. It couldn't, it just couldn't be possible that Marco had chosen this morning of all mornings to be out somewhere—at the market, the artisanal cheesemakers, the vineyard. As she approached, her knees felt weak beneath her.

The restaurant was open; she could hear the chefs chatting and singing inside. She knocked timidly on the glass of the open door. One of the sous chefs appeared and smiled in recognition.

"Is…?" Darcy began. "Is Marco here? Si!" As the sous chef disappeared, Darcy leant briefly against the lintel to counter the rush of relief.

Within seconds, he was in the doorway, filling the frame with his body, wiping his hands on a tea towel. Immediately, she felt that her lips were the biggest and most prominent thing on her face. "Hi," she said primly.

"How are you?" he asked, looking at her anxiously.

"Come and sit down." As he led her to a table, seemingly careful not to touch her arm, Darcy sensed a restraint about Marco that had not been there before.

Had she but known it, Marco's reserve sprang from a desperate urge not to put a foot wrong. He had not slept from the moment their last meeting ended. There had been a closeness then that surely he had not imagined. And yet days had passed since, without any sight of her. He had heard the film had been called off and the actors leaving; such a seismic event in the hospitality trade didn't take long to penetrate Rocolo. He had been full of fear that Darcy had gone too.

As he looked at her helplessly, Darcy stepped forward and smiled. "I want to ask you something."

Hs heart raced. "Anything!" he declared, waving his hands and putting into the gesture all the feeling he could not express in words.

"You told me once that your restaurant philosophy is all about giving your staff time to have a real life. They don't work long hours, they get paid properly…"

He frowned. Why was she interviewing him about his management techniques? "Ye-es…" he said cautiously. "Yes, that's right."

Darcy smoothed a hair behind her ear.

"Well, I was wondering," Darcy smiled, showing white teeth in pink gums. She looked about sixteen, with those freckles and candid coffee bean–eyes, he thought.

Her heart hammered. She took a deep breath and squeezed her hands together. "I was wondering…whether you might have a job for a friend of mine."

"A friend…of yours?"

At the beginning of the sentence he had, with a leap of the heart, started to form the thought that she was asking for a job for herself. Apparently not.

"Yes. A homeless woman. One who's never cooked very much before."

He shrugged.

Darcy's heart sank. "So you don't employ homeless women who can't cook?"

"I have no problem with a homeless woman," he replied. "That is fine. Anyone can make a mistake, huh?"

His eyes seemed to Darcy to be boring into her with particular meaning.

"Presuming she is willing, clean, hardworking, and of good character…" He looked enquiringly at Darcy. She nodded hard.

"If she is, then I am sure I can help find her somewhere to live. I know a lot of people in this town, after all." He waved a hand expansively around. "There are flats, rooms in people's houses. We can sort something out."

Darcy felt jittery with joy. He had passed the test beautifully.

"However"—Marco pressed a finger to his full, wide lips—"it is more of a problem that she can't cook."

"Is it?" Darcy managed from a suddenly dry throat.

"Mmm. Most people applying for jobs in restaurants can cook already." He shook his shaggy head. "No, that is a real problem. A big, big problem."

"But…" Darcy objected. "But…if she is really passionate about food? Really, really wants to learn?"

He shrugged his big shoulders. "That would help. In some ways, of course, that is the most important thing."

"So keen to learn that she would be happy to peel vegetables, sweep up, do anything. And you wouldn't have to pay her much either, not at first."

Marco looked at her and smiled. "Not until she became a Michelin-starred chef, eh?"

Darcy blushed. "That's right."

"She sounds good," Marco said, nodding. "Yes, I'd like to meet this homeless woman. What's her name?"

He felt a pair of slender arms round his neck. "As if you didn't know," giggled Darcy into his neck.

Marco bent to kiss her, a long, lingering kiss to which Darcy responded with an ardour that meant neither of them were any longer in any doubt about anything. The sun finally broke the clouds and flooded the square in dazzling sunshine.

"Oh, Marco," Darcy, her eyes closed, murmured into the salty, soapy, warm-skin scent of his hair and neck. "I love you."

"And I you." He pulled her tighter, even though it wasn't really possible.

She breathed, as best she could, a deep, happy sigh. "I can hardly believe it," she told him happily, his curls tickling her lips as she spoke. "My life's been such bollocks until now. Without meaning, without direction, and now it's suddenly as if, I don't know, the clouds have parted or something, and it's all so clear." She raised her head and beamed at him. "There's so much I can learn from you. You can show me so much…you're such an artist, such a man…"

To her surprise, instead of looking delighted at this outburst, the round brown eyes, so melting a second ago, now fixed on her in concern. A chill feeling now swept through Darcy; had she said something wrong? "What's the matter?" she stammered, her throat clenched with fear.

Marco's brow lowered. He stared intensely from below it at Darcy.

"What have I said?" she burst out in panic. Her last words jangled hysterically through her mind, like a runaway train. But they had been all praise and love, surely?

Marco took a deep, slow breath and gently put her from him. The air was warm, but, released unwillingly from the tight, hot circle of his strong arms, Darcy felt cold. She stared at him, eyes ping-ponging frantically about his face, feeling her knees start to tremble.

"If we are to be together," Marco now informed her in a slow, grave voice, his eyes steady and never leaving hers, "there is something you must know about me. Something that might change your entire view of me."

Chapter Fifty-eight

HOT AND COLD WAVES of panic were coursing through her body. Was he about to reveal the existence of a wife? An entire other family? A penchant for cross-dressing? She gazed at him helplessly.

"I have a weakness," Marco admitted, now looking at the cobbled floor.

Nausea was pushing in her throat. Her palms and forehead felt clammy. Weakness?

Her thoughts raced. Drugs? Alcohol? Was he gay? Oh, it was so unfair. She had been so happy, so excited, so hopeful; finally her life had had a direction. And now all was to be shattered.

He was walking away from her now, towards the restaurant. "Come with me," he called, without turning round. As if in a dream she followed, stumbling, one leg planting itself shakily before the other, her eyes fixed on the broad white back before her, topped by its ball of dark curls. The sounds around her—the passersby in the street behind, singing birds, her own panicked breathing—swelled in her ears with cataclysmic, hyper-real volume.

She watched as he went through the door. Whatever he was about to reveal was to be revealed in the restaurant. Bodies in the freezer? What horrors—and Darcy had no doubt now that they were horrors—was she about to be told?

Darcy, following the tall-white-clad figure through the tables, had only the vaguest impression of what was around her. Tables, chairs, white walls. She banged painfully into the corner of a table;

the sharp edge bit into her thigh and would no doubt cause a bruise. Darting through the boiling sea of impressions that constituted Darcy's thoughts came the memory of Sam. Her one-time model agent had been full of instructions about avoiding leg injuries and always, but always, putting on mosquito lotion as careers were ruined by bites in the wrong places. How happily, Darcy remembered, she had received the news that her own career was ruined by a combination of overeating on her own part and bad driving on Christian's.

Parting company with Sam had been such an intense relief, but would she now, Darcy wondered miserably, have to pick up the acting and modelling baton again?

Marco had disappeared through a door in the side of the room now, and Darcy followed him to find a small stone stairwell. At the top, she emerged, still in a dreamlike state, into a small, hot, noisy room full of shiny things, noisy chatter, and people in white; the kitchen, she slowly realised. The cacophonous noise now stopped as suddenly as if someone had turned it off. Darcy passed through the people, the shiny surfaces, the bowls and glinting knifes, in silence.

Marco had vanished again; through a shadowy doorway at the end, Darcy now saw as she reached it. She could see his white form moving about among the gloom inside. She stepped in after it, knowing with a clammy, immense sensation that whatever took place here, in this small, dark room, would affect her forever.

He was slapping about on the walls. She could make out dim shelves, full of bags of things. It smelt of flour. There were savoury tangs with sweet undercurrents. It did not seem especially sinister; it looked, in fact, like the kitchen storeroom.

"Here's the light." He snapped it on. Yellow brilliance flooded her eyes, and she blinked, looking at bags of pasta and flour with ornate labels. Jars and bottles of olive oil gleamed like jewels; with odd detachment, she admired the range of colours from yellow topaz to emerald. She shook her head slightly as she looked at him, her mind now utterly empty. All she could do was look.

He was bending now. His hand seemed to have closed over something on the bottom shelf. "What I am about to show you," he said softly into the wall in a tense monotone, "might change everything. And if it does, I promise you I will understand. I must warn you now that not many women would be able to understand. Italian women especially."

"Right," croaked Darcy, whose very feet were now fizzing with tension. Her back ached suddenly, unbearably.

"But you seem to see me as some sort of hero, and I have to show you that I am just a man, and weaker than most…"

"Show me," Darcy croaked, feeling that, however awful whatever he was about to show her was, it could not possibly be more awful than the suspense. She tensed herself, cringing slightly with narrowed eyes, ready to be shattered, ready for her fragile dream, so frail and recent of construct, to fall finally, conclusively apart.

He turned. He held something in both his hands. Her breath caught in her throat. He opened his hands. Standing on his palm was a tin of spaghetti.

She frowned and blinked, not understanding. "What's in there?" Crazy thoughts whirled in her brain. Was he a drug smuggler? Did he use tins as a cover?

He proffered the spaghetti. "Spaghetti. Spaghetti's in there." He spoke in a broken voice; his eyes, as he looked at her, were doleful and full of shame. "Can you still love me?" he asked, his voice now a whisper.

"Love you…?" She whirled her head from side to side. "I don't understand…what's spaghetti got to do with it…"

"I am an Italian man. A chef…"

Understanding burst in on her as brightly as the light had just done. Following close on its heels was a gigantic wave of relief. This was his weakness. She remembered, in a series of flashes, the small blonde girl asking for tinned spaghetti outside the restaurant. He had been so understanding…this was why. No wonder he had met her demands with such little fuss. The laughter came from somewhere around her navel, rose, inflated, and burst hysterically out.

"…have always loved it," Marco was saying sorrowfully. "I can't help it. Sometimes, after a hard night in the kitchen, it's all I want to eat. Of course, I know it's gunk; it's nothing like real, proper, Italian pasta. God knows what grade of flour it's made with, and it's never al dente. And that slimy sauce, but somehow it works, and I love it. I know I shouldn't. And it doesn't mean that I don't love the food I cook, the real Italian food I believe in, with every nerve in my body." A flash of pride illumined his features before the hangdog expression returned. "If the news got out, I'd be ruined. My brigade…"—he shook his curly head in the direction of the kitchen—"they know, of course. They had to know. And there are others…"

"Others?" Darcy was trying to control her mirth now. It was obviously an extremely serious matter for Marco.

"There's a whole society of us. In Italy. We're called the Societa Fapirollo, and we meet in secret every month. We have to. Italians are very proud of their pasta…you can imagine…and me a chef as well…" He stopped, as she was laughing again, a helpless hiccupping mirth.

"You don't mind?" There was wonder in his voice. "You can live with that, with knowing my secret? You don't blame me? Can you love me?"

Can! Darcy, forcing away her smile, sternly held his gaze. She had considered teasing him, pretending she did care, as retaliation for the agonies he had caused her. But his worried gaze and his crumpled, puppy face melted her heart. She pressed herself into him, shaking her head and smiling. "You know, I think I just…can."

Farm Fatale

BANG ON 8 A.M., the car alarm that had been shrieking all night finally stopped. After a two-second pause, the road drills began. Rosie could hold back no longer.

"Mark? You know we've been talking about moving to the countryside…"

"*You've* been talking about it, you mean," corrected Mark, hunched over his bowl of Cheerios and flicking rapidly through the newspapers. "I don't believe it." He groaned.

"I know." Rosie pressed her hands to her ears. "They only dug up that patch a week ago. Something to do with cable TV."

"Not that," said Mark, his spoon dripping milk as he shook it at the center spread of a tabloid. "This. The *Mail*'s got Matt Locke. We've been trying to get him for ages."

"Who's Matt Locke?"

Mark looked at her, exasperated. "Honestly, you're like that judge who asked, 'Who is Gazza?' Don't you ever *read* the papers?"

"You know I don't. Apart from the horoscopes." No doubt, Rosie thought, she was missing something, but she failed to share the awe with which Mark regarded newspapers in general and his job on one in particular. After all, it wasn't as if he was setting the national agenda, exposing Nazis, or bringing corrupt politicians to book. As far as Rosie could make out, Mark's job as assistant editor on a Sunday lifestyle section mostly involved rewriting other people's articles—"tickling up" as he called it—and attempting to persuade celebrities to give interviews about everything from their cystitis (for "Disease of the Week") to the contents of their refrigerator (for the "Chillin'" slot).

"Matt Locke, m'lud," Mark explained with elaborate patience, "is an extremely successful singer. The chisel-cheeked champion of howling rock 'n' roll angst, he burst on the scene two years ago with the number one platinum album *Posh Totty*, an epoch-making elegy to soaring strings, gutsy guitar, melancholy blues, and a touch of country and western, following it up with the even more successful *What Did Your Last One Die Of?* Then, at the height of his fame, he crashed and burned amid claims that the stress was too much."

"Oh," said Rosie, peering at the newspaper photograph of a girlish-looking youth with elaborately tousled hair and huge lips. He did not look particularly stressed. Actually, he looked half asleep.

She winced as the road drills outside changed to an even more brain-penetrating key. "Darling, you know you said you'd think about it. The countryside, I mean."

"Recycled interviews, of course," Mark muttered, pressing his nose almost against the newspaper. "Nothing that's not been printed before. Apart from these aerial pictures of Matt in his garden, although they're so blurry it's probably one of the gnomes."

"Two-thirds of people living in cities want to live in the country," Rosie persevered, hoping she'd remembered the figures properly. "Thousands are migrating every month."

"So if we stay in London," Mark said flippantly, "everyone else will eventually leave, house prices will go down, and we'll end up with a mansion on Regent's Park Road."

"Oh, *Mark*."

"Look," Mark said, putting the newspaper down at last. "I know I said last night that I'd think about it, but it was the wine speaking. I don't want to leave London. I'm a townie born and bred. Crowds and noise are my lifeblood; filth is my friend. I can't breathe anything but carbon monoxide. A landscape of brutalist shopping precincts, down-at-the-heel Tube stations, and municipal concrete bunkers is the only sort of scenery I have time for. Besides," he added, stretching with satisfaction, "I'm going to be promoted. At long last, the paper's going to give me a column of my own."

"It *is*? But you never mentioned that last night."

"Well, it's not quite sorted out yet."

"So it's still 'Driving Miss Daisy' for the moment?"

The main column in Mark's section, "Driving Miss Daisy," recorded the adventures of Househusband, a stay-at-home father who looked after his infant daughter, Daisy, while his wife, a successful futures trader, went to work. Desperate for a column of his own, Mark despised the weekly chore of extracting the material out of Househusband and writing up the results himself. The fact that Househusband was incapable of stringing a sentence together, much less coming up with ideas, was, as Mark often savagely pointed out, not unconnected to the fact that he was the brother-in-law of the paper's editor.

Mark's brows drew together crossly. "For the moment, yes. But they've obviously given me that to train me for better things." He raked a hand through his rumpled golden hair. "Rosie, I can't leave. I'm on the brink of a promising career."

"Look," she said persuasively. "Why don't you ask the paper for a writing contract? Or go freelance, if they won't do it. You'd enjoy it much more. We could live anywhere we liked then. You can't really want to stay here." The hand she waved at their rented flat's dust-bloomed windows jerked involuntarily as a backfiring car joined the shrilling symphony of drills. "Imagine. Clean air. Cottages with roses round the door. Sun-dappled country lanes, empty of traffic."

Mark merely shrugged at this. Her dreams, Rosie realized miserably, were not his. In which case she'd target his nightmares, namely the dentist and going bald. "Water that doesn't cause tartar buildup behind your teeth. Rain that's clean and doesn't poison your hair follicles." As he still looked unimpressed, she added desperately, "Struggling into the office on the crappy, broken-down old Tube with your face pushed into someone's bottom. Or armpit."

"You don't have to struggle on the Tube anyway," Mark cut in self-righteously. "You're a freelance illustrator. You can lie around all day if you want."

Rosie rolled her eyes but refrained from pointing out that the endless illustrations for the food and horoscope pages of various glossy magazines in which she seemed to have become a specialist left little time for bon-bons on the couch. The fact that paintings of scallops and Scorpio were relatively poorly paid was, Rosie thought, another argument in favor of the move. Her fees would go further in the country.

"But what about everything we'd leave behind?" demanded Mark. "Restaurants, the theater, the cinema, and all that."

"But you decided a while ago we couldn't afford to eat out anymore," Rosie said gently. "We never go to the cinema and I can't remember the last time I saw the inside of a theater." In fact, she added silently, the most cultural thing we've probably done all year was eat Marks & Spencer's ravioli in front of *The Charlie Rose Show*. "We don't really make use of London these days," she pressed. "If you went freelance, we could live anywhere in the country. So why not live somewhere that's nice?"

Mark's handsome face was preoccupied. He was, Rosie knew, searching for the defining argument against, the ultimate no.

"But I'm on the fast track. The managing editor told me the other day that anything could happen. Which can only mean one thing. They're seriously thinking about giving me my own column."

"But wasn't he just saying anything could happen now that everyone's combining jobs because of the cutbacks? I mean, now the fashion editor's the foreign editor, too, so he's got a point."

"As I believe I mentioned," Mark said defensively, "the only reason Tallulah covered the military coup in Zwanwe was because she was doing a bikini shoot in the disputed border area at the time. Getting her to do a few interviews while she was there was only sensible."

"Even if her scathing criticism of the local warlords' dress sense wasn't," muttered Rosie, suddenly tired of arguing. "Darling, listen to me," she pleaded. "Moving out's not a mad idea. A recent survey said seventy-one percent of all people thought the countryside was more peaceful than the town. Fifty-four percent like the feeling of space and, um, fifty percent like the trees and forests." She was gabbling now, she knew.

"Fascinating," said Mark. Rosie looked at him sharply. Was he being sarcastic? The smooth dips and planes of his face, however, expressed only thoughtfulness.

Rosie waited, stiff with hope, watching Mark anxiously. Odd how, straight from bed, clad only in crumpled boxer shorts and an ancient T-shirt, he still managed to look devastating. She drew her toweling robe around herself, conscious of gray calves so long un-shaved they probably needed a combine harvester by now. "So what do you think?" she ventured.

"I think," Mark said, slinging the spoon back into the pool of milk in his bowl, "that I might suggest it to the editor as a features idea."

Rosie ground her teeth and decided to drop the subject of the countryside. For now.

AN EXCERPT FROM

Bad Heir Day

THE BRIDE HAD STILL not arrived. Beside Anna, Seb fidgeted, sighed and tutted, and the surrounding cacophony of wailing babies and coughing increased. There seemed, Anna saw as she glanced around the candlelit chapel, to be an awful lot of people there. All better dressed than herself. As she caught the haughty eye of a skinny and impeccably turned-out brunette, Anna dropped her gaze to her feet. Realising that there had been no time even to clean her shoes, she immediately wished she hadn't.

Everything had been such a rush. After breakfasting at his usual leisurely pace, Seb had glanced at the invitation properly for the first time and, after much panicked scanning of the Scottish mainland, eventually discovered the location of the wedding in the middle of the Atlantic.

"Fucking hell, I thought it was in Edinburgh," he roared. "It's practically in Iceland." Seb thrust the *AA Road Atlas* at her, his stabbing finger a good quarter inch off the far northwest coast of Scotland. Anna stared at the white island amid the blue, whose shape bore a startling resemblance to a hand making an uncomplimentary gesture with its middle finger. She glanced at the invitation.

"Dampie Castle, Island of Skul," she read. "Well, I suppose getting married in a castle is rather romantic…"

"Castle my arse," cursed Seb. "Why can't they get married in Knightsbridge like everybody else?"

"Perhaps we shouldn't bother going," Anna said soothingly.

After all, she had met neither component of the unit of Thoby and Miranda whose merger they were invited to celebrate. All she knew was that Thoby, or Bollocks, as Seb insisted on calling him, was a schoolfriend of his. There seemed to be very few men who weren't. While his habit of referring to Miranda as Melons confirmed Anna's suspicions that she was one of his ex-girlfriends. Again, there seemed to be very few women who weren't.

Seb, however, was hell-bent on putting in an appearance. Abandoning plans to drive to Scotland, they flew first class from Heathrow to Inverness instead and drove like the wind in a hired Fiesta to the ferryport for Skul, Seb in a rage all the way. Being stopped by a highway patrol car and asked, "Having trouble taking off, sir?" had hardly improved his temper. In the end, they had arrived at Dampie too late to be shown their room, too late to look around the castle, too late to look at the castle at all in fact, as darkness had long since fallen. Too late to do anything but rush to the chapel, where the evening service would, Seb snarled as they screeched up the driveway, be halfway through by now at least. Only it wasn't.

❖❖❖

Ten more brideless minutes passed, during which a small, sailor-suit-clad boy in front of Anna proceeded to climb all over the pew and fix anyone who happened to catch his eye with the most contemptuous of stares. Anna returned his gaze coolly as he bared his infant teeth at her. "I'm going to kill *all* the bridesmaids," he declared, producing a plastic sword from the depths of the pew and waving it threateningly about.

"I'm feeling rather the same way toward Melons," murmured Seb, testily, when, after a further half hour, the bride was still conspicuous by her absence. "Then again, she always did take bloody ages to come." He sniggered to himself. Anna pretended not to have heard.

"Thoby should think himself lucky," whispered a woman behind them as the vision in ivory finally appeared at the door. "Miranda is only fifty-five minutes late turning up to marry him. She's always at least an *hour* late whenever she arranges to meet *me*."

"There's probably a good reason for that," muttered Seb.

"Shhh," said Anna, digging him in the ribs and noting enviously that Thoby clearly *did* think himself lucky. His inbred features positively blazed with pride as Miranda, her tiny waist pinched almost to invisibility by her champagne satin bustier, drew up beside him at the altar on a cloud of tulle and the arm of a distinguished-looking man with silver hair and a second-home-in-Provence tan.

"Stella McCartney," whispered the woman behind.

"*Where?*" hissed her companion.

"No, the dress, darling. *Achingly* hip."

"Aching hips, as well, I should think. It looks like agony. Poor Miranda."

"Still, it's worth it. Mrs. Thoby Boucher de Croix-Duroy sounds *terribly* grand. If not *terribly* Scottish."

"No. They're about as Scottish as pizza," whispered the second woman. "Hired this place because Miranda was *desperate* to get married in a castle. And I hear Thoby isn't quite so grand as he seems anyway. Apparently he's called Boucher de Croix-Duroy because his grandfather was a butcher from King's Cross."

"*No!*"

"*Yes!* Sush, we've got to sing now. *Damn*, where *is* my order of service?"

As everyone vowed to thee, their country, Anna sneaked a proud, sidelong glance at Seb and felt her stomach begin its familiar yoyo of lust. His tanned neck rose from his brilliantly white collar, his tall frame, drooping slightly (Seb *hated* standing up), looked its best in a perfectly cut morning suit innocent of the merest hint of dandruff and his long lashes almost brushed his Himalayan cheekbones. He might make the odd thoughtless remark, but he was the best-looking man in the chapel by a mile, even—Anna prayed not to be struck down—counting the high-cheekboned, soft-lipped representation of Jesus languishing elegantly against his cross. Seb was *gorgeous*. And, source though that was of the fiercest pride and delight, it was also rather terrifying. Seb attracted women like magnets attracted iron filings—and in about the same numbers. If being in love with a beautiful woman was hard, Anna thought, it was nothing to being in love with a beautiful man.

About the Author

WENDY HOLDEN WAS A journalist for the *Sunday Times, Tatler,* and the *Mail on Sunday* before becoming a full-time author. She has now published nine novels, all being top ten bestsellers in the UK, and she is married with two young children. Her novels include *Farm Fatale, Bad Heir Day, Simply Divine, Gossip Hound, The Wives of Bath, The School for Husbands, Azur Like It,* and *Filthy Rich.*

Krestine Havemann

Bonus reading group guide available online at
www.sourcebooks.com/readingguides.

A Comedy of Country Manors

farm fatale

wendy holden

INTERNATIONAL BESTSELLING AUTHOR

Farm Fatale
Wendy Holden

A witty, beloved novel of heart and heartland, *Farm Fatale* skewers the culture clash of city vs. country in the snappy, observant style that made Wendy Holden famous.

Cash-strapped Rosie and her boyfriend Mark are city folk longing for a country cottage. Rampantly nouveaux riches Samantha and Guy are also searching for rustic bliss—in the biggest mansion money can buy. The village of Eight Mile Bottom seems quiet enough, despite a nosy postman, a reclusive rock star, a glamorous Bond Girl, and a ghost with a knife in its back. But there are unexpected thrills in the hills, and Rosie is rapidly discovering that country life isn't so simple after all. Or is it?

Praise for *Farm Fatale*

"Wendy Holden writes with delicious verve and energy."

—Mail on Sunday

"Clever, naughty."

—Sunday Times

"This lighthearted romp, surprisingly unpredictable, smart, and fun, is refreshing fare readers can turn to."

—Publishers Weekly

"A light, sexy, and entertaining novel…will please fans of contemporary and comic romances."

—Bookreporter.com

"Every character here is deliciously ridiculous, and every rustic detail a grand satirical opportunity."

—Baltimore Sun

"Wickedly funny."

—Kirkus

978-1-4022-3716-4 • $14.99 U.S.

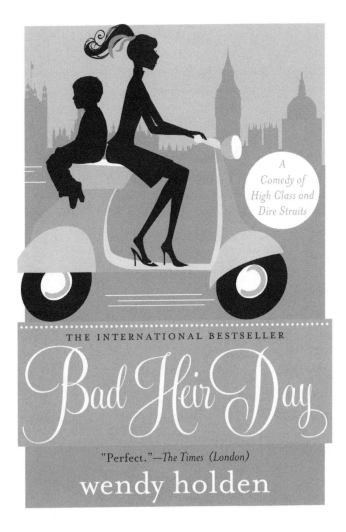

THE INTERNATIONAL BESTSELLER

Bad Heir Day

"Perfect."—*The Times* (London)

wendy holden

Bad Heir Day
WENDY HOLDEN

After being dumped by her rich, handsome boyfriend, Anna vows to give up men forever. She takes a job as a nanny in the ritzy Kensington home of the Knights. Armed with a vacuum in one hand and *Harry Potter* in the other, Anna finds herself living with the family from hell: Cassandra, a social-climbing romance novelist with writer's block; Jett, Cassandra's cheating rock-star spouse; and Zak, their spawn-of-Satan son. So when Anna meets Jamie, the dashing heir to a castle in Scotland, she figures he's too good to be true. And she just may be right…

Praise for *Bad Heir Day*

"Perfect."

—*Times* (London)

"Devilish satire."

—*Elle* (UK)

"Savagely amusing…the satire is deadly, the plot addictive, and the pace exhilarating."

—*Metro London*

"A romp of a novel…Wendy Holden writes with delicious verve and energy."

—*Sunday Mail* (UK)

"Well observed and witty."

—*Mirror*

"Holden not only dissects social trends but also restores the pun to literary respectability—an amazing feat."

—*Esquire* (UK)

"Laugh-out-loud funny…a treat."

—*Express*

978-1-4022-4061-4 • $14.99 U.S.